WAVES AND WICKEDNESS

WOLF SHIFTER KINGS
BOOK FOUR

BELLA MOONDRAGON

For Micah, the guy who let Jules die.

CONTENTS

1

———

CIVIL WAR

Finn

"Finn!" My Beta, Elian, pounds on my body beneath the covers like I'm a drum.

I kick at him without even opening my eyes, and he dodges back with a laugh.

"It cannot be time to wake yet."

"Time to wake came and went," Elian replies. "You are bordering on late, and Kieran wants to speak with you before the Tansy Beach delegation arrives."

I groan and burrow deeper beneath my covers. There is nothing wrong with Tansy Beach arriving—other than the circumstances. I even like their prince; over the last few years, we've spent enough events standing next to each other that I could be compelled to call Xander my friend.

The problem is morning. I hate it. There's a reason we have a Moon Goddess rather than a sun one. The sun is all grabby fingers, noise, and expectation. If I could never wake up in the morning again, I might actually be happy.

"Come on." Elian flips the covers off me.

"You're lucky it is not winter." I crack an eye, take in the grin under his shag of blond hair. To cause the prince the loss of a toe is treason, I'm fairly certain.

Elian rolls his eyes. With another groan, I heave myself out of bed. The stone underfoot is already sun-warmed, promising he didn't lie about the time. Dammit.

I may have been a prince all my life, but to be *the* prince now still feels strange. Altair's birth two and a half years ago ended my brief reign as crown prince, and his new sister, Vespera, has nudged me well down the line of succession. Nevertheless, with Kieran on the throne and Anwen in Sundrop, I am the prince. The only one who can truly talk, at least. It's bizarre to have so many people looking to me for opinions.

"Meet with Kieran, official welcome, banquet… anything else?" I trudge toward my wardrobe. If Kieran needed me, he would have mind-linked—or sent Ingrid. Elian, I can ignore. Our littlest sister knows how to make ignoring her impossible.

"Not that I've been told of." Elian perches on the end of the bed. "But you like Xander, don't you?"

Tansy Beach's prince. When we first met, I thought he was a macho ass. Then, he decided he liked me, and I learned he was a macho ass with the ability to take a joke. "Well enough. It's better than hosting Cirrus Summit again," I say.

Prince Rex was a talker. And not just a talker, he expected me to respond. To everything. Frankly, I was shocked to discover he was only a year younger than me, not fifteen or sixteen as I expected.

Elian laughs at the sneer that must've crossed my face. I need to wake up. I might like Xander, but his father is paranoid, and I suspect, controlling enough to rival my own at his worst. King Alden merely bothers to put on a front for company.

"But liking him will not be enough to make *this* meeting any simpler." I pull on a tunic in royal silver and blue over fitted trousers. A few swipes through my hair, and I believe nothing else could be asked of me.

Elian grimaces. "Are you going to ask him about it?"

"His mother not only left his father but took half the kingdom with her?" I scoff. "We haven't talked about anything deeper than how much crowns pinch during official events."

Elian shrugs and says, "He might wish he had someone to talk to."

"He's got a whole king—well, *half* a kingdom to rely on for that." I straighten my tunic one last time and pray Kieran is waiting for me with a breakfast spread. "A stranger he sometimes talks with at formal functions is hardly going to be his first choice of shoulder to cry on."

That makes Elian snort a laugh. "Somehow, I can't imagine Xander crying."

I chuckle as we step into the hall. Xander carries himself like, if he ever met an emotion, he'd bite its head off before looking it in the eye. It makes him a fun night of company but seems as if it would become tiresome quickly.

Outside my room, courtiers bustle back and forth like particularly industrious bugs. Some carry papers, others banquet supplies, and still others nothing but their own worries. Elian and I cut through the chaos smoothly. In the years since Dun's Crossing's reintroduction to the world as something other than the monster under everyone's beds, these diplomatic visits have become far more frequent, but they've never yet failed to send everyone into a tizzy.

Sometimes, I miss the bad old days when no one wanted to come here. They were quieter, at least. And half the courtiers didn't trip over themselves to bow to me while the other half continued to ignore me.

"Kieran." I swing open the door to his office and discover not just him but Raven and Altair inside. "And company."

Raven puts down the quill she was writing with and waves while still bouncing Altair on her knee. I don't think I've seen her without a thousand things to do since the revitalization of Escuro. Her parents are still in good health, but they correspond constantly so she can stay up to date on affairs in the kingdom she'll someday lead.

"Vespera remains asleep," he says. The bags under Kieran's eyes show just how difficult a feat that has been to achieve lately. "And I am hoping she'll remain so long enough that Raven can join us at the welcome, but…."

"What do you need from me?" The strangest part of everyone disappearing to various corners of the globe is how much Kieran asks of me now. For most of my childhood, we barely talked. He and Anwen were a pair, if a contentious one, and so were Candace and Ingrid. Since spending time with Raven was a recipe for a beating, I spent a lot of time alone.

"Everyone knows King Alden is coming to request military aid." Kieran scrubs a hand over his face. "Our forces are stretched thinner than I'd like, especially without Father's conscription laws, but if the new kingdom—"

"Moonlight Hollow," Raven supplies.

He nods to her. "If Moonlight Hollow decides the land they have isn't sufficient, we do share a border with them."

"You want me to get a read on how likely that is?"

He shakes his head. "I want you to build goodwill. Can you show the prince, Alexander, a good enough time that our alliance remains strong no matter what decision I'm forced to make?"

So, I'm to be Candace today. Something burns in my chest. "Of course."

"Thank you." The relief is genuine in his voice, and that burn dies out a little. He needs me. Or at least, he believes he does.

In most ways, I cannot tell Kieran is Father's son anymore. But in the way he relies on people with Solberg blood—and Raven—above the extensive network he has at his fingertips, is classic Father. If I ever end up leaving this place, he'll be alone with Ingrid.

Perhaps I'll visit the day he asks her to be Candace.

"Carriage pulling up to the castle," one of the gate guards informs us all through the mind-link.

"That would be our cue." Kieran stands and then winces.

Raven winces at the same time. "Vespera is awake."

Wordlessly, Kieran takes Altair from her, and she hurries off to the royal bedroom while the rest of us make our way down.

Summer hangs thick and humid in the air outside. If it's warm here, I can't imagine what it's like south, in Tansy Beach. I tug surreptitiously at the collar of my tunic as the gates swing open.

A carriage rattles through the opening. It's unassuming, the sides a faded shade of their royal indigo with only a few copper fixtures to complete the association. It looks as though they had to sneak out of their own territory. I heard things were tense, but not that fighting had actually started. My shoulders tighten as the door to the carriage opens.

King Alden steps out first, a picture of courtly poise. Tall and broad-shouldered, his brown hair catches the copper shades from his simple crown and becomes almost red. Quickly behind him, though, is Xander. He carries himself with the same confidence as his father, but those big, broad-shouldered traits must skip a generation. Xander looks more like a wolf who hasn't quite grown into his paws yet—reedy, or possibly lanky is a better word. Not that he lets that keep him from looking the castle up and down like it's his.

"Dun's Crossing welcomes you." Kieran steps forward as a few other people, non-royals, continue to climb from the carriage, and offers the best bow he can with an increasingly rowdy Altair in his arms. "It is good to see you again, though I wish it were under better circumstances."

King Alden returns a wan smile and also bows. "I would agree. You know my son, Prince Alexander Mlakar, but perhaps not his Beta, Councilor Corwyn Hajni."

Corwyn, a man a few years older than us with caramel-colored hair and strangely familiar olive eyes, stands behind the prince. Xander meets my gaze and bows. Amusement sparkles in his hazel gaze, mocking the performance of politeness when nobody can think of anything but the civil war they left behind. Or perhaps just mocking the distance between our two families when we've been close allies for a few years now. I bow back with a smirk.

On the first night he decided he liked me, I ended up the winner of an arm-wrestling contest held at the back of a formal ball. If he didn't drag me over, I'd have avoided it like the plague. Too much drawing attention to myself, making a mess when I could just linger on the sidelines and listen to what people thought I didn't care to hear them saying.

It was one of the best parties I'd ever been to. So I'd play Candace for the length of their stay—with a guy like Xander, it would be easy, even with the threats in the air.

2

____

A NIGHT OUT

Xander

THAT NIGHT, FATHER STANDS FROM HIS SEAT NEXT TO ME. "AS A TOKEN of gratitude for how you've welcomed us, we would like to offer you this chest, hand-painted by my own mother in anticipation of our trip."

That is our cue. I reach under the table, and at the same moment as my Beta, Corwyn, lift the three-foot-long chest onto the edge of the partially cleared banquet table. Nonna's delicate brushstrokes swirl across the slick, black surface in reds, greens, and purples. Father is lying, of course. Nonna's hands shake like the last autumn leaves of late; she painted this chest some years ago, and he stored it in one of our rare water-tight rooms for an occasion such as this. But it has the intended effect. Oohs and ahhs ripple up and down the table from the dully dressed Dun's Crossing nobles.

Alpha Kieran stands and runs his hand across the lid. "This is an incredible gift. Give your mother my deepest thanks."

There's a beat. Father's shoulders tighten. In Tansy Beach, host gifts like this are customary. If Alpha Kieran hasn't bothered to learn enough about us to have one prepared, Father is going to take that as an extremely bad sign of the negotiations to come. My palms slick with sweat.

Seated on his brother's left, Finn's gaze goes hazy with a mind-link. Servants begin moving in the corner of my eye, and I swallow a smile. The moment I saw him, I knew that bored, disinterested posture was a mask. He knows exactly what is about to go wrong here.

Alpha Kieran's eyes haze for a heartbeat before he says, "And in return for the difficulties of your travel to us, I extend a goblet jeweled with sapphires mined at the north edge of our kingdom."

Father nods with barely disguised relief. He didn't spot Finn's intervention, and though the gift is obviously less personal, the sapphires are dark enough to seem to be a nod to our royal colors.

"Do you see the dust around the settings?" Corwyn demands. *"They barely brushed it off."*

"We dusted Nonna's chest at our last stop today," I remind him.

He still huffs, his olive-green gaze sharp for any signs of disrespect. I'm just waiting for the moment we get to sit back down. As much as my whole life has been an endless tightrope of saying and doing the right thing, the pressure has been cranked to impossible levels of late. Even a moment where I can hide my expression behind a goblet of wine is a relief.

Finally, Father accepts the gift with the traditional thanks, and a pair of valets take the chest from Corwyn and I. One step down, about a hundred more to go before we learn if we can rely on Dun's Crossing for military support.

Nausea curls in my gut as I sit. I argued against coming here at all. Even with the semi-subtle carriage, this is a line drawn in the sand. Dun's Crossing is still the foremost military power on the continent. And perhaps there have been rumors that Mother's—Moonlight Hollow–is gathering allies for a potential attack, but nothing more has come of them yet. I don't want to take up arms until we're forced to.

What I want hasn't mattered yet, though.

"It is good to break bread with friends," Kieran declares. "And it is equally good to let friends rest after a perilous journey. I'll be having a nightcap in my sitting room with the door open, but I won't make you stay here any longer."

Laughter rumbles along the table. Father's eyes glint, and I know he'll be in that sitting room. But he doesn't ask me to go, so I push back from the table and leave. The meal was good, but heavy, too warm for the summer months even here. I need to walk it off.

Perhaps I'll run it off. My wolf is the only other shred of peace I get.

A few steps outside the massive hall, Finn catches up to me. All the Solbergs do look shockingly alike—except for Candace, of course. His ice-blond hair hangs straight around his razor-sharp cheekbones, and his ice-blue eyes shine just as sharply, no matter how he tries to dull them.

"Should I get used to you following me around?" I ask, though I don't mind. He really is decent company, once he gets over himself.

"You're my assignment for the week." He falls into step beside me. "I think Kieran would manacle us together if he thought it would help."

I raise an eyebrow. "Why do you want to keep on our good side?"

He shrugs, boredom swallowing his features like a mask. The other thing I've learned about Finn Solberg? He is more stubborn than anyone I've met in my life, other than Father.

"Well, if you're my shadow, can we at least do something more interesting than hold court with your brother?"

"Please." He rolls his eyes. "There's a place in town. Follow me."

He leads me along increasingly labyrinthine halls, a few of which can only be accessed through secret doors. King Gavin's paranoia is hard to miss. Some of these have to predate him, but there's no other reason why his children would have such a perfect knowledge of them.

Long minutes of walking lead us outside the castle without seeing a single guard or opening more than an iron portcullis over the mouth of a tunnel.

"I wish Tansy Tower had that," I mutter.

"Ask me how many times they've been used against the royal family, then tell me that again," he deadpans.

I shake my head. "No more politics."

"When I start following your orders, then you should start worrying."

That pulls a laugh from my throat, one of the first since I woke up to the news Mother was gone.

But that is not a chest I can open, even alone in the dark with a prince I believe I call my friend. There is too much to do—too much to protect. Finn is expecting the brash, cocksure Prince Xander he knows. My only responsibility now is to provide. Shoulders back, for whatever breadth and intimidation I can get, and stance wide. Be what they expect.

The town below Solberg Castle is quiet but far from dead. Pubs lining the harbor glow with light, and I'm surprised when Finn turns away from them. Instead, he shoulders open the door to a smaller tavern called the Dusty Battleaxe.

Warm smells of hoppy beer and more heavy stew pour out into the night on a current of music and laughter. Round tables dot the main floor, about half full, just like the stools at the bar. On the far end, next to a roaring hearth I am grateful for after the unexpectedly cold night, sits a pair of musicians. One plucks a lute and sings roughly half the words to a drinking song I recognize the tune of while the other handles a flute with shocking mastery. The barkeep, a plump woman, smacks a patron with the rag in her hand, and the patron only laughs.

Finn nudges me toward a table next to the wall, seemingly unaffected by the atmosphere. "The drinks are good, and there are enough people to make some noise, but not enough that you can't move without being recognized."

I slouch into a hard, wooden chair. Somehow, the place already feels familiar. I have never been out drinking in Tansy Beach—no matter how small the pub, I would be mobbed the moment someone spotted me.

"Are the drinks good enough that you think you can out-drink me?" I ask before he can start a conversation I don't want to have.

The corners of his lips twitch. "Depends. How confident are you that I can't?"

A pouch of gold sits in my room back at the castle, but betting gold is a weak man's game. "Loser makes breakfast for the other."

A true smirk. "Deal. Fastest to down a half-dozen pints?"

I stick my hand out, and Finn claps his into it to shake. My blood races with the rush of competition. Because of the way I was born, I have to stay out of the thick of things more often than not. Moments like this, though, Father can't worry away from me. Finn signals the barkeep, and two tankards of beer arrive at our table.

"Keep them coming," he tells her.

I raise my tankard, knock it against his when he does the same. "May the best man win."

"Oh, he will."

I tip the glass to my lips and almost choke on the head of foam. Finn doesn't flinch. In seconds, his first tankard hits the table, empty. Goddess above, I shouldn't have let him pick the drink. If he wanted me to take a half-dozen shots of sourplum brandy, I'd already be done.

Be what they expect.

I open my throat and become nothing but a vessel. My first tankard follows his swiftly, and with the delay from the barkeep, I beat him to finishing the second. Attention drifts our way, then patrons themselves.

"Is that Prince Finn?" someone whispers as I slam down my third.

The hairs on the back of my neck prickle, and I am slow grabbing the fourth. Finn's gaze darts to me.

"Nobody else could beat Xander's ass," he says indolently, lingering over picking up his own next tankard.

I recognize the blatant favor, but the prickling turns to the feeling of pins clicking up my spine as he says my name.

No one reacts to it. There is no mob, no pushing, no demands for my attention on this or that measure at the next council meeting. Or his.

Finn catches my eye. The ice in his looks anything but cold—it is challenging, asking if I'm really going to let such a little thing as this stop me. His next tankard reaches his mouth.

The challenge ignites me. I snatch the mug and drink for all I am worth. Chants split the crowd. Some holler my name, others his. A pair on my side attempt to slow the delivery of his next pint, and I laugh as I snatch mine.

When we reach the final tankard, mere heartbeats separate us. Did he bring his to his lips first? Did I? Is the thick head of foam that I'm certain now the barkeep is sabotaging me with going to make me sick?

Should I win, for the sake of the war?

I push those thoughts from my mind. No politics. No worry. Nothing but the challenge in Finn's gaze and the last few sips of hoppy beer, pouring down my throat.

Slam! Slam!

Our mugs hit the table one after the next. I stare at him, breathing hard, barely able to get enough air into my lungs through the constriction of my clothes, and wait for the verdict.

The barkeep grabs my wrist and raises my hand. "Xander wins!"

Applause thunders over the music. I smirk at Finn, but concern starts to creep back in. Surely, now the people will begin making their demands. The evening's entertainment is complete, and politics must return.

The barkeep brings us a pair of shots of something brown, on the house, and our small crowd melts away.

"Breakfast of choice?" Finn asks.

3

DIPLOMACY

Finn

The next day, I knock on Xander's bedroom door with a plate of food in my hands.

"Enter," he calls.

I march inside with my best approximation of the staff's invisible poise, then fake a curtsy before presenting the requested breakfast: toast with jam, a pastry, and a steaming cup of coffee. His personal steward, a tall, pale man whose name I don't know, stares at me in blank confusion. I don't see a single sign of Xander.

"Uh—"

Xander steps out from behind a hinged partition, fixing his tunic, and laughs. "Remind me, did I bet that you would make me breakfast after another six pints?"

I drop the platter on the low table in front of the barely lit hearth. "No, but I wish I had."

He sits on the couch and begins picking up the elements one by one. "A child could have done a superior job spreading jam."

"There is a little on the crust." I stuff my hands in my pockets. The kitchen staff stared at me the whole time I was putting this together, clearly wondering what possessed me to do such a thing but not saying a word. "The bread crumbled."

"And the pastry? I asked for something light and flaky." He holds up a dense, highly creviced biscuit.

I scoff. "Dun's Crossing pastries are never light and flaky. That was your mistake."

"You must come visit. You have not lived if you have not tasted a true pastry." He shakes his head, then sips the coffee and grimaces. "For the honor of your kingdom, I shall not ask what occurred there."

I've made tea. Coffee, I have discovered, is a different beast altogether. I took a sip of the sludge on his tray and almost lost my own quick breakfast.

"Perhaps this is a good thing." Xander stands, holding only the toast. "Father has just informed me the first round of negotiations are beginning shortly, so I haven't time to eat."

"You're going?"

"The heir belongs at the king's side," Xander recites before grinning at me. "Breakfast or no breakfast."

* * *

We enter the eastern war room, which is already getting crowded. Clearly, Kieran picked the smallest one because he hoped it would constrain both parties. No such thing has occurred. At his end of the table, Taner, Jase, Raven, and a squirming Altair cluster around him. On the other, King Alden sits with Corwyn and a pair of nobles whose names I haven't yet learned. Xander sighs so subtly that if I hadn't been standing close enough to watch his chest move, I would never have noticed, before joining his father. I slouch over to the wall and lean against it. There aren't enough seats anyway.

"News of your kingdom's… troubles have reached us," Kieran says carefully.

Even that sets off a cascade of response from the Tansy Beach end of the table. A scowl flickers across King Alden's face before disappearing. Xander tenses slightly. Corwyn's sneer lingers barely longer than his king's scowl. The other two look to King Alden for their marching orders.

I've never been as good at this as Anwen, but some cues aren't difficult to pick up. King Alden isn't just hurt by his wife's departure —he's furious about it. Corwyn, too, is angrier than he is hurt. Xander and the nobles are harder to read.

"That is good." King Alden's voice is tight. "I had not wished to explain. Have you also heard the news from Birchmint Valley? Oakspring Dunes?"

Kieran nods steadily. Those are the two packs Moonlight Hollow is rumored to be allying with for some kind of attack. "I am equally aware there has been no movement from either of those packs yet."

Corwyn clears his throat. "Forgive me, Alpha, but by the time either moves, will it not be too late to act? Dun's Crossing shares a border now exclusively with Moonlight Hollow; Tansy Beach borders both of these other packs as well and could be easily pincered."

King Alden nods. "There is a reason we did not wait to travel to you, despite the risks."

"Does Moonlight Hollow patrol the borders?" Kieran asks.

Xander glances at his father. "Not in the way you imply. They merely watch."

"Then what risk did you accrue, Councilor Corwyn?"

I know Tansy Beach has some sort of strange inheritance system that means the crown does not always fall to the Mlakar family, but I didn't realize how much it would affect their politics. Kieran answers every question lobbed to his side of the table. The only person who ever attempts to interrupt him is an increasingly bored Altair, and only with pleas for "up," a game where Kieran tosses his son in the air. On the Tansy Beach side, however, answers come from almost every mouth.

The cacophony, the endless circles of asking one person only for another to reply, starts to wear on Kieran. When he cuts something just short of a glare at Altair's umpteenth interruption, and Raven squeezes their son protectively close, I decide I can play two of my siblings at once, no matter what Kieran asked of me.

"*King Alden is on the fence,*" I tell him just as Anwen would have. "*He's furious about what Queen Maris did, but he doesn't exactly crave bloodshed.*"

Kieran's gaze flicks to me for a second. "*Xander?*"

"*Diplomat.*" I think. He still wears his usual bravado, which mutes down many of his expressions into a flat confidence. But every time the matter of all-out war comes up, Xander offers a counterargument.

"*Councilor Corwyn?*" Kieran's mental voice is flat, disdainful.

I eye the Beta. He talks like an etiquette manual, every word a little too rehearsed, but he doesn't have the oily reek of a liar like Floyd.

"*The opposite,*" I say finally. "*A war hawk if I've ever seen one. I just don't know why.*"

"My nephew speaks the truth, though more baldly than I would have." King Alden inclines his head toward Corwyn, and a few things make more sense. "We come in the hopes you will commit troops."

"Troops?" Kieran's eyebrows shoot up. "We have nothing but a few rumors, and you want me to commit my people's lives?"

"If you do not, the people of Tansy Beach will have no choice but to die," Corwyn says.

"Unless the rumors prove untrue," Xander replies before Kieran even can.

I blink. I thought he was more peaceful, but I didn't expect him to disagree outright with one of his own people. King Alden is clearly thinking something similar. The corners of his mouth tug down for a heartbeat as he looks between his son and his nephew.

"Which they very well may." Kieran nods at Xander. "Can we not discuss a more diplomatic solution first? Have you attempted negotiations?"

"All routes of communication have been severed." King Alden's voice echoes off the tight walls so bitterly that Raven even stops amusing Altair to wince. He shifts, hiding the edge of a splash-shaped mating bite peeking from his sleeve.

King Alden and Queen Maris were mates. This kind of division between a couple like that borders on unheard of—yet another reason I'm not especially upset about how many Hazes have come and gone without finding anyone. A mate bond is work, like any other relationship, and it comes with a permanent, physical reminder when it fails. I wonder how much pain he's in.

I wonder what he did to make Queen Maris decide to leave anyway.

"Can they not be reopened?" Kieran spreads his hands in front of him, a disarming gesture.

"Attempts have been made," Corwyn snaps. "They have been rebuffed, and we are not foolish enough to sit around with our underbelly exposed, hoping Queen Maris might see fit to change her mind."

Her name lands like devouring ice in the center of the room. Xander freezes first, then King Alden. Kieran cannot resist long. Soon, I find myself in a room of statues rather than people, all trying to figure out what to say in the wake of someone finally naming the problem.

"You want our help; in exchange, we're only asking one favor," I say.

Every gaze in the room lands on me, heavy as rocks. I flatten my voice even further, check for dirt under my nails.

"You're here for a week already. Make one last attempt, and if nothing comes of it by the end of the week, we'll talk about troop commitment."

Kieran melts first, nodding slowly. "Yes. A compromise. Seek peace, and then we'll know we're not charging blindly into war."

King Alden folds his lips into a tight line. "Might we use one of your messengers? We believe their… familiarity with ours may have been part of the issue."

"Happily." Something like a smile grows on Kieran's face, though he doesn't look at me. "I do not want to leave our allies unprotected."

The king's answering expression lands halfway between a smile and a frown.

"Well?" Kieran says.

I study King Alden, the bags beneath his eyes, his white knuckles in his folded hands. If Anwen was here, he could read the king like an open book. But we are stuck with me.

"He's not lying," I say. *"He will send the message, and in earnest. But...."* I glance around the room, then peer at the Alpha one last time. There's no denying he's not happy with this solution, but that's no surprise. No, there's something else that's making me hesitate. Something lurking in the depths of his gaze or behind the wall of his teeth.

"I don't know," I admit. *"But I do not believe this is over."*

4

TOURNEY

Xander

I LEAN AGAINST ONE OF SOLBERG CASTLE'S PARAPETS, WATCHING STAFF members scurry back and forth below. They carry straw targets onto an archery field, construct brightly colored stands, and string flags from tree to tree.

Next to me, Father shakes his head. "King Kieran says this tourney will display their strength."

I raise an eyebrow. There are a few competitions that place their wolves at the forefront—races, sparring matches, tests of agility—but most of the displays being built before us highlight human capabilities. Capabilities that will never see a battlefield, no matter how impressive they may be. I know others consider our focus on our wolves strange, but I think their human-obsession makes far less sense.

He chuckles at my expression. "I believe my response was something similar."

The laughter is stiff, however. Bare inches of wall separate us, as they always have. Those inches seem far more relevant now that Mother isn't here to fill them.

A door creaks open, and the scent of ginger and moss reaches my nose. Finn. He has been dedicated to King Kieran's instruction to keep me occupied. We've spent days trading dares back and forth, and it is fun, but I attempted to slip his attention this morning because I'm getting tired of the production of princely camaraderie. I needed a break.

"King Alden." He bows as he approaches us. "Prince Xander."

Father and I bow.

"Watching the preparations?" he asks.

I nod, slouching into my lean a little further. "Sizing up your competition?"

He smirks. "You and I, in the same competition?"

I roll my eyes, but he's not wrong. Finn has at least four inches over me, and I've packed as much strength into my frame as I can, but last night's arm-wrestling rematch reminded me of the corded strength of his arms alone. Once, I caught sight of his wolf through some trees. He was a silver ghost of muscle, pure power pouring along the forest floor.

"Finally admitting you could not challenge me anywhere outside of a wrestling match?" I ask.

In the corner of my gaze, Father's eyes flash dangerously. I know what he's thinking. I hope he will not risk contradicting me in front of a foreign prince. There is a rush in playing these games with Finn, watching him come alive like he does in so few other places.

Finn joins me along the wall. "All kidding aside, there will be a Grand Melee, all wolves. Taner—my brother's Beta—is locked up with a few of his men, designing the perfect terrain for it right now."

That sounds… like a lot of fun. The diplomatic gesture is obvious, a concession to our preferences about wolves, but the terrain would give me more of an advantage than he thinks. Speed and strength are never going to be my strong suit, but I can jump surprisingly high, and my dappled coat makes it simple to hide. Handing Finn his ass in the center of a screaming arena, battle-rush pumping through my veins—

"Prince Xander will not be competing," Father says before I can reply.

His heavy hand landing on my shoulder is a reminder of every reason I hadn't even looked at the list of events. I straighten under it and nod.

"We do not like to publicize this, but he was born early." Father leans forward with the small, conspiratorial eyebrow raise I have seen so often. "He is slightly too frail to show his strength without displaying weakness to our enemies."

I shoot Finn a half-apologetic smile. It is a perfectly choreographed routine. Father doesn't need to say he trusts Finn or Dun's Crossing, doesn't even need to tell them the truth to make it seem like this is a win for them.

Finn's cool blue eyes flicker from Father to me, lingering on his hand on my shoulder. A step out of time. Usually, the recipient offers a gesture in kind or simply thanks us at this stage. But Finn is still looking. Those icy eyes shiver down my spine. What does he think he is going to find?

"Understood." Finn turns and leaves without another word.

Father releases me with a sigh and begins to walk away. "Why do you taunt that boy?"

I hurry after him. "He likes being taunted."

That only earns me another heavy sigh. "I don't need to remind you—"

The morning everything changed, the decree staked to the palace door, flashes through my mind's eye. "No, you don't."

He grits his jaw as we enter a dark tower, and strange voices float up; a pair of Dun's Crossing nobles, also headed for the prime tourney-watching vantage point. Silence hangs heavy between us as Father leads me back to our room.

All I can think about is that decree. It's been three weeks. Three weeks of outrunning the thought of it, and now he's made it unavoidable.

When I woke up, all I noticed was that the castle was quiet at first. I couldn't find Corwyn anywhere. But slowly, I followed the trails of looks and staff to the front door. The decree was still pinned in place by what I instantly recognized as Mother's letter opener, and my stomach dropped.

She'd been kidnapped.

I shoved through the crowd until I could read the paper, until I found Father and Corwyn at the front. Until I saw, in Mother's own looping hand, a declaration. Henceforth, the lands west of the Grayhead River would belong to Moonlight Hollow, a pack ruled by Luna Queen Maris.

Father opens the door into our suite and marches through to the private garden attached. He always says walls have ears. Sometimes, I wonder if that was one of the things Mother was running away from.

In the center of the garden, beside a babbling fountain, he coaxes even louder with a flick of his wrist, he looks at me. His hazel eyes are as heavy as his iron hand on my shoulder.

"I am not a young man," he begins.

"And the crown is not guaranteed," I finish. "I know, Father. But won't others someday notice that I am not nearly as frail as you claim?"

"Not if we stay the course." He looks up at the sky, and I know he's wishing for his favorite holy woman, Nomi. "Our family has held the throne for three generations, Xander. If we are careful, we can secure a fourth."

"The most cantankerous councilors are no longer members of Tansy Beach," I remind him. "What do we have to fear now?"

Another strange difference about visiting other places—they have one royal family, who hand the crown down one to the next. Though Finn is sharp, capable, the clear choice, the crown prince is his nephew who still wets himself. In Tansy Beach, eight great houses have always ruled by council supporting the current Alpha, and when that Alpha dies, it is from among those eight houses that the next Alpha is chosen. If there is a male heir of age in the former Alpha's line, they tend to be a shoo-in. Lord Denidor has a promising son a few years older than me, Lord Andrija objects—objected to Father's policies whenever he could, and Lord Zdenko is of age to take the throne himself, but all three of them defected.

Only five great families remain. Four and a half, really.

"Upon my death, there will be a vote," he says. "Votes can be swayed."

"Anything can be swayed." I shake my head. "Lord Juraj is frailer than ash, but he has the ear of half the generals; he could decide tomorrow that a military coup would be the best for his family and end all our worrying here and now. But if I am a king with no achievements to my name—"

"No achievements?" Father scoffs. "You have read every book in the library."

"Twice," I mutter.

"You are the reigning champion of bolar."

An ancient strategy game Father revived some years ago, it requires planning a semi-realistic attack on your opponent's pieces, and the winner is the one with the fewest casualties. He's right, but it's another skill I've developed in my room.

"I simply do not believe that kings are supposed to spend this much time in hiding." I stare at the grass under my feet, crushing the stems to paste with the toes of my boots.

Father stands. "Alexander. Are we going to have a problem?"

"No," I say, keeping my voice steady. "I understand why we are doing this. I always have."

His shadow falls over me, cooling the warm day. He's trying to keep me safe, I know. Perhaps the Grand Melee is particularly well-suited to my skills, but that doesn't stop some enterprising noble from taking the opportunity to end the Mlakar line with one conveniently ill-placed strike. It is reckless for any heir to enter such a battle, not merely me. But something new bubbles under my skin, something that makes me itch for more—a chance to prove I am more than just a continuation of the Mlakar line.

Father's pause is pregnant with words he is not saying. Words we cannot say to each other, here or anywhere. Finally, he turns for the door.

"Stay inside." His voice is low, almost distant. "Absence will raise fewer questions than sitting on the sidelines."

I nod as my gut knots around itself. Mother would have sat beside me in the stands, faking faint and claiming she needed her strong boy to support her through such a difficult time.

Or perhaps she wouldn't have. A few weeks ago, I would have guessed that, if Mother decided to leave, she would have taken me with her.

5

CREEPING HAZE

Finn

CHEERS RICOCHET OFF THE WALLS OF THE QUICK-BUILD ARENA, deafening, as one wolf shoulders another out of the jousting lane. I think both of them are from Dun's Crossing. In theory, they ought to be wearing our colors. Hell, they might be. But I've barely been paying attention.

Most of my attention is on the thin wisps of silver-gray mist threaded through the clouds. The very first sign of a Haze settling in.

Kieran said this might happen. As communication and cooperation grows, it's becoming more obvious that, though the Haze always comes somewhat randomly, big gatherings of wolves are likelier to be hit. Especially big gatherings that blend kingdoms, giving mates that ordinarily wouldn't be able to reach each other more chance to mingle. Yet another reason to wish the diplomatic visits would slow. Every Haze since I've come of age is just another opportunity to risk ending up in a messy situation I can never extract myself from.

Ingrid shoots out of her seat beside me, shouting as she lifts Altair to the sky. Jousting is apparently her newest hobby, but she thinks our soldiers always let her win, so she refuses to face them. I shake my head and look away as Kieran pulls his—perfectly safe—son from her grasp.

He looks like King Alden, stopping Xander from fighting in a melee with several hundred eyes on it. Worrying too much.

Elian elbows me. "He's up!"

I turn back toward the events where two more wolves are lining up. One, narrower than you usually see in a joust and pure white, prances in place. When he sees Elian waving from the royal box, he tosses his head and howls.

Fitting, given that wolf is Howell, Elian's mate.

On the other end is a Tansy Beach bruiser I don't recognize. Howell's reputation precedes him. Despite his size, he's one of the best Dun's Crossing has ever produced.

A trumpet sounds, and the two wolves barrel down the lanes. Deftly, Howell avoids the bruiser's graceless shoulder-slam and whips his tail across the bastard's eyes. The split-second of stumble is all he needs—a hip to the back knee, and the bruiser splashes into a puddle of mud.

The crowd goes wild once more.

"Oh, I have to talk to him." Ingrid leaps out of her seat and sprints from the box.

Before I'm done shaking my head, her seat is full once more. In honor of the deal we're striking, Kieran decided the Tansy Beach delegation should share our royal box. Xander hasn't made an appearance, but King Alden and Xander's Beta, Corwyn, have been here all day, watching intently from their corner. As soon as Ingrid abandons her chair beside me, Corwyn fills it with easy grace, like it already belongs to him.

"Interesting tactic," he says. "I've never seen anything like it. Do you know the jouster?"

Elian drops back into his seat with a wild grin. "He's my mate."

Every rumor about Tansy Beach speaks to their traditionalism, but even a place like that doesn't sneer at a mate bond between two men, as much as they might if the Goddess wasn't involved.

"I would appreciate your assistance in getting him to show me how he discovered it, then. I am not much for this sport, but I believe it could be useful on the battlefield...."

"Elian. Finn's Beta." He extends his hand and laughs. "Howell will love that." Corwyn shakes his hand amicably.

Over our mind-link, while "watching" the next match, I say, *Don't be flattered. He tries this hard with everyone.*

Harsh? Perhaps. But something about Corwyn rubs me the wrong way. Elian's smile dims a notch.

"Wonderful. I expect we'll see battle before long." Corwyn's gaze grows distant, thoughtful. "What do you think, Prince Finn?"

I cross my arms and lean back in my seat. "About?"

His eyebrows tick up. "The situation in Moonlight Hollow. Do you expect it to devolve into fighting?"

I glance over Corwyn's shoulder. A second empty seat now separates me from Kieran. Raven has disappeared, presumably to tend to something with Vespera. It would be easy enough to mind-link Kieran, but Corwyn would catch the look in my eyes. He's blocked me off from them anyway, like the physical shield of his body is enough to stop my thoughts.

He wants an answer, he wants it privately, and he wants it now. I've got no clue why. Kieran barely listens to me more than the average soldier, and I'm not crown prince anymore. The amount of influence I have here is negligible. Maybe he just wants to know if he can shake up our camp with a dissenter.

He should've done better research. There's no one less likely to shake the camp than me.

"Not sure," I reply, my gaze still on the match below.

His teeth click sharply together. "Beta Elian? What about you?"

Elian knows me too well to even look at me before snorting. "They don't let me into those meetings. I just play with all the little tents. I once stacked them twelve high before they collapsed."

"Ah." Corwyn's politeness strains at the edges already. Almost too easy. "Have you read the reports from the border, Prince Finn?"

"Wasn't aware there were any."

"You were in a meeting in which we discussed them," he nearly snaps.

"Was I?" I offer him half a laconic smile. "I figured out how to sleep with my eyes open a few years back. You really should try it. I've never been better rested."

"Perhaps I shall." Somehow, all that pseudo-charm he wielded in the meeting snaps instantly back into place. The smile, the warmth, all of it. He rakes a hand through his hair then bows to me and leaves.

I stare after him. There's simply no way I was imagining the tension. Tansy Beach wears busy, highly embroidered tunics, but even that couldn't hide the knots in his shoulders. And yet, for all the liars and snakes I know, there isn't a person among them who can put themselves back together that quickly, that perfectly, when nothing has changed.

Did you see that? I ask Elian.

I'm not sure, he replies.

* * *

THAT EVENING, I RAP ON THE DOOR TO KIERAN'S OFFICE.

"Come in," he calls.

I step inside. For once, Raven isn't here—Ingrid mentioned some kind of tea with the *one* woman Tansy Beach brought, and I assume that's now. Kieran sits at his desk, poring over piles of handwritten paperwork.

"What is all that?" I ask, moving a chair next to him.

"A proposal from Tansy Beach." He shakes his head and sits back. "They have some very specific requests, as well as the message they sent to Luna Mavis, witnessed by several credible people."

I grimace. "Goddess above, you'd think they want us to hate them."

"With a royal structure like theirs, I imagine they need all this protocol." He sighs, takes a sip from a glass of wine, and looks at me. "What can I do for you? Is it Prince Xander?"

I wish. He never even made an appearance at the tourney, which surprised me. I figured we'd bet on the whole thing, even if we didn't compete. I even prepared a few forfeits for that exact situation.

"His Beta, Corwyn. He…." I shake my head. "I have concerns about him."

"He's certainly a war hawk." Kieran glances back at the pile of paperwork. "I get the sense some of these requests have come directly from him."

"Not the king?"

Kieran sighs. "They sound like him, but despite our alliance, I haven't spent enough time with King Alden to be sure. I would like to, before I start making promises."

And if I was Anwen, he'd ask me to do it. They might be scattered to the corners of the globe, but it's like our siblings are still sitting between us. I'm still his third choice. There is no way he didn't notice Corwyn approaching Elian and me today, but I still had to come start the conversation with him, rather than the other way around.

"Corwyn seems to have a lot of sway over him," I say instead of any of that. It's not like he would hear me if I did.

"I'm not sure." Kieran runs his hand over the nearest page. "When I have spoken to him, he seems level-headed. He doesn't push for war, preemptive strikes." He frowns.

"What?" I know I need to ask.

"I expected him to be more hurt by Luna Maris's defection," he admits.

With the Haze hanging in the air, tingling over my skin, his words land heavier. Yet another reminder that matehood turns you into half of yourself. Kieran would be a shell if Raven left. King Alden might be, and Corwyn could be what's filling that shell.

"Corwyn seems willing to try anything," I say, "even cornering me for answers. I just think we should keep an eye on him."

"That, I am happy to do. But I think we can trust some of the delegation, even if they are different than we expect."

"Agreed. Xander has been basically nothing but upfront with me." His absence from the tournament and the strange moment where his father refused the tourney for him notwithstanding. I just don't get the feeling he's lying to me. At least not about anything important. He's the only one of them I actually find pleasant.

Kieran nods slowly. "And we'll see about the rest."

6

———

THE JOURNEY BEGINS

Xander

"YOU SEEM DISTRACTED," VEDRAN, MY PINK-EYED ATTENDANT, SAYS AS he finishes fastening the line of buttons down the back of my tunic.

I stare out the window at the cloud-studded Dun's Crossing sky. The tourney flags are all gone or hanging at odd angles, three days of celebrations melting the somewhat elegant presentation I've only ever seen through this window. "I suppose I'm surprised we are leaving this quickly."

"I thought you said King Kieran and your father had agreed." He smooths down the fabric, and my skin prickles with the familiar wave of his magic.

Mages are rare in Tansy Beach—across the whole world, really. Vedran is the only one I have ever met. His mother and mine crossed paths when we were first newborns, and Mother insisted Vedran come to the castle. The healer had already told her I was the only child she was likely to have, and Father had already begun worrying about the line of succession. A mage like Vedran, specializing in glamors as he now does, would be a miracle in terms of making sure I

31

looked like the sort of Alpha Tansy Beach needed. In exchange, he was educated as well as I was, and if I ever stop needing him, he'll have his pick of generous retirements.

"They have, but…." One more look out the window belies the real reason why we're leaving. Ribbons of blue Haze slice through the sky. If it doesn't descend tonight, it will be a miracle. There are thousands of little things that could affect my ascendancy to the throne, and potentially the largest of all reaches down from the clouds with hungry fingers.

Vedran follows my gaze and frowns with understanding. He knows me better than even my own Beta.

"Better to simply get this over with." I straighten my tunic one last time and step from my quarters into Father's attached room.

Trunks line the floor, waiting to be carried out by the flurry of staff darting to and fro. Still, Father feels a need to direct every single one, as though we will not all arrive in the same place and repeat the procedure in reverse at home.

"Go to the carriages," he barks. "I will manage this end, you, that."

Certainly better than being pressed into service carrying trunks. I leave the chaos for the slightly different chaos of the hall.

"Did he expel you, too?" Corwyn saunters up to Vedran and me, a traveling cloak draped over one shoulder.

"I'm to manage the carriages." I shake my head. We all know that's the same as being kicked out. Father has always been particular, and each trunk already has a single location it is destined for, come hell or high water.

"Regardless, I am beyond glad to be leaving. I thought King Kieran would never agree."

"To your proposal? He wouldn't have, cousin."

Corwyn snorts. "I don't know when you turned soft on me."

When the enemy on the other side of the board ceased to be pieces of carved stone or even foreign strangers but my own bloodline. He is my cousin through Mother; I don't know how he can be so cavalier.

I laugh at him. "Soft? Why would wanting territory I can use rather than blasted wastelands be soft? You're simply shortsighted."

"In these last few years, our very allies have proven even the worst wastelands can be revived." Corwyn looks at the hints of Escuro black amongst the Dun's Crossing blue in the decorations here.

"Our very allies have promised troops in three weeks." Three weeks during which, according to the lesser messengers scurrying back and forth, Mother *may* meet with him to discuss peace. Nothing has come directly from her yet. Somehow, I feel like I would know if it did. "So I suppose we shall discover who is correct."

I offer a silent prayer to the Goddess that it is not Corwyn. Perhaps the land can be revived, but those killed never can.

"Three weeks." He scoffs. "They may as well have turned us around at the door. They want us to flounder while they reinforce their own border."

King Kieran seemed frustrated when he first suggested sending troops in a month. Three weeks is a compromise—and, like all compromises, one no one is particularly happy with. Corwyn squeezes the ruby-studded hilt of the knife at his waist. How he, of all people, is taking this dispute most personally, I have no idea.

Outside, Finn leans against a wall within eyesight of the carriages, looking like he's not watching them load up. There will be a proper, formal goodbye once everything is prepared. We shall depart before noon, earlier if Father has his way. But I don't want to recite Finn's royal title and follow it up with the perfect bow.

"Watch the carriages," I tell Vedran before peeling off to talk to him.

"Surprised to see you out of bed." Finn smirks.

We spent last night drinking at that same little tavern until we could barely stumble to the castle, but the Haze infuses me with adrenaline.

"Ah, so you were drunk." I slump into an impression of him on the walk back. "M'not… even a li'l alcoval."

He rolls his eyes. "Don't worry about a goodbye. I'll remember you by the vomit you left on my shoes."

Now, that, I forgot about. It explains the taste in my mouth this morning, though.

I stick my hand out. A blatant violation of protocol—a challenge. Finn eyes it for a heartbeat then claps his palm against mine.

Static zings between us, like touching a doorknob at the end of a carpeted hallway. His fingers swallow mine, and his grip is powerful, almost crushing. I squeeze back. The faint ache in my joints barely registers over the gleam of competition, of laughter in his blue eyes.

I pull back. Any longer, and he'll notice just how much smaller my hands are. "One last win for you. Consider it a parting gift."

He shakes his head. "Whatever you say."

* * *

Father and I share a private carriage. He always claims Vedran makes him uncomfortable—a common enough complaint about the albino mage I've never understood. As usual, we sit across from each other, reading separate books. Or, in Father's case, sheafs of letters. I flip absently through a book of military strategy I first finished before age twelve.

The sun is setting, the moon beginning to peek above the horizon, and my bones feel like they are rattling in my flesh. It is time to go. My mate is out there. My wolf needs this—the run, the rush, the hunt.

I look at Father. He looks at me.

Without a word, he raps on the front of the carriage. "Find a stopping place. It will rain tomorrow, and my hip can take no more riding."

In an ancient border spat with Lightning Cape, before the reign of King Gavin, he once took an arrow to the hip. It does bother him when the weather sours, but fair skies are predicted for our whole journey home.

Still, mind-links ripple down the line as the coachman spreads the news, and before long, we are pulling into a tiny way-town. The well-kept inn and stables alongside ramshackle houses show this place survives by those who need overnight lodgings alone. In the morning, perhaps I'll convince Father to re-provision.

My wolf shrieks. Father dismounts the carriage to make arrangements, leaving his crown but wearing his royal colors. I dig my nails into the meat of my palms, letting them grow into the skin until the coppery scent of blood joins the stink of manure in the air. Only a few more moments.

I've endured two years of Hazes since coming of age. There is nothing new about tonight.

When he returns, I offer him my shoulder to "lean" on. He barely places any weight on me, instead crushing me to his side like I might change my mind and bolt. I almost remind him of the two years, but words seem almost impossible. Too human. Instinct is eating me alive.

He and I have private rooms on the first floor, everyone else above. Nearly private. Vedran will sleep in mine, probably already has the key. For now, I move through the wooden door and throw the heavy lock.

I take a deep breath. Another. The Haze shimmers in through the cracks in the shutters, rich with scent. Wet grass. Wet noses. The wet puff of another's breath on my fur.

I belong out there. Wild. Free. Hunting.

No, I belong on the throne. I squeeze my eyes shut and picture my royal portrait. The heavy copper crown I'll one day wear. Only a strong head can hold it up. I pull iron manacles from my bag, preparing to chain myself to the bed like usual.

A howl splits the night, and something inside me snaps.

I throw open the shutters and launch myself into the night.

7

WILD CONNECTION

Finn

A FEW MINUTES AGO—TIME DISAPPEARED WITH ALL MY LOGICAL thought, it seems—I was drinking in town with Elian and Howell, just like we do every Haze. They like to consider it an anniversary rather than keeping track of a specific date, and I know that the high of whatever the Moon Goddess is doing will keep me from getting too hungover.

This time, something is different. And I don't just mean the broken, squeaking bar door I left in my wake. All day, I've been strange. Off. Feeling the excitement drain the rest of the castle usually does when a delegation leaves.

When Xander left… shit, I almost wished he wasn't. Keeping track of him gave me something half-pleasant to do every day.

The deeper I charge into the Haze, though, the harder those thoughts get to hold onto. Any thoughts. Alcohol ribbons through my veins, fuzzing my vision. The seamless slide of muscles under fur and thudding rhythm of my paw pads on the cobblestones become all I am. That, and my nose pointed to the air. There's something out there. *Someone* out there.

I smell her.

My mate.

Aniseed and clove. Warm and unique. Unforgettable. I charge through the streets, chasing my heart. The people skittering out of my way with soft screams hardly matter in the face of her.

I understand why everyone wants this. Why they throw themselves into the Goddess's arms every time they get the chance. I have never been more whole, even with Haze and liquor distorting my thoughts.

The full moon overhead is like a spotlight, guiding my footsteps. Out of town, south, through the forest. Every step brings me closer. The Goddess urges me, gifts me the stamina I need, speeds my steps

There she is.

Across a clearing, I lock eyes with my mate. Clove and aniseed blind me to everything else. There's no hesitation, no game, no wondering what comes next. A heartbeat after we see each other, we are sprinting the remaining distance. Maybe I can't see quite clearly. Nothing could possibly matter less when her coat brushes mine, thick fur tangling. I twist around her, the shift starting to take me.

And she bolts past. Her tongue lolls from her mouth, halfway to a smile. An irritated bark slips from my lips—why not here? As soon as we found each other?

Her answering yip oozes challenge. The Haze grabs me again, urges me after her. She might be mine, but I have to prove it—to her, if no one else.

I take off after her. She weaves through trees, hides in low bushes, even ends up chasing me in one blurry moment. Liquor slows my reactions—tomorrow, I will show her just what I am capable of. She may be brilliant, but I can keep up.

She is brilliant. I don't realize she's led us to one of the tents Kieran sets up for the event until we arrive at it. I pause, brace to jump and tackle her into the tent if she isn't intending to stop, but my mate is a miracle. She charges inside without breaking stride.

I shift in the doorway of the tent. My human eyes are blurrier even than my wolf ones, but I see the shape on the cot, bare and welcoming. Human sight—human thought is a waste of time with my mate before me.

Our mouths crash together. Aniseed and clove twine on my tongue as she pushes hungrily into my mouth. I scrape my hands over the silken skin of her sides. Muscle cloaks her ribs, her stomach, but she's still so soft. She hisses in pleasure, and the sound shoots through me like an arrow from a master's bow. My cock, already hard, springs to impossible attention. I need to be inside her.

She bites my lower lip. I snarl and bite her right back. Aniseed and clove and copper on my tongue, a few drops of precious blood spilled. I lap them up in half-apology, half-hunger. She barely lets me, still intent on devouring my mouth.

Her hands knot in my hair. I grasp at every inch of skin I can reach. No matter where I touch, she responds, willing, wanting. I reach for the apex of her legs. If she is this pliant, surely—

Before I can touch her, she wraps her hand around the base of my cock, and I groan as I jerk into her touch. With a few nudges, she guides me to her mouth. My body screams with want. When she lays my tip on her tongue, whatever last, desperate reserve of self-control I might've been holding onto shatters like a dropped glass. I fuck into her warmth, her wetness.

She is like nothing I've ever experienced. Distantly, I am aware I've had sex. After Anwen, half the women in the castle wouldn't go anywhere near me, but the other half was more than happy to indulge a few awkward, teenage fumblings. I learned on my own, learned quietly where my brothers were loud. I know how to make a woman squirm, even weep.

Learning left little time for exploring everything that could be done to me. I'm sure some woman somewhere knows the taste of my cock. With my mate wrapped around me for the very first time, I have no idea who she is, and I don't want to. My mate rolls her tongue along my underside, grabs my hips to pull me closer. She is tight and welcoming, swallowing me deeper. I brush the roof of her mouth, and the spasming of her muscles almost sends me careening over the edge.

Some deeper instinct than pleasure screams in the back of my mind. I can't finish without her, outside of her. Where I cannot reach her vulnerable skin with my teeth to mark her forever mine. She stares up at me, eyes full of moonlight through the opening at the top of the tent, and I know she wouldn't begrudge me if I did.

She would count it a win.

I grit my teeth, slow the rhythm of my hips. She's mine. I will prove it to her. She groans, vibrations shimmering up my cock, and I barely resist losing myself. Instead, I slide a hand into her hair—shorter than I would have expected—and pull her back. She fights me every inch, scraping her teeth softly over my skin and dragging her nails down the backs of my thighs in teasing stripes. But she cannot resist me.

The tip pops from her lips as I stare into those moonlight eyes, sparkling with something beyond the animal. She is daring me to make the next move.

I am more than happy to.

My muscles ripple as I flip us. She sits over me, backlit, but I won't give her a chance to take this as a position of power. I line my saliva-soaked cock up with her entrance and pull her down onto it.

She keens, high, somewhere between pain and pleasure. Guilt tears through me—I should have been more careful, should have made sure she was wet instead of trusting the lubrication already provided. But then, she rolls her hips.

Her mouth was magical. This? This is a fucking miracle.

She's so tight it almost hurts, impossibly hot, and still, she tries to take more. She impales herself on me, inch by inch. I squeeze her hips, setting a rhythm, but she has control over the depth. She's my mate, and that means I need to protect her.

When her hips meet mine, sticky skin on skin, I know this is where I belong.

I pull her up, throw her back down. Her thighs tense as she moves with me, leaning into my punishing rhythm. Those high, desperate moans build in volume. Mine join her in harmony. I press my fingerprints into her hips, holding on like she might disappear if I let go for a single second.

She leans down and buries her teeth in the muscles of my chest. My groan snaps in the middle, wound too tight to hold itself together as I spear deeper into her than ever before. I grab a fist of her hair and drag her close enough to my mouth to mark. The tender skin of her shoulder brushes my lips, knotted with tension. I bare my teeth and bite.

As my mate shakes on top of me, my mind goes white. Pleasure, blood, and her combine into a cocktail more potent than anything I drank earlier. I fly, and judging by her scream, she flies with me.

The next thing I'm aware of is her muscles fluttering around my cock. Satiated exhaustion weighs me down. I can't imagine moving an inch. As I wrap my arms around my mate and bury my nose in her air, the tent overhead spins slightly.

Oh, Goddess, I pray, not feeling ridiculous at all. *Let me remember this tomorrow. Every second of it.*

Sleep claims me as my mate starts to stir.

8

REALIZATION

Finn

Morning comes faster than I expect. Last night, it was... I don't have the words to describe it. I thought it would last forever, away from sunlight and anybody else's opinions. A hangover clusters at my temples, informing me the Haze's effects only chase those off if you spend it alone. Memories of last night only exist in flashes, but I'd still rather have those than no headache.

The scent of clove and aniseed still hangs heavy in the air. Her. My mate. Months of avoiding the Haze, resenting it, feeling stupid in the wake of her come to mind. Something rustles, and I open my eyes.

She bends elegantly over, displaying an ass I know I'm going to dream about, even if I can barely remember it from last night. Disappointingly, she's already dressed, so I have to imagine the ass without the interfering pants. Her arms move quickly, sharply as she laces up a pair of boots. The clothes usually left in the tents for the Haze hang loosely on her frame, hiding her curves.

Curves my hands remember, even if my mind doesn't. I rub my

fingers against each other. The silken touch of her skin remains, at least.

She straightens, but only halfway. Why? The tent ceiling isn't that—

Realization strikes like a punch to the gut. She's attempting to sneak out. She doesn't want to see me.

"Hey." I push up onto one elbow. She can't escape that easily—at least, not while I am hungover enough not to regret asking her to stay.

All my fuzzy excitement grinds to a screeching halt as I watch my mate turn around. Auburn hair swings out of the way to reveal a familiar face

Not a stranger. Not the sole woman in the Tansy Beach contingent.

Xander stands as far away from me as he can in the tiny tent, brows drawn tight against each other.

My mouth falls open. I snap it shut. This isn't possible. I would've known. I'm not gay. I did not have sex with a man last night.

The high, frantic noise he made when I entered him echoes in my memories.

No. There is only one answer.

I burst out laughing.

"I knew you were funny." I swipe a tear from one of my eyes. "But this is a level I was not expecting."

"What, exactly, about this is funny?" he asks, his voice rough with sleep, shoulders still knotted with tension like I haven't caught him in the joke of the century. I have to appreciate his commitment to his role, at least.

Otherwise, I'd have to consider that I've heard that voice before, or nearly. It didn't shoot through me then like it does now.

"Come on." I sit up, blanket pooling around my waist. My chest throbs with a fresh mate's mark. "Bring in Elian and the girl I had sex with last night. He must be involved."

"I am relatively certain your Beta was not *involved* last night," Xander says tightly.

Hangover pain and bite pain throb in unison. My mind rejects the conclusion laid out before me. That would be simply impossible. I was drunk, caught up in the Haze, but I could not have missed all that. I would have recognized Xander, at least.

Distantly, I remember that Kieran and Raven fucked their presumed twins during the Haze without noticing. As quickly as I think of that, I shove it away.

"Ha-ha," I say, all actual laughter swiftly dying. "You've gotten me. Now, where is my mate? She deserves her own congratulations for messing with me like this on our very first morning together."

Xander's jaw works. Emotions flash through his hazel eyes like schools of fish through disturbed water. I've never realized quite how many colors there are in his eyes; gray, green, hints of sky and sapphire blue. They shine like mica, hiding how special they are behind the façade of plainness.

What under the Goddess's light am I thinking?

Xander answers that question for me by pulling back the curtain of his hair and tugging aside the neck of his tunic. There, emblazoned on his neck like a brand, sits the swollen, red outline of a sun-shaped mate mark.

Discovering who was standing in my tent hit me like a fist. This hits me like a battering ram to the skull. I drop back onto the thin pillow, mind spinning. A thousand thoughts fight for my attention, but all I can focus on is one: the tempting curve of his neck and how much I want to put my mouth on it again. It sweeps up into the angle of his chin, a perfect contrast.

I put my hand on my cock over the blanket and close my eyes. He can't see its swift reaction, how much I want to pull him back onto this shitty mattress for another round—one I can actually remember. And I cannot see his reaction to that.

Disconnected images swirl through my mind. His hand wrapped around mine, last night or in some competition. The column of his throat bobbing as he knocked back pint after pint. The sparkle of laughter in his eyes whenever court grows too boring.

He is leaving.

My mark aches, throbbing on my chest, and reality knocks my teeth in. This is exactly what I was avoiding. Mating bonds are a gift from the Goddess, a promise this person *could* make you the happiest in the whole world, but they're also a fucking curse. Just because, in theory, Xander could make me happy, his unhappiness will torture me for the rest of my life.

"You never told me you were gay," I say.

Silence falls like a heavy blanket. I cannot imagine a more useless set of words to throw down, but I cannot imagine any others to say either. I didn't tell him I was gay—because I'm not. Or I didn't believe I was.

My headache intensifies. Hangovers aren't meant for mornings such as this.

"I'm not," Xander snaps, turning away, toward the door of the tent.

Another lightning bolt of pain. I grit my teeth.

"This… it doesn't mean anything." He scrapes a hand through his hair, not looking at me. "It was a mistake."

"What?"

Fuck everything I've thought so far this morning. I'd give up everything that happened last night for my life being my own again. Especially with how disgusted he seems.

"We are not talking about this," he hisses through gritted teeth.

That shouldn't even hurt. Xander shouldn't be anything more than a guy who occasionally makes me laugh at galas. An ally, at most. I feel like I've been pulled out of bed and dropped in the middle of a thunderstorm—nothing makes sense, and I did not ask for any of it.

Still, I can't stop thinking about his now-hidden mark. The location should have been another clue—why would I have avoided my mate's chest unless I was protecting myself from something I didn't want to know?

I stand. My shadow swallows Xander's on the tent wall. "Yes, we are."

He shudders, sways. Pain redoubles in my mark—whatever we are to each other now, I shouldn't be treating him like that. But I need to talk to someone, and I cannot exactly imagine sauntering back into the castle and asking Kieran for advice. No matter what I did, the gossip would spread like wildfire, and I can only imagine what that would do to the alliance.

"Threaten me all you like, Prince Finn." Xander straightens, faces me, wields as much of his less impressive height as he can. "You do not scare me."

"I'll be in Tansy Beach in three weeks." It's all I can say. Three weeks, and then we shall have to face this, one way or another.

"Unless peace talks are successful." A muscle flickers, tense, in his jaw.

"Right." I don't mean to sound like I don't believe him. But King Alden has spent a week complaining that Luna Maris will not negotiate with him for a reason; she still hasn't, and the only thing forcing her to the table now is the threat of Dun's Crossing's additional strength.

Silence stretches between us, and I know I've said the wrong thing. Maybe he still wants his mother to return. I cannot imagine wanting my mother anywhere other than buried under a few seasons of ice in Snowcrest, but Luna Maris seemed nice enough.

"It makes no difference where you or I will be," Xander says tightly. "This cannot have happened. It did not."

My knees almost buckle as agony screams from my mark out into the rest of my body. Goddessdamned bond! Rejection shouldn't hurt like this. I shouldn't be forced, for a chance at happiness, to take every refusal like a crushing blow. I have spent far too long getting good at rejection to lose it all like this.

But perhaps Xander has spent that same time improving his ability to dole it out because he uses my moment of distraction to flee the tent entirely, leaving me alone.

9

———

THE TRUTH BEHIND CLOSED DOORS

Xander

I PRY OPEN THE SHUTTERS ON MY ROOM WITH MY FINGERNAILS, WOOD splintering. My neck burns, as it has since I left Finn standing in the tent.

Why did it have to be Finn? Why couldn't it be some boy from this tiny way station I would never see again, or some lesser noble I could intimidate into silence? Something sparked in his eyes when he saw it was me—confusion, shock, the blatant attempt to hide from himself what had occurred by accusing me of making fun of him, certainly, but something beyond that. Something I already know will haunt me for the rest of my days.

But those aren't the sorts of thoughts I can be having right now. I clutch the loose Dun's Crossing tunic around my chest, desperately grateful for their strange blend of modesty and wildness as I slip in through the window.

Vedran sits in a chair in the center of the room, pink eyes muzzy with sleep but clearly waiting for me. "Your father is already stirring next door."

I let out a loud breath. Of course, Vedran will keep this secret, just as he keeps the rest of the things I've confessed to him. I close the shutters, shed the Dun's Crossing clothes, and submit to my morning routine.

He's quick, like always. Before I even dress, he traces the line of my jaw, my brow, with his tingling magic. Princes are supposed to look a certain way, and every little bit of help I can get, I shall take. Additionally, he has recently figured out a glamor to shield my facial expressions in little ways, which he swipes over my lips and eyes.

The work on my body is clinical as always. He hides muscle tone in one place, enhances it in another, smooths and roughens and intensifies as needed. When I was younger, Mother and Father set the regimen of spells I endured. Since coming of age, my appearance has been left more in my own hands, but I have changed very little. The people of Tansy Beach have come to depend on Prince Xander looking a certain way, and I intend to deliver.

There is one departure from routine, though. Vedran pauses at my neck on the raised redness of Finn's bite. I haven't seen it, turned my eyes away from the one creek I passed religiously, like I could make it disappear if I only ignored it, but it is impossible not to feel. Impossible not to know why Vedran has stopped and what he's thinking.

Without a word, he steps over to his bag and pulls out a book. The daily spells, he knows by heart, but he is capable of more, scrawled in tight hand in a heavy, leather tome he carries everywhere.

Father's footsteps pound down the hallway. We have only a few more seconds, and if I cannot hide this, all is lost. I don't know what he will do. Ever since Mother—

Vedran races back to me, lays his palm fully on my neck, and whispers a word in silvertongue, the ancient language. Magic prickles like little hooks, sharper than usual.

Father doesn't bother knocking. As always, there are three keys to my room—mine, Vedran's, and his. I barely have time to pull on a long tunic before the door slams into the wall.

He strides inside, shutting the door behind him with routine precision, then looks me up and down. "The Haze has passed."

"I can feel it," I reply as I reach for a pair of trousers Vedran already has in hand.

"How was your evening?" He turns away from me, inspecting the walls.

Fuck. On most Hazes, I spend the evening clawing at anything I can reach, desperate to escape my own restraints. There are no gouges in these walls. The only blessing I can name is the manacles, laying on the floor where I dropped them before my flight. I could well have bound and freed myself.

Anger sears through me, brighter and louder than any pain in my mark. Years of practice, of success. And I failed on the very first Haze where I was close enough to Finn for it to matter. I should have been more prepared, should have asked to stop sooner, should have—

I swallow. "Dull. You would be surprised how similar they become, after a time."

"Is that so?" He circles the room slowly. "I assume that would be why I heard less of you than usual."

Icy fear weaves through the burn of anger. Yet another detail I've missed.

"Prince Xander worried that his howls might alert the entourage to the truth of his location," Vedran says quickly. "He had me work a spell to bind his tongue."

"Hmm." Father looks from my attendant to me, his eyes sharp. He seems all at once like the man I knew before Mother's betrayal; clever, put-together, no longer so out of sorts.

The lie twists like a knife in my chest. All my life, the three of us— four of us, truly, because Vedran's contributions cannot be under- stated—have been a bulwark against the world. The continuation of the family name, the legacy, has been our heart. Mother destabilized the balance. Father's unpredictability knocked me asunder. Vedran has held steady, but alone, he cannot keep all the threads in this tapestry. Lying as I have feels like grabbing one of the threads and pulling. If Father and I cannot trust each other…

"I am pleased to hear it," he says. "Hopefully, that is something that could be continued upon our return."

Of course, he believes us. What cause have I given him not to? The manacles were my very own idea, after enduring my first agonizing Haze with only my own willpower and a few locks on the doors.

"I did come to you for a purpose." He withdraws a scroll from a fold in his cloak. "I have received word from the other side."

That's what he calls Moonlight Hollow, Mother, and everyone who went with her. He says he will recognize any kingdom who earns their name, not those who steal it.

Still, my heart skips beat after beat. Either Mother has refused the offer, and Dun's Crossing will arrive in Tansy Beach far sooner than three weeks, or Mother has accepted, and this all stands a chance of coming to an amicable end.

"What did she say?" I take a step forward.

Father unrolls the scroll and reads. "We will meet you in the Beddingsea Grove, twelve days hence. If terms can be agreed to, a peace can be found between our… kingdoms."

Beddingsea is a tiny forest, right on the border of the split lands. Neutral territory, or as close as any in a civil war can get to such a thing.

"She's willing to negotiate." Something as close to a smile as I can manage on a morning like this pulls at my lips. "I'll be going with you, of course."

Father's brow knits, and he turns the scroll around to show the paragraphs he didn't read. "No. They have a number of terms to ensure this meeting is *safe for all who attend*."

With a hollow thud, I realize the words don't sound like Mother's, though. They have the careful pronoun-avoidance of some undersecretary writing for the queen and wishing not to overstep. The legalese smacks of Lord Denidor, though I doubt he set his hand to the paper. It does not even truly say she will be there.

"Ah." I saunter over to the bed and drop onto it. "I suppose that makes sense."

"I believe the meeting shall be private." He scans the writing intently. "Between her and myself alone."

Were he meeting with any other kingdom, Father would say that this was a trap. Beddingsea is barely neutral ground—both sides have claimed it–but Moonlight Hollow uses it most frequently. And I don't believe Mother would stoop so low, but Lord Zdenko has always advocated those sorts of underhanded techniques. He should take someone with him.

He should take me. If any other soul deserves to be in this meeting, it is the crown prince and scion of the two warring houses. I am living, breathing neutral territory—or I ought to be. Perhaps I am not certain how Mother thinks of me at this time, but I know how she treated me. How she loved me. In a castle where appearances are paramount, she loved me more in private than she ever did with the eyes of the court on us.

I open my mouth to tell Father this and realize he is still staring at the scroll. He runs a thumb over the stamped seal at the bottom. That, too, was likely impressed into the paper by some secretary. I'm not even sure where Mother would have gotten such a thing. But he strokes it as if she made every dent with her very own nails.

My neck throbs, and my words catch in my throat. His mate left him. He has been living with pain like this—perhaps worse—for months. I owe him a moment of privacy with her, for the lie if nothing else.

Though I cannot regret lying to him. The last thing the family needs is another threat. And for all I cannot intimidate or avoid Finn, I don't believe he will reveal what happened between us. That would risk far too much of himself. Frankly, I am shocked he didn't take my refusal and leave himself.

Another ache. I am something he cares about enough to fight for.

I kick my legs up and slaughter all these thoughts. "Planning to seduce her back home?"

Father looks at me, startled, then laughs. "You shall have to stop talking like that if I do."

10

A MISTAKE

Finn

My paws thud over dirt. Wind tousles my fur. Here, in my wolf form, I can almost hide from all the thoughts whirling through my head and lose myself in the simple, animal pleasures.

Those simple, animal pleasures being exactly what fucked me in the first place.

Still, my body hums with energy. Excitement. It screams for me to forget the castle, to turn around and charge after the Tansy Beach contingent. I can chase them all the way to the border before I risk causing an international incident. My legs ache for the stretch, my lungs for the challenge.

I ignore it. It's nothing more than Haze-hangover to go with the more classic one throbbing in my temples. I have no idea what came over me in the tent. Asking Xander to stay, to face what happened… what the hell did I expect? He'd already decided to leave, and if I think about it for more than one Goddess-damned moment, I know that he's right.

What happened between us was a mistake.

After all my siblings, I am not foolish enough to pretend that the Goddess Herself is wrong; She never is. I'd rather not waste my energy pretending there's some magical loophole either of us can exploit to escape, or that She was as drunk as I was last night. No, it's a much more average mistake. The sort of thing we both ignore like it never happened.

Maybe, in another world, the two of us could've made each other happy. In this one, where he's got a warring kingdom on his shoulders, and I am…the same as I always have been, it's better for both of us to pretend we both stayed in last night.

As soon as I'm back within the walls of the castle that will feel as true as it sounds. All I need is a little normalcy.

I lope up to the front gates of the castle, still in wolf form. *"Open up."*

"Prince Finn?" the guard on duty replies.

"Who else?"

I cannot shift to prove my point. It's most efficient to include one set of male clothes and one set of female in each tent for the Haze. Since Xander woke first and either didn't realize that or didn't care, I have nothing but my pelt to keep me decent.

In most situations, I wouldn't care if our own soldiers saw me naked. I trained with most of them occasionally. But the day after the Haze?

I'm already losing the race against the rumor mill, if I know anything about the castle.

The gates creak open slowly, and I slither inside as soon as there's a gap. A few gasps chase my path—it's not exactly common to enter as a wolf. I snarl, realizing there's only one way to protect whatever shred of a chance I have at not being the next big topic.

I channel Elian into a dopey, wolfish smile and knock a pile of papers out of a nearby courtier's hands. He starts to object then recognizes my silver coat and forces a laugh. Nauseating. But I force myself to tug on the end of a soldier's halberd, play with the tassels on the hem of a lady's dress, whatever I can imagine making Elian laugh on the long, long trip to my room.

Finally, I reach my door, shift, and dart inside before anyone sees me.

Sweet peace and quiet. Wind whistles in through open windows, cooling my overheated skin. My usual hangover breakfast sits on the table in front of my couch, at least an hour old by now. I still grab a thick slice of fried bread as I walk toward my bedroom to ring for some time to come and run my bath and put on my robe.

The servants arrive swiftly, and I cover myself in enough pillows and blankets that they don't ask any questions of me as they go about their tasks. This is what I need. Privacy. An opportunity to organize my thoughts without Xander's smell in the air, muddling them.

When the door shuts behind them, I shed my robe and pad into the bathroom. Steam rises off the tub. Soap eddies within, white like the crests of waves—

I shake my head and climb inside. All thoughts of Xander, or at least those which do not directly concern the situation with Moonlight Hollow, are forbidden until I've at least had a bath. At that point, I stand a chance of feeling like myself.

The soap I requested is the most fragrant in the castle, made with sap from pine trees to the north that blot out almost every other smell. It's strangely thick, clinging to my fingers when I try to scrub, but it does what I need it to do. Within moments of sitting down, the idea of smelling clove or aniseed seems impossible. There has only ever been pine.

Perhaps I'll regret that later, but at least Candace is no longer here to forbid it for the headaches it gave her.

Washing myself, though, draws my attention back to the mating mark on my chest. This early, I can barely see the shape. If I hadn't spotted part of King Alden's, I would have no idea what the blurry outline was, other than another sun. Instead, I know the two crescent moons of Xander's teeth sit at the center of a splash, splatter across my pectoral and through my pale chest hair like a bead of water dropped on my skin from a height. If it were any larger, it would be visible through the lacing of some tunics.

Something thuds. I'm starting to turn when I smell it—ink and some purple flower I can never remember the name of.

Shit. My time is up.

I scrape bubbles toward my chest a heartbeat before the bathroom door slams open with a *thud* that instantly explains the first noise I heard. Graceful as a herd of bulls, Ingrid careens into my bathroom.

"I heard you were *out* last night." She waggles her eyebrows as if she hasn't broken into my room to harass me about half a rumor.

Yet another sibling missing those who have gone. Before Candace moved to Snowcrest Canyon, Ingrid would barely have noticed if I walked in proclaiming a new mate and my impromptu wedding. We've just never had much in common—that, and she and Candace lived in each other's pockets.

"I always go out for the Haze." I gesture at the door. "You can go ask Elian and Howell about it instead."

Mistake. I haven't asked either of them to lie for me. Elian might know without being asked—or remain asleep at this time—but Howell is his better half in many ways, most of which are primed to fuck me today. Maybe I can use the mind-link to warn them.

"You are just trying to distract me with the idea of jousting." She boosts herself up onto the counter and kicks her feet, revealing surprisingly heavy boots under her thin summer dress. "That means there is something to know, and I want to know it first."

"Gossip your latest hobby?" I raise a tired eyebrow.

I cannot mind-link to him now. She'll notice and pounce. I just need a distraction.

"And here I thought Candace said you were secretly paying attention." She shakes her head, blonde braids whipping into a cloud. "No, Dario is a gossip, and if I bring him something particularly juicy he'll train me."

Dario is Kieran's new Master-at-Arms, yet another in a long line of bastards Father left behind. Sometimes, it seems like Kieran will never be able to weed them all out. Dario is a transplant from across the Lonely Sea, so gossip doesn't surprise me. He's still trying to find his place here.

Somehow, that does not make it any less exhausting to be hounded.

"Then I suppose you're not getting trained." I yawn elaborately. "I got extremely drunk and passed out in some alleyway. End of story."

"Come on," she wheedles, leaning closer and batting her eyelashes teasingly.

That would work on Candace. It would work on Kieran, probably. Hell, it would've worked on Father. And I'm not any of them.

"Believe it or not, you cannot will me into being someone you can manipulate just because everyone else has left," I snap. "Maybe making some actual friends instead of relying on blood relations should be your next hobby."

Ingrid blinks. Have I...actually hurt her? It probably makes me an awful person that all I can think about is that at least she'll leave if I have.

She throws back her head and laughs. "I'm here because you cannot make any other friends, Finn, not the other way around."

"Elian and Howell—"

"The Beta Father picked out for you and his mate?" She laughs again. "Now who's falling back on blood relations?"

I grit my teeth. "Leave. I'm done talking about this."

Instantly, I wish I hadn't said it like that. Images of Xander, framed in muted morning sunlight, saying the same thing, consume my thoughts. Ending conversations like that never works, no matter how much you want it to. In three weeks, I'll be face-to-face with him again, and we'll both know there's more to say.

"But I'm not." She leans away when I splash her. "If nothing happened, why were you acting so strange on the way in?"

"Still drunk," I mumble. Goddess above, I wish I was still drunk. Numbness would be a blessing.

If I were still drunk, I wouldn't have felt that rush of electricity when he showed me his collarbone, the imprint of my teeth in ruby red. I wouldn't have wanted to fit my mouth over it to see if he still tasted as sweet.

"All right, I'll guess." She narrows her eyes. "You found your mate, and it's the married bartender from that bar you like, so you can never go back."

"No. She's mated." I don't know that I can never go back, but I suspect I'll need at least a month before I can hear anything but Xander's laughter bouncing off the ceiling.

"Hmm…the Goddess came to you and told you She was your mate." She laughs.

"No, that's it," I deadpan. "I'm moving into the sky next week."

My mark throbs. If I could speak to the Goddess directly, I wouldn't have anything that pleasant to say to Her.

She rolls her eyes. "You didn't find your mate, but you did sleep with someone with the absolute worst timing."

"By the Goddess, can you shut up?" My words lash out, fast and sharp. "I haven't met anyone in a full year of Hazes. I've been out late on almost everyone. At some point, you and everyone else are going to have to accept that I'm never going to meet my mate. There is no one out there for someone like me."

Silence falls. Ingrid studies my face, eyes sharp.

At last, she hops down off the counter and starts to leave. "Certainly not with that attitude."

I duck beneath the water until I hear the door close behind her.

11

RISING TENSION

Xander

WE ARRIVE HOME IN TANSY BEACH ONLY A DAY LATER. FATHER PUSHED the horses hard, changing them whenever we could purchase new ones. As soon as the carriage rolls to a halt, he throws the door open and leaps out.

"There is much to prepare," he says before I've even stood.

Corwyn appears at his shoulder. "Agreed. What can Xander and I assist with?"

I climb, achingly, from the carriage as Father nods appreciatively at Corwyn.

"I was hoping the two of you might shoulder some details so I might prepare for the peace talk." He glances at the low-slung, sand-stone castle behind him, and I imagine he's picturing Mother waving from the open-air walkway once more. "Corwyn, you have to keep the Council in order. Run the meetings and ensure those fools do not gain the floor for long. Xander, you can hear petitions from the people, yes?"

I nod. Petitions are few and far between these days, our people just as shredded as our kingdom, but that only means I will have time to do many other things.

Father hands out more responsibilities. Corwyn is to cultivate any other alliances he deems valuable, as he has been able to make more—or at least, more reputable—connections with other kingdoms. I will manage the palace and ensure all remains steady. We will work together on a few prospective attack and defense plans, focused on all relevant borders. And so on.

The more I agree, the more my mark throbs. There is so much to do and only three weeks to do it in. When Finn arrives…I have no idea what will happen.

* * *

"No, to the east." Corwyn points at a corner of the map laid out on the table before us. "We have a weak point in the line there."

I nudge the small wooden tent representing a squadron to the spot he indicates. "We left that weak point on purpose, I thought. To funnel troops into this stronghold."

He eyes the circle of tents directly behind the one I just pushed into place. It's been a week since our arrival home, and I haven't seen Father for more than half an hour at a time since. Corwyn and I have been spending nearly every waking moment together. He may be running the Council, but I'm still required to attend. I may be answering what few petitions we have, but he stands at my side as a representative of the Hajni family. I love my cousin, but I am swiftly growing tired of having him as my only company.

"That was your idea, wasn't it?"

I gesture over my shoulder at one of the thick tomes of military strategy on the shelf. "Poropat's idea, really."

"Right." His gaze flickers quickly to the book then back to the map. "And was Poropat subject to a civil war?"

"No, Poropat fought—"

"Then he was not prepared for enemies who know our terrain and tactics as well as we do." Corwyn scoops the circle of troops off the map. "We would be better off attempting to invent our own tactics than using anything out of those books."

"Those are big words from someone who has never yet defeated me in *bolar*." I grab his wrist, and for a second, we become children again, wrestling for some dessert or prize.

He's strong, but there is no one in this world I know how to fight better than him. I duck a swinging fist and twist his arm back until he releases the tents. Corwyn may not be my brother, but he might as well be. In everything but heritability, that is. His two years over me would ensure his ascent to the throne if he was.

Corwyn snaps at me with a teasing smile. "I thought the fragile little prince had to let his words do his fighting for him."

"I thought the cocky counselor could see through Father's bullshit." I release him, stand, and dump the tents on the table.

In truth, I couldn't care less whether we use my plan or his. We are imagining potential scenarios, preparing for eventualities. It's bloodless. Boring. And the closest I'll ever be allowed to actual fighting. In this scenario, Moonlight Hollow attacks with the full might of Oakspring Dunes, Birchmint Valley, and another neighbor we haven't yet named. No matter how much has changed, I do not see Mother doing that.

I see her coming to this peace talk with Father earnestly. Agreeing to terms. Ending the violence before it spreads. But I don't much see her starting this war, and the rumors of her alliance with other kingdoms continue to intensify.

Corwyn smirks. "Let us leave this for now, then. I shall take a look at Poropat and see if he has anything of value to offer."

"I doubt you could read a word." I snatch the book off the shelf and drop it heavily in front of him. My cousin is many things, but as our years sharing a tutor can attest, *studious* is not one of them.

"I told you not to spread word of my near illiteracy." He pulls a sheaf of papers he was scribbling on before a pair of undersecretaries brought the map in over to him. "I've heard from Lightning Cape."

Swallowing my grimace is a struggle. Lightning Cape was one of the first packs to return from its conquering by King Gavin after

Escuro, and they have wasted no time establishing themselves as a power in the region.

A military power. Alpha Iraj wastes no opportunity to show off that the pack's ancestral wind powers are staggeringly strong in him and that he has hand-picked his army for the same. Of course, his alliance is the first Corwyn would seek. No matter how often I suggest this might not come to all-out war, he insists that that must be a decision we make, rather than leaving it to those who already betrayed us.

"What do they say?"

"Alpha Iraj is interested in our plight." Corwyn's smile grows slowly. "He would like to bury old hatchets and assist us, if assistance is what we seek."

"Assist us how?" My mind drifts to Dun's Crossing and their hesitancy, how long it took to secure an agreement. As it does every time I think of Finn, my mark groans. I scratch at it absently. It grows easier and easier to endure the pain. "And for what cost?"

"He doesn't mention cost here, but I would imagine he seeks a promise in kind, should fighting ever reach their shores." Corwyn scans the letter again. "It would be reasonable, with their recent re-establishment."

"You are not foolish enough to sign a promise with no idea what you are promising." I reach for the papers, and he pulls them away.

"Sometimes, I think how far Uncle keeps you from battle makes you naïve," he says absently. "Careful planning is the luxury of those without enemies on their doorstep."

I grit my teeth and make another grab instead of trying to reply. I cannot disagree. Father has allowed me adequate self-defense training so that I can fight if my hand is ever forced, and nothing makes my blood pump quite as vibrantly. It's immediate, all-consuming. It rips me from my endless parade of thoughts and worries, forces me to be a body in a single moment with no concerns but surviving to the next. It is visceral like nothing else in my life is.

Unbidden, my mind fills with memories of my one night with

Finn. If visceral is what I want, there is no higher mark. I never felt more present, more undeniably *there* than on that night.

And just like battle, my position means I'll never really be able to have it.

"Why are you always scratching your neck?" Corwyn asks.

I whip my hand back down to my lap. Ice freezes my veins. I didn't even realize I was doing it that time.

Say something, anything.

"I went on a run a few days ago, forgot to check my surroundings before scratching an itch on a trunk." I shrug and try to push my loose hair over my shoulder to block his view as casually as possible. "Missed a patch of demon's roadweed."

Eons pass slower than a snail. Corwyn stares at me, sharp olive gaze unwavering. If he sees my neck clearly enough, he'll know I'm lying. Demon's roadweed leaves a red, raised rash. Though perhaps I've been scratching enough to redden the skin despite Vedran's glamor.

There are so many things that even my cousin does not—will never—know about me. I have no doubt about what he would do if he discovered this. Father would know within the hour.

"You should see the royal healer. I'm sure she has a paste or salve she could give you." He turns back to his letter.

I exhale a held breath silently through pursed lips. Perhaps Vedran can magic my hands to keep them at my sides. Perhaps Miralyn's salve would dispel even this itching. I don't know, but I know I need something. Corwyn is not studious, but he is brilliant. I cannot keep relying on my own clearly weak will to protect me.

Yet again, I cannot think of anything but Finn's arrival in now two scant weeks. The pain is growing manageable, but the itch only seems to intensify. When he's here, anything could become true. I need to be able to resist it, resist him, no matter what temptations lay before me. The fate of the Mlakar family depends on it.

And I will have to do so for the rest of my life. This conflict will end, but there will be balls, diplomatic visits, more troubles I can't yet imagine. Years of keeping my hands folded in my lap and gritting my teeth stretch out before me, long and lonely.

Not especially different from the life I was planning for myself before my stumble. I know my lot in life. I just need a salve for the itch, and I can manage this as I've managed the rest.

For the rest of the day, I keep feeling the weight of Corwyn's gaze on my shoulders, as if he's trying to see through my tunic to the skin underneath. Every time I look at him, though, he's looking somewhere else.

It must be my imagination. Simple paranoia. Keeping two secrets for a lifetime is no harder than keeping one.

Still, when I get to lock my door behind me and strip out of all of Vedran's glamors, it feels like shedding my manacles at the end of a Haze. There's only one person in the world I want to talk to about this.

And she lies on the other side of a contested border.

1 2

THE STRUGGLE WITHIN

Finn

"Is that so?" Lady Marita, a visiting noblewoman from Snowcrest Canyon, leans forward over our private dining table, pressing her breasts forward in her gown.

"It is." I glance at her miles of pale cleavage then away. Somehow, all I can think is that she should really be careful—any more leaning, and she's going to pop right out of the low corset. "You should ask Queen Raven to tell you the story of how they used those tunnels to free the castle from my mother's clutches someday."

"Oh, I'd much rather hear it from you." She bats her eyes, dark and green as a stagnant pond, as she twirls a lock of red hair, so bright I wouldn't be surprised to learn she colors it, around one finger.

"I wasn't there." I prod my nearly untouched bread pudding and glance over my shoulder. Dinner at the high table is almost finished as well, so I'll get to escape soon enough. "Well, I was, but not for the tunnels part."

"Could you show them to me?" She strokes a finger along my arm. "We could make our own stories instead."

"Maybe." I pull my arm back and stuff it under the table. Why, under the Goddess-damned sky, can't I just say yes? I've certainly had worse dinner companions. Marita knows how to ask simple questions that keep the conversation plodding along without overdoing it. She doesn't seem to resent the occasional silence. She is, objectively, a beautiful woman.

And I couldn't care less. I may as well be eating with Ingrid. If I challenged her to an arm-wrestling contest right now, she would leave the table in disgust. If we were mates, and I found her in the Haze, she would run toward me instead of away.

I clench my jaw. I need to make an effort to find something in this woman—in some woman. If I do not, I will have to spend the rest of my life in this castle.

"What about you?" I ask through gritted teeth. "Any interesting stories about… tunnels?"

"Not exactly." She offers me a small, tight smile.

Of course. I just rejected her. I have been all night. If I wanted to make an effort, I should've started at the beginning of the fucking meal—or, hell, when she arrived this morning.

Metal rings against metal, and I look over my shoulder. As expected, Kieran is standing and knocking his fork against the side of his goblet.

"Vespera has started insisting I wrap this dinner up," he says with a grin. "So we are off. Drinks will be served in—"

"Give Alpha Kieran my best." She stands and marches out the door of the hall before he even finishes his sentence.

I knock back the rest of the whiskey in my goblet and wipe my mouth on the back of my arm. At least the alcohol burn almost disguises the burn of my mark. Other nobles leave the room in pairs and trios, chattering. More than a few glances point my way, and I know Marita's exit is going to be a topic for at least the next few days.

Splendid. Ingrid still hasn't stopped hounding me, and since I asked Elian and Howell to say I was out with them, Elian keeps shooting me puppy-dog looks I know mean he wants me to tell him why. More gossip will certainly improve my week.

I signal a steward to fill my glass again. Sleep hasn't exactly been coming easily either. The more I relax, the harder it is not to think about… him.

With my hands clenched, I shove the thought away. The steward returns with a decanter and begins to tip it over my glass.

"No."

He stops immediately, straightening to a waiting posture. Kieran, one of the only people in this castle who can stop me from drinking, drops into Marita's abandoned seat.

"Thank you, but Prince Finn is done for the night," he says.

"What the hell?" I lift my goblet, hunting for any drops of liquid remaining. Nothing.

"I should be asking you the same thing." Kieran crosses his arms. "You know Candace picked out Lady Marita especially for you."

"I don't know why." I set the cup down and stare over my brother's shoulder, already bored of this conversation. He cannot say anything I don't already know.

"Because she is well on her way to becoming one of the most valuable spies in Snowcrest's network, a fact you would have known if you asked her a single question." He shakes his head. "Something is going on with you."

No shit. Honestly, I'm surprised it only took him a week and a half to realize that. He's been up to his neck in preparing the troops for potential movement to Tansy Beach, and it isn't like we make time to hang out at the most peaceful of times.

"Let me guess, you talked to Ingrid."

"Should I?" He looks around like she has not certainly already disappeared for something she finds more interesting. Maybe he actually doesn't know. He was close enough with Candace, but Ingrid is more than five years his junior. I doubt he sees her as anything more than the baby.

"No."

Kieran stares at me like he can pry the answers he's looking for out of my skull. I stare dully back at him. We'll never be close, that's more than clear. But at least I don't have to wear his frustration with how incomprehensible I am to him as a bruise for the rest of my Goddess-damned life. Being alone is easier without the additional insult on injury.

"Is this about how often you've been going out?" he asks. "You're well on your way to giving Anwen a run for his money."

I would be, if anything had worked out. There's a small parade of women in town who now think I'm a tease. Blondes, brunettes, redheads. Beautiful women. Ugly ones. Older and younger, desperate and standoffish. Kieran is right about one thing, I have been at some bar or pub every single night since Tansy Beach left. Tripping over my words and attempting to convince myself that the next woman is the one who will convince me to put in the effort that so easily used to win them back to my bed.

"Write to him about it, then." I stand. "Maybe he'll actually give a shit, because I know I don't."

Kieran stands as well, blocking my path. The dining hall has emptied around us, leaving us alone with nothing but a few staff clearing the last plates. So he doesn't hesitate to get in my face, showing off the inch he has over me. I don't flinch. It has been a long, long time since Father used to have us spar so he always knew which of us was the strongest. I've filled out, grown strong in ways Kieran has no idea about.

"I can fight you for it, if you want," he says. "But you are going to tell me what's going on with you if it kills us both."

I blink. Memories flicker through my mind—parents, tutors, siblings all leaving when I stopped acting bored and lashed out. Years and years of it. A perfect fucking system.

Part of me expects to see Father's rage burning in Kieran's eyes when I look, but they're just hard. Determined, I could call them. He's not pissed. He's not walking away. He's not lashing out in turn or laughing at me. He's just… staying.

Does he actually want to know? For more than political reasons?

"What if I'm not who I thought I was?" I find myself saying.

Stupid. Childish. If he laughs now, I won't even blame him.

"Who is?" He drops back into his seat. "I married my twin sister and murdered my father."

I remain standing, looking at him. My heart pounds in my throat. I'm going to be sick. "What if it's… deeper than that?" I wince. "Not deeper. Don't—not that. Uh, more… integral."

He raises an eyebrow. "Can you explain a little more?"

No. My lips won't wrap around the word *gay*, not with him looking at me. But I can't walk away with this half-finished. It feels like I spent the last week walking around on the ceiling and everybody else just acted like everything was the same. If someone just noticed, everything would be different.

Or that's another lie I'm convincing myself of. Only one way to find out.

"I thought my favorite color was red," I blurt. "And now, something is making me wonder if it might be green. But I've never even wondered about that before." I stuff my hands in my pockets, knot them into fists. "You know?"

"Hmm." Kieran nods slowly then shakes his head. "No. I'm sorry."

I groan in frustration. I'm not supposed to be one of the ones who has to worry about eloquence, always saying the right thing.

With my lungs threatening to strangle themselves to death, I grab the neck of my tunic and pull it down, just slightly. Enough that he can see the raised redness of the mark but not its shape.

"Oh." He rocks back in his seat. "You thought you liked… Finn, did you mate with a man?"

I release my tunic and stare at a point over his shoulder. It was a mistake. I don't even care. My face is not burning.

Kieran puts a comforting hand on my shoulder. "You should know that was never going to bother me. And I don't know if that really is a more…*integral* issue than mating with your twin sister. You thought one thing was true; it isn't. All that matters when it comes to our mates is that the Goddess knows best."

I sink my teeth into my tongue to keep from asking if that's supposed to help me. He's trying, and hell, that's something. It's certainly something Altair and Vespera are going to need. But he still knows me about as well as any random groom out of the stables, and his advice shows it.

"Thanks." I leave the hall before he can do something stupid, like ask me who it was.

13

———

PEACE TALKS

Xander

VEDRAN LUNGES AT MY FLANK, AND I WHIP OUT OF THE WAY BEFORE HE can sink his teeth into my skin. He's silent, as always, a pale ghost against the sand of the training area. I dart left, then right, aiming to scrape a blunted claw over his underbelly. My pulse pounds. Impulses fire into actions before I can finish the thought. For a single moment, everything in my body makes sense.

I make contact with thin skin, and he yelps, tumbling away.

"Point Xander," I say through the mind-link.

"Disembowelment," he replies. *"That's new."*

"You know me too well." I trot over to him and lean my shoulder against his. *"If I don't ever try anything new, you'll win every fight."*

"Only because of our terms."

Vedran's eyesight is weak in his human form, but it's nearly nonexistent as a wolf. He has a thousand blind spots I could exploit for easy win after easy win. He expected me to, when we first started doing this. I never even considered it.

"Again?" I ask.

He squares up.

This is the only way I could have spent this time without destroying myself. Father is at Beddingsea now, negotiating for our kingdom's future. He took an escort halfway before insisting they stay behind, something Beta Stjepan told me with great irritation through the mind-link.

That mind-link is truly what consumes my thoughts. I forgot just how near the palace Beddingsea Grove truly is. It's at the very edge of mind-link range but not outside of it. I could chastise Father for his recklessness.

Or, far more vitally, I could contact Mother.

Vedran charges, and I throw myself into the fight. For the length of it, my mind goes blank. I'm merely a set of weapons strung along muscles. But Vedran and I both are too good for any single match to last long anymore. He knocks my back legs out from underneath me, sending me sprawling to the sand with a grunt.

He doesn't ask if I'm all right, and that's why I'm here with him, instead of with Corwyn, as Father suggested. My cousin would've not only wanted to talk, but to talk about the meeting. Ceaselessly. I would have torn my hair out—or his.

Vedran circles over to a bubbling water fountain for a drink. I jog in place, practice the dodge-leap I should have used to avoid his strike, but nothing quiets my thoughts as well as fighting.

Father—and most of Tansy Beach—would consider mind-linking to Mother treason, even if we talked of nothing but the weather. Unless the meeting is going well enough that we will be one kingdom by sundown, which is an option I will not disregard.

I should make the attempt. Perhaps this has all been a misunderstanding—or perhaps I can sway the tide.

Another option breathes down my neck, forcing me to acknowledge it. I might reach out to her and discover that I cannot reach her anymore. That we are, in some intangible way, now members of two separate packs. A knife the size and shape of her letter-opener pinning that last message to the door twists in my gut.

Vedran returns, tongue still lolling from his mouth. *"Another? Yes."*

* * *

"IT IS OVER," FATHER SAYS FAR MORE THAN AN HOUR LATER. *"I WILL MEET you at the south gate shortly."*

I shift, throw on clothes, and sprint for the south gate so quickly that even my irritation that he didn't inform us the moment negotiations ended can't catch up. He survived. There's something he wants to hide, which is the only reason to go to the south gate—perhaps that something is Mother herself. Regardless, he will be the first person to have seen her since that last night. Nothing can slow me on the way to that information.

When I reach the gate, I find it already open. There's no sign of Father, nor any of the usual guards. My heart races as I step outside.

"Cousin!" Corwyn smiles at me. "I've prepared everything for Uncle Alden's arrival. I thought he might like some privacy."

As I would have, I think to myself. My first scraps of information about Mother in three months will come with an audience.

I shake the thought away as soon as I have it. Tansy Beach wouldn't have survived these last two weeks if Corwyn and I were not working together to keep it afloat. He can focus on the political details of whatever Father has to say. He's said very little about his Aunt Maris, after all.

Father's salty scent whips toward us on the wind, and we both turn at stiff attention. He runs out of a small copse of trees alone, no sign of his escort. Or Mother. At least he doesn't seem injured.

He shifts as he approaches. Corwyn offers him an armful of clothes, which he dons quickly. I only have eyes for his face. The deep lines and creases he's gathered in the past few months still remain, and he won't meet my gaze.

My stomach sinks.

"How was it?" I ask.

He sneers. "How would you think a reasonable conversation with a woman too impulsive to bid her own family a proper goodbye would go? I cannot begin to imagine why Dun's Crossing would have staked their hopes on it."

My sinking stomach plummets through the dirt, and funeral bells ring in my ears. "Surely, it wasn't all bad?"

"My apologies, I misspoke." He puts a mocking hand to his chest. "The Goddess's most impulsive woman *and* her most objectionable man, in the form of Lord Andrija."

"Wasn't this intended to be a private meeting?" Corwyn crosses his arms.

"I had a very similar question!" Father laughs viciously, not a hint of amusement in his eyes. "Apparently, those were rules I was to follow, as the aggressor in the situation."

"Aggressor?" Moonlight Hollow seceded; such insanity doesn't sound like Mother at all.

"To hear Andrija tell it, certainly." Father begins pacing, hammering his footprints into the dirt. "And as the aggressor, they expect certain concessions from us."

"Ha!" Corwyn's eyes glow with the same irritation infecting Father.

I elbow him as hard as I dare. This is my mother we're talking about. I may not be able to stop Father, but I can stop my ridiculous cousin from feeding the fire.

"I tried to talk to her. Make her see reason." Father throws his hands up. "She wouldn't hear a word of it. Not that she would hear a word of anything else I said. I would be surprised if I finished a single sentence, between the two of them."

"Mother spoke over you?" Lord Andrija, I believe that of. He has always had a mouth bigger than his station and no real compunctions about acting as if there is no mismatch. Half the Council meetings I remember attending from a young age were spent convincing him that someone else's obviously beneficial ideas wouldn't somehow bankrupt his house simply because he hadn't come up with them.

"Like she had been waiting her whole life to do nothing but." He sneers, disgust sharp as a claw. "Truly, I do not see a shred of the woman I married when I look into her face now."

Something hot surges through me, and I step into Father's path. "How did you treat her that she responded like that? Because I don't believe the woman who loved us both for twenty-two years could disappear in three months without some help."

His face contorts. My heart hammers. I've never spoken to him like that before—but he's never talked about Mother like that before. I don't care, at this moment, if she left me behind intentionally or because she was forced to. I only care that someone stands up for her, and clearly, I'm the only one who will.

"I reminded her she had selected the day I asked for her hand in marriage as our meeting," he snarls at me. "Foolishly, I thought that would mean something. Just as you foolishly believe she was not leaving us for a long, long time before she strode out the doors. Who saw her?"

"You." I struggle to stand my ground in the face of an anger I've never faced before. "But—"

"But nothing, Xander," he bellows. "I saw a woman with ice where her heart should be, and as your father, I expect you to respect that."

He storms around me, forging a new path rather than waiting for me to move.

"I'd say respect is the core of what she lacks as well." Corwyn tugs me back gently, like he's trying to protect me. I rip my arm out of his grasp. "After all, you are her Alpha."

"I am!" Father snaps. "The world is not hers to control. She cannot make up a new set of rules to a game we've all spent centuries playing."

"Just like Andrija." Corwyn steps up beside me instead. The only remaining marker of my resistance are Father's footprints in the dirt, charging through us. They will be gone tonight, judging by the humidity hanging in the air.

"Andrija." Father clutches the air in front of him as if he is wringing Lord Andrija's neck. "Shall I tell you how the so-called meeting ended?"

"Please," he says.

I bite the inside of my cheek harder and harder until I taste blood. There. That will linger. Proof I tried to settle this before Corwyn gets his way and paints our land with our people's blood. Proof I put myself in the path of the oncoming storm and forced it to go around.

Proof there's some reason, other than my name, that I might someday deserve the crown perched on Father's head.

"She rattles off her list of demands, ending in"—he barks a sour laugh—"free travel between the two new kingdoms. After I finish explaining how many of those demands are perfectly impossible, Andrija shoots to his feet. Slams a hand on the vegetable cart we were using as a table and flips the Goddess-damned thing."

"He has always been dramatic," Corwyn says.

"At this point, I would call him delusional." Father shakes his head as if trying to loosen the memory from its moorings. "He declares that *I* never intended to make a deal, drags her to her feet, and the two of them storm off!"

"He dragged her away?" My buried gut twists with nausea. Did Mother even leave of her own volition, or have Andrija and the other renegade councilors simply claimed her?

How has it taken me this long to wonder that?

Corwyn raises his eyebrows, the picture of surprise. "You must be right about her, Uncle. Anyone with half a brain in their heads could see you've been striving to make a deal ever since they betrayed us."

"You would think I refused even their minuscule handful of reasonable terms and closed negotiations myself," he spits. "I'm going to my chambers. Corwyn, if you could inform the relevant parties of the most vital details."

Corwyn. Not me. Father storms away, and my cousin has only an apologetic bow to offer me before he leaves as well. I stand alone at the open south gate, neck itching furiously, half wishing the full might of Moonlight Hollow would pour past me and end this torment.

There's only one choice left to make.

Mother? I say tentatively. She could be long gone, far outside my range. She did leave the meeting first, according to Father's telling of it.

All the logical justifications in the world don't stop me from falling to my knees, sick with something I can't name, when I don't even feel the link connect.

14

THE PATH OF DOUBT

Finn

I could've asked Kerr, my personal steward, to pack my bag. He probably would've done a better job of it than I am. A mountain of half-folded clothes looms at me, asking if that's really how I'm going to show up to a foreign kingdom.

Putting my back to it is easier than answering. I need a few things out of the bathroom regardless. A bar of that pine soap, at least.

My head has been spinning since Kerr woke me early this morning with a message from Kieran. He'd finally gotten a letter from Tansy Beach, nearly at the end of our agreed-upon time frame. If we didn't hear in the next three days, we'd be leaving no matter what and assuming the worst.

I hoped the last-minute letter meant they'd managed to find terms. Should've known I'm not that lucky.

In goes the pine soap, next to the three tunics Elian has been trying to convince me to turn to rags for almost a year now. One is a horrifying, blotchy, shit-brown, a leftover from Ingrid's ill-fated time as a dyer. The next was once Father's, and it shows in the many patched holes, one of which is sewn in my own crooked hand because Elian and I had been too far from the castle to return when it tore. The last, I've never understood why Elian hates. The fit is too boxy, or not boxy enough… all I know is that he says it makes me look awful, and that's enough for me.

The trip to Tansy Beach is going to take a week. Apparently, it's about two and a half days by carriage, but we have too many bodies to move for that. Father never bothered much with the southern kingdoms, claimed they didn't have anything worth taking when he already owned the whole eastern shore. I wish I could take his stance. But after that attempted talk with Kieran, I know any resistance about Tansy Beach will make it all too easy for him to put two and two together. He already gives me enough comforting, semi-private pats on the shoulder.

"Semi" both because he rarely actually waits for a room to empty and because Raven has started shooting me *keep-your-head-up* smiles that she has no reason for unless Kieran told her everything.

Yet another reason why I don't want a mate. I would like to have some parts of my life that stay mine. The way mates become two halves of the same whole, just like in the old legend, makes me sick.

That's what I need to hold onto. The nausea. Between that and a set of clothing choices I know would irritate the sensibilities of at least one gay man, Xander and I won't stand a chance of changing our minds.

Bored and nauseous. I'm going to be one hell of a guest.

* * *

I drop my knapsack in the dirt by the side of the road and roll out my aching shoulders. After four days of walking at the head of a hundred-strong battalion, I'm really beginning to regret packing the third tunic. Sunset turns the sky orange and red on my left. The first few days, I actually kind of enjoyed getting to see that change happen. By this point, novelty is a dead concept. My feet grumble every time I take a step, and army rations are all identical.

Elian skips dropping the bag in favor of just dropping himself on the ground with a groan. "We have to be almost there."

"More than—" Kieran's eyes glaze over. Yet another mind-link. Since we left, he's barely had time to piss between people needing him. Taner and Lucias are supposed to be helping manage the troops, but if they are, he should've had a few others helping out as well. "I'll be back."

With a sigh, I pull out his bedroll and lay it out. He'll eat at a half-dozen different cook fires where someone just *has* to talk to him, and by the time he gets back, he'll collapse on the ground if his spot isn't already set up.

Raven's voice rings in my memory. *"You have to take care of him while I can't. You know he won't do it."*

She wasn't wrong—though it was about the first conversation we'd had since Vespera's birth. Kieran will burn himself to ashes before we even reach Tansy Beach if I let him.

Elian groans again, clearly unsatisfied with how much attention he'd gotten.

"What?"

"I'm dying." He shoves up on one elbow, proving himself immediately wrong. "If I have to sleep on the ground one more night, I'm going to die."

"You're just pissed Howell stayed in Dun's Crossing." I tug a sack of fire supplies I've been collecting out of a small cart and start setting up a fire.

"I'm without my other half," he says thoughtfully. "But, no, I'm certain it's the ground. My bones can't take it."

"Sleep as a wolf. You know that's more comfortable." I line rocks up in a neat circle. My mark isn't screaming so loud it makes my hands shake. I don't care about this conversation.

"But I sleep like shit as a wolf." He slumps over and lays next to me, staring up at the sky.

"Tough."

But that makes Elian stop talking. Somehow, I've started relying on his constant complaining. It gives me something to think about.

Something other than what I'm going to say when I see Xander. What he's going to say to me. The single nice-looking tunic, squirreled away in the depths of my bag like I wouldn't notice myself packing it. Elian thinks he sleeps like shit? I've been dreaming about that sliver of Xander's neck for days, reconstructing the night we spent together that I can barely remember as soon as I close my eyes.

My cock starts to stiffen just thinking about it. I pull the bag of supplies into my lap. It is the only part of me interested in my sleepless nights.

"Come on, don't you hate something else?" I nudge my sprawled Beta.

"Always." He pops up. "But you usually don't prompt me for it."

Goddess above, I would've figured out how to lie better if I knew this was going to be how my life went. I shrug and hope that's sufficient.

Of course not. Elian sits up and studies me.

"A portrait lasts longer." I set up a triangle of sticks, surround it with larger logs, and reach for the flint.

"This is about the Haze," he declares. "When you disappeared and asked us to lie."

There it is again. Us. Like he and Howell are one entity.

"I'll beg if you want me to," he says.

I ignore him. This far into the trip, the flint is starting to wear thin, but I manage to send a spark flying. The wood starts to catch

Elian throws himself on the ground and nearly shrieks, "Oh, please, fair Prince Finn, tell me what you keep so mysteriously alluding to! I am a simple worm, pleading for kindness. I will do anything you ask."

"Shit!" I flinch back and slap a hand over his mouth. "I'll tell you if you shut up, all right?"

He nods excitedly. I exhale through my teeth. I should've known he'd try something like that.

With my hand still on his mouth, I stare into the growing flames. "When your target is a man… do you attempt to attract them differently?"

Elian's eyes grow wide, swallowing the flames. *"Attract them? As in flirting?"*

I regret ever opening my mouth.

"First, and I don't know where you got this idea, but you don't have to talk like a dictionary."

I throw a few twigs I didn't use at him, and he rolls out of the way, freeing his mouth. My mark aches. It's the only thing that wants this answer, not me. I intend to forget it just as soon as I learn it—that is, if Elian can stop being a dick for long enough to give me anything like an answer.

He rolls back and sits up with a wide grin. "That Haze you disappeared, did you—"

"No questions." I feed more kindling to the fire, trying to convince the outer logs to catch.

"You know this only works because one of us is familiar with the concept of laughter." He brushes dirt and sticks from his ponytail. "But all right, serious time. The truth is… it's exactly the same."

"Then why don't I understand why you hate that blue tunic?" I ask before I can kill the words for ever existing.

"That's a matter of taste, which you still lack." He laughs. "Flirting is much simpler. People are people. They want to laugh, to blush, to know you're interested in them. Nothing more."

Finally, one of the larger logs starts to smolder, putting off a plume of smoke.

"The gentleman we're talking about—"

"No. Questions."

15

———

TENSION CONTINUES

Xander

"Apologies." Lord Edvard bows, dark hair braided back away from his face, and hurries to his seat at the council table. "There was word of a skirmish at the edge of my lands, and it required my attention."

Father gestures dismissively. "There are rumors of skirmishes on all our lands, Edvard. I would thank you to keep your attention on protecting Tansy Beach rather than the holdings of House Arbanas."

Lord Edvard takes his seat with a slight grimace, but he doesn't dare push back against Father. Ever since his return from the meeting in Beddingsea, very few people do. Despite his attempts at secrecy, word spread quickly. Everyone knows.

Peace is not coming. Or at the very least, not without a price.

That's why tension already hangs heavy in the council's air. We've talked of nothing but the war, and I don't expect that to change soon. Every person at this table has a lifetime of legacy to lose, and they're barking orders with that in mind.

Corwyn clears his throat. "As I was saying, I believe Hillwe Strait is our strongest point of attack."

"As I was saying," Lord Juraj rasps, "such a position only shows your youth. I have never seen a water position held strongest."

"If we turn to the history books…."

My thoughts drift from the conversation, no matter how hard I fight to keep them there. The mark on my throat throbs like a second heartbeat, a half-step out of time so I can never forget it's there. I twist my hands in my lap to keep from clawing at it just to silence it.

It's not as though I don't know why it's so active. Our scouts were very clear—the reinforcements from Dun's Crossing arrive today.

Perhaps that's why I've felt lower than dirt since I woke up this morning. In addition to the throbbing, my stomach ties itself in knots, and my head pounds. Were this anything less than the first full council meeting since Father spoke with Mother, I would have stayed in bed.

"I was reading Poropat," Corwyn says.

I shoot him a look. He winks at me. At least he knows where the idea came from—and by the glint in Father's eye, so does he.

Lord Kresimir, usually the most even-handed and reliable of the councilors, leans forward. "Well, if young Hajni has an idea, what are we waiting for?"

My heart drops. "Moonlight Hollow hasn't attacked yet."

"I have no doubt they will," Father replies, his voice heavy as an anchor. "And we shall not sit unprotected and waiting for their sword. However, Prince Xander is right that some care in planning must be taken."

That isn't what I said, but I'm already sure there's no point in arguing. Father doesn't like disagreeing with me in front of the council; he thinks it will make it easier for them to disobey me when I take the throne. So he has once again twisted my words into something he can agree with in order to give the illusion that we are on the same page.

My neck throbs, and I wonder, not for the first time, just what my life would look like if I stripped away all the illusions.

"Hillwe Strait is only a position of power if we strike at night," Corwyn says. "The narrow channel is easy enough to hold, but we need the element of surprise to claim the initial advantage."

I drag my gaze over the map. Simply moving my eyes burns, like I spent all night hunched over books rather than snoring away in my bed. Hillwe, Hillwe….

There. Mere inches, though I know those inches become hundreds of feet, from one of the most productive farming villages in the territory Moonlight Hollow now occupies. Abruptly, I realize exactly what strategy Corwyn is advocating for.

"You're going to starve them," I say softly, horrified.

He swallows. "It's brutal, I know, but I want us positioned to have that option if they continue to force our hand."

"Force?" I shoot to my feet, and the whole room sways around me. Only my fingers, clamped on the edges of the long, wooden table keep me upright. "How, exactly, have our own people forced us to slaughter them?"

"Our people?" Corwyn looks incredulously around at the other councilors. My blood boils. "Cousin, they have declared quite clearly that they are *not* our people. They wish to be their own."

Nods circle the table. First Kresimir, whose lands border Moonlight Hollow most closely. Then Edvard, with the distant look of someone still struggling to catch up. Last, reluctantly, Juraj's aging head wags in agreement.

I meet Father's eyes down the length of the table. When he first put me on the council, I assumed I would sit at his right hand. Everything I'd read about politics indicated that was the prince's position. But Father put me at the opposite end of the table, saying this way we could control the whole room. Encircle any enemies and overwhelm them. It has worked out more often than not, but now, I wish I could be close enough to read all the tiniest fluctuations of his expression. I need to know what he's thinking.

"Will we put them to death when we reunite our land?" The wood of the table bites into my palms from how hard I'm clasping it. "That is what you are suggesting now."

"I admire your foresight." Corwyn smiles apologetically—he tries not to disagree with me before the council either, but we've never been at such opposite ends of an issue before. "But we cannot win a war while protecting the other side. And the other side are the ones who have declared there must be war. I would have us all reunited by dinner, but they have dug their heels in. You drew my eyes to the methods of yore, cousin." He taps the tome in front of him. "I know they are brutal, perhaps even cruel, but the faster this war ends, the more lives will be saved, will they not?"

Father stands. He looks between Corwyn and I. A bead of sweat slips down my face. Is this room getting hotter, or is that simply me?

"Prince Xander is correct that the small folk have done us no wrong and deserve our grace." He scans the map. "With that said, these farms most directly feed the barracks to the north, barracks I'm certain the other side intends to make use of."

I sink back into my seat, shaking slightly. The decision is made. Standing is a waste of my apparently waning strength.

Will ending this faster truly save lives if we take more in civilian death than we would have on any battlefield?

Corwyn appears at my elbow, having left his seat beside Father, with a glass of clear water. "Apologies for that. I have to ask, though— are you well?"

He may as well have thrown the water on me. Realization strikes like lightning—the aches, the nausea, the headache. I ought to have recognized the symptoms and already removed myself for my monthly *prayer retreat*.

I snort and push the water away. "What, I have to be ill to disagree with you? No, I just have to piss."

He jumps back before I spill the whole glass on him by standing up into it. Too fast. The edges of my vision gray slightly, and my stomach lurches. Usually, the symptoms are not this bad this quickly. I barely maintain my swagger while I escape the council room. A brief nod to the two indigo-clad guards beside the door, and as soon as I am out of their sight, I'm running.

Washrooms are too far. Windows are too far. I skid around a

corner and duck into an alcove half-shaded by a tapestry some Mlakar ancestor slaved over before I am violently sick.

I slump onto the edge of a potted plant.

"Vedran!" I call through the mind-link, describing my location. He always escorts me to my retreats. There's simply a bit more to hide this time.

The acrid stink of it should make me ill again, but the nausea clears like a summer storm. My stomach even rumbles—I am ravenous when I couldn't stomach a bite this morning. I cup my hands around the moisture in the air, and my palms fill with water cooler and clearer than anything Corwyn could have offered me. It slakes something deep inside me like no other drink can.

By the time Vedran arrives, I have drank a pitcher's worth of water, and my mouth no longer tastes like a carcass left in the sun.

He purses his lips as he looks at the mess. "Do not worry about this, Your Highness. But you should know—you are late for your prayer retreat."

What? No.

"Your Majesty," one of the guards at the front gate says. *"King Kieran and Prince Finn have arrived."*

16

———

THE DISTANCE BETWEEN

Finn

Kieran leads the charge to the heavy, beaten-copper gate at the top of the winding, shell-strewn path. I do my damnedest not to choke on my heart, which seems to have taken up permanent residence in my throat. I also give myself the gift of not looking at Elian. Even in just my peripheral vision, I can see him looking back and forth between my face at the gate, primed to attempt to guess which of the eligible young men inside forced me to open up to him.

I don't know why I'm wasting the energy. No matter what happens in there, Xander and I will not be the same as we were before, and Elian will spot that from a mile away. All I can do is hope the rest of the courtiers can be fooled.

The gate opens a crack—just enough for one reedy man in an indigo robe to wriggle out and face Kieran. It's clear from the way the man looks over Kieran's shoulder at the battalion first that they didn't exactly send their strongest soldier. He goes white as a sheet before turning to my brother.

"Good morning." He bows. "I am Undersecretary Mislav."

93

"We were expecting King Alden," Kieran says. "We've come a long way."

"And King Alden understands that." Mislav bobs another anxious bow.

I should've recognized the look sooner. He isn't just a coward—he's a coward who's been sent to get rid of a powerful king and his army. King Alden, or maybe Xander himself, has changed their minds. We have to march all the way back, and with my luck, thank them for the time we spent marching here. I begin planning how I am going to keep Elian from becoming so irritating I actually have to kill him.

"As your timing was so uncertain, our great houses are in council at this time. I would be honored to escort you and Prince Finn, as well as any other envoys, to where they are meeting, where King Alden believes your experience would be invaluable. Your men will be housed and fed while you tend to matters of state."

Kieran sighs. "I had hoped for a moment to clean up. We traveled with our men."

Yet another bow. "Apologies, Your Majesty, but I have been told to bring you and all envoys to the council chamber at once."

"Lead the way, then."

The gate creaks open, this time wide enough for a few more people. Kieran exchanges a look with Taner that I know means his Beta is staying behind to make sure our soldiers are taken care of properly. As Elian steps forward, I tell him the same, despite his scowl.

That will mean one less set of eyes on me the first time I see Xander in almost a month. I'll take the scowl without complaint.

Mislav leads us inside. My mark keeps time like a drum on my ribcage. I haven't been able to escape the taste of salt for hours already, but it's even thicker here. The Windy Ocean is so close that I can hear the faint hiss of waves even after the gate closes behind us.

Tansy Tower is a strange castle, as castles go. Striations of a hundred different browns, reds, and tans run through its stone like a massive layer cake. Here and there, shells and preserved sea creatures stud the surface. Spires rise from all corners, not half the height of those in Snowcrest and strung across with open-air bridges swaying under the weight of staff crossing them. Overall, it looks… fragile. Like one of the Windy Ocean's famed waves could wash it away. Somehow, it has stood for centuries.

Inside isn't much different except for the oppressive feeling in the air. We don't pass a single person who pauses for longer than a half-second, just enough time to give us the most basic courtesy. The sounds of wolves locked in battle echo from somewhere beyond the path Mislav leads us down—training, if I had to guess. Half the windows we pass are shuttered and bolted; the others are barely open.

This is a castle preparing for the worst. Waiting for the other shoe to drop.

Fuck, Xander has been living in this.

Mislav pauses at a double door made of the same beaten copper as the gates. The surface bears eight inscribed names, four on each door. I pick out Mlakar, Xander's name, and Hajni, which I'm almost sure was Corwyn's. Thick black lines cross out three of the names.

"I go no farther," the undersecretary says. "Enjoy your stay in our home."

With another bow, he hurries away. Kieran takes a deep breath but doesn't even look at me before pushing the door open.

A long wooden table covered in maps and tactical pawns dominates the room. Six men sit or stand at various points along the table. My Goddess-damned mind will only focus on one.

At the far end of the table from his father, Xander looks up as we walk in. His auburn hair is braided back away from his face like all Tansy Beach men, revealing sharp cheekbones and lips I have held between my teeth. Vividly red lips. Far redder than I remember. In fact, he looks pale, like he's spent every second of these last three weeks inside without sleeping.

Something hot and urgent surges inside me. I want to grab him, drag him out of here, and then…I'm not sure what. Vague memories of the Haze war with thoughts of him in bed where that wrinkle between his brow was smoothed.

Xander's gaze meets mine, and I couldn't think about anything else if I wanted to. I never realized the hazel of his eyes is as layered as his castle's stone, just as deep and distracting. I lean slightly forward.

"It is disappointing," Corwyn says.

Everyone in the room turns to him. My mark shrieks as Xander looks away.

"What is?" Kieran asks as a steward in the room pulls two more chairs up to the table on King Alden's left.

"That Luna Raven could not join you," King Alden says. "Her powers would have been invaluable."

That sounds like Corwyn's words in the king's mouth, but I hardly notice. It's almost like the Haze all over again; I am a creature of instinct, and every instinct drags me toward Xander.

He's not looking at me. I sit as loudly as I can, but his gaze remains fixed on his cousin.

Dammit.

"Apologies." Kieran stands next to me. "But Queen Raven has responsibilities at home. She is ruling Dun's Crossing in my absence."

"If we could spin up a storm over the strait…" Corwyn says, tapping his chin.

"My wife is a woman, not a weapon," Kieran says brusquely.

"Of course." He inclines his head. "I was merely mourning the limitations of Tansy Beach's abilities a few moments ago, and your lady wife came up in that context, which you could not have had."

"My nephew is right. We forget ourselves." King Alden stands. "We have neither the time nor spare resources to greet you as we ought to, with a ball and days of feasting, but you and any family you travel with should join Prince Alexander and myself for *kafi* this evening."

"Thank you." Kieran sits obviously mollified.

I clear my throat loudly. "Thank you from me, as well."

Xander does not even glance my way. He studies the papers in front of him—papers I can see are blank—like they hold more interest. I resist the urge to kick him, just to get him to look up.

Three weeks apart. Days of travel. Dirt clinging to my skin. An ancient-looking nobleman shoots me a look that informs me I'm coming across as very strange.

This is why I didn't want a mate. I'm making a complete fool of myself because of some connection I never asked for, never sought out. It shouldn't matter whether he looks at me or how perfectly he was able to hide the shape of my teeth on his pale neck. I dig my nails into my palms and force myself to slouch back in my chair.

I don't give a fuck about anything, least of all the crown prince of Tansy Beach. I'm just here because Kieran dragged me along.

Xander lifts his head. Every nerve in my body springs to attention —but he's just looking at his father, who is saying something about a plan of attack.

"How many men did you bring exactly?" Corwyn asks.

"As many as agreed upon," Kieran replies. "A hundred of our best fighters."

He frowns as he plucks a few wooden tents from a pile to add to the map. A muscle in Kieran's jaw flickers. It's ridiculous that the prince's Beta wouldn't bother hiding his displeasure with a foreign Alpha. Ridiculous that his king wouldn't stop him.

"Along the east side," is all King Alden says.

"If we're using Poropat"—Xander's voice sounds like a blade drawn from a sheath, scraping straight past my ribs—"splitting them between east and west would be better."

"Thank you, cousin," Corwyn says.

My mark howls. I rub my chest, trying to silence it. Let Xander talk to whoever the hell else he wants. I'll be here, surviving this meeting until Kieran lets me go home.

It seems like that's all I can do.

17

KAFI

Xander

"HE'S HERE," VEDRAN SAYS IN MY ROOM AS HE HELPS ME PREPARE FOR *kafi*.

I meet his pink eyes in the window's reflection. "How did you know?"

Vedran taps one of my shoulders lightly. "Every time someone mentions their arrival, you tighten. Why do you think you have woken so sore in the mornings?"

The war. Father's behavior. This illness I seem to be coming down with—ever since the nausea passed, it has settled into a dull throb of a headache but nothing worse. Perhaps, maybe, a bit of concern about Finn's imminent arrival.

My mark throbs. I reach for the pot of salve Miralyn gave me last week, but the attendant itch doesn't follow.

If I consider the pain, which I've been trying not to, I'm forced to admit that, too, is less intense since he arrived.

Vedran watches me withdraw my hand from the row of bottles in the wardrobe. "What will you do?"

"Nothing," I say immediately. "There is nothing to do. You know that."

He purses his lips. I do not need or want his opinions right now, though. Both the headache and the mark pain may be lessened, but they still work in irritating concert. Holding onto a thought is an achievement.

"Which vest?" he asks.

"Any of them." I flip my hand dismissively.

He returns with a light indigo piece, heavily embroidered. Another heirloom in a palace full of them.

I frown. "You know that one has always been loose on me."

"*Kafi* is not a gentle beverage on the stomach," he says, helping me into it.

"Earlier, that was…." I have no idea. But it hasn't made a reappearance, so I believe all my worries about needing a prayer retreat were overblown. "I am fine, Vedran."

"A visit to Miralyn would not be out of order," he says. "Your father would order it."

"Then it's a good thing he isn't here." I adjust the slightly oversized vest until it sits right on the ghost of my reflection in the evening window. When Father gave it to me, he tailored the shoulders, so I didn't exactly look like a child who'd found their way into their parent's closet. Still, the lightweight fabric hangs loose from my body, clearly insinuating this would be better suited for the barrel-chested Mlakar men of yore than me. "Corwyn has become obsessed with the idea that Moonlight Hollow has spies in the Tower."

Vedran raises an eyebrow.

"If he's right, I can't show weakness by visiting the healer twice in as many weeks," I say.

Vedran sighs. He knows when he's fighting a losing battle, at least. While I make final adjustments, he turns to his chest in the corner of my room. Perhaps he has some spell to kill the lingering headache.

He returns with a handful of off-white bandages and offers them to me.

My stomach drops, and I push his hand away. "I said I had no need of a prayer retreat now. It was a false alarm. A fluke."

"Your Highness—"

Someone raps on the door. I roll out my shoulders, trying to chase off that tension Vedran mentioned, and saunter over to answer it.

Corwyn stands in the entry, a hazy expression on his face. Something between amusement and irritation.

"I have to go shortly." I turn and walk back inside, trusting he'll follow.

He doesn't. "Uncle sent me as an escort. We were discussing the council meeting, and he said he wanted to ensure you weren't late."

A mind-link would've done just as well. I sigh quietly then nod to Vedran and turn back. "By which he means five minutes early?"

"Ten." There, that is clearly a grimace. He's irritated at playing errand boy; he knows as well as I do that Father could've told me directly. I wonder how their conversation ended for Corwyn to be sent away like this. "Shall we?"

I join him in the hall, and we begin the winding walk to the *kafi* room.

"I thought this was to be immediate blood relations only," I say.

"It is." Another grimace. He's equally frustrated at being kept out. "For us, at least. No one quite knows how many people Alpha Kieran is bringing yet."

At least one. "He is just rationing the beans."

"I know." Corwyn shakes his head. "I only want to be there because, to be frank, I don't much trust either of them."

"Really?"

"Alpha Kieran is so terrified of his father's legacy that he treats war like a snake about to bite him," Corwyn says decisively. "And Prince Finn has all the interest in politics of my left pinkie finger."

"Harsh." I force a laugh as my mark stings. "Why would that make Prince Finn untrustworthy?"

"I suppose you're friends with him." He cuts his gaze to me, evaluating if he's overstepped.

I school my expression tightly, tracing the constellations of seashells studded in the walls like I used to when I was a child. This hall contains only Great Fish, but at the next turn, I'll be faced with Less Great Fish, Bunch of Trees, and Splat.

It is very obvious at times that I also named these when I was a child.

Finally, Corwyn sighs. "There're two ways it could be trouble. The first is that someone who doesn't care is easily convinced. He has no principles to adhere to. The second is much simpler, likely true regardless: there is no space in Tansy Tower for those disinterested in politics at this time. I would stay away from him, or people may begin thinking you hold similar opinions."

I suspect—I very nearly know—there is more to Finn than that, but I cannot disagree with Corwyn without prompting further questions.

"I would worry less." I smirk. "It makes you sound like an egghead."

"This, from the man who's read every book in the library—twice!"

We bicker the rest of the way to the *kafi* room. Past the engraved door, Father waits with our nicest *kafi* set—twisting tubes and receptacles of beaten copper, cups and saucers of porcelain painted almost to match.

"Ten minutes," he says. "You have recovered from earlier?"

Perhaps the guards heard me get sick. Perhaps he is just worried I'll run out. Regardless, I take the low-backed armchair beside him and say, "Of course."

* * *

Father and I are already standing when King Kieran steps in, just as the clock strikes the appointed hour. I bow as I am supposed to. My pulse pounding in my mark warns me who I am going to see when I straighten.

Somehow, that does not make it any easier.

The low, flickering evening light casts Finn's raw-boned face in dramatic shadow, carving hollows beneath his high cheekbones and the sharp angle of his jaw. His pale eyes, however, shine like pearls in the deep. As does the inside of his mouth, which opens slightly when he sees me.

I quickly drop into another bow, though protocol does not demand it. My racing heart does.

Father endures this, though he shoots me a bemused look when I am done. "Would you—"

"First," King Kieran produces a parcel from behind his back, "as a token of our gratitude, even in these trying times, for offering such a warm and welcoming home."

Corwyn may be right. King Kieran may be devoted to diplomacy at nearly all costs, but at least he is a clever hand at it. Father unwraps the parcel to reveal a pair of intricately filigreed gold and silver hand mirrors.

"Once, these are what Dun's Crossing was known for," he says. "Fine metalwork, the likes of which could not be replicated. I would like to be known for such things again, and I would be honored for you to hold a piece of that history."

A much better gift as well. Father produces ours in turn—a tapestry from some ancient Mlakar whose name no one truly remembers, which is received with appropriate excitement. From Kieran, at least. I have not looked at Finn since he entered the room.

As in the council meeting earlier, that is a mistake I intend to make only once. My body and my mark have been very clear—my willpower is not strong enough to endure looking at him for long.

Father prepares the *kafi*, an intricate process of measuring ink-black beans, boiling in a series of alembics, and patience. King Kieran sits, as he ought, in the chair across from Father. Finn skips the one beside his brother to sit a single seat closer to me. Not quite enough to draw Father's attention.

Certainly enough to draw mine.

"How do you do this?" King Kieran asks Father.

In the corner of my eye, I watch Finn turn to me and know I have lost. Father will explain *kafi* until the war ends around us with no interest in whatever I might see fit to do. I may as well be alone with Finn.

My mate.

My greatest mistake.

"Not a lot of opportunity to go to a pub around here, huh?" he says.

By the Goddess, he is attempting normalcy. As if I can feel anything but this throbbing headache and the mark pounding the off-beats. As if I am not painfully aware of the inches between his knee and mine.

"At another time, I could show you a whole host of places that would stare at us like fish in a bowl," I manage.

"Sounds like fun?"

"Not especially." I dig my nails into the embroidered velvet of my chair. The *kafi* room used to be larger; I'm certain of it. Those in Finn's chair have always been farther from me.

"Right." He leans back, glances at the bubbling *kafi* apparatus. "Is there anything fun to do in the castle?"

For nearly a month, I have done nothing but attend tense council meetings and plot battle strategies. The last time I had fun was—

His breath on my neck, his eyes blue and hazy, his hands hard on my hips.

"Not really," I say.

The apparatus hisses and sputters out the first palm-sized cup of *kafi*. Father hands it to Kieran. I drum my fingers on the arm of my chair. An entire lifetime of keeping myself under control, of denying the messy, bloody, animal impulses in my gut, turns to nothing in front of Finn. It's humiliating.

The second cup. I seize it before Father can even offer it to me. My hands are shaking too badly to hold the saucer as I ought without clattering the two against each other, so I set it in my lap and take a searing sip.

Warm, bitter, with a familiar edge of burnt nuttiness. I try to exhale, letting the ancient ritual settle me.

Finn hums softly as he tastes his own, a noise that shoots directly to my gut.

"Apologies." I stand, look at Father. "Lord Corwyn needs my eyes on a new strategy, and it is urgent."

His eyes flash. I'm not to leave.

I turn and flee before I can disobey his foremost rule instead.

18

CONTROL

Xander

Lukewarm night air whispers through my private garden. One of the many strange things about Dun's Crossing is how far off they seemed to keep the natural world. Buildings cover all the land within their walls, or they have flattened it into fields. I appreciate they went to the trouble of allowing us a courtyard, but it was nearly impossible to find another. These gardens pockmark Tansy Tower.

This one, however, is mine. My pride and joy. I dance my fingers over broad-leaved ferns and tip my nose into the fragrant bloom of a night mallow. There's a path, only a few crushed shells and stones, and my feet find it by instinct rather than relying on something as shallow as sight. The plants grow so thickly that I'm not truly sure I could see it.

It's almost enough to make me forget I just fled a diplomatic meeting with an excuse so paper-thin I would be shocked if the *kafi* itself could not sense my lie.

I drop to a low, nearly hidden bench along the path. Leaves I have tended enfold me like arms. Behind me, the sole fountain in my garden sings.

The laughing cedar droops under the weight of its summer fruit. It always needs extra attention at this time of year. I hum in harmony with the song of the fountain, curling my wrist as though dancing.

Water springs out of the air at my call and patters over the twisted roots of the cedar. Even though it doesn't touch me, it feels like someone is dabbing my face with a cool washcloth. Like a trustworthy voice murmuring in my ear that all is not lost. Like I have control over this one thing in my life, so tightly and so masterfully that it may well be enough to cancel out the rest.

I survived the council meeting. There were more people, more distance between Finn and me. That's something I could maintain. And however long the war might be, however long they intend to lend their troops for, I sincerely doubt the king and prince of a pack will stay with us for longer than a few weeks, no matter how competent a leader Luna Raven is.

The creeper heather beneath the cedar sprouts an extra inch, vines deepening to emerald and flowers blooming amethyst. I release the stream of water and exhale slowly then tilt my head back against the welcoming trunk of a corkscrew silver bell.

Above the froth of greenery, I can just make out one walkway studded with pockets of lantern light. In one, a figure stands outlined. My mark yelps.

Finn. Looking down at me, his pale eyes intent.

My stomach twists. He turns and hurries back through the nearer door. Somehow, I know what he's thinking. That he's trying to trace the castle to find this place. And I know I could—should leave before he succeeds.

But that patch of lamb's ear needs some water.

Finn arrives through the side door, the only one accessible without going through my quarters. The one I used tonight and intended to lock behind me. I expect to hear him crashing through the plants as he hunts for the invisible path, to be able to shout at him for his destruction when he reaches me. Instead, only the faintest rustling reaches my ears before the scent of ginger and moss.

He parts a fern and steps through, pauses a few feet away. "Corwyn, huh?"

I shrug. "I grew tired of listening to my father talk and knew what excuse he'd accept."

"So you left me to listen." He stuffs his hands in his pockets. "Thoughtful."

With a simple gesture, I cut off the stream of water spattering his shoes. The moment I do, I regret the choice. That makes it seem as if I want to talk.

I'm not allowed to want that, no matter how the pulsating pain at my throat does.

"If we keep dancing around each other like this," he says, "everyone is going to figure out we're ma—"

"Busy," I say sharply. "That is all we are, Prince Finn. Busy people."

Of all the many reasons I'm not supposed to look at him, the last I expected was that hurt would punch through his gaze with all the force of a blow and knock the wind from my lungs. I tear my gaze back to the vague ribbon of path at our feet. Safety lies in picking out every shattered stone and nowhere else.

"Understood." His voice becomes brusque, a door closed in my face. "I'm only here for a few days. Shouldn't be too hard. You need to stop looking like a deer who's just smelled a wolf every time I walk into the room, though."

In my memory, his eyes pierce the night, pinning me before him like prey. My mark writhes beneath Vedran's magic, burning like it wishes to make itself visible.

I scratch my neck, curse myself for not applying the salve as a safety measure. "And you need to stop acting like a baby chick who has picked the farmer as its mother."

He scoffs. "I've barely spoken to you. Three, maybe four sentences?"

"And your choice of chair?"

"Utterly political." His shirt crunches, likely his arms crossing. "I need to get in good with the crown prince to make this entire operation run smoothly."

Laughable. We need their good graces, not the other way around. But my mind whirls out of my grasp, imagining a reverse scenario, how he would come to me for help and have to obey.

"Tell your brother you have, and stay out of my way," I say.

His answering snort says everything he won't. Finn risked chasing me down after I ran away from him—the second time, really—because I knew he was trying to catch me after the council meeting. He chiseled the first chink out of his wall of disaffected boredom. I'm the one mortaring it over.

It's for the best. Even if he keeps adjusting his feet to stand as carefully on the shadow of the path as he can, protecting plants he doesn't even know I care about.

"Fine, then," I blurt. "It's a bet. If I win, we keep our distance. If you win—"

"We attempt to look normal." His smirk is hollow. "Fight me for it."

My blood trips over itself in my veins. A true fight, with stakes. My very first.

Before I can agree, he adds, "As humans."

It goes against the ancient interpretation of the Goddess's word by one of our holy women. With tensions this high, it might be considered treason.

"It's a bet."

Something fills his smirk, but it's sour and thorny. He sloughs off his doublet and drops it on the bench beside me. I add my vest to the pile then pull off my rings when he nods to them. He frees a single golden loop from the top of his ear and lifts his hands.

"To the pin," he says. "Or the tap—if you're done, you can slap the ground to yield."

I nod. "No weapons."

He eyes me. "No location is off limits."

I've read about fights like this. He's saying that we can pull hair, jab eyes, punch below the belt.

I stick out my hand. Finn shakes it.

"Go." His hand snakes up my wrist, clamps down, and he yanks me forward.

I stumble, almost into him. My lips part to call *foul*.

But I'm not fighting Vedran, who is not only in my head but trying to sharpen my skills. Finn slams an unyielding fist into my side. I grunt as a bruise blossoms and cant to the side.

I'm not fighting Vedran. I don't need to return to the center of his vision. My heart hammers. My leg snaps out, contacts the center of his thigh. Finn huffs a breath and grabs for my ankle.

"I don't fall for the same move twice." I circle his grasping hands and dart to the side.

He's strong, faster than I might've expected, but I'm faster. I swing a fist and slam into his shoulder.

The impact spiders up my arm, bones crunching against bones. Finn's mouth falls open—pain? Surprise?—and a wild smile paints my face. I cannot sink my teeth into his lower lip like I want to, but that doesn't matter, because I can duck the swoop of his fist and drive my elbow into his side. His breath gusts over my face, hot and reeking of him. He grabs a fistful of hair, sparks of pain shooting to my gut, and holds me in place long enough to crash another bruising blow against my side.

My other side, where the bruise aches but doesn't shriek.

"Taking it easy on me?" I grab his wrist with both hands and twist in opposite directions, friction-burning his skin.

He hisses. "Not anymore."

He tries to sweep my feet, but I know not to believe him.

Perhaps he shouldn't believe me either. When this ends, I want to see myself splattered over his skin in vivid color, but nothing more. My mark scorches through me, sealing the promise. Nothing worse than proof we once touched each other, even if it was with violence between us as a shield.

What an abominable shield. My pulse pounds. My heart races. The headache has disappeared somewhere far behind us, and nausea is a forgotten dream. He encircles my neck with his arms, dragging me tight against his body in a way that sets my spine groaning and allows me only a whistle of air. The cedar is near enough to reach if I wish to tap.

I bite his forearm, teeth sharpening, and the copper taste of blood mingles with the salt of his sweat. He yanks back with a curse. Leaves crush beneath my feet, but their green scent can't compete with his. My memory replays the throaty moan he offered the last time I sank teeth beneath his skin, and the two harmonize rather than clashing. Two sides of the same cursed coin, still spinning in the air.

I whip toward the bench, use it as a springboard, and careen through the air toward him. He turns too slow, and I hook my arms around his neck, my legs around his waist, backpacking myself onto him. With all the strength pounding through my muscles, I clench my arms around his neck tighter. This close, I'll feel his tap along his skin before I hear it. I can feel the very breath whispering down his windpipe.

He steps forward, then charges backward, nearly as fast as a regular run. I slam into the trunk of the cedar, setting the leaves rustling against each other in their namesake laughter. My breath explodes out of my control, and my grip loosens.

With a laugh, Finn spins me around him until I cling to his front then falls forward. I expect to hit the ground just as hard—harder— perhaps even jar my headache back to life. Our momentum jerks to a stop a heartbeat before that, his outstretched arms hitting the vines. Like I wouldn't notice, he lowers himself atop me a second later and grunts.

"You—" My accusation dies on my lips.

Because Finn's chest presses tight to mine, and he looks at me with dawning horror.

He can feel me.

19

TRUTH REVEALED

Finn

When I grabbed Xander in the headlock, I thought his tunic was kind of lumpy. Probably just a side effect of how loosely they wear them under those vests. When Xander climbed onto my back, I thought…well, mostly I thought that he'd set me up to win.

Now, with the entire line of my body pressed against Xander's, there's no other explanation I can invent for the soft rise of flesh beneath my chest. They're small, compact, like they're being crushed by something other than me, but unmistakable.

Xander has breasts.

I scrape through my memories of the Haze again—lips, hands, hips… nothing. Just a few flashes I can barely put together into the rest of the body before me, much less this.

Her hazel eyes go wide, swallowing the scraps of starlight above. "It's not—"

"You have breasts," I interrupt.

"No—well—"

"You're a woman." The words dissolve like a cloud of sugar on my tongue. On the trip here, back in Dun's Crossing, they felt so important. An affirmation that I am who I thought.

Now, I barely hear what Xander says when he—she–opens her mouth. Her brows pinch in the middle, and I know she's denying it again. That's fine with me. I'll say whatever she likes, just as long as she doesn't stop my hand creeping up her side, beneath her tunic. I brush my thumb along a line of rough linen.

"Finn," she breathes.

A high, fragile voice. I'm going to break something if I keep going.

But she's not saying no. She's not pushing my hand away.

My mark and my heart throb in unison. Deep in a cloud of aniseed and clover, a scent I didn't even realize haunted my every dream since the Haze, I can't resist their combined arguments.

I palm the linen that compresses her breasts almost out of existence, and she arches up into me like a pulled bowstring.

Something breaks.

I crush my mouth down onto Xander's. She crushes back up, bites me with razor-edged teeth like the ones that put holes in my arm. Words are dead to us now. Maybe they always have been. There's a reason she didn't tell me, that we were talking in bullshit circles before I suggested we fight. All the lies and pretty language belong out there. In here, between us, our bodies know the score better than either of us.

She reaches up underneath her tunic, hot fingers brushing mine, and the linen loosens. I palm the revealed flesh hungrily. Xander whimpers softly into my mouth as I twirl one of her nipples between my fingers. If I could record that sound, I'd play it for the rest of my days.

One thing's for sure: this time, I'm not forgetting anything.

I trace the shape of her lips with my tongue. Full and pouting like the bright orange flowers I had to walk past to find her. She snaps at my tongue, impatient, and I drink the pain like wine before pinching her in return. When she rolls us over until roots scratch at my bruised back, I drag my nails down her side in long stripes, pulling the strips of linen down and away. A growl rumbles between us. I don't know whose throat it started in.

She rolls her hips against mine. Pleasure crests, becomes pain, and circles back again. My pinned cock begs for release.

I pull back from her mouth, grab her chin and hold her in place when she tries to stop me. Want burns in her hazel eyes even as she twists to bite my hand.

With my other hand, I yank her tunic up, baring her to my eyes. Her breasts hang free, just the size of my palm, nipples dusky pink and desperately upright from the attention I've already given them.

I drag her closer and press my mouth between their peaks. She whines, and I push three fingers from the hand on her chin between her lips, muffling the sound. I've already won—if she wants the upper hand, she's going to have to fucking take it from me.

And with clove and aniseed heady on my tongue, I'll fight damn near to the death for it.

Xander sucks on my fingers like she did my cock. I drag teeth over her breasts, her nipples. Her skin pebbles under my touch like it can't wait to get closer to me.

I can't wait anymore either. I sharpen my claws and shred the belt holding her trousers up then yank them down as far as they'll go. Just enough to show a tempting thatch of auburn curls. Xander moans around my fingers. My cock jerks, begs.

I've won, and that means I get every inch of her. I drag her up my body until I can strip a few more inches of pants and reveal her wetness to my eyes. A droplet lands on my lip, and I lap it up hungrily.

My groan vibrates against the slick skin of her thigh. I pull her down and open my mouth.

I should've known better than to think she would sit back and let me take her. She clamps her legs around my head, crushes herself into me. My nose aches, threatening to crunch. My lungs beg for air.

Who gives a fuck about them? I wrap an arm around one of Xander's thighs and paint lacework with my tongue until she barely chokes down a scream. There. I repeat the gesture. Again. Her legs shake, clench and unclench. Fragments of bark rain down on my chest as she grabs the tree for support.

Wetness rich with the taste of her spills over my chin as she garbles something around my fingers and trembles. I don't slow. She's been more than clear about what she can take.

Her sounds, and her hips, climb in speed again as I fumble open the tie of my pants. I barely even need to move them before my cock springs into the night air, achingly hard.

This time, I'll remember exactly how she feels.

I roll my tongue across her one last time then flip us and surge upward in one movement. Her ankles remain hooked over my shoulders, hefting her legs high, but she doesn't complain.

And I stop. Slivers of moonlight filter down through the leaves, casting her in mottled shadow. Her hair, frizzed out of its braid, pools around her head like simmering lava—still lethal if you break the crust. Want, distant and deliriously needy, fogs her eyes. Her tunic remains caught above her breasts, and her pants scrunch between us, not blocking a centimeter of my view.

She's fucking beautiful.

She grabs a fistful of my hair, tight, and huffs. I smirk in reply. She doesn't need words to demand things from me, and I don't need them to deny her.

But only for a second. My willpower is already dust beneath us, and my cock is hungry.

I plunge into her wetness and hilt myself in a single motion. Impossibly tight, impossibly hot. She keens, just like before, and drags my mouth back to her breasts. That's a fight I'm happy to lose.

My hips synchronize with the pounding of her heart under my lips, swift and frantic. I'm nearly bending her in half, but that doesn't stop her from rolling back into me with every thrust. Just as fast, just as hard, just as wanting. With teeth and tongue, I leave my mark on her breasts like I did with the bruises on her sides.

She squeezes even tighter, and this time, I know exactly what she says.

"Finn!"

"Xander." I jerk as the apex of my pleasure slams into me like a kick to the thigh.

When that fades, though, I'm left with the moment of discovery again.

I unsheathe slowly, like I need space for all my thoughts. Xander is a woman. She lied to me, to everyone, but she's a woman. I just never noticed. Anger steps on the heels of my confusion, racing to get to the head of the line. If she'd just been honest, I wouldn't have spent the last three weeks driving myself insane over who I *really* was.

And maybe I wouldn't be sitting here, pants around my ankles, next to a mate who I can't trust. One that wants nothing to do with me because of what I might do to her precious secret. Where the fuck do we go from here?

Xander rolls into a sitting position and yanks the strips of linen back into place around her breasts. "Whatever you may think you know, you do not."

I blink. "I'm pretty sure—"

"And if you did know something,"—she spears me with a glare—"it would be best for everyone involved if you forgot it."

She pulls her tunic down, her pants up, and hurries away through a different door, hand on her hip clearly to keep her pants up without their shredded belt as subtly as possible.

What the fuck?

20

THE WEIGHT OF TRUTH

Xander

My door slams shut behind me, and it's far from enough. I want to lock it, bar it, drag furniture in front of it, but before I can do any of that, my stomach lunges up my throat.

The washroom. Feet pound, heart pounds, mark screams. I land on my knees in front of the toilet and lose the *kafi*, along with everything else I've eaten since the last time I found myself like this.

When I'm empty, alone with the stink, my nausea doesn't fade. I wish this were as simple as a cold, but whatever is making me sick is buried deep in my bones, lodged under my skin. It throbs in the shape of a sun on my collarbone, crawling up my neck. In my mind's eye, over and over again, I reach past Finn's hands and loosen the tie on my breast binding.

Foolish. Ridiculous. What was I hoping would happen? What under the moon could have helped my situation? In twenty-two years, no one has discovered my secret, which my parents and I did not choose. Six people, not counting myself, have ever known. The midwife who helped Mother through the birth is still enjoying her

119

retirement in the countryside with her family, far away from town and with the promise of royal favor for generations. Vedran wouldn't dare breathe a word, though loyalty now outweighs the benefits he has reaped from this situation. Miralyn was raised in a temple and considers protecting my true gender from the world a sacred duty.

Twenty-two years, and I threw them all away for nothing when the stakes could not possibly be higher.

There is a threat from Moonlight Hollow, perhaps, but Mother leaving weakened Father's position in the eyes of the council. I've seen how the other lords look at him now. The threat of a coup hangs heavy alongside the threat of war. If Finn so much as whispers the truth to the wrong ear, the other great families will seize on it. Only a male heir can inherit.

I conjure water, rinse my mouth in the basin. The law of male primogeniture has been the guiding principle of my life. Mother's labor was difficult; the midwife said the strain damaged something inside of her, something that meant she could never have another child. So, my parents looked at the squalling baby girl in their arms and made an impossible decision.

A decision they spent my early years impressing the importance of onto me. A decision I have protected with everything I am. Until some smirking, eye-rolling *boy* from a kingdom to the north looked at me.

The mark pounds a heady tempo into my tirade, reminding me he's not merely some boy. Some boy could be gotten rid of. Finn is my mate. Our destinies are knotted together like a pair of hopelessly tangled laces, no matter what we do.

Which makes it all the more foolish that I risked everything to have him again. The branches of the laughing cedar should have hid us from view, his fingers in my mouth should have muffled us enough, but I cannot be sure. There are no sufficient safeguards I can put in place for a risk like this.

None but what Father recommended so long ago—that I withdraw from public life and become a letter-writing king. Blame religious obsession or similar. Eccentric but acceptable.

A woman on the throne is unacceptable.

I sink back to the washroom floor, savoring the cool of the stone under my hands, and blink back tears. Men don't cry, not even alone in the dead of night.

Vedran peeks into the doorway. "Your Highness—"

"Not now," I snap.

He leaves without another word. Of course, he does. There are only three people in all the world who wouldn't. Father does not follow anyone else's orders. Corwyn does not follow my orders without an audience.

Finn somehow already knows better than to listen. And there is no one I can speak to about this less than him.

I'll have to content myself with burning eyes and the constellations of seashells on my ceiling.

* * *

THE NEXT DAY, I CONTRIVE AN EXCUSE TO GET FINN OUT OF THE meeting between Kieran, Father, and I. Pleading distraction, I take my meals in my room. Vedran and I train furiously, though even that is different now. It's impossible not to see how carefully my attendant touches me after Finn's bruising blows. Finn's not scared for me, or of me.

Which is why I turn and walk the other way when I smell ginger and moss drifting through the halls.

A note slides under my door that night. *I won the bet. You're welching.*

I douse the paper until the ink bleeds to nothingness then have Vedran burn it. Let him think I'm a coward. I have too much to lose.

Days begin stumbling by, marked by near-sightings of him and spells of dizziness or nausea. Our first shared council meeting is like sitting on a brazier of coals. Every point I make comes out garbled, and I don't even look at his side of the room. But I survive. And as all remains quiet, rumors circulate that Dun's Crossing will leave soon. There's no point in housing soldiers without a war to fight.

Four days after *that night*, Father and I eat lunch on his balcony. He eats lunch, that is. I prod at a plate of reeking fish that I would have loved a week ago.

"The other day, Corwyn said—" He straightens, gaze going hazy with a mind-link.

Fighting in Drumtemple, a voice I don't recognize pants. *They... started it.*

The link breaks like the man dropped unconscious from exhaustion. Drumtemple is a village on the border, so if he ran all the way here, I would not be surprised. I turn to Father, who glowers at his own half-empty plate.

"He was right."

"Who?" I ask.

"Corwyn." Father whips his gaze at me. "The other side struck first, and we weren't ready."

Another voice. *Apologies, sirs. The scout reports we won the day—Hajni troops saved the town from destruction.*

"I thought we agreed not to ready troops until we agreed on a plan of attack," I say.

"I have never been better ignored." Father's grin is jagged. "This is war."

I poke at the flaky white flesh on my plate. "We should meet."

"Tonight." He stands. "I need to speak with your cousin."

Ice crawls up my throat. *Were you in Drumtemple?*

If only, Corwyn replies, seemingly in good health. *I sent them plans, no more.*

I exhale. "He is safe."

Father nods, already halfway to the door. "Oh, Xander?"

"Yes?"

"Are you quite well?" He looks at my full plate then my face. "You look pale."

The ice returns, growing, and I wish it were only Corwyn I had to be worried about.

* * *

"I'm sick once or twice a day," I say as Miralyn twitches a lock of chestnut hair out of her face. Vedran's voice echoes in my mind, sharp with concern. "Perhaps three times."

"Vomiting, that is?" She runs her cool hands along my neck.

"Occasional dizzy spells as well." I stare straight ahead. There is no room in the palace more frequently checked for spies, magical or mundane. There is also no room in the palace in which I am more honest. "They come and go, like lighting a torch."

She checks my torso, hands bumping disinterestedly over the shallow rise of my bound breasts. "Anything else?"

"Headaches, sometimes." Miralyn's bluntness is the only thing that makes this less painful; I appreciated it when my monthly bleeding began, and she did not flinch, and I appreciate it now. "Oh, and I've noticed a change in my appetite, starting today. The kitchen served roasted haskor, right in season, and I couldn't stomach a bite."

She hums, steps away, and checks something in her desk. I study the bottled remedies lining the walls, all labeled in her jagged hand.

"You are late," she says. "More than late."

She cannot mean what I think.

Miralyn returns to the side of the low examination couch, frowning. She runs her hand over my torso—my stomach—and stops just above my navel. It's tender to the touch. Likely just a result of all the vomiting.

"You are pregnant." Graceful as a hammer to the skull. "I would say you have a month at most before you start showing."

My stomach lurches, but there is nothing in it to lose. I take back all I've said about her bluntness; I want this news cushioned so heavily I cannot see it for the tassels.

I do not want this news at all.

Numb, I stumble off the couch, shaking my head.

"Apologies," Miralyn says, not unkindly.

"That's not possible." The words sound false to me. A lie. An image, and one everyone can see me clinging to by the tips of my fingernails.

She rubs my shoulder. "Perhaps Vedran can extend how long you have?"

Perhaps…but not forever. There's a life inside me, put there by a man I have been avoiding for days. A man I cannot so much as share air with and keep my head.

My mate.

This is why, when I came of age, we agreed I would lock myself in my room during the Hazes. Even if Tansy Beach could accept a gay king, I would never have been able to avoid this fate forever. Not if I wanted to enjoy my mate.

The glass bottles reflect myself back at me in twisted and strange shapes. A thousand sets of hazel eyes, all asking me how I landed them here. Why.

A scream builds in my throat. They don't undergo an hour of careful glamors each morning before leaving their rooms—glamors that never truly stop itching, that limit my movement so I never step outside of them. They don't have to tailor every coat to enhance characteristics they never truly had. They don't bind their breasts, painstakingly losing air because glamors don't remove physical mass.

They do not, cannot, understand. Even those who know the truth, who help me hide it, cannot understand.

As they cannot understand the gut-wrenching pain of watching all those illusions crack like a split breastplate. Cracks spread—and once they do, they will take everything I've worked for with them.

"There are options," Miralyn says. "I would be willing to help."

The options are simple: either I abandon the court I've lived my whole life in service of, or I destroy the tiny life inside me for my mistakes.

How could I possibly choose either of them?

21

THE COST OF SECRECY

Finn

A COUPLE OF DAYS, KIERAN SAID WHEN WE LEFT. WE'LL BE IN TANSY Beach for a couple of days, maybe a week. Enough to get the soldiers settled, to make sure they actually tried peace like they promised, to be certain they have the military capabilities to not simply get our people killed. When I walked away from my second encounter with Xander, I was counting on those few days. An escape.

Now, somehow, a week has disappeared, and my brother hasn't even mentioned leaving.

Honestly, I should've known this would happen. Dun's Crossing still outstrips nearly every other kingdom in terms of sheer military force and prowess, even this long after Father's death. Since Kieran doesn't have any plans toward world domination, he's started taking on problems like this—ones more military *might* solve, if applied right. I may never be the same after our fortnight freeing Yewbrush Stream from the so-called "Solberg Purists," who believed Kieran had falsely claimed the throne and intended to rebuild Father's kingdom, starting in one not-so-forgotten corner.

Tansy Beach was exactly the sort of problem Kieran could no longer resist. An under-armed, under-prepared group up against a mysterious enemy he had reason to believe was acting unfairly. I barely saw him, but he was running to some council meeting or troop review.

I barely saw anyone in the days after my discovery, if I could help it.

The morning after, Elian bounced into my room with his usual grin and asked what we were doing for the day. Holding my tongue has never been a problem for me before, but I nearly told him everything. When he asked about the deep purple bruise Xander had left behind, I bit my tongue until I tasted blood.

Until it hurt as much as the mark on my chest.

Nearly.

The look in Xander's eyes when she told me to forget anything I thought I knew… I spent that night intending to remember every second, which meant each time I closed my eyes, I could picture that heady blend of disgust and fear. Tansy Beach only accepted male heirs, that I know. And there is something with the council and family lines. But there was more than the usual fear of disappointment or failure in her eyes. That was something bone-deep, almost instinctual.

Not that I cared. I just didn't want to make the situation any more complicated and convince Kieran we should stay any longer. Plain and simple.

Plain and simple was what led me to assign Elian to be Taner's right hand, managing things from the troop side. He knew I was getting rid of him, but he also knew that I was giving him his equivalent of a promotion. Letting him pretend we'd both inherit command someday, instead of lingering in second place for the rest of our lives. So he went, and I spent my days wandering around Tansy Tower.

Not thinking. Drinking, if it ever came too close to that. There was nothing to think about—Xander was clear about that. Her secret, why ever she was keeping it, meant more to her than a mate ever could.

I understand that. I'd give almost anything to scrape this brand off my skin. Then, I could spend this trip laughing and getting drunk with my friend instead of falling asleep on out-of-the-way benches for a change of scenery.

After the first time I miss a council meeting, Kieran asks. I tell him what he wants to hear—I'll be there next time, just got distracted. After the second missed meeting, he's frustrated. After the third, he doesn't bother tracking me down. Pretty soon, half the palace treats me more like a seashell embedded in the wall than a foreign prince.

Just the way I like it.

A day after that, I'm studying another hand-painted box on display in the easternmost spire when a pair of undersecretaries wander by without so much as a bow. They genuinely may not recognize me; it's not as though I wear a crown, and they would have no reason to keep track of me in their reports. One belongs to Lord Juraj, I believe, and the other to the one called something like Edward.

"I heard another tale," Juraj's man says.

The other one scoffs. "If I offer you a ratified report, you say you've heard another tale. When you provide me with any shred of proof something you've heard is true, I'll take the time to listen to it, Vito."

Vito huffs a sharp breath. "If I had sworn before the whole cadre that I'd tasted Lord Edvard's lady wife, I might not sniff so much at others' words."

Edvard's man turns slightly purple in the corner of my eye. "I—the brandy—oh, spin your useless yarn."

Vito preens like a cat presenting a caught mouse. "My sister married a Hajni foot soldier. Infuriated my father, but she writes to me sometimes of what is actually occurring on our borders."

"Third-hand information, then."

"But information all the same," Vito insists. "She says the fighting came from our side. That there was an order for Hajni troops to attack, Of course, she claims it was in response to movement on the other side of the border, but I have my suspicions…."

"Our first victory?" Disbelief rings through the hall as if it's empty. "That's what you wish to challenge? I—"

The two of them turn a corner away from me, and I shake my head. Morons. At least I know those exist in all kingdoms—and that Anwen wasted his time with all his sneaking and skulking. If you seem bored enough, people will act like you're invisible even when you're standing right in front of them.

Meet me after lunch, I tell Kieran through the mind-link.

*　　*　　*

I SIT AT MY USUAL TABLE IN THE LIBRARY, GNAWING ON A HUNK OF DARK bread, when Kieran finds me. He looks tired. Or maybe he's just pissed I dragged him away from all his precious meetings.

I don't ask how he knew I would be here. His whole "ignoring me" act is just that—an act. I would be shocked if he didn't know I spent most of my days here, studying books of military theory. The blowhards can argue over which is best in the council meetings; I work best alone, where I can actually finish a thought.

"What?" He takes the seat across from me.

"There is a rumor that Hajni troops started the fighting at Drumtemple," I say. "Third-hand. One of Juraj's secretary's sister's husbands, but I heard it from the secretary."

Kieran sighs and scrubs his hands over his face. "That would be difficult. Corwyn's location is accounted for from the beginning of the fighting to the end."

I glance at him. "You already suspected this?"

"The first battle of a simmering war, on the war hawk's home ground?" He smiles tiredly. "Father taught me the trick for my fifteenth birthday."

Father mostly taught me I was in a fallback position. I'd still prefer that to the heaviness in Kieran's voice every time he mentions him.

"Then we should send a party to look into it. Substantiate the rumors."

"We should bring it before the council," he says.

"You have my blessing." I wave vaguely and pull my book back. He should know I won't be going.

"I don't know why you waste everybody's time with this act," he says. "If you didn't care, why tell me at all?"

"I really hate Corwyn." I've already finished the book in front of me, but I reread the last paragraph intently.

With another sigh, Kieran leaves me.

It's better than fighting with him. He can't force me to do anything here, with so many eyes on us. He has other strangers to save.

I stand and go to grab another book from the shelf. Tansy Beach's strategy differs from anything I've ever read before. They're used to fighting on shifting sands, avoiding or using tides. They have no wall of brute force to conquer the day, just careful use of the land itself.

The tome slides back into place with a dull *thud*, and I grab the one next to it.

The Haze, the Goddess, and Our Other Selves.

Misfiled. Obviously not military theory. I should put it back.

My mark throbs.

Covering the title, I bring it back to my table and open it quickly. The writing is heavy-handed, alternately dry and downright poetic. Of course, all the poetic shit is reserved for how the mating mark *feels*. The rightness of being reunited with your other half. Finally becoming your whole self.

I skim, flipping page after page, like there are going to be any answers in here. What a stupid waste of time. I know there's no way out.

The word *markless* catches my eye, and I pause.

In a brief paragraph, the author explains the markless. People who, for whatever reason, never find a mate. The author suspects they are mates simply born too isolated from each other, but in a single sentence, he admits to another possibility—maybe the markless just don't have mates.

Envy stabs me through the chest. Those lucky few, complete in themselves. Not trapped in this impossible hell, this web of royal expectation and desire. Fuck, I'd give just about anything to be one of them.

A horn blows, low and resonant. I cock my head. I haven't heard that before.

Moonlight Hollow is attacking, Kieran says urgently. *Here.*

2 2

ON THE SIDELINES

Xander

   "They're coming in from all sides!"
   "Goddess above, where are they coming from!"
   "Flank right, you ridiculous—"

I wince and try to drown out the noise of mind-links flying back and forth. It's hard to say how long ago the alarm went up now, but I know I've been standing on the nearest balcony ever since, staring at the distant dunes over which I know the battle is happening. Dun's Crossing fights alongside us, but I cannot quite tell how many Moonlight Hollow has. Orders soar through my mind, but more than that, I can hear their screams. They're so loud I cannot quite tell whether they're in my mind or truly echoing through the evening air.

An attack on Tansy Tower—or nearly, though technically it is our closest outpost that has been hit. The news of Drumtemple surprised me; that Moonlight Hollow was able to penetrate so deeply through our borders and that they would risk such a maneuver feels almost incomprehensible.

131

In my mind's eye, I see Mother, curled with me around one of our military texts. *You see this?* she asks, dragging a fond finger along a diagram. *This is our history. Tansy Beach has survived as long as we have, pulling apart as we are at our own seams, through these tactics. None can challenge us but ourselves.*

I cannot see the woman who spoke those words in the fighting over the distant dunes. It's not even clever, a full-frontal assault like this when they don't have the territory for a tactical retreat.

Still, my heart thrums to the beat of the chaos. Father's voice threads through the noise, barking orders from above. I could be at his side, directing our troops.

But even standing here, a million miles from anything that matters, makes me feel more alive than the dead air of the war room I know he occupies. Evening breezes tousle my hair. I can almost scent blood on the wind. Those pained, heart-racing screams—a sick, sour part of me wants to taste one tearing up my throat. I want to know how it feels.

Father says books teach more about war than any fight, but I don't know how he expects me to send our people to their deaths without knowing what it feels like to face the same. He spent his days on the battlefield, brief though they were. And my opportunities to try such things are running short.

Isolated on this balcony, I allow myself to place a hand on my still mostly flat stomach. Father would never let me join the fighting, even though that's where a prince ought to be. For my whole life, I have understood his caution, even as I tempered it with Mother's insistence that I live as much of my life as I could.

Now, the part of me that refused Miralyn's offer of *help* is glad of his paranoia. No one can see the lethal secret coiled inside me yet, but that does not protect it against scraping claws or gnashing teeth.

Not that I have made any sort of decision. To abandon a life created through no fault of its own or my life, for which I have abandoned everything and turned myself inside out, is an impossible choice. Making it alone is even more impossible yet.

Who would I talk to, though? Vedran may be as close to me as a second skin, but I cannot ask him to keep this secret as well. Not when I know what price Father would lie on him for that knowledge. I certainly cannot talk to Father; in the best of all worlds, he takes the decision away from me, and my newest secret dies. In the worst, I die with it.

I scratch my neck as my mark gnaws. That possibility does not even bear considering.

"Knock knock," Corwyn says behind me.

I turn to see my cousin stepping into the sitting room, half-armored despite the fact that the armor will only fall away when he shifts. It's a ritual, a mental protection more than a physical one, and since he has never attempted to fight in human form, Father allows it.

"I am surprised to see you here," he says.

"As I am surprised to see you. Should you not already be part of the fighting?"

He shakes his head. "When you didn't arrive at the war room, Uncle insisted I stay."

I look away. That's simply nausea bubbling in my gut, not guilt. Corwyn has seen enough fighting that I don't need to feel sorry for robbing him of this.

Though he is a brilliant fighter–against anyone but me. He could have saved lives out there. Guilt overwhelms nausea, but like a crashing wave hitting a beach, I know the nausea will remain when guilt finally recedes. It's my constant companion these days.

"He didn't call for me," I mumble.

Corwyn takes a step closer. "To be frank, I assumed you were out there."

My heart pounds a marching beat against my sternum. "Why?"

He laughs. "No one refuses Uncle."

No one but Mother. Even I didn't by staying here. He assumed I would join him so instinctively that he didn't even ask.

"Well, you know how it goes," I say noncommittally.

"Difficult labor." He nods. "Of course. I should have realized."

The fading sunlight catches his eyes, making something I can't quite name shine within. His smile twists slightly.

"Father's over-concern," I say, trying to dim whatever that shine is before it becomes a problem. "He worries he'll have no heir when the time comes, if I am allowed to test myself in battle."

Corwyn keeps nodding, but he seems to accept this glimmer of truth. Though he would technically be in contention for the throne, were I to disappear, the Hajni family has enjoyed endless privileges in its current position, and he is my Beta.

"Apologies," he says. "I assumed it was your weak constitution because you've been so peaky, visiting Miralyn so often of late."

He says it like it means nothing, but my stomach yanks, knots around itself. My skin burns hotter than the sinking summer sun.

He knows.

He can't know. I have been so cautious. Since Miralyn laid her hand on me and told me my careful future was little more than shattered glass, I've only been to see her myself once, despite her requests to the contrary. I've sent Vedran to her for the various potions and powders she recommended, should I decide to keep the ticking time bomb in my gut. Certainly, I've been ill, and hiding my bouts of nausea gets harder and harder as council meetings stretch longer and longer, but that cannot be enough for Corwyn to truly suspect something, much less confront me with it like this.

Right?

His gaze hangs heavy around my neck like a yoke. I'm letting too much time pass.

I smirk, saunter another step forward, and poke him in the chest hard enough that he rocks back on his heels. "If you're implying that you think I can't still take you—"

"I was implying nothing!" He holds his hands up, laughter dancing in his eyes like this was all a big joke. My stomach starts to unknot. That sounds like something Corwyn would do. "Forgive a subject for worrying about his prince."

"Subject?" My eyebrows shoot up. "Now I know you're simply making fun of me. Or are you stalling because you're too frightened to join the fighting?"

"Spread that rumor." He takes a step back, arms wide. "It will only make it more impressive when I return with the heads of those traitors impaled on my claws."

"An extremely impressive limping return." I smirk at him and wave him off. "Let us see if you can keep the promise. I'll be here, worth protecting from a premature death."

He leaves me alone with my thoughts, the breeze, and the torrent of mind-links. The ice on my skin melts slowly. He cannot have known, have been implying what I feared he was. It's simply not possible.

But it's only impossible for now. I fold my hands on the railing of the balcony so they don't fall to my stomach or rise to my neck. Before long, the secret I'm hiding within my very body —that being growing there—will make my decision for me. A few weeks, Miralyn said. In that time, I doubt the war will even have ended. So little time to make a decision that will reshape my entire life.

A howl soars over the dunes. Perhaps it's my imagination, but I think it sounds like Mother. Instinct surges too fast for me to catch it back.

"If you are out there," I say to her through the mind-link, *"I need to talk to you. I have to make a choice, Mother, and I cannot do it alone. You would know what to do."*

For all my trouble, I don't even receive the simple ease of connection. She may not be out there. She may be many miles away, giving orders from a distance, like Father.

Or she may no longer be part of my pack.

My eyes sting. I lower my forehead to the balcony to hide my face from whoever else may see fit to visit the errant prince, tucked away in a corner of the castle. What would Mother say, anyway? Clearly, she did not much mind the idea of abandoning all she had built, of destroying her only child in the process. Either option might sound palatable to her.

That damnable mark on my neck all but dances for my attention. It knows who I want—need to talk to.

I start to quash the feeling, but I can't quite manage it. Six days have passed since Finn and I... and he hasn't breathed a word. Or, if he has, his words have not reached Tansy Beach ears. Even the slightest whisper in a climate this fraught could call for the sort of investigation that would bring everything crashing down. He has been avoiding me, I thought, but perhaps he's avoiding everything. Perhaps I can trust him with one more secret.

Except he is fighting for his life on the other side of these dunes.

I lift my head and tune into the stream of orders once more.

2 3

———

WHAT REMAINS

Finn

I DIVE TO THE SIDE AS A CLAW SCYTHES DOWN, AND MY BLEEDING LEFT flank crumples underneath me. Slammed to the ground, I swallow a mouthful of dirt, but I don't collect another injury. The Moonlight Hollow wolf bares his teeth, about to snap at my throat.

Only fighting as wolves shrinks their imagination of what we can really do. And it helps that I'm larger, stronger than almost anyone from this beachside kingdom. So when I throw my weight forward and barrel into his ankles, he goes down like a pile of twigs.

And then kicks stinging sand into my eyes. I wince. He shuffles, but I don't know where he's heading.

"Enemy report," I spit through the mind-link. *"Can anyone—"*

A lupine grunt ends the quiet, followed by the fresh reek of blood. My tear ducts manage to clear the sand from my gaze just in time to see a tawny wolf with familiar, olive-green eyes standing over the fallen Moonlight Hollow wolf.

Dead? Unconscious? It's hard to say. All that matters is that he's not an issue any longer.

I struggle to my feet, limbs whining with exhaustion, and look around for the next enemy. It's simpler than facing the wolf before me and the simmering resentment that Corwyn saved my life.

But there are no other enemies, really. I watch tails whip away through the tall grass they were attacking from—a full retreat. One of them drags another away, cutting a path wide enough to follow.

Despite my injured leg, I shoulder in front of Corwyn and block his way forward. The scent of blood hangs heavy in the air. Everywhere I look, the sand is stained or torn by claw and fang to reveal paler sand beneath. If Moonlight Hollow is taking their injured, there are as many, if not more, injured—or dead—on our side. We've taken enough losses.

Before my eyes, he shifts. Not into Corwyn, but into someone who looks like a younger, leaner version of him, swaying with exhaustion. I know him.

I shift. "Ty?"

He offers me something to the left of a smile. "And here I thought you wouldn't remember me."

I met him during the revitalization of Escuro. And, if I'm remembering correctly, there's a real chance the sway in his step is drunkenness rather than tiredness.

"Corwyn's brother?" I pull on a pair of breeches, and we trudge toward a gathering column of wolves and humans. Strength in numbers, for the short march back to Tansy Tower. My left leg screams at the scrape of fabric.

Ty ducks under my arm wordlessly, forcing me to rest my weight on him. "The lesser Lord Hajni, at your service."

His awkward bow almost dumps me back onto the sand. I wheeze something like a laugh.

"See those lights?" Ty gestures toward Tansy Tower as we struggle up a dune.

Points of greenish light jump and dance like fire. I nod.

"Branches we pull out of the ocean burn like that," he says tiredly. "We only light them for the dead."

They light our path back, two amidst a bleeding crowd.

"How is it looking?" I ask Elian.

"Heavy casualties," he replies. *"We're more injured than dead, but Tansy Beach is the opposite."*

I grimace. Injuries heal, but…shit, this level of organization in Moonlight Hollow was unexpected. They weren't supposed to be assassins, stealing out of grass like shadows rather than creatures.

"You?" I ask.

"Scratched up, nothing too serious." He laughs. *"You'd think I tasted bad."*

He and Ty should be together. They'd laugh the entire way back.

I free myself from the lesser Lord Hajni when we reach the trees closer to the castle and brace myself on low branches instead. Ty wanders off to check in with a few of what seem to be his friends, clapping them on the shoulder.

Clove and aniseed. I twist toward the smell before I can stop myself, leg pulsating.

Through the trees, I can just barely make out a glimpse of auburn hair. Hazel eyes catch mine, hold for a heartbeat, then turn away.

Xander wasn't part of the battle. I searched for her, even though I promised I wouldn't. Maybe she's just watching us plod home, counting heads.

Or maybe she's watching me.

The mark I can't escape no matter how Goddess-damned hard I try peels me away from the group and sends me through the small forest toward her. Her scent barely punctures the stench of blood, but I think I finally know what it's like to be Candace. Right now, I could track it anywhere.

Anywhere, apparently, being a low-slung cabin made of sun-bleached wood supported by columns of shell-studded stone. Xander stands on the porch, hands clenched so tight around the railing her knuckles are turning white.

This is the closest we've been since that night, and she looks like she wants to run away. Of course, she does. I inhale slowly. Whatever comes next, I need my strength to be able to hobble away on my destroyed leg.

This far from the battlefield, I realize something is different. She doesn't just smell of aniseed and clove. There's something new, something rich and earthy I can't name.

"I need to speak with you," she says.

"It looks like you dragged me out here to kill me while I'm already weak," I reply. The cabin is painfully clean and completely isolated from anything else around.

A ghost of a smile flits across her lips. "Once a moon, I require somewhere I can devote myself to private prayer."

She doesn't say it like a lie, but she doesn't need to. There's only one reason someone like her would need privacy—far enough that she couldn't be smelled—once a moon.

Suddenly, the cabin looks less like a trap and more like an olive branch. And, as my leg scream, even more like somewhere that might have chairs.

"I need to speak with my friend," she says as I take a step forward. "Can you be that again?"

My mark throbs in harmony with my leg. For her, for a place to sit, I'll do anything. I nod.

She lets me up the single stair, then opens the door. The room inside is cool and comfortable. A small kitchen crouches against one wall, cupping a two-seat table. A bed piled with pillows and blankets hugs the opposite.

The wooden chair creaks when I drop into it. She eyes my bleeding leg then strides to a cabinet on the wall. From it, she withdraws a few bottles of what look like herbs.

"This is just for the pain." Her voice scrapes out of her throat as if pulled. "You'll still need stitches."

Pain relief I will take. She cuts away the fabric of my pant leg to bare the weeping slash then starts mixing the herbs in a mortar wordlessly. A few times, she looks up at me like she's going to say something, then looks away again. Her fingers burn against my skin, spots of heat that linger even through the pain. My cock jumps when she brushes too high on my leg.

I promised friendship, but that's much harder to remember when she's on her knees before me.

A cool rush, like the first sip of a drink after chewing mint leaves, washes through me as she applies her poultice and ties it in place. I exhale sharply, and the throbbing abates.

One throbbing. The mark on my chest screams into first place, especially as she sits back on her heels. Surprisingly vulnerable, she chews on her lower lip.

"I bet you won't tell me," I breathe.

She snorts, but I don't think I'm imagining the note of relief in it. "I bet you won't like it when I do."

"There's only one way to win that bet."

She takes a deep breath, throws her gaze at mine with all the weight of an anchor. "I'm pregnant."

Blood roars in my ears. I slump against the chair. There's no point in asking whose it is. Her voice keens in my memory. I doubt she's kissed anyone other than me.

"I need to speak with someone—with my friend—about what to do."

Her voice may as well be the wind. I'm a father. There isn't any space for other words in my skull.

"Finn?" Xander snaps her fingers in front of my face.

I blink. Her words filter in slowly. "What do you mean, what to do?"

Xander shoves to her feet and begins pacing back and forth, her voice climbing in pitch as she talks. A complete history spills out before me like blood on sand. Her mother's arduous labor, meaning there would be no more Mlakar heirs. An impossible decision about an infant baby girl. A legacy to protect.

And I'm listening, I really am. But at the end of every sentence, *you're a father* echoes through the air. There is a life growing in this very room, and I am the only father that life will ever have. An exclusive role, a place I will always belong exactly as myself.

"And earlier today, during the battle, I briefly thought Corwyn alluded to knowing something about my secret—secrets, now." She shakes her head. "Carrying this alone is making me increasingly para-noid, seeing shadows where there are none. I needed to ask someone else's opinion."

The hairs on the back of my neck rise. Corwyn isn't getting anywhere near my baby if I have anything to say about it.

Then, the weight of her words settles in. She's not asking me how to hide it; she's asking me whether hiding it is worth the trouble. Whether she should destroy the only proof of our time together, now that the bruises are fading.

A yell bubbles in my throat, short and simple: *no*. But a memory corks it in place: Xander's voice as she told me I should forget what-ever I thought I knew. This cabin is a place where court doesn't exist. That's its purpose. Here, she can ask me what to do about our baby. Outside these walls, the mark shrieking over my heart is a mistake again.

"I don't know," I say as casually as I can. "What do you want to do?"

Something in her eyes breaks like I pushed one of the glass jars off the table. "You have no thoughts on the matter?"

The yell shoves against the cork, trying to burst free. If she asks me to, I'll kill for this baby, this chance.

I shake my head.

Xander blinks and looks at the floor. "Of course. You should…you ought to be celebrating with the other soldiers. I'll let you go."

I start to stand when I smell it. Barely. Just a little more salt in this salt-stained kingdom. I hear it a second later, the whisper of a drop of water hitting the ground.

Xander is crying.

My leg doesn't hurt, but it drags behind me as I struggle the few steps between us and crush her to my bare chest.

"You're the only one I can ask," she mumbles against my skin. "Anyone else…they would kill me or get killed for it."

She needs me. This baby needs me.

The cork pops, and the seal of my lips breaks. "I want my baby."

24

———

THE WORLD SHIFTS

Xander

I EXPECTED MANY THINGS WHEN I PULLED FINN AWAY FROM THE OTHER soldiers after the battle. I thought he might ignore me entirely, might flee, might do exactly what he seemed to be doing a moment ago and refuse to give me any kind of answer.

In no world did I expect the words that just dropped from his lips.

I stare into the icy depths of his eyes and try to find the wink of amusement, the sparkle of a joke. He offers me no such reassurance. Just cold, clear certainty.

In the back corners of my mind, a clock starts ticking. I can only boggle at his confession for so long before he will pull back, retract it, take my silence alone as an answer. It might be slightly longer this time; though I don't find laughter in his eyes, I do find something uncomfortably like desperation. Like I've offered water to a man who thought he was going to spend the rest of his life dying slowly as he crawled across a desert. He wants this more than I almost knew it was possible to want something.

My mark itches into my notice.

Perhaps not more than I knew was possible after all.

Our baby. Words I haven't dared to think. Baby alone is impossibly heavy, but ours? Something hot, sharp, and undeniable stabs through me.

Finn does not back away. He leans forward, his gaze dropping to my lips. He is offering me everything I can't have.

I close my eyes, and his mouth brushes over mine. Slow. Hesitant, like he is waiting for me to run. Perhaps he is. But he tastes like ginger and moss, sharp and soft in one, and the world shifts under my feet.

For nearly a decade, this cabin has been my retreat, the place I go when I can no longer hide the secrets I carry inside me, not even with magic. I have danced here, cried here, wished I could rejoin the palace and wished I never had to, all within these walls. This is the place where something like what I would have been, if my parents hadn't made that fateful decision, exists.

And I know exactly what that version of me wants. She has been screaming it since a powerful silver wolf stepped out from between two trees and gave chase.

Here, if nowhere else, I can indulge her.

I shove my fingers into Finn's hair, loosen sand that falls between us with a soft hiss like rain, and lick along the seam of his mouth. His lips curl into a smile before parting.

Mine. My mate.

As I plunge my tongue into his mouth, he grabs my hips and hauls me closer. A voice in the back of my brain mumbles about his injury, but that careful, protective voice doesn't belong here. I shove it away and straddle his lap like he so clearly wants me to. The growing bulge of his cock presses up into my center, and I don't bother trying not to moan.

No one can hear us here.

His answering groan rumbles against my mouth, and my eyes sting with something like tears again, but I cannot imagine feeling sad right now. All I can feel is him—his cock between my legs, his tongue intertwined with mine.

His hands, hungry but careful on my thighs, like he is worried about pushing this too far.

I have no interest in the careful, controlled, *bored* Finn he shows the world. Achingly, I pry myself off his mouth and stand. He stares at me, glass-eyed, a frown pinching his brow.

"I'm not going anywhere." I pull my tunic off over my head then untie the crushing bindings keeping my chest flat.

I could stop here. The cautious voice in the back of my head begs me to. Somehow, there is still something to lose.

But I'm not listening to that voice now. I'm tired of living alone with it and my secrets. I want, for one night, to be able to truly lean on another person. The person I most want to lean on.

I shed the rest of my clothes and stand fully naked before him.

His pale eyes drink in the details of my body. His mouth goes slightly slack. I'm not sure how long it's been since anyone has seen me like this, but certainly a number of years. My skin stings like a nerve rubbed raw.

Finn grabs the table, shoves to his feet, and wraps himself around me. No more careful hands. His fingers roam, possessive, ravenous. I arch into his touch and begin leading us backward toward the bed where I've spent so many nights alone. He cups my breasts, teases them. I whimper, and the smile he gives me looks downright dangerous.

When my knees hit the edge of the bed, he shoves.

I fall for what feels like a thousand years, staring up at him. Blood streaks his bare chest in vivid red. The white of the bandage stands out against his thigh. He looks like a conqueror—a king.

What am I, if that's what he is?

I hit the bed, and he lands on top of me, tracing a line with his mouth along my neck. He ghosts over where my mark claims me as his, and lightning shoots through me. As if he felt it, he returns, harder. I writhe beneath him, want building in my gut like a wave caught behind a dam.

The tension in my chest, the weight of all my secrets, starts to ease for the first time since I knew I had secrets to keep. He can be the king, the conqueror. I thread a hand between us, find the top of his shredded pants, and cup his cock. He jerks into my palm, and I grin.

As everyone knows, as Mother and Luna Raven make more than clear, the queen is usually the true power.

I loosen his pants until I can reach skin, and begin stroking him in rhythm with his wild feast on my neck. His groan vibrates through my whole body. Fingertips dance over the apex of my thighs, teasing.

I bet I can last longer. The words whisper through my mind, almost reach my lips. At first, I think they belong to the mask that is Xander. But as Finn smiles against my throat when I roll my hips into him, I know they belong to the laughter between us.

Right now, though, I don't feel like laughing.

I feel hungry.

"I want to taste you," I manage.

He drags his lips away from my skin, presses them to mine. His taste is stronger here, but it's not enough. I shake my head, stroke his cock.

Realization dawns on him with a choked groan. He shoves his pants off, away, but he doesn't instantly bring his cock to my lips. Instead, he turns, positioning himself just out of reach while he kisses down the slope of my still flat stomach.

"So do I," he murmurs.

Every remaining thought in my head shoots between my thighs. That's the secret—it doesn't matter who's king or queen or anything else. All that matters is the word that makes the world shift under my feet like loose sand. *Our.* Our pleasure is more palpable than that of one of us alone.

His cock bumps against my lips, and everything else ceases to matter. Finn buries his mouth between my legs as I swallow him down. Ginger, moss, and the salt of him burst against my tongue. I moan, and he moans in turns, a circle of vibrations shivering up my spine and down his.

We start moving in unison. Ravenous. Each pushing the other higher, faster. He is longer than I remember, but relaxation is simple with the cascades of want he sends through me. His tongue is a masterwork, dancing some pattern I don't know but need to learn over my wetness. I chase his rhythm, laving him with my tongue, grasping his hips for whatever shred of stability I can find in the middle of this storm.

My legs clench. The apex of pleasure looms on the horizon. I want —need–him inside me, but the sun has barely set. There will be time, at least tonight.

Finn has no such patience. He pulls back, gasps for me to stop, bites my inner thigh until I do. I hiss and release him.

He doesn't ask, just flips me off the top with a slight wince—the pain poultice Miralyn gives me the ingredients for is beginning to fade—and lines himself up. The explosion of pain and pleasure when he first did this felt like the initial step under a waterfall, uncertain whether one's feet will last beneath the power of the water.

Now, it's intense, but I know this waterfall all too well. It's like slipping into a favorite hiding place, secure in the knowledge no one will find you there.

It's like finding the person that completes you and dragging them as far into yourself as possible.

My body pulses. My mark sings. The girl who only exists within these walls dances in sheer, wild delight.

I grab Finn's hips and shove him back then pull him forward again. He rasps a laugh and lets me set the pace, fucking myself with him. The dam inside me quavers, ready to burst. Neither of us have long like this.

But perhaps the night doesn't have to stop here.

I roll, writhe, grind. He puts his power behind my instructions, slamming me into the bed like he wants to break it. Someone is moaning, hasn't stopped moaning for a long time—and somehow, that high, fragile voice is mine.

Finn cups my face and meets my gaze. In his eyes, I see that desperation again.

Is it for me as well?

Pleasure crashes through my last restraints, catching me in its arms and dragging me under. My whole body shakes. I garble something and cling to his shoulders. He stutters and goes stiff over me, my pleasure becoming ours.

When it's over, he rolls off me with a slight wince. There's barely enough room on this bed built for one, but he doesn't leave. Instead, he takes my hand.

"We've never held hands before," I say, startled by the realization.

He doesn't say anything poetic about how we'll do it again. He doesn't breathe a word about the future, the world outside this cabin. Finn just kisses the back of my hand and smiles softly at me.

He wants this baby. Perhaps he wants me. And I don't know what any of that means for me or for Tansy Beach. But I know I want to hold his hand and lay beside him in a too-small bed.

So I close my lips around all the tomorrows and pillow my head on his shoulder.

25

IN THE SUN

Finn

THE SUN IS HIGH IN THE SKY BY THE TIME I PEEL MY EYES OPEN THE next morning. My leg aches, but a second application of that herb shit before we finally collapsed to sleep keeps it from being the nightmare I'm sure it would be otherwise.

That, and Xander's head on my chest, her mouth open with sleep and auburn hair splayed everywhere. Her face looks surprisingly like it does when pleasure overwhelms her completely—just about relaxed, with the faintest smile. My cock reacts to the thought.

I shake my head. Dawn was threatening when we finally ran out of ways to try each other's bodies or the stamina to come up with them. I fought a battle yesterday. And Xander—

My fingers drift instinctively from her hip, cupping the tiny swell of her stomach. The Haze was only a little over a month ago now. She has some time before the bump of our baby will be impossible to hide, but she still sought me out. Maybe because other interventions have to happen faster. Or maybe because she wanted me to tell her to keep them—wanted to know if I wanted them.

Fuck, I want this baby. Our baby.

Anyone else would kill me or get killed for this, she said.

My hand tightens protectively. I won't let that happen.

Her brow starts to furrow in her sleep, like my worries are infecting her. I slowly release my grasp, and she relaxes once again.

She looks different in the morning light. Actually… she looks like she did the morning after the Haze. And the morning I had to bring her a hangover breakfast. Every time, I've chalked it up to lack of sleep, but didn't she say something about glamors last night?

I trace the softened curve of her jaw, her slightly fuller lips, her higher cheekbone. The changes are small; I can still see the prince in her features. But like this, she looks….

She looks like the girl of my dreams. Soft enough to need me, hard enough to take everything life throws at her. To not take my shit.

And they made her hide this. Her Goddess-damned face. Her whole Goddess-damned self, once a month. This is probably why King Alden wouldn't let her fight in the tourney, even though I saw the way her body language shifted when I asked her. She wanted to. Badly.

How much has she had to give up? Hell, who even knows? Her parents, of course, but is there anyone else in this castle she can actually be herself with?

No. Everyone looks at her expecting the person they want to see, not who she actually is.

I brush a kiss over her forehead, wishing that made a little less sense to me.

Her eyes flutter open. I pull back to watch them catch the sunlight in strands of gold, shades of blue and green. She looks at me hazily, a smile still curled on her lips, and I lean in to kiss her.

"What time is it?" she demands, shooting up off the bed and out of range.

I blink. "Not sure. Doesn't look like early morning."

She looks past me, out the window. "No, it looks like we're sneaking up on noon. Shit, shit, shit."

"What?"

She grabs her pants from where she left them lying on the floor and begins shoving one of her legs into them. "I failed to tell anyone other than Vedran that I was leaving, much less coming here."

Vedran… it takes a moment, but finally I connect the name to the pale, red-eyed attendant I've caught glimpses of here and there. "Vedran, who does your glamors?"

"You were listening." She pauses, eyes me for a moment. There's something in her gaze that warms me as much as the beam of sunlight her abrupt departure has rolled me into. "Yes, that Vedran. He is comfortable lying for me, but after a day like yesterday, even his best work won't hold up for very long."

My leg aches, a throbbing reminder of exactly what yesterday entailed. "Kieran said you were all confident Moonlight Hollow wouldn't try something that far over the border any time soon."

"We were." She has one leg of her pants up and wobbles as she tries to hop into the other.

Instinct fires before my brain can catch up, and I lurch out of bed to catch her only to fall on my ass when my injured leg won't support me. Xander tries to grab me like she has her balance, and the two of us land in a groaning pile on the wooden floor.

The pain fades in comparison to the warmth of her skin on mine. A laugh bubbles out of my throat. We must look ridiculous, a tangle of mostly nude limbs, bandaged, bloodstained, and tired.

After a heartbeat, she laughs with me. Her laugh is different, too. Maybe her whole voice. Once again, it's not unrecognizable. Xander always had a little husk to his words, like he had something caught in his throat, and that remains. She's just a little higher, a little clearer, like the magic sanded off the edges of her words.

My mark hums that I could listen to her laugh forever.

Instead, of course, she shakes her head. "You're not listening, Finn. Moonlight Hollow just made an impossible incursion deep behind our borders, and now the prince is missing. How does that look?"

"Vedran will say you're somewhere." I stroke her hair back from her face and absolutely don't help as she struggles to free herself. "Not prince-napped."

"I have no idea how the battle even turned out–if we won." She manages to disentangle from me and stand.

I offer her my hand for balance as she slides on the other leg of her pants. "We did, with heavy losses."

"There are funerals to conduct. I need to be there." She closes her eyes for a long moment. All the tension is back now, maybe doubled. That, I can't argue with. No matter how much I'd like to. "Where is my binding?"

She spins in a tight circle, searching for the strip of linen trapped under her heel. I free it and stand. With a slight, grateful smile, she tries to take it from me.

"Show me," I rasp, trying not to show how unsteady I am on my feet.

"Finn—"

"I'd bet Altair's claim on the throne that it's faster when someone else does it." And I won't give up what might be my last chance this morning to touch her skin. "So show me."

Xander inhales deeply, shakily. She takes one end of the strip and holds it to the middle of her chest, below and between her breasts. "Wrap. Overlap each strip a little with the last one. And go as tight as you can, until I tell you to ease off."

Slow, methodical work has never been my strong suit. Even when I study, I tend to have a half dozen books out at once and trade between them. It's only here, where I thought that would make me look too interested, that I've been trying not to.

It's easy to focus on the thin line of cream, Xander's bracing finger, the inches of skin disappearing. Last night—what I said— looms between us. One of us is going to have to say something, and Goddess above, I hope it's not me.

I glance up at her face and find her chewing on her lip, gaze distant. It's not going to be her, it seems. Last night was an outlier.

"Have you made a decision?" I cover half of a purple bruise shaped like my lips, too large for a single strip to hide.

"It's ours," she says simply. "I won't take it from you."

Something knotted in my gut unravels. "How are we going to hide the pregnancy, then?"

"You mean how am I going to hide it?"

I shake my head.

She exhales sharply, loose hair swinging. "You know magic, then? Or you're an apothecary? Anything I can actually use?"

I yank on the binding, pulling it so tight she hisses. "I'm the fucking father, and we can't just waltz out of here without a plan."

"We have no time," she replies through gritted teeth. "Every second I spend here is another second during which my people might decide to question me. Once those questions start, they will never stop. My whole life is built from choices that keep people from having those seconds, and I do not intend to change that now, when my people need me more than they ever have."

My chest aches as I reach the end of the binding. I may not be an expert, but I know she doesn't have long. Raven needed new dresses halfway through her second month. Estrella made it to the third, according to Anwen's latest letter, but regardless, we're talking about a matter of weeks.

"Knot it," she says. "As tight as you can. Make sure it won't come undone."

My fingers twitch and refuse to obey the command for a heartbeat. The irritating little voice that seems to have sprouted inside my mark begs me to grab her, carry her out of here, and declare her mine.

Ruin her life in one selfish blow.

I tie the knot. Tighter. Again. She exhales a slow breath, one that stops long before I expect it to.

Of course. With how tight I tied that, I'm surprised she can breathe at all.

"Vedran can tighten it," she mutters as she turns for her tunic.

A memory floats back to me from the Haze, still spotty with liquor and hormones. Deep, almost blood-red lines sketched across the sides of her chest. Marks from the bindings.

I open my mouth to tell her that can't be safe then close it again. She probably knows. And a scheme like this doesn't work unless it's been happening since the day she was born. I don't know if she even has a choice at this point.

"Make me a wager," I say instead.

"I don't have time—"

"I already have the parameters," I interrupt.

She twists her tunic between her fingers but nods.

"I'll act like everything is the way it was between us. Before the Haze." Even if I can't touch her the way I want to, staying away feels impossible now that I know I wouldn't just be avoiding her.

"And if you succeed?"

"You tell me your real name." I smile.

She looks at the floor. "I don't—pick another forfeit."

I have no idea whether she doesn't have one or she won't tell me. I don't know which is worse.

"If I win, you meet me at night," I say. "You pick the place, and I'll be there."

"All right." She slips her tunic on, straightens, and suddenly, I barely notice the tiny differences in her face, her voice, her body. She is Prince Xander. "Tonight, if you can do this."

I toss her a cocky salute, trying to lessen the knots in her shoulders.

No luck. She just shakes her head at me as she pulls her hair up in a simple tie and walks away. My mark bellows to go after her, but I stay planted in a single shaft of sunlight.

In the doorway, she pauses.

"Thank you," she says, her voice barely above a whisper.

She slips out the door and closes it behind her before I can even ask what she thinks she's thanking me for. The cabin falls silent. Just me, the sunlight, and my thoughts.

I'm a father.

2 6

AFTERMATH

Xander

"Secluded in prayer?" I ask Vedran as he dances magic over my skin. "I'm going to develop a reputation for religiosity if we're not careful."

"Can you think of another reason why the prince would disappear at such a time?"

His magic bites slightly deeper with unspoken judgment. I swallow my wince. He has every right to judge. I abandoned him here in an impossible situation and then demanded he sneak to this far-off corner of the castle to fix my mistakes.

Still, as he covers one of the many red marks Finn left on my skin, I can only bring myself to regret how little I told Vedran. And, perhaps, that I did not ask for a wake-up call. It was impossibly dangerous, and how much Finn wants this baby will make the coming weeks that much harder.

And I cannot give up the way Finn looked at me when he said, *our baby*.

"I'm sorry. I'll communicate better the next time this happens."

He raises a pale eyebrow. "Next time?"

I can only nod. Last night feels like a fading dream, something too fragile to hold on to. Explaining it now threatens to break it.

With a sigh, Vedran offers me a clean tunic.

* * *

"MAY THE GODDESS HERSELF TAKE THEM BY THE HAND," FATHER'S favorite holy woman, Nomi, prays over a line of reed canoes loaded with the bodies of the fallen.

I stand at Father's side, trying for perhaps the thousandth time to count just how many there are. More than I expected, even with Finn's warning. My chest aches like a bruise. My selfish absence from command resulted in the loss of so many lives. Father is a brilliant fighter, but he occasionally fails to see the entire field and leads our people into foreseeable dangers. If I had been at his side yesterday, how many lives could I have saved?

Twenty-five canoes, and I lose count again as Nomi raises her arms for us all to chorus the final send-off.

"May they find their place among the stars."

One by one, the friends and loved ones of each person in each canoe push them into the roiling waters of the river that feed the nearby sea. Splashes harmonize with tears. Twenty-five canoes, at least, and I count perhaps ten mating marks among them. Lifelong bonds severed by senseless violence.

When every canoe has hit the surface, Father and I raise our hands in unison. I've presided over funerals before, but none with this many subjects. Nomi sings a hymn of peace as we move like two branches of the same tree. Hand, wrist, turn. The water of the river parts like a hungry mouth and swallows the line of canoes in a single gulp. The ocean will carry them beneath the surface, and they will settle into their final resting places amidst the element that gave them power.

May they find their places amongst the stars.

Nomi's song ends, and Father steps forward.

"This evening, Prince Xander and I will be available to speak with those grieving the brave warriors we lost yesterday," he says. "For now, however, we are needed in the infirmary."

He pivots on his heel and marches away, expecting me to catch up. I scurry after him.

"The infirmary?" I ask as soon as we're out of earshot.

"Had you been in your bed this morning, you would have known the schedule." He clips the ends of his words sharply; not disbelief of Vedran's excuse, exactly, but irritation that an excuse was needed. "If you are not careful—"

"I'll develop a reputation for religiosity." I sigh. "Yes, I know."

We step through the gates, and Father scowls. "If you are not careful, the other side will catch you unaware. Imagine the demands they could make if they had our prince."

I glance at him. Under the scowl, sleep still crusts the corners of his eyes, and his taut, straight posture looks even more strained than usual, like a marionette on over-tightened strings. All those canoes… Father is just as aware as I am that they are not simply numbers lost in a war but lives destroyed by his hand. That must be weighing on him–and him alone.

Finn's smile ghosts through my mind, and I push it away. Right now, this is where I belong. Nowhere else.

Father leads me to the infirmary, a converted minor banquet hall near Miralyn's office. Bodies of all sorts pack one against the next on long tables. The reek of blended herbs and blood hangs heavy in the air, buoyed on a chorus of pained groans.

My stomach churns, and I barely manage not to be sick simply because I haven't yet eaten. I belong here now. I belonged at Father's side—or on the battlefield—yesterday. My people cannot suffer like this while I remain above the fray.

I look at Father. This, I've never done before.

He nods to the closest man. "They need to know we haven't forgotten them."

Chin high, I march up to a writhing man. Stained bandages cover the stump where the end of his left arm should be. His face twists in pain. "Hello," I say.

He doesn't respond.

"You have served the crown honorably," Father says. "You'll never have to worry about your fa—"

The man punches through Father's words with something verging on a shriek. One of the maids Miralyn has obviously pressed into service hurries over, offering us an apologetic smile, and spoons something into the man's mouth.

She curtsies as the man starts to settle. "Would you like me at your side?"

"Keep to the regimen Miralyn assigned you," I answer before Father can. This man clearly needed attention, but I will not pull any aid from anyone else who does.

Father presses his lips into a thin line as we step to the next man. Carnage piles up like kindling, just waiting for a spark to light the pyre ablaze. Even those cogent enough to speak are gravely injured. I think of Finn's bleeding leg—surely, there must be more injured like him, but perhaps those are in another room. Or no room at all, to make space for those who may soon occupy the next wave of reed canoes. Dun's Crossing wounded lay amongst our own, and I catch sight of King Kieran's Beta making similar rounds.

"The next steps are simple," Father says between visitations.

I stare out over the agony. "We ought to ask for the assistance of Sundrop Gem. They have healers, do they not?"

"No, your cousin was correct." He clenches his jaw; a forest fire of rage briefly replaces tiredness. "We'll take the fight to them. They are monsters, savages, and I will play no more waiting games while they devour what people we have left. Healers will come later."

My mouth falls slightly open. How can he look at this and think more of it is the way forward? We visit a few more men before I can work the words out of my mouth.

"They're all our people," I repeat through numb lips. "The border drawn between us is imaginary."

"Clearly, those on the other side do not believe so." He sweeps the room with his gaze. "*She* does not."

I sway, nausea and dizziness threatening to steal my feet from me.

All these wounded… some injuries are vicious, painful in a way guaranteed not to kill. The sort of injuries which don't occur unless some commander gave the word to make sure the attack hurt. And there is no higher commander in Moonlight Hollow than the queen.

Mother.

"Now, you understand." Father offers me a grim smile. "Today we grieve, clean up the aftermath. Tomorrow, I intend to call everyone to council and lock the doors until we have a plan of attack."

After that, every visit and word exchanged blurs. I don't know how many hours we spend in the infirmary. All I know is that, by the time I leave, my head throbs. Whether it's the smell or the implication of Father's words that makes it do so, I can't say.

I stumble to the kitchen, where Cook is kind enough to ply me with a simple bread and cheese lunch. Halfway through it, my stomach turns, and the cheese reeks like death. I barely manage to choke down the remainder of the bread and offer the good cheese to a maid I'm almost certain I saw in the infirmary. Judging by how ravenously she falls on it, she needed it, even if I'm wrong.

Tension muddies the air as I walk through the castle. Patrols are doubled; Dun's Crossing boots march beside our own because we no longer have the bodies for increased security. The slightly off rhythm is another reminder. I watch a young, usually pleasant, undersecretary shove a steward out of the way, and the resulting fight almost comes to blows before I separate them.

"Fire!" someone yells.

I sprint toward the sound. Magical powers are not nearly as common in Tansy Beach as in some other kingdoms, and I may be the only soul around with the ability to halt the destruction inside our very walls.

The cry brings me to the edge of an open walkway overlooking a courtyard. The crowd parts to let me to the front. I grab the edge, prepare to vault down and hope I land on my feet or in a particularly lush bush.

And I see what they're burning.

Impaled on a tall stake of wood is a portrait I haven't seen since

Father ordered it banished to a storeroom three months ago. Mother's royal portrait burns as a crowd watches. Some cheer. Some bellow insults. Others simply grin.

Water dribbles off my fingertips, somehow freezing cold. Or perhaps I'm too hot. The world narrows to Mother's laughing eyes, which blacken and curl away to nothingness. Dust in the wind.

My vision goes gray.

* * *

I blink my eyes open to see a stone ceiling, a hard surface beneath me. My mouth tastes like vomit, and the scent of char clogs my nostrils.

"Ah, you're awake." Miralyn bustles into view. Blood streaks her forehead, a rusty red that promises it belonged to someone else, and exhaustion slows her movements.

"What happened?" I struggle to sit up. She shouldn't be here with me in her chamber. There are so many others who need her more.

"You fainted." She holds a cup to my lips. "Drink."

Cool, clean water. It washes the taste from my mouth, but the smell remains.

The smell of Mother burning.

Miralyn sets the cup on the table next to me. "I have less time than usual, Your Highness, so I'll be brief. You are overworked, straining yourself too far. You need to tend to your body at times like these, not drag it around like a younger cousin."

A muscle in my stomach twinges as I finally manage to sit. "Find me a person in this castle who is relaxed, and I'll make you my personal undersecretary."

She crosses her arms, unamused. She never is. "You either need to be rid of this pregnancy—"

I shake my head, Finn's desperation burning bright in my mind. I will see him tonight, no matter how he acts, because I need to.

"Then you need to stay in bed. This much stress risks the baby's life."

"I—"

She scowls. Smeared in blood, she looks more dangerous than the few bottles of poison I know she has squirreled away in her somewhere.

"Understood." I flip her a salute, like Finn would.

Miralyn shoots me one last glare before leaving. I hop off the hard bed but catch myself when I wobble. The dizziness seems to linger this time.

I can manage that. But my kingdom couldn't make do without their prince for a single morning. I certainly can't disappear on them now.

Not without an excuse any of them would believe.

2 7

THE NOOSE TIGHTENS

Finn

Xander jostles me awake, his hazel eyes urgent. "You have to get up."

I blink and stretch. Although my leg has mostly healed, new muscles ache. I'm not used to this much sitting.

After what people have started calling the Battle of Tansy Tower, everything changes. Kieran demands I come with him to marathon council meetings and watch the other players in the room. I roll my eyes at him—I'm still not Anwen—but once I'm in the room, it's obvious he wants me there as another voice. We don't quite get votes, as foreigners, but every bastard around that big wooden table has turned into a war hawk. With their borders breached, they now favor bloodshed over peace talks. Kieran keeps arguing for caution, at least, and Xander ventures the occasional agreement, but other than that, I'm the only person on his side.

Most of the time. Even though Corwyn is the most aggressive, the most slash-and-burn of all of them, he has the worst habit of offering the occasional good idea. And everyone at that Goddess-damned

163

table knows it, even if they can't tell which are the good ones, so he holds more sway than anyone only a couple years older than me ought to. The meetings where I'm forced to agree with him are the worst.

"What's the rush?" I graze a thumb over her bare nipple just to watch it stiffen.

She swallows a soft noise of pleasure. "We have busy days ahead of us."

She's not wrong. When the council meetings end, Kieran sends me to the barracks. Most of the barely wounded are there, and healing decently, but that doesn't mean it's not a wasteland. Taner is still in charge of the uninjured troops and is throwing himself into training the two groups together so we can work better as a unit. That leaves Elian with the injured. On the first day after the battle, he looked tired. The second day, he looked wiped. By the third, and now fourth, he barely smiles anymore. It's like someone is sucking the life out of my Beta. I find myself making jokes to try to pull him out of his slump, a reversal I'm not fully comfortable with.

I don't stop toying with her, though. "Thought you picked this place because you were tired of running out."

"I was tired of both of us running out." She glances at the pale light slivering in between the drawn curtains. "You still have to, or this all threatens to fall apart."

I flop back. These last few days have been exhausting, but the nights have made putting up with the rest of the shit worth it. At dinner every night, a different servant or secretary passes me a slip of paper with a location to meet her at. Luckily, they're growing more comfortable as she gets more confident; the closet of the first night was not an experience I'm looking to repeat. We don't always have sex—just most of the time. Between that, she teaches me a game called *bolar*, which I'm terrible at. I take revenge by fleecing her at a card game I make up on the spot. Sometimes it seems like the hidden rooms she picks are the only place in the castle anyone is allowed to laugh.

Last night, though, the paper contained a tiny riddle, mostly inside jokes, that led me to her bedroom. A whole set of rooms, just for us— and a royal mattress to put through its paces.

"I'll go," I grumble before she can threaten to revoke my nightly visits again.

"Thank you." She exhales a sigh of relief and slides out of bed. The sliver of predawn light lines her curves in silver. I'm probably imagining the swell of her stomach.

But I don't want to be. If these past few days have proven one thing, it's how right my first instinct was. I've covered her dizzy spells during council meetings, ordered overly complicated food with a thousand options so I'm sure she'll have something to eat, even held her hair back while she was sick. The only thing I haven't done is attend her occasional visits to the healer, but that's because she says it would be too obvious if we went at once.

"I still don't know your name." I climb out of bed and wrap my arms around her waist.

She tenses. She always does when I bring this up. This time, I don't let go. Battle plans are just about finished. There are troops traveling to border skirmishes as distractions as we speak. Corwyn keeps suggesting we establish field commanders, send the most competent tacticians away to oversee in person, and she's too smart not to be at the top of that list. Tansy Beach is truly at war, and I don't know how much more time we're going to have.

"It feels wrong to call you Xander now," I admit into the cloud of her hair, the skin of her neck. "That's not who you are to me."

She doesn't turn, doesn't even relax, but she says, "I don't have another name. The woman you're looking for… she doesn't exist."

I spin her in my arms so I can see her face. "Yes, she does. I'm holding her right now. She's carrying our baby."

Xander shakes her head. "You're not listening. There is no name I'm hiding. I was brought into the light of the Moon Goddess as Alexander."

"Would you like one?"

She cuts her gaze up at me. "I don't know."

I've gotten used to her like this, all the glamors faded in the night.

I'm not sure exactly when they wear off, but I'm pretty sure I've caught the moment of change once or twice, when we're still awake because tiredness seems a hell of a lot less dangerous than tomorrow. Every time, it surprises me how similar she is, and how different.

"What about Alexandra?" I ask. "Xandra for short?"

"Xandra." She rolls the name on her tongue, tasting it. "That wo… I like that."

"For us." I kiss her on the top of the head. "But now, I really have to go before we're both late."

Her eyes go wide, and together we rush through throwing on clothes. I brought a spare tunic, so I didn't look like I slept here. But finding it takes forever through sleep-hazed eyes and the fact that she doesn't put on pants until well over halfway through. The name Xandra flies back and forth between us on currents of laughter.

Finally, though, I slip out through her private garden, lock the door behind me, and turn toward the guest quarters where Kieran and I are staying. This early, the staff is barely awake, and I memorized the patrol schedule. I just have to avoid—

I turn the corner and nearly slam face-first into Corwyn.

"Watch where you're walking," I spit as I stumble back a step.

"Apologies, Prince Finn. Almost no one uses this breezeway." He smiles tightly around the term I've learned they use for their open hallways, wind whisking in behind him. "It only leads to my quarters and, circuitously, to Prince Xander's."

His gaze darts down. I don't need to follow it to feel the bite of metal in my palm; the key to the garden door, still out.

"I like to walk when I'm thinking." I stuff both my hands in my pockets and lean against the wall. "Still learning the palace."

"And here I heard you were a late riser."

Normally, but once Xandra wakes up, I tend to follow shortly after. It's been strange. Elian is barely going to recognize me.

I look him up and down. "There's a war on. Haven't you heard?"

His chuckle curdles. "All is well, Your Highness. I know you have many reasons to be in this part of Tansy Tower these days."

"Like what?" Lightning strikes down my spine. I've blown it for her.

"Oh, you and Prince Xander have gotten so close." Another tight smile. "I would imagine you have many things to discuss. About the war, of course. That is, unless Prince Xander intends to have another spark of religious feeling when every battle starts."

My mark roars, and only the teeth of the key cutting into my hands keeps me from roaring with it. I can take anything this bastard throws at me. It can't touch half the shit Father said when he thought we weren't listening. But nobody, not even her smarmy war hawk cousin, talks about my mate that way.

I step forward, crowding Corwyn against the railing that opens out into empty air. I tower a few inches over him, and he's got a diplomat's frame. On the first floor, he'd only topple into some bushes, but I want him to feel the threat of the rail, feel just how much bigger I am.

"Explain to me why that's any of your Goddess-damned business," I growl.

He stares steadily up at me, olive gaze unflinching. "I care about my prince and my kingdom."

"You think so?" I lean closer. "I think you're pissed because you're not even in second place for the throne. You're not worth that. So you end up in a pile of candidates, fighting your way to a crown that's never going to be yours." Another few inches. I can smell his breath. "I think you're jealous."

Corwyn purses his lips. "In Tansy Beach, those are the sort of words that make two men fight."

"I'd love nothing more than to hand your ass to you." I smirk. "A formal duel, I assume? For your fragile constitution?"

He swallows, but I don't see any fear in his face. He's got balls. "I don't think that would satisfy either of us. We'll fight outside the walls, where no one else can intervene."

"My pleasure."

* * *

THAT NIGHT, CORWYN MAKES EYE CONTACT WITH ME, THEN SLIPS OUT of *kafi* early with an excuse about needing to finish something. I'm not stupid. I wait a few minutes and then follow him.

He's waiting for me. A dozen feet apart, we escape the castle, then the walls. He takes me to a cove blocked from anyone's view by a jagged rock then shifts.

His wolf, a coppery tan, is no larger than he is. I snort before throwing myself into my shift—all silver muscle and hungry jaws. We haven't set parameters, can't talk anymore, but we don't need to.

This is animal.

One of us lunges first. Impossible to say who. We crash into each other, the collision almost louder than the waves, and slam into wet sand. Human thought melts away. Claws rake and teeth snap, never more than an inch from vital flesh. Corwyn fights like he's desperate, which makes him strong and sloppy. Sand flies around us as we wrestle for position. Blows ache, but none of them sear with split skin. The only salt in the air comes from the ocean.

I offer him an opening—my vulnerable stomach. He dives for it, and that's all I need. Roll, twist, tackle, and he's on his back with his head in the surf. I press a paw to his throat. He sputters.

We didn't set a forfeit. I'm happy to pick my own. I rear back, slashing claws across his face. Blood spills into the water, and I howl in victory.

2 8

———

RED-HANDED

Xandra

I PICK AT BREAKFAST, TRYING TO QUELL THE RIOT IN MY STOMACH. Next to me, Father darts his gaze at my plate. If I don't manage to get something down, he'll ask if I'm well again. He might even insist on coming with me to visit Miralyn, and though I've been very clear with her that I'm not telling anyone about this until I'm forced to, I don't want to put her in the position to lie to her king. She's a terrible liar, anyway.

Everything has changed. I've lost so much. But I still know how to hide disgust behind my teeth. I force myself to take a bite of flatbread and wash it down with a sip of tea.

Father looks away, and I exhale slowly.

Across the small, round table at the southernmost point of the room, in the position of honor beneath banners of House Mlakar and of Dun's Crossing, Finn cuts his eyes at me. I shake my head surreptitiously. We sit in the middle of a crowded dining hall, surrounded by nobles and secretaries alike. Five days after the battle, soldiers have

169

been promptly banished from anywhere those with noble blood might see them accidentally.

He nods and starts a conversation with King Kieran about something from their home that I don't know about. I hide a small smile behind another tiny bite of bread. He's been doing an… impressive job acting like there's nothing between us since our night in my retreat. Just having him here, knowing he's aware and paying attention, has relieved a shocking amount of pressure. There is someone else watching my back; I don't always need to twist myself in knots to do so.

And that has been particularly helpful, now that my back is so often bent in sickness. Miralyn says the nausea should abate soon—would do so faster if I would simply stay in bed. I'm hopeful she's right about the first, at least.

"We must send another set of thought-beads to Lord Juraj," Father says.

I wrench my attention from my thoughts. "Why?"

"He's fallen ill again." He waves his fork dismissively. Once, in private, he confessed to me that he thought House Dolenec ought to have replaced Lord Juraj as their councilor years ago. His health has been failing for some time. "Miralyn sent word."

"Miralyn?" Usually, we hear from Lord Juraj's pretty young wife. She likes the attention of an ailing husband.

He nods. "She seemed—"

The door to the dining hall slams open. Half the room looks first to the windows. This close to the shore, we are subject to powerful gusts sweeping over the Windy Ocean. But the waves in the distance look nearly becalmed.

Every turned head whips around when Corwyn declares, "The prince of Dun's Crossing has attacked me."

Time seems to slow, and details drift toward me like kelp underwater. A bruise purples Corwyn's eye. A set of garish red slashes, spaced like claws, mars his face from eyebrow to opposite cheekbone. Garish, because it is fresh. As late as last night, perhaps, but no later.

"Do you have any proof?" King Kieran stands, towering over the rest of us.

Father stands to meet him. "He does not need proof. I've nearly raised Corwyn myself, since he lost his sainted mother on the day he was born. Have you any proof to the contrary?"

"You would push blame back onto a prince?" King Kieran's eyebrows raise in disbelief.

If Corwyn's lying, this is an outrageously risky lie. He is accusing the third in line to a foreign throne, brother of the man whose soldiers are the only things keeping us alive. He… he would not do that.

I look at Finn. He does not look back at me. Instead, he leans back in his chair and folds his hands behind his head.

"I gave him that bruise," Finn says. "But I didn't attack him. He challenged me to a duel. Is winning against the rules now?"

My stomach drops. Duels have been illegal in Tansy Beach for nearly a century now, based on the first declaration of King Pavao—my grandfather. Corwyn would have known that, but Finn wouldn't have.

Discussion ripples through the dining hall. Father's gaze flashing across the assembled crowd is calculating. Corwyn finally reaches us, his face red beneath the blood. He is furious like I've never seen him.

"We will discuss this," Father says tightly, "away from the ears of the public. Follow me."

I stand automatically, and Corwyn and I fall into line behind Father. Me first, him a step back, as always. Today doesn't seem like the kind of day where he would try to get on my nerves by stepping on the backs of my shoes, like he used to. When footsteps don't follow, I glance over my shoulder. King Kieran glares at Finn as mind-links obviously fly between them. Finally, with a sigh, Finn gets to his feet.

That's his act, of course. He would not actually attack my Beta and then refuse to even discuss the consequences.

Though I have no idea what he was thinking fighting Corwyn in the first place. Even if there was a duel, even if it wasn't illegal, he knew it was unsanctioned. He had to know what it would look like. Why would he let himself be goaded?

Why would he put me in this position?

Father leads us to a tiny sitting room, usually used by the lowest undersecretaries. Right now, though, it's the nearest privacy we can reach. Sharply, he points Corwyn to one chair and Finn to another.

Corwyn obeys. Finn does not.

"There is no dueling in Tansy Beach." Father crosses his arms.

Finn looks at me as if for confirmation. I don't give it to him. He has to stop looking at me.

"How was I supposed to know?" He shrugs. "He was the one who challenged me."

"I would never!" Corwyn winces with the intensity of his own reply. "I know the laws of the land I'm living in."

Finn rolls his eyes. "Duels aren't illegal back home, but they are archaic. Why would I bother?"

"Perhaps because you find us *archaic*." Father stares at Finn's legs like he can will the prince to sit down.

"That's uncalled for," King Kieran says. "Prince Finn has insulted no one, though he ought to have paid closer attention to his diplomatic briefing. It seems like this was just a little boyish fun."

"Boyish fun?" Father gestures to Corwyn's face. "Perhaps I shouldn't be surprised about what passes for fun in King Gavin's court, but in Tansy Tower, amusement rarely includes blood."

"I do not lead my father's court," King Kieran replies icily. "I lead my own, and you know as well as I do that both of those will be gone in less than seventy-two hours, with a little attention."

My head spins. The few bites of bread I managed to swallow riot in my stomach. Who is telling the truth? How do I keep this from escaping my control completely?

"What if both Finn and Corwyn tell us the entire story from the beginning?" I suggest. "That should make it easier to see where fault— if any needs to be assigned—lies."

Father's jaw clenches. He will not directly contradict me here. "*Lord* Corwyn?"

My cousin nods. "I ran into Finn in the hallway and mentioned how pleased I was that he was getting so comfortable in Tansy Tower. He took that as an insult about the more… pacifistic policies he and Alpha King Kieran have been advocating for and threatened me. I thought taking the fight outside of the castle was the safest thing I could do."

"Oh, come on." Finn shakes his head. "That doesn't even sound like it could be true."

Father scowls. "I believe—"

"Finn?" King Kieran says. "How would you say this happened?"

Finn's gaze flits over to me, and my sunken stomach plunges deep into the ground. I know exactly what set him off—Corwyn said something about me.

"We ran into each other," Finn says slowly.

When? Where? I look at Corwyn, who meets my gaze steadily. Is that a smirk, a hint of laughter? How much does he know?

Is this Finn's fault or mine?

"But he didn't say he was pleased I was getting comfortable." He finally drops into the chair Father indicated. "He insulted someone I really care about. Uh, Princess Ingrid."

Kieran's eyebrows soar along with the tension knotting his body. It's a good lie, one his brother is likely to believe.

But it makes Father turn red. "Now, who is spewing obvious lies? I do not even believe Lord Corwyn met Princess Ingrid. What purpose would he have in insulting her?"

"Thank you, Uncle." Corwyn smiles. "I think we can see the actual truth here."

"I certainly can," Kieran says. "Every other word out of your mouth seems to be a sideways comment about me or my family. Don't think I've forgotten what you said about my wife."

"That she is a powerful fighter we would benefit from the assistance of?" Corwyn looks like the picture of bloodstained innocence.

"Did you have a witness?" I ask desperately. "To the duel?"

"I didn't want anyone to see what I'd been forced into," Corwyn says. "I thought I could win and end this. It was foolish, and I'm sorry."

"You see?" Father says. "How can you disbelieve him when your prince lounges and sneers at the very idea of accountability?"

"If he has nothing to be accountable for," King Kieran starts.

"It strikes me," Father turns his back on the foreign king, a grave insult, "that having both the prince and the king within our walls is quite a lot of oversight for a single battalion of men, is it not?"

I watch King Kieran draw in a long breath through his nose and regain some shred of his composure. "We are all needed in a council meeting shortly. King Alden, can I host you in my quarters for *kafi* afterward? I've been learning the art, and I believe discussing this with something warm in our hands rather than with breakfast cooling on the table behind us might yield better results."

"We need his men," I remind Father. *"Especially after this last battle."*

"They insulted your cousin and broke your grandfather's law—"

"And how many men has Lightning Cape promised thus far?"

His shoulders heave with a sigh, and I know I have him. Alpha Iraj has been dragging his feet on troops, clearly waiting to see which way the tide is turning. Dun's Crossing is all we have.

"After the meeting," Father says. "I shall bring my second-best set."

"You honor me." King Kieran bows and leaves the room first.

Father nearly drags Corwyn away a moment later. No matter what else happened here, Corwyn humiliated us by creating a scene in the middle of breakfast, and Father will not let that slide.

This leaves Finn and I alone. I step to the door and ease it shut.

"I thought he'd take it like a man," Finn grumbles. "I should've known, based on how he—"

"What were you thinking?" I hiss.

He blinks. "I… he insulted you."

"And I'm, what? A damsel in distress?" I prowl closer, anger building now. "Corwyn is my cousin, and he is a loudmouth. He has insulted me before. I'd wager he'll do it again. You can't bloody his face for it."

Finn stiffens. "It's different now."

"What is?" I cross my arms. I want to hear him say it.

"Us." He gestures at my neck, where his mark hides.

"Us or me?" I press my chest against his. "If you still thought I was Xander, would you have fought my fucking cousin, or just told me about it?"

Finn opens his mouth, then closes it.

"That's what I thought."

TIME TO GO

Finn

Fuck the council meeting. Xandra doesn't need me to cover her near-constant nausea-induced lapses in thought. That's what I'd do for a damsel, not my Goddess-damned mate—

Or my Goddess-damned friend. Whatever. If Elian were sick and hiding it from people, I'd do the exact same thing for him.

Clearly, Kieran doesn't need me either. He didn't get angry until I mentioned Ingrid. If I had thought of it, I would've said Corwyn insulted Raven instead. Maybe then he would've stood up for me as more than just an international incident waiting to happen. I didn't miss that every defense was about me as a prince, as a member of Dun's Crossing. Even King Alden defended Corwyn based on his character. Not me. I'd just do this because I care so little.

Sometimes, I miss Candace. It took her ages, but she finally saw through me. She might've been the only Solberg who ever did.

When I first started avoiding council meetings after we arrived, I thought Kieran might look for me. A few ambling conversations with old enough members of staff, and I knew exactly what parts of Tansy Tower nobody used anymore.

I shoulder open the door that I wedge back shut every time I leave and duck into the Old South Tower.

A cloud of dust puffs up at me. I cough and wave it away. There's no glass in the windows here, just storm-barred shutters, so the dust isn't going to leave. According to the ancient maid I spoke to, this place was barred up after a long period of war gave way to an era of peace. The Alpha at the time, a Hajni one, though you'd never believe that by the way Corwyn acts, declared they didn't need this stack of war rooms anymore. Barring it was symbolic—the kingdom was back at war within the century—but breaking the old king's word is bad luck.

I'd like to see a little bad luck screw me over worse than I already am.

Faded maps droop off the walls. Chipped versions of the precise little tokens everyone is pushing around on a much neater map scatter the shelves below them. I pick one up and twirl it between my fingers. A week in the library, and I'm still not sure what war they were fighting. The enemy tokens are red, but that could be a royal color or just something aggressive.

I pull a handful of scrolls from the shelf and then free the map from its pins. Tansy Beach has some secret way of processing parchment that makes it transparent, one they may have lost, judging by how little I've seen it outside of this tower. These scrolls sit over the map and detail troop movements in sweeping arrows labeled in different types of cramped handwriting.

Eight, to be precise. I can picture an ancient council sitting at this table, yelling at each other just like the current council is right now and has been for days.

These things never fucking change.

Still, I keep pulling out scrolls. Laying them over the map. Seeing how tactics have changed, what they knew to use and what they didn't. Some of my anger starts to burn off.

When I open the last scroll on the shelf, something a lot less translucent floats out. I grab the scrap of paper—it looks like a note that somebody scribbled out.

Anwen's voice whispers through my mind. *"You can recover destroyed writing by…."*

I grab one of the maps and position the mostly blank corner over the paper. With a hunk of coal from a long-dead fireplace, I rub back and forth over the parchment until the shadow of words starts appearing.

Only some of them. *"Reached M… soon, but… Astralis."*

And that is why I do not normally take Anwen's advice. The word *Astralis* doesn't even mean anything to me, and it's not like anyone else has been in this tower. I found part of a centuries-old conspiracy in which all the conspiracists are dead.

All my frustration rushes back, and I shove the ancient cartography away. Maybe Elian wants to blow off his responsibilities too.

* * *

I stumble back up from the cellar, my thoughts swimming with sourplum brandy. Apparently, taking care of all the slightly less wounded has its benefits—one of the soldiers usually guards the brandy cellar, and he was more than happy to give Elian a way in as thanks for all he did.

At least Elian laughed when I told him about the look on Corwyn's face. Somebody as cocky as him should be able to back it up in a fight.

I'm humming Howell's favorite drinking song—Elian's brutally homesick—when I round the corner onto the hall where my quarters are and see Kieran standing outside my door.

"I was looking for you." He takes me in slowly. "A much better use of your time than backing me up, as I asked you to."

"Yeah, it was." I amble past him, trying to keep all my limbs in order long enough to unlock my door. Xandra hasn't asked to meet in my room yet, and I don't know if she ever will, but I'm getting people used to the idea of the door being locked just in case.

Kieran follows me into the room, even though I'm pretty sure I didn't invite him in.

"Make yourself at home." I fling an arm out grandly and then drop onto the nicest couch, taking up all of it. Let him have the over-embroidered armchair.

He stays standing. "I spoke with King Alden."

Oh, shit. Has it really been that long? We missed lunch.

"We've come to an agreement. Taner and Elian will stay here to manage the men. You and I leave for Dun's Crossing tomorrow, and we'll be taking his Beta, Stjepan, with us to ensure a constant line of communication for both parties."

"I'm not leaving," I mumble into the arm of the couch. Xandra's not getting rid of me that easily; not with our baby growing inside her. I'll burn this whole damn kingdom down to be a part of his or her life.

I can't decide whether I want a boy or a girl more. A boy would have an easier time of it here, but a little girl I could spoil and raise as tough as her mother would be—

"Finn?" Kieran snaps his fingers in front of my face. I struggle to focus my blurry gaze on the movement. "Are you drunk, or are you serious?"

I sit up, my head swimming. "Drunk and serious."

Kieran closes his eyes for a long moment. Then, he turns and strides away. Before I can marshal my thoughts enough to wonder where he's going, he throws a glass of freezing water in my face.

"What the fuck?" I leap up, drunkenness dripping away on slivers of ice. The good couch is soaked, and so am I. On instinct, I start to take off my shirt.

And pause abruptly, grateful for the noxious sobriety Kieran is forcing on me. I can't reveal my mark.

"Serious or drunk?" he asks again.

I lower my tunic back into place. "Serious."

Surprise splashes over his face, undeniable. "You're actually refusing to do something."

I sit in the over-embroidered chair. It's better than standing—my head might be clear, but my legs are very inebriated. This is my last chance to back out, to leave like I normally would. Like I still want to, especially without the taste of plum so heavy on my tongue. Clearly, Xandra doesn't want me around. I'm not going to stay where I'm not wanted.

But the baby, our baby, wants me. Innately, unquestioningly. Hell, I wanted my father around more often than I wanted him gone, and I'm going to blow him out of the water.

"I seem to be."

Kieran looks at me for a long moment. He takes in the soaked tunic I didn't shed, the resolute, if drunken, set of my shoulders. And, fuck, I know what he's thinking before he even says it.

"Corwyn didn't say anything about Ingrid, did he?"

Kieran's leaving tomorrow. Nothing I say can change that, especially if he made a deal with King Alden.

I shake my head.

He sits on the sodden couch and scrubs his hands over his face. The first person, other than Xandra herself, who knows who my mate is, and he looks like I just told him the palace burned down. Perhaps it's not the strongest sign for my relationship.

"And Corwyn is dangerous," I say. "He's got King Alden almost entirely in his pocket, and Taner and Elian don't have the political capital to fight him."

"He's at every meeting," Kieran says.

"Then I'll be at every meeting." I resent the words stumbling off my tongue and wish I could blame them on the brandy. Every meeting means hours and hours out of every day doing my best not to strangle Corwyn.

For my baby, I'll do it, but Goddess above....

"Mates are harder than they have any right to be," he says softly. "Especially for people in our positions. You cannot just have a relationship—you need to balance kingdoms and armies with what your heart is telling you."

"Do I?" I offer him a thin smile. "I'm third in line to some much younger competitors."

"Altair's age cuts both ways." He looks at me. "If something happens to Raven and me, you become regent until Altair comes of age. Over Dun's Crossing and, someday, Escuro."

The realization hits me like a club—or perhaps that's still the brandy, making everything feel bigger. I knew that, on some level, but not in so many words.

"It's not fair that so much rides on what should be so personal, but that's the price of power." Kieran brushes his hands off on his pants. "The Goddess gave us mates to test us and to make us our best selves. Maybe that's your challenge—listening to what you want and what you know."

"You sound like a holy woman." I smirk.

"You sound like a drunk asshole." He stands, a new expression in his eyes. "Forget the philosophy—he has something you're lacking. Find that, hold on to it for all you're worth, and we all might come out of this okay."

I nod slowly. Xandra has about a million things that I don't, but despite the insistence of one brandy-soaked voice in the back of my head, I don't think Kieran means *auburn hair*.

"I'm leaving tomorrow," he says. "If you stay, that draws a line in the sand."

"Does it break an agreement?"

"Not exactly. You won't be a delegate of Dun's Crossing. You'll just be a visiting prince."

I can smell a loophole—one he only would've left if a part of him thought I might refuse. If he noticed something about me—specifically.

"I won't be able to be seen supporting you." He sticks out his hand. "In order to keep our alliance with Tansy Beach healthy."

I shake it from where I sit sprawled, and it actually feels like signing a deal. Like he's saying, for the first time, I trust you to figure out what to do next. Not anyone else, but you. He can't be seen supporting me, but by not forcing me to leave, he's saying all he needs to.

"Have a safe trip," I say.

"Have a safe war," he replies.

3 0

HALF MEASURES

Xandra

I LEAN AGAINST THE WALL OF THE BARRACKS AS HEALED TROOPS PARADE before me in Dun's Crossing's pale blue and Tansy Beach's rich indigo. If Father were here, he'd lecture me about my posture, about failing to stand at attention for these brave men who've risked so much for our kingdom. But if I try to stand upright, the gray at the edges of my vision stands a real chance of taking over entirely, and I've managed not to faint in public since I saw them burning Mother's portrait.

Things have only intensified since King Kieran's departure nearly a week ago. Father has somewhat officially banned Finn from the council meetings. Beta Taner sits in on most of them as the representative for Dun's Crossing, and he cannot technically refuse a prince where a Beta is allowed, but the message has been conveyed: Finn can enter the room—if he wishes to face the consequences.

No one is quite clear on what those consequences will be. Yet, Father's glower does not encourage me to find out.

The soldiers snap a crisp salute, about face, and march away. Elian

185

bounces up to me. Finn and I haven't spoken about our fight—him staying was all I needed to know about his commitment, but he hasn't apologized, and I don't intend to ask him to. But ignoring it has proven far more pleasant than ignoring him, so I've gotten to know his sunny Beta well enough to pass the occasional message. Nothing that gives us away; just friendly invitations. Elian even tags along with us sometimes.

"Well?" he says.

"Taner was right," I manage without losing my lunch. "They are in far better shape."

Elian punches the air hard enough to spin around. "They've been working like hell. So you'll vouch for them in the next meeting?"

"Happily." It's always easy to agree to anything that makes someone who looks so tired smile so brightly, especially with all the sourness around the castle these days.

"He said you were the best." He claps me on the shoulder.

He may as well have shoved me. My entire world cants to the side. Wood scrapes along my back, and I am falling.

"Whoa!" Elian barely catches me.

Nausea claws at my throat. My head spins, throbs. "I need—"

"A healer."

"My room."

Elian slings his arm around my shoulders reluctantly. "He said you were damn stubborn, too."

* * *

Vedran presses a cold compress to my forehead. "Your next council meeting starts in a quarter hour."

"I need my notes." I start to stand, and the room swirls around me. My knees give. I sit back down on the bed heavily.

"You need rest." Vedran pushes the compress harder against my skin, forcing me to lay back. "Miralyn said—"

"I know what Miralyn said. Do you know what Father said? Corwyn? Lord Juraj?"

"I do, Your Highness." His thin lips become paler as he presses them tight. "As I know you will be no heir if you die before you can claim the throne."

A memory floats through my mind on the same lazy whirl as the walls. Mother, the one time someone asked her why she had never tried for another child. She turned white and stiff as a statue before saying it "was not worth the risk when she had one child to live for." I imagine myself lifeless on Miralyn's table and Finn alone with a squalling baby.

And I lay down. Buoyed by my pillows and blankets, I can float more easily through the sea of nausea and dizziness. The compress actually threatens to soothe.

A smile flickers over Vedran's mouth. "I'll send word that you are busy."

"Thank you," I mumble.

"Shall I send for anything else?" he asks.

I shake my head. Water is only a flick of the wrist away, I can't imagine eating, and Miralyn is still tending to the worst of the soldiers.

"Anyone?" Vedran says, the picture of innocence.

Finn. He means Finn. Everything in me lunges toward the suggestion—I need him next to me, holding my hand, another anchor in the storm.

"No." Last time he was in my quarters, he fought Corwyn. Nothing good can come of this.

Vedran nods, starts to leave, then stops. "I know it's not my place—"

"Nothing is in their places these days." And he is the only other person in this castle I wholly trust.

"Your father half-conceded to your mother's requests, to yours, and look at where that has landed us," he says. "Half measures, especially ones where you accept only the worst of things, are what brought Tansy Beach to this point. Accept some of the good before it is too late."

I stare at my attendant. I've confided in him for years, and he accepts it with little nods, frowns, and furrowed brows. The most advice he's offered me is on clothes to disguise my secret. He was well-trained, unfortunately.

"Send for Prince Finn." If it's worth Vedran abandoning propriety, it's worth doing.

The knock comes shortly after I'm undressed and tucked below layers of covers. Finn steps through without waiting for an invitation, and I catch a brief nod from Vedran in the open door, who doesn't come back inside my bedroom.

"Are you okay?" Finn hurries to my side and dips the cloth back into the bowl of water to dab my head.

"Just dizzy." I try to bat his hand away and miss horribly.

"Uh-huh." He swipes cool water across my forehead, and I try not to show how pleasant it is. "That's what I thought."

Our fight looms between us. If Xander were ill, Finn wouldn't be doing this. But it's difficult to deny how much a part of me wants him to. Why can't I have both?

"The *bolar* set is in my nightstand," I say. "I bet I can still whip your ass."

He doesn't move, just strokes damp hair off my forehead. "Stakes?"

"You can tell Cook what to make for dessert tonight." He's been complaining about how sticky our cakes are for ages now. "And…I'll let you prod at me with wet rags."

There it is—his rare and laughing smile. "If you keep offering prizes like that, I'll figure out how to cheat at this game."

A tired grin is all I can give him, but he takes it all the same. The yellow and red *bolar* set comes out, and I fix my pillows so I can sit up before he can, earning myself an eye roll for my trouble. The room sways slightly. I grab his hand.

The walls won't stay put, but he does. And with him, I can, too. I'm in the eye of the storm, just for a moment. With his other hand, he sets out pieces in the starting formation I taught him—my favorite, the Tinker's Star. Most new players start with the Honest Man, but Finn can earn his wins if he wants them.

"East-seven takes east-eight," I declare.

"Don't I go first?" he replies.

"This is war." I smile. "The last winner always acts first."

* * *

"North-fourteen takes…uh…." Finn scans the board, looking for a way out of my trap.

I smirk. "Noth—"

The door to my bedroom slams open, revealing Father and Corwyn. I scramble for my blankets. Vedran's magic should remain, but my breasts are unbound in a loose top.

"You see?" Corwyn says.

"Prince Finn." Father steps into my room, murder in his eyes.

"Are friends not allowed to play games together?" I demand, ice and fire warring in my veins. What does Corwyn hope to prove?

Why does he look so sure?

"Not during *vital* council meetings," Father replies. "Not when Moonlight Hollow spies line our very halls."

Corwyn's idea, presented without a speck of hesitation. Ice begins to win out.

Finn stands between us. "He's doing his diplomatic duty."

"Diplomacy?" Corwyn yanks his hand across his chest, a gesture so rushed I don't recognize it until a tendril of water reaches out of the bowl at my side and rips back my covers, revealing the scant swell of my stomach. "Is that what you call impregnating our not-quite-prince?"

My world narrows to Father's face. He drags his gaze down. His brows furrow and then flatten. His mouth twitches toward a grimace. Red crawls up his neck in bloody rivers. His gaze stumbles back up to my face, and it's as if he doesn't recognize me.

Finn backhands the tendril of water away, splashing us both, and pulls my blankets back. "Better than your fang-and-claw diplomacy, I'd say."

"Do not speak to my nephew," Father thunders. "Or my son—ever again."

I flinch. Corwyn sneers. Finn clenches his fists.

If he fights them, he loses. Because he is not just fighting them, he's fighting two decades of lies, five centuries of tradition. There is no moving this stone.

Not from the outside.

Grabbing a robe, I struggle to my feet, clinging to Finn's arm for support. There's no use in hiding now. "And how do you intend to stop me from speaking to him?"

"You—" Father glares at a point over my shoulder, as if he cannot look at me. "You will listen. I will make you listen."

It's all hot air. If he had a threat, he would make it.

"I sincerely doubt that." I sway as I stare at him. "Prince Finn is not only the father of my child, he is my mate, and we *will* have our baby."

I've never said the words before. They sing off my tongue, the only thing I could say now. Enough denial. Enough hiding. Let Father face the truth he's been denying since my birth.

He crosses the room in two steps and backhands me. Pain cracks, hot and sharp, down my spine. I crash into Finn, who barely keeps his feet. It's all that prevents him from attacking my father for striking me.

"I will die before you end the Mlakar line like this."

Ice melts. Rage burns. Fear kept me behind doors he first locked, telling lies he first scripted. "If that has to be the way—"

Behind him, Corwyn shifts and sinks his teeth into Finn's free arm. Corwyn drags him away from me as he shouts in pain. Several guards pour into the room to help subdue Finn, to keep him away from me. My mark shrieks. I collapse onto the mattress. Father towers over me.

"*Miralyn,*" he says through the mind-link he makes certain I can hear. "*Prepare whatever you need to end a pregnancy.*"

"*Yes, Your Majesty.*"

Miralyn betrayed me.

"*However,*" she says.

Hesitation? She never hesitates.

"That will take some time. Perhaps as many as five hours, depending on the ingredients."

"Whatever you need, it's yours," he replies.

Miralyn promised me she could have the potion ready in an hour or less.

She is lying to him.

I look at Corwyn, snarling around Finn's arm. He is willing to destroy me—what else is he willing to do?

And to what end?

"Take him to the dungeon," Father spits. "This will all be over soon."

Corwyn and the guards drag Finn out of my bedroom. Father follows close on his heels. He has nothing more to say to me, not even a look to spare. In the hallway past my sitting room, I hear him call over a pair of guards and tell them to stay at my door.

The door to the hallway swings shut.

I'm trapped with five hours until he tries to slaughter my baby. And I am alone, barely able to stand.

Vedran steps into the doorway connecting my bedroom to my sitting room, holding his book of spells. "No half-measures."

3 1

LAST RESORT

Finn

CORWYN SPITS ME OUT AT THE FEET OF THE TEAM OF GUARDS, ALL IN Tansy Beach indigo, who helped him subdue me. My arm burns, but it's nowhere near as bad as my mark, which feels like it's sinking white-hot claws into my heart. I have to go back. Xandra needs me.

A shift tingles in the back of my mind. I know I can beat Corwyn —or at least, I think I can. I glance over my shoulder at the mostly healed gash across his face. He could've let me do that so he could make that Goddess-damned scene. To get rid of Kieran.

After what he just did to Xandra, I can't put anything past him.

So I sit on the ground, oozing blood, until he's done mind-linking orders to these soldiers and pads away. I don't know what he's done, but I know I stand a better chance at just about anything with him far away.

One of the soldiers hauls me to my feet by the injured arm.

"Can you use the other one?" I snap.

He rolls his eyes. Another closes thick, iron manacles around my wrists.

The one holding my injured arm drags me down the hallway, even farther from Xandra. I glance over my shoulder like I can still see her. That bastard Alden ordered guards to watch her room; he's worried she's going to try to escape, and he's right to. When she stood up, faced her father, I didn't see how pale she's gotten or how shaky she was. All I could see was my mate, brave and fucking beautiful, defending our baby. I would've kissed her right there if Corwyn hadn't gotten me.

I'm surprised that touching her after that didn't burn Alden. She looked like a fire spirit, despite the water in her blood. Light caught every strand of red in her hair, and her eyes burned.

Of course, she doesn't need me to protect her. But she deserves not to have to protect herself all the time. I need to get back to her.

I study all four of the guards' faces. If Elian helped any of them, I've got an in. For some reason, he's not responding to my attempt at mind-linking right now.

Shit, I really should've looked at the soldiers he was treating more closely. I sort of recognize all of them.

"Elian is my Beta," I say.

One of them snorts. Not encouraging.

"I told him to—"

"Shut up." The one holding my arm digs his thumb into the gash. My eyes water when he lets a nail sharpen into a claw, shredding vulnerable flesh.

"Much better." The one with a stripe on his shoulder that marks him as a lieutenant, a higher rank than the rest of these bastards, unlocks a door.

As expected, I stare at the mouth of a staircase headed down. What I didn't expect was the rumbling sound that issues up.

"Like it?" The lieutenant sneers at me. "The dungeon is under the river. You'll never believe what kind of stuff they can do down there."

"Show me something my father didn't show me first." I smirk as best I can.

A soldier behind me kicks the back of my knee, and I crumple, allowing the rest of them to haul me bodily down the stairs. I go limp. If I can't stop them yet, I can at least make it as hard as possible.

The one with his nail in my arms curses, but they don't stop.

Not until they reach a surprisingly large cell with a flow of water pouring down the back wall. There's a ledge to step over, and once inside, I realize why. The whole cell is covered with an inch of standing water.

And there's no bed.

"Enjoy, lord-killer," the lieutenant says.

"What the fuck does that mean?"

"We were Lord Juraj's personal guard," another sneers. "You can't lie to us."

I surge forward, water sloshing. "I don't—"

The door slams in my face.

I slam my fist into it in reply. They can't fucking do this to me. Kieran might not be here, but he knows where the fuck I am. Tansy Beach still needs our men—

My heart skips a beat.

"Elian!" I yell through the mind-link, desperately trying again..

"Yeah?" he finally replies.

Casual. Alive. Probably not arrested.

"Wherever you are, get out. Start running. I don't care what direction."

"What the hell?" he demands.

"I'll explain." I exhale sharply. *"Later. For now, every second you spend talking to me is one you've wasted. I'll be behind you as soon as I can."*

"Shit. All right."

The link goes quiet, and I wish like hell I could sit down. The water bubbles mockingly.

"I didn't forget," I snap.

It certainly didn't take me long in solitary confinement to lose my mind. I run my hands through my hair and try to think about anything other than my arm, my mark, and Xandra.

Maybe next, I'll try to learn how to fly.

No, Xandra needs me. If I can break out, I can reach her.

The guards said something about Lord Juraj. They said they were his men, but I've been to enough of those ridiculous council meetings to know that any soldiers leant by a specific lord still owe their loyalty to him first.

Juraj is dead.

And they think I killed him.

I grind my teeth so hard my jaw aches. Corwyn brought me to them on purpose—people he could be sure wouldn't listen to a word I said. I wouldn't be surprised if he killed Juraj himself, though I have no idea why. Last I heard, the old man was sick for the thousandth time.

None of this is helping me get out. I peer through the tiny, barred window of my otherwise fully solid cell. A bit of wall. No sign of any soldiers, much less the ones who brought me down.

Inside, I've got…just about nothing. A bucket for waste. The waterfall I can't do anything with. Several pebbles.

Once again, I wish we'd kept Sundrop Gem's powers when we crossed the Lonely Sea. A little ability to melt metal would come in more than handy here.

A key rasps in the lock, and I brace.

Xandra scuttles in, a hood drawn over her head and something red smeared on her cheek.

There are a thousand questions I could—probably should—ask, but I just slam into her, wrap my arms around her. She hugs me back, but only for a second.

"We have to move fast," she hisses, extending a hand toward the waterfall.

"How are you here?" I ask. "Are you hurt?"

Water wavers out of the flow and feeds into a few cracks in the stone. "Not enough to worry about right now."

"So yes." I swipe my thumb through the blood on her cheek, anger building, but there's no injury underneath.

"We can speak when we are out." Her voice strains with concentration. "Don't make me think now."

The edge of desperation in her voice makes my mark throb. She's here. She's free. Our baby is safe.

"What can I do?" I ask.

"Dig."

I sprout claws, step up to the wall, and start tearing at the stone she's weakening. Water splatters my face, and sandstone crumbles beneath my fingers.

"There are old tunnels," she says. "Condemned, completely unsafe —and unwatched. Our way out."

A small, terrified part of me goes silent when she says, *our way out.* Despite everything, I thought she might not leave with me. That she might be saving my life at the expense of hers–or the baby's.

I dig at the wall with renewed fervor. Behind the stone, I catch a whiff of thick, musty air.

"How sure are you these still have an exit?"

"Surer than I am that we can save ourselves any other way."

She is on fire again, like she was facing down her father. Like this, I'll follow her anywhere.

A block of stone crumbles away. Darkness yawns beyond.

"Two more," she says through gritted teeth.

"Three," I reply. "You'd hear any alarms raised, and you'll fit better through a bigger opening."

She scowls at me. "If I—"

"Well, that's not the situation we're in." I glance at her over my shoulder, already pale and swaying. "Three, or I'm not going."

She slices a look at me but doesn't waste the time fighting. I don't care if she hates me. I'm keeping both of them safe.

The third block turns to nothing but sand, and we start on the fourth.

Xandra tenses. "There's the alarm. It sounds like they found the bodies, not Vedran."

"Vedran?"

"Helped me." The jet of water intensifies, splattering me, pounding at the stone. "He's running."

"So's Elian." I haul back and smash my fist through the next block, scraping my knuckles to shit. It shatters, though. "Let's move."

I boost her through the hole, then wriggle in after her, stone shards scraping at my broad shoulders. She nudges the waterfall over the opening, a pitiful cover that destroys any comfort from standing on dry land again, then takes my hand.

Her eyes shine in the dark. "Run."

Behind us, footsteps clatter downstairs. We take off. The passage is ancient, slick with growing things that make every step a potential fall, and too narrow for either of us to shift. My arm burns. I have no idea how the woman I, not more than an hour ago, had to help move pieces on a game board is sprinting along beside me.

Maybe she's thinking the same thing I am right now—that there is no future, is no baby, if we die in Tansy Tower. Maybe that's enough to push past everything else.

We drag each other down the tunnel, our linked hands the only real thing in the seemingly endless darkness. There are no words, just our harsh breathing echoing off the exposed stone. My heart hammers. Sweat drenches every inch of me, pools between our palms.

Shouts start echoing behind us—the tunnel has been discovered. But we've got one hell of a head start, and judging by some scrabbling and whines, the soldiers tried for the additional speed of a wolf and got stuck.

"Here," she gasps suddenly. "The exit should be here."

I reach a hand out. Stone, wood. A door, bound and locked in metal so rusted it flakes off under my touch. There's no opening it.

"Can you do the water trick again?"

"I'm spent." She sounds it, her voice barely a whistle.

The shouts grow louder. My mate, my baby.

No one will touch them.

"Back up," I growl.

For once, Xandra doesn't fight me.

I need the power of my wolf to get through this in time. That leaves me one option. I take a few steps back, inhale slowly.

Then, I run.

One step. Two. The door looms. I kick off my third step, and before I hit the ground on my fourth, I shift. Stone bites into my fur, but I hit the ancient wood and metal with full lupine strength.

It explodes into splinters and the memory of iron. Pale moonlight floods the tunnel. Xandra vaults onto my back, clenching her fingers in my fur, and we take off into the night.

"Will your brother hide us?" she asks, barely audible over the whipping wind.

Kieran's last words echo in my mind. A line in the sand. Tansy Beach can't fight a war on two fronts—but I won't force Kieran into that position.

I shake my head. I don't know for sure, but it's not worth the risk.

Silence falls. I run through other options—we'd never make it to Escuro or Sundrop Gem, all the local packs have chosen sides and mostly Tansy Beach, neither of us has the survival skills to simply hide out.

She says what I'm thinking before I have to wonder whether it's worth shifting. "Then we have to go to my mother and pray."

I turn my nose east.

3 2

———

HOLLOW

Xandra

"Through the river!" I hiss, leaning low over Finn's back, though that makes the high grass whip across my face.

I don't know how long we've been running. The moon has long passed the apex of the sky and is sinking toward morning. Howls echo around us. Dunes hump along the horizon to the south, and trees offer a dark welcome ahead. There's no point in looking behind us; Finn's speed leaves no hope we're not cutting a trail that will be as easy to follow as a line on a map come morning. For the first time, I wish we were a more northerly kingdom, half-covered in forests where we could lose our pursuers easily.

"Head them off," Father shouts. *"They cannot escape."*

Of course, he knows where I am going. He taught me most of what I know, and the rest, I've taught him. But that doesn't make it any worse of a plan. Until dawn, they can only track us by smell. We need to disrupt that. The bulk of the force remains behind us, only those already outside the palace and not bottlenecked by the prison when the alarm was raised are ahead.

201

Finn leaps over a small boulder, and I jounce against his spine as he lands. My stomach revolts. Vedran's spell to strengthen me through the escape is waning, but I need it to last just a little longer. Once we're in the forest, we can rest.

We will have to rest. Even someone as strong as Finn can't run like this forever. I clutch the tiny bag of provisions I was able to scrounge from around my room and pray it is enough to support us.

All the way to Mother. Who might turn us away the moment we reach her.

"Davor, Vanja, flank left," Lieutenant Jakov orders. *"I'll pincer right."*

Is it a mercy or a mistake that they still allow me to hear them? I may never know.

"Go right," I tell Finn. "Defenses are weaker there."

He adjusts instantly. Jakov is an old veteran and one of Lord Juraj's favorite men. He won't hesitate to attack if he finds us, but he's neither the fastest nor the cleverest soldier in Tansy Beach. We can evade him.

The river sings to me as we approach it, so near it almost changes the rhythm of my heart. More howls pierce the night. Two left, one right. I loop one arm around Finn's neck and throw the other out toward the river.

Water splashes like sprinting footsteps between the two groups. The howls coagulate there. I wish I had the strength to reorient the current; though the Tansy River is only a tributary of the thundering Grayhead River Mother declared the border between the kingdoms, we have lost more than a few lives to its power. It's all I can do to quiet Finn's first plunge into the rapids.

He sputters, paddles wildly.

"There's nothing here," Jakov cries.

"Spread out," Father demands.

"I bet our lives you can't swim faster," I whisper in Finn's ear with a grim chuckle.

Any answer is lost in the noise of the river, but he seems to pick up speed. I spot the vague shape of another wolf in the water and crush myself closer to Finn.

He breaks free of the bank.

'They've crossed,' Jakov spits.

Let him. We burst into the tree line, and foliage so thick it blocks out the moon surrounds us. They have no chance, not without searching every inch.

"Find a tree with striated bark and purple-veined leaves," I tell Finn.

He actually spares a glance at me, dry and irritable. He can't see color as fine as veins like this.

"I'll look." I stroke the thick, soft fur of his neck in apology as he slows to a canter. I steal glimpses between tree branches I have to duck and patches of total darkness. Sourplum trees are famed for their strange trunks; we just need to find a wild one. I only know them from the palace orchard.

The scent of rotted fruit whisks by on the wind. They're out of season—any unpicked fruit would lie fallow on the ground. I urge Finn toward it until the distinctive tree comes into view.

And, as always, it has a yawning hollow in the base of its trunk. I dismount, stumble—Vedran's spell really is failing.

"Inside." I start grabbing loose branches off the ground to cover the entrance.

He shifts, and it takes what shaky willpower I have left to keep working rather than staring at him. There are two spare sets of clothes in my bag; I could easily offer him pants. But really, I should wait until we're safe. He doesn't enter the hollow in the tree, not yet.

"Elian is out," he says at one point. "I've told him we're going to Moonlight Hollow, but not to join us until we're sure it's safe. He could go home."

"Good." I want to say Father wouldn't take this out on him, but I can't. Not when my cheek still throbs.

"Vedran?" I ask as I position branches over the entrance.

"I have made it to the forest," he replies. *"They don't seem to be following me any longer. Should I continue on to Moonlight Hollow?"*

"Could Kieran hide one attendant?" I ask Finn. "If Moonlight Hollow...."

"He'd be pissed if I didn't let him try," Finn replies tiredly.

"No. Go to Dun's Crossing. King Kieran will grant you asylum, especially if you can find Elian along the way."

"May the stars light your way," Vedran replies.

"And yours." I shuffle the last branch into place—covered, except for one opening, which I gesture Finn at.

He grabs my hand—a silent question. He's still not sure I'm going to follow him. I gesture with the final branch—I'm just going to close us in.

Finn crawls into uncertain darkness at my request for the second time tonight. I take a deep breath—the reek of rotting sourplums may also help disguise us—and follow him.

Quiet settles softly around us. My heartbeat slows, and I can feel something other than windburn and fear. The trunk is smaller than I thought. To fit, I have to tuck right up against him, my body curled into all the hollows of his. Clothes are going to have to wait; I'm not sure I could even reach the bag in here. Finn's heat spills through my layers, softening knots of tension in my muscles like a warm bath. Spent, ears still pricked for whatever else might come after us, I reach back for his arm and draw it around my waist.

Finn clutches me tighter, just above the swell of my stomach I didn't even realize was visible until tonight.

My mind shies back from the events of this evening. Father's eyes, the crack of his hand on my cheek. The blood I spilled to reach Finn —it was necessary, but I've known those men for years. And I did it brutally, with a knife, like a monster. But a shift would've drawn more attention, left more evidence. We are ready to deal with wolves. But humans?

No honorable person would fight like that.

My eyes sting. Have they been open too long, or is that the specter of useless tears? I blink regardless. Tears are the luxury of those not currently being hunted.

Finn kisses the top of my head softly. I lean into him, but that only gives him purchase to graze his teeth along the shell of my ear. His hand on my chest spans half my ribcage, his thumb resting on the bottom of one of my unbound breasts.

I have bindings, in case it's safer for me to travel as a man. But tonight, I needed air more than my secrets.

And tucked away in here like this, my mark sings louder than the river that I need Finn more than I need air.

I have nothing left to give. Distantly, I knew power exhaustion was a possibility, but I've never felt it before. It's like I've run a marathon on an empty stomach. I quiver like one of the leaves overhead, and every twitch ripples soreness through my body.

But Finn is perfectly content to hold me, to drag slow kisses over what little of me he can reach, to breathe with me. My eyes sting again. Corwyn's face dances in my mind.

My Beta. My cousin. My betrayer.

I push him away. Outside of this earthy hollow, where Finn's scent folds back in on itself and becomes so intense I feel drunk on it, I can worry about hows, whys, and what nexts. Now, there is just this. Him. Us.

It all feels worth it–for now.

"Thank you," I mumble, my eyelids heavy.

"For what?" His reply rumbles against my neck.

"You didn't have to risk all of this for me." I lay a hand on my stomach, just below his. "For us."

His breathing continues, low and slow, but he doesn't speak. I wish I could see his face, read his thoughts through his eyes.

"I wouldn't have made it this far without you," I admit. "And I am…glad I did. Consequences be what they may."

"You know I can't back down from a challenge," he replies, his voice a shade off.

Or I believe it is. Sleep threatens to drag me below its numbing waves with every breath. What I know is that my mark stings, just a whisper of the agony I've lived with for weeks, but it's still there. He's not saying he regrets nothing. That he will stand by me always.

Before these thoughts can cloud out the warmth and comfort of his body, exhaustion claims me, and my world goes dark.

33

ACROSS THE RIVER

Finn

Xandra wakes me in the morning by crawling out of the hollow in the tree to be noisily sick outside. My stomach churns. Empty. And I have no idea what is or isn't safe to eat in this part of the world.

Worse, I don't know if she was awake enough to realize how badly I responded to her last night. There's no reason why. I would do anything for our baby. Keeping both of them safe is my highest priority. But curled up like that, her words sounded so nearly like a confession of love… my tongue just froze to the roof of my mouth.

I squeeze myself out of the trunk as she sits back on her heels, wiping her mouth. She looks at me. I look at her.

"There should only be another few hours of running before we reach the border," she says.

Probably clever. I can smell other wolves in these woods, and now that we don't have the protection of the tree, they'll be on us before long.

I stretch my aching arm. "Do you want to ride again?"

She peeks up at me through her lashes and then looks away. "No.

The symptoms are easier to manage after I shift. Last night, shifting alone would've been too much."

"Probably smart." A few scabs flake off Corwyn's bite, and new blood oozes. Running with her on my back wasn't exactly easy. "Then, we can get over the border without being recognized."

She looks toward the horizon. "Hopefully."

* * *

As soon as we leave the sourplum tree that sheltered us all night, the other wolves close in. Xandra and I trade the lead easily. She can hear them, but I know how to run and hide in the woods better than she does. We travel in short sprints between gaps in patrols, waiting in shadows and nooks when we can't move. The sun drifts across the sky as I grow used to the feeling of her warmth beside me, rising and falling with frantic breaths, pressed up against me.

Eventually, she nips my right leg. The signal that we're approaching the Grayhead River—the one that separates the two packs. I turn in a quick circle—understood. She charges forward. For the final stretch, not falling into Tansy Beach hands matters most.

Xandra dodges left, ducking low beneath a spray of leaves. They spatter dew across my face as I charge after her. The rumbling growl of a river reaches my ears. It's far larger than the one that almost swept me away last night, and this time, she doesn't have her powers.

We're going to have to swim.

But that comes second to following her through a tight slalom of trees. We pause behind another sourplum. Her panting is barely audible anymore. The river drowns everything else out.

Xandra explodes out of the cover, and some part of me knows this is the last stretch. My muscles strain as I push them harder. Strength and speed are always closer cousins than anyone thinks. In a few strides, I am running beside her.

We see the river emerge from the trees simultaneously.

It's maybe twenty or thirty feet across. Gray-white with rapids.

Stones poke from the surface here and there, sharp in a way that promises further dangers beneath the water.

Xandra dives into it headfirst, no hesitation.

Of course, she does.

Howls split the air as I line up my leap for maximum distance. If I'm caught, King Alden will kill me, but Xandra and our baby will be safe. Maybe I should stay and fight them, buy her a little more time.

She splutters, and I throw myself after her.

Ice. Like the worst snowstorm I've ever been out in, except there's no ground to find my feet on. I tumble head over heels, smashing into unseen obstacles.

Teeth clamp around my scruff and drag me. My head breaks the water.

Xandra's hazel gaze meets mine, concerned and furious. I nod to the far bank. She can yell at me later.

Her answering snort promises she intends to, but she starts swimming. The current fights like it's alive, but slowly, I realize she's using the lethal stones as supports, moving from one to the next. They break the unending force just enough that I don't go under again.

We reach the bank together. I struggle out, clawing up chunks of mud, and collapse. The pressure of the ground on my side is less intense than the current.

Xandra jerks her head up.

A trio of wolves steps out of the trees, led by a human woman in patchwork armor.

"Halt," she says.

I wasn't going anywhere. Xandra steps in front of me, and a spear of protective anger coaxes me to shaking feet.

"You've crossed into the sovereign kingdom of Moonlight Hollow," the woman says. "State your business."

Xandra's brow furrows, but after a moment, the woman's gaze goes hazy with a mind-link.

So, she can still reach them. It's just difficult. That complicates just how sovereign the two kingdoms are.

"Refugees, huh?" the woman says. "And why are you defecting from Tansy Beach?"

Xandra looks at me. I don't need words to know that she's asking whether to tell the truth. I stare back at her, trying to force the thought that we should only reveal ourselves to her mother as deep into her mind as I can.

She turns back to the woman. A few beats of silence pass.

The woman laughs derisively. "Luna Maris? You must—"

One of her wolves nudges her, looks at me. Not surprising. In a crowd of red-brown coats, my silver one is the only outlier.

The woman sighs. "All right. Follow us. But if you try anything—"

Xandra shakes her head, clearly indicating we won't. I hold up one paw to support the idea. The woman rolls her eyes and starts leading us through the woods.

Her trio of wolves surround Xandra and me. Well, two of them start to, and one has to nip the third to get them into position. That about matches the disagreement in front of potential hostiles and the woman's armor. What it doesn't match is the lethal machine I faced outside of Tansy Tower.

Are they only sending their strongest to fight? Is border security not a priority?

Or is it another smoke-and-mirrors game, like the tiny tricks that made everyone believe Xandra was a guy for so many years?

We arrive at what looks like a small camp before long. Clustered on the edge of the woods, simple houses circle a central area, and farmland stretches beyond. It's a waypoint, I suppose. Queen Maris wouldn't stay so close to the border simply for her safety. But the trees start to break up so I can see more of the land beyond.

It looks… pretty much the same as Tansy Beach. Mostly flatland, some hills, a coastline to the south. Fertile and welcoming. Nothing like a war zone.

Xandra's vehement defenses of the land itself make even more sense.

"Hana," a younger man says as he runs up to us.

"Lieutenant Hana," she corrects. "Please, Dario."

"Right." He shakes his head. "Is this them?"

She glances over her shoulder at us, as if making sure the other three haven't lost us since she last looked back. "They are. Luna Maris?"

"Preparing herself. She says to take them to the apothecary."

Lieutenant Hana sighs. "All right."

She nudges one of the other wolves, and we're moving again. Is Queen Maris... here? I look around the seeming hamlet with new eyes.

The first thing I notice is the roaring fire pit in the center of town. A handful of spits turn, roasting large carcasses that send up warm smells. The people turning them—men and women—sing a quiet song that matches the rhythm of their turns, as well as the rhythm of a rope game some children play behind them. Civilians, not soldiers. Not that Dario seemed very much like a soldier.

We're pushed into a wooden hut. Lieutenant Hana pauses in the door.

"If you wish to talk to the Luna Queen, you're going to need mouths that can do so." She glowers. "And if you touch any of my herbs, I'll kill you no matter what she says."

With that, the door slams between us and the rest of the village. A heavy lock chunks into place on the opposite side.

I shift. "Do you think we're in here because it's the only door that locks?"

Xandra shifts more slowly, looking around for a long moment before she turns to me. "I wouldn't be surprised. Hana has some remedies in here I know Miralyn would kill for."

"But why are they here?" I scan the bottles and can't make any sense of them. A large window, currently shuttered, occupies one wall. There's a bed, a table, and half a dozen implements we could use as weapons. It borders on stupid to lock us in here if they're worried about what they're going to do.

"Tansy Tower is our only palace." Xandra pulls clothes out of the bag she's been carrying—including clothes for me, which she certainly did not offer last night. "There are a few manors, but staying in another of the great families' manors holds enormous meaning."

"So she's camped on the border?" I pull on pants.

Xandra stares at the door like she can see through it. "Perhaps she wanted to be closer to the fighting, now that no one could refuse her."

The reality of the situation crashes down on my shoulders, and I drop everything to hug her. She's about to see her mother for the first time since she was abandoned. I remember what it felt like, looking behind us on the trip to Escuro for the revitalization ceremony and seeing the prison cart there. I never visited Mother; she would've refused me if I tried, and I had nothing to say to her anyway. She only had eyes for Kieran and the girls. But facing her again—I don't know. Father died far away, on a battlefield I'll never see. Mother looked us in the eye as we left her.

"Can you do this?" I ask. "Because we can turn around."

"And go where?" Xandra asks against my chest.

"Anywhere." I'll find a way to carve out a life for us.

"I have to face her someday." She sighs shakily. "I know that. I just… the woman who raised me is the one who built this place. Who puts children alongside soldiers so no one is separated from their families and no one forgets what they're fighting for. Not the one who orchestrates the attacks we've seen. I have no idea who we are going to meet." She laughs, on the line between humor and delirium. "Meeting my own mother. I feel like I am losing my mind."

"You aren't." I kiss the top of her head. "The world has lost its mind. You're simply doing what you can."

She huffs a breath. "We are."

"We are." I lay my hand on the tiny swell of her stomach.

Her smile curves against my bare chest.

"Luna Maris will see you now," Hana says from behind the closed door.

34

LUNA QUEEN MARIS

Xandra

I PULL MY HOOD LOWER OVER MY FACE AND BARELY RESIST THE URGE TO pick at the effects of the only potion Vedran was able to send us with —two bitter sips, choked down in the heartbeat between when Hana, a woman I remember vaguely from around the palace, knocked on the door and when she opened it, painted half my face with a grisly scar. Everyone who looked at us knew Finn wasn't from here, knew he was likely associated with Dun's Crossing, but they would not recognize him.

Me, however?

My stomach threatens to crawl out of my throat and heave itself onto the floor. I keep seeing faces I recognize; soldiers, staff, even commoners I think I saw on some visit or tour. And none of them can compete with what lies ahead.

Mother.

It has been nearly five months since I saw her last. Since I faced that note staked to the door. Before I needed her, I had no idea what I would say when I saw her again. Now, anything that might be words churns into bile.

Finn takes my hand. I start to twitch away—there's no reason to reveal our relationship before we have to—but the first brush of his skin over mine makes me sway. The worst of last night's dizziness is gone; my mark simply screams for me to throw myself into his arms, to let him face all the dangers for me.

I hold his hand, but I square my shoulders and lift my chin as much as is safe. I am not some squirming little girl who needs the protection of a brave man. My mother is mine to face.

Lieutenant Hana pauses before a door flanked by two soldiers. A perfectly average door, like any other in the village. I peer around the side—it's attached to a perfectly normal house.

Or so it seems at first. The wind rises, and camouflaged bridges in the air, networking this house to three others, bounce. It's still not much of a palace, but it's enough space to house the amount of people I expected, if they are packed in quite close.

The soldiers nod at Hana. She nods back at them. And the doors swing open.

Despite my brave words, only Finn's hand on mine keeps me moving forward. Sunbaked tile greets my feet as we step into a magnificent—for this place—entry hall. At the opposite end, close enough that I could reach it in three bounds, sits a chair behind a desk. And in that chair—

"Bow to Luna Queen Maris," Hana intones.

I obey automatically. A bow, not a curtsy. I've never learned how to do those, and I think I might trip over my ankles if I try. And this means I don't have to look at her yet.

"Clear the room." Her warm, familiar voice, tinged with a hint of husk that means she hasn't been sleeping enough, rings through the small hall.

"Your Majesty—"

"You heard me, Lieutenant. These two pose no threat. Clear the hall."

I hold my bow. This can only mean one thing. Footsteps shuffle around us, leaving through a variety of doors I haven't spotted yet. At last, a final door shuts, and silence falls.

"Xander?" she asks softly.

I straighten, intending to face her like the man she raised me to be. But when I look into her eyes, darker than mine or Father's and soft with something I can't name, that crumples. I burst into tears. It's been so long since she—since anyone looked at me like that.

Those are not the eyes of a mother who leaves her child behind.

"Oh, my darling."

Through the haze of tears, I can barely see the dark shape of her hurry out from behind the desk. It's my only warning before she wraps her arms around me, and I'm surrounded by her lily-and-sour-plum smell.

I intend to resist the embrace as well. She is the woman I remember now, but she left me behind. Disappeared in the night without a word. It couldn't have been that much harder to leave me my own note, if she truly cared as much as she seems to. That stings deep in my bones.

But I am tired, sick, and pregnant. I want my mother. So I sag against her shoulder and hold her in return.

"I have spent my life seeing my daughter through disguises," she murmurs in my ear. "Did you really think this would trick me?"

I shake my head. Others, perhaps, but I avoided any reflections in the healer's house in case the weakness of my disguise robbed me of my nerve. Leather dents my cheek, unlike the light silks and satins I am used to her wearing. I didn't even look at her outfit; I barely looked at her. But this feels like… like armor.

I pull back and take her in for the first time. Wetness beads in her eyes; new lines bracket her mouth and brows. Her strawberry-blonde, graying hair is pinned severely back, and over a sober gown, she does, in fact, wear a leather breastplate.

"So much has changed." She smiles self-consciously and lifts her dull skirt. "I miss the dresses, but they are a price I'd pay over and again."

"And me?" The words burst from my lips before I can catch them. "Was I a worthy price for playing rebel?"

Something in her face cracks, and she looks away from me. "I fought for you."

"Fought who? Everyone obeys you here." I gesture at the empty room—nearly empty, that is. Finn stands slightly to the side, his hands in his pockets, clearly trying not to intrude.

"The other lords are not so subservient," she replies crisply, then shakes her head. "What has your father told you about what we are doing here?"

I raise an eyebrow. "Doing? You are splitting the kingdom in half."

"The kingdom is tearing itself apart at the seams." Something I've never seen in her before lights her eyes—passion. "Can't you feel it? Tansy Beach is overburdened by the weight of its own traditions, and your father would rather die than release an iota of them. He told me so himself. They mean more to him than the safety of his people, the continuance of Tansy Beach as an idea, if not under the Mlakar line."

I blink. My head spins. "And Moonlight Hollow…."

"Stands as a refutation of that," she declares. "A haven for all those who believe we can be more than what we have been. A way forward. We don't want to destroy Tansy Beach—we want to save it."

"Chair," I say.

"What?" Her brow furrows.

Before she can ask again, wood scrapes across the floor, and Finn slides a chair in behind me. I sit heavily.

The spinning slows, just slightly. Enough that I can string together half a thought. "You never mentioned this to me."

"I couldn't." She cups my cheek, glances at Finn with a question in her eyes that I don't intend to answer until all of mine are satisfied. "You were your father's pride and joy. His greatest achievement and last hope. I could barely speak to the other lords often enough to gather support. A whisper of this, and he would've had me declared a traitor."

I start to shake my head, but my cheek stings in memory. That man—the one who ordered the destruction of a life because it challenged his line—he would've killed or imprisoned my mother for these thoughts. And perhaps these thoughts are the very thing that brings that man out of him.

"I couldn't take you with me," she murmurs. "He would have stopped at nothing to bring you home, and he would have destroyed our fledgling project before it had a chance to discover if it could fly. You understand, don't you?"

"Why couldn't you leave me my own note?" My voice cracks, fragile and worthless. I don't understand—and I do.

"After some discussion, we all came around to Denidor's point of view. No matter what protections we took, a second note was too likely to fall into your father's hands. I couldn't prove how much they could trust you,"—she shoots a look at Finn, clearly wondering just how much he knows—"and I worried you might leave of your own accord if you knew the truth."

I would have. Of course, I would have. I think. I glance at Finn; perhaps I only think I would leave because he has made it so clear how much life lies outside of what I have been prescribed.

Mother stares at me, begging me to understand with her eyes. Even just being escorted through the village outside as prisoners, I can see the difference she was talking about. I have never seen anywhere in Tansy Beach quite so light or free.

But she left me behind to do it. She still bowed to the whims of the other great families. How different is this really?

She looks at Finn again, and I swallow my concerns like a bitter pill. It's different enough, with all her ideals, that I doubt she will send us away.

"We do come seeking refuge," I admit.

Her face lights. She thinks this is acceptance, understanding. I plunge forward with the story before that can stop me.

"This is Prince Finn, of Dun's Crossing. He is also my mate, and," —I swallow, place a hand on my stomach—"the father of my child."

Mother's gaze flickers between us quickly. A heartbeat later, she offers me a beatific grin. "I'm so happy for you."

"Father didn't feel the same." I can't face her excitement, how quickly she put the pieces together when Father had to be told while we were living under his roof. "He attempted to force me to end the pregnancy, so we fled. We cannot return. Finn's family would be endangered if we went there. So...."

"So you've come to me." She hugs me again, impulsively. Like this, she reminds me far more of the beautiful but immaterial mother I knew. That almost feels worse than facing down a warrior queen that was hidden from me. "Of course, you can stay."

"Thank you, Queen Maris," Finn says.

She releases me and hugs him instead. "That is far too formal. We're family now."

He stares at me, wide-eyed, begging me to free him.

"What of Father, though?" I ask.

She releases Finn and looks at the two of us. Her smile fades, and I see where all those new lines have come from. "I cannot deny that we can't exactly withstand a full-frontal assault from Tansy Beach at this time. Announcing your presence would be dangerous."

Somehow, I know what's going to happen before it does.

"Would you be willing to stay in disguise?"

THE COMMON LIFE

Finn

I sit on the edge of a thin straw mattress in a tiny room, one of many honeycombing what was once a playhouse. Crooked nails jut from equally thin walls, clearly constructed as quickly as possible when the townsfolk discovered they were going to be hosting their new queen and a not insignificant portion of her army. Laughter echoes over the tops, where they don't quite reach the ceiling.

"It's safe," I tell Elian through the mind-link. *"Or about as safe as anything is."*

"Where should I go?"

I give him directions as best I can. *"If that fails, you want the town of Tarrin."*

"And the crown prince?"

"Not exactly."

I pick at my rough pants and glance at the slim curtain sectioning off a tiny corner of our room. It rustles, an elbow jutting into it, or maybe a knee. Behind there, Xandra changes into her last disguise. *Hopefully,* her last disguise. If I have anything to say about it, it will be.

"Silas and Anica Tanner. I'll explain when you get here."

"Whatever you say."

The link to Elian goes quiet, and I turn our new backstory over in my head. I'm Silas now, a twenty-five-year-old tanner drawn across the border from Dun's Crossing during the Haze a few years ago who never went back. Anica—Xandra—is a year younger than me, a farmer's daughter and scribe. Apparently, there's a significant call for people who can write, and far less for those who can make leather, so the fact that I don't possess that skill matters less.

We're mates. Married mates, awaiting our first child. No matter where we go here, no matter who can see us, there's no reason for me not to grab her and kiss her. No reason to hide. The thought frissons through me, hot and sharp.

I mouth the words, "my mate," testing them on my tongue. No matter how much I fought them, they fit there. I just wish I could call her by her name.

"You have to promise not to laugh at me," she says from behind the curtain.

"Why would I laugh?" I lean back on the bed we're going to share for the length of our stay here.

"There are a thousand reasons." Her voice takes on an edge of irritation. "I have never worn a dress before this moment. I'm not sure how to sit, or walk, or stand, or—"

"I swear by the light of the stars, I will not laugh." A smile plays at the edges of my lips. I won't break my promise, but it's hard to picture her in a dress, even now. So much of Xander still clings to her. Part of me imagines she might look a little like Howell did the one time he put on a maid's dress and flounced around all day for a joke on Elian's birthday.

The curtain slides aside, and my breath catches.

I am a moron.

A skirt of the same rough-hewn, brownish material as my pants swirls around her legs, not quite reaching the floor. A few inches of bare ankle promise she, too, is avoiding the lumpy stockings that will protect our feet from the ill-fitting boots as long as possible in this heat. At her waist, a belt of simple rope both holds up the skirt and highlights the gentle slope of her hips I know mostly by how they fit under my palms. Above that, a blouse of undyed linen clings loosely to her breasts. Miles of tanned skin lays bare above the neckline, which offers a teasing hint of cleavage. Half-sleeves highlight the lean muscle of her arms, a lifetime of training impossible to disguise with a few swaths of fabric.

And at the center of it all, equally impossible to hide without layers of magic and clothing built intentionally to shield, her belly swells softly with the growing life inside.

She pushes her hair, now partially pinned, back. It's a looser version of the style her mother wears, flowing over her shoulder. "Silence might be worse than laughing."

"I'm sorry." I stand and drift the few feet to her in our tiny room. "You look…." Like Xandra. Like the glimpses of a woman I've seen when we lie naked beside each other, when she stops thinking about everyone else for slivers of seconds. "Incredible."

She snorts. "You have to say that."

"I do not." I brush a kiss over her cheekbone. "I need to say something kind, so you don't hit me, but I've gotten very good at non-compliments."

"Is that so?" She smirks up at me, a challenge sparkling in her eyes.

"I could say that brown brings out your eyes." I grin. "Or that you look convincingly like a commoner."

"Hey!"

"You asked!" I hold her tighter as she tries to squirm away, carefully above the bump. "I think you look like a miracle, probably the best thing to ever happen to these clothes."

Her squirming slows. She peeks up at me. "Really?"

I put a finger under her chin and tilt her face up to mine. "Really."

She smiles as I drop a kiss on her mouth. Queen Maris wanted to see us after we were finished "settling in," as she called it. I should stop there. We have personas to establish, secrets to keep even as we tell more of the truth than we've been able to yet.

But her lips part under mine with a quiet intake of breath. The sound whistles through me, just as warm and perfectly fitted as the words, *my mate*, moments ago. She is mine. No matter what I have to call her, no matter what story I tell about how we met, she will take my hand, kiss me, and laugh where the entire world can see.

I drag her closer, reason burning away. She pushes back into me. My legs hit the bed unexpectedly, and we fall.

Protect them.

I twist, land on my back, and cushion her against the unforgiving straw. Breath gasps from my lungs. Still, I open my eyes to make sure she's all right.

Xandra laughs. Not laughs—she giggles, a sound I've never heard from her before.

"Oh, Silas," she says, sighing. "What would I do without you?"

My smile grows to match hers. "Nothing good, Anica, dear."

"Thank the Goddess we don't have to wonder, *dear.*" She rolls her hips slowly. Skirts shift, and the warm skin of her thigh meets my stomach, where my shirt has pulled up.

My cock reacts. Bless skirts. Bless the easy endearment falling from her lips, even though I know she's just teasing me. Silas and Anica love each other, I suddenly know. They say it often and easily.

Maybe it's a game. But just for now, I want to fuck my mate like I've already told her I love her.

I caress her cheek. She turns her face to kiss my palm, hips still undulating. I push up on one arm, pull her closer, and drag my mouth along her neck. Slow. Like we've got all the time in the world. I lap the taste of her off her skin and chase my tongue with the barest hint of teeth. Noises of pleasure mumble past her lips—she's holding back–for the sake of our neighbors.

We'll see how long that lasts.

For now, I use what little she gives me to map the sweetest places. She half-gasps when I linger over her pulse point, barely hums across the center, whines when I place my mouth over my first mark once more. I stay there for long moments, kissing it like she once whispered she loved. A constant rumble of sounds pours from her, needy but not yet demanding. My cock strains against the constraints of my pants.

The moment before that balance tips, I move from her throat, down the long path to the neck of her tunic. The linen moves obligingly out of my way, even props her breasts closer when I lower it beneath them. She hisses softly.

And I take my time once more. Let the queen—the world–wait. My mate has been put through hell. She's lost and gained and changed. She needs time, someone to take care of her, even if she'll never admit it.

She fists one hand in my hair, her hips moving more and more insistently. Wetness slides between us. Want made physical. I groan against her skin.

"Shush, Silas," she mumbles.

"I'm not ashamed," I reply. "Let everyone know just how well I fuck my wife."

A moan stutters past her control. I slip a hand beneath her skirts and find her core. She is moving too fast, too desperately, for me to do anything but offer her friction right now. Xandra grinds against my fingers, my palm. More moans barely catch behind her teeth.

I sit up, forcing her to straddle my lap. With my other hand, I make quick work of my pants and free my cock. Xandra buries her head in my shoulder to smother another moan, and one of her hands joins mine. She encircles my cock, strokes it slowly, as if I am not on the precipice just seeing her like this.

But we have time. Whatever we can't—or don't—do now, we can do tonight. Or tomorrow. Or any moment we have alone in this room we share. So I let my mate coax me nearly to the edge.

With a smirk, she meets my gaze. "Please, Silas."

Xandra would never beg. Not unless I had far more time and patience than I do now. And she is the only barrier between me and where I want to be most, but I'll play along.

I always will, for her.

"Whatever you want, dear." I pull my cock from her grasp, line it up, and sink deep inside her.

She parts to fit me, all searing wetness. Her mouth falls open. I palm one of her breasts, just watching her for a moment.

So she moves. It's a symphony of movement, really. Thighs, hips, breasts. All soft. All on various degrees of display in the ruins of her dress. And my mind goes blank. The apex of pleasure still waits ahead of me, but I can't form enough of a thought to even meet her rhythm. She fucks herself on me, beautiful and unashamed.

I love her.

That thought shocks through me, leaving enough space for others. I roll my hips in time, fit a hand back between us to push her over the edge. She throws her head back, and a full, throaty moan escapes.

I explode. Euphoria shakes my limbs, tumbles out of my mouth. My mate, my wife, my love clenches around me as she follows swiftly after.

In the aftermath, once I've landed, and she is still shaking around me, I hope hazily that she knows that wasn't just a game.

3 6

―――――

NEEDED

Xandra

"I approach Tarrin from the southwest", Vedran says the next day. *"With Beta Elian in tow."*

I nearly drop my quill. Sanja, the weaver for whom I'm penning a letter to her family still in Tansy Beach, looks at me questioningly. Finn braces around the log he's hauling a few feet away.

"Our friends are arriving," I say, shocked by the sheer intensity of relief crashing through my body. This is the longest I have been away from Vedran since he came to the castle. I have less to hide than I ever did, and his daily spells are no longer necessary, but the lack of his quiet presence by my side has left a hole nothing else quite fills.

"Go," Sanja says warmly.

Finn smiles, drags the log into place, and loops his arm through mine with a new ease. "Get ready for a whole lot of complaining."

"I will be glad to hear it," I say

I try twice to mind-link a warning to Lieutenant Sime, the soldier leading the southeastern scouts, before it goes through. Truthfully, we should've laid in backstories for them already. Elian's less pure coloring makes him less obviously Dun's Crossing, but rumors of our escape will reach Tarrin proper eventually.

Still, that's hard to consider when I can smell Vedran on the wind. I pull Finn through the war-town toward the scent, but judging by his grin, he feels similarly.

Vedran and Elian break through the trees in unison, a pair of white wolves behind Lieutenant Sime. The only ways to tell them apart are the shades of yellow in Elian's coat and Vedran's ruby-red eyes. They shift, pull on loose trousers, and I break free of Finn's hold.

I've never touched Vedran unofficially. A careful boundary of propriety, of appropriate masculine affection, has always separated us.

For the very first time, I hug my best friend. "How did you fare?" I demand as he slowly embraces me in return.

"I took a few scratches in my escape."

"I told you that you wouldn't fit through that window."

"I fit." He hisses softly through his teeth. "Not well enough for a graceful landing, but I did fit."

The image of him, sprawled in the bushes below the window in his quarters makes me laugh and squeeze him tighter.

"… Anica," I hear from the conversation next to us.

One glance tells me all I need—Finn left every detail of our situation, *my* situation, until he could explain them to his Beta in person. Elian looks me up and down, wide-eyed. Am I going to have to worry about another man fretting over me as if I've become a delicate flower overnight?

I shoot Elian a rude gesture and a wink. He blinks, then responds in kind.

Perhaps Finn has something to learn from his Beta.

"And the days in the forest?" I ask Vedran.

"A hot meal would not go unwelcome, and I have never resented my coloring quite so much, but I discovered Elian the day before last, and we have been traveling together since." He releases me, steps back, and takes me in. "And you… Anica?"

"Well." I put my hand on my growing stomach. "The Luna Queen is merciful, and Silas has been attentive."

Lieutenant Sime clears his throat. "I ought to take these two to our Luna Queen."

"No need." I smile at him. "I have a lunch with her shortly. I'll explain everything and get them settled."

His eyebrows shoot up. "*You* have—"

"My mother was her nursemaid." I lie easily.

That settles the lieutenant quickly enough. I'll have to warn Finn, who hasn't overheard, before someone asks him. For now, the four of us set off deeper into Tarrin.

"I always wanted to be called Tobias," Elian muses.

"I'll call you Toby," Finn replies.

"Or Ass," I add with a smile.

"Three days in the forest for you." Elian scowls. "And this is the thanks I get!"

"I shall keep my name." Vedran cuts him off smoothly, a testament to the time they've spent together. "You might be called Milo. It is an unoffensive name that transverses borders."

"Milo." Elian nods thoughtfully. "Milo, the leatherworker. I take your goods and turn them into something usable, Silas."

Finn rolls his eyes. "Careful. That might land you with a needle in your hands."

"And how do you know I couldn't handle it?" Elian wiggles his fingers.

"Zlata will settle you with supplies," I say. "And jobs. But I truly am needed elsewhere, unfortunately."

"With Luna Maris?" Vedran asks quietly.

I nod. Mother invited me to a private lunch, a chance to catch up on all we've missed without other eyes on our shoulders. Mixed emotions still roil in my gut, but I would like to speak with her like I used to.

"I'll take care of them." Finn claps both men on the shoulders. Vedran nearly jumps in surprise, and I turn toward Mother's makeshift palace with a smile.

At her instructions, I enter through one of the other networked houses—directly into a sweltering kitchen. The heat goes straight to my head, and I'm forced to catch a counter as my knees weaken. A young girl with a laden tray darts around me. An older man scowls and wriggles a dish out from under my hand.

"Anica!" Mother calls from across the chaos.

It barely stills for her, but she cuts through it like a hot knife. In moments, she's at my side, weaving an arm under mine to support me. I forgot how much taller than her I am—only a few inches–but the difference feels massive as her shoulder slots nearly beneath my own. She takes a few steps back, and the relative cool of the breeze whips through my hair.

Instantly, she releases me and resumes a court posture. She looks no more formal than she did yesterday, but I can still see the Luna throne behind her, her standing before it as Lunas must while their Alphas sit.

"Please accept my apology," she says.

"You couldn't have known the heat—"

"Not for that." She smiles ruefully. "General Zdenko has just returned from a mission with vital information. The four of us are meeting now."

"Oh." I deflate like a sail that has lost the wind. "Another day, then."

She looks at me, posture taut but a thread of worry in her eyes. "Now that you are here, there will be no hiding the truth from them. Not for long."

I glance down at my belly. My face is wholly undisguised, Vedran's potion long since having worn away. We are relying on the confusion of my pregnancy to keep those here from recognizing me.

"We could confront them first," she says. "Tell them the truth before they have a chance to reason it out and nip the scandal in the bud."

"That sounds like Father talking." But she is offering me a chance to be a part of the war effort. A part of her life. Temptation sings sweet songs in my ear.

"Perhaps, but he is a clever man, if nothing else."

"He struck me," I blurt.

I don't know why I bothered to say it until I see the change in her face. Her eyes turn to storms. Fury knots her brow and weighs down the corners of her mouth. "And he will not do so again," she growls.

Something unknots in my gut. A deep, sour worry that I misremembered Mother, that, if put in Father's position, she would make the same choices. She would never lay a hand on me, and she would never have permitted him to, were she there.

A small voice murmurs a warning—my knees still tremble, my head still swims. I haven't even told Finn that Miralyn ordered me to stay in bed more permanently than the night we fled Tansy Beach. After an encounter like mine with the kitchen, I ought to return to our room and rest.

But Mother needs me. Otherwise, she would not offer this.

"All right," I say. "Let us face the music."

* * *

"Who is this?" Lord—General Zdenko demands in the tight cellar they apparently hold their most vital meetings in.

Lord Denidor peers through the thin gloom left behind by the pair of flickering lamps, and the undersecretary he apparently goes nowhere without mirrors him. "I may recognize her."

"You do," I say before Lord Andrija has a chance to weigh in. "You know me as Prince Xander."

As if choreographed, three councilors of the great houses look from my face to my stomach, then back again, in perfect unison.

"I knew Alden was lying," Lord Andrija mutters.

"As was I," Mother says. "To protect our kingdom and our line. Now, the truth is more important."

Down here, she is even more perfect, even more the queen I remember. Father may as well have his hand on her shoulder or the back of her neck, as he so often did.

Lord Denidor splutters, graying hair falling loose from his braids.

"Then my Petar ought to have been training for a chance at the crown."

"Ought he?" Mother spears him with a look. "I lead Moonlight Hollow. My daughter has as much right to inherit as your son."

He turns red in the low light.

General Zdenko crosses his arms over his breastplate. "Alden will come after him."

"Her," I correct. A lifetime of swallowing that word; I would expect it to be harder to pry off my tongue. But watching General Zdenko nod in simple acknowledgment is so sweet that I doubt I'll ever hold it back again. "And my presence isn't known to any but those I arrived with and you."

I let the sentence hang in the air, a quiet threat. Another of Father's tricks. If we are betrayed, we will know someone in this room is to blame.

Andrija shakes his head slowly, firelight playing over his red curls in brilliant spikes that hurt my eyes. The close air of this cellar does me no favors.

"Would you like to meet, or would you like to argue over the details of my genitals?" I snap.

"Who is the father?" Lord Denidor asks abruptly.

"I believe my daughter told you the topic was closed." Mother takes a seat at the head of the table. "General, what did you learn?"

Denidor's gaze lingers on me as I sit beside her.

"Border skirmishes continue to slant in their favor." Andrija grimaces. "Our tactics fail to persuade."

"The tactics of brutality?" My unbound tongue springs to life without my say-so. "You leave so many maimed, it is difficult to tell them from the dead."

Mother's mouth opens slightly—did she truly not know?

"You outnumber us at every turn," Andrija snarls. "If we cannot convince you we are more than we are, we will all die. Or do you believe your father has mercy on his mind?"

"I think that, if you wish to be better, you ought to be better." I stand, and my vision starts to swim once more. The earth isn't enough to cool air this full of fire. "What principles will others believe of you if this is how you show them?"

"What principals will matter when Moonlight Hollow is nothing but a gravestone?" he spits. "You have not been here—"

"And whose choice was that?" I slam a hand down on the table and lean as much weight as it can take onto it. "I am a member of this council. I know what you've been doing. And I say it has to change."

"You little b—" Andrija stands abruptly, knocking into the board that passes as our table.

My hold tips. My vision tips with it.

I am falling.

THE TRUTH

Finn

I PACE BACK AND FORTH IN THE CRAMPED CONFINES OF THE HEALER'S house once more.

"Stand the fuck still for five minutes, will you?" Lieutenant Hana snaps.

The word *no* boils on my tongue. But ever since Xandra collapsed in some kind of meeting with her mother and the other three lords—definitely not the lunch she said she was going to—Hana has been bent over my mate, sweating buckets as she mixes herbs, powders, and some other shit I don't really want to ask about into poultices, potions, and wraps. Sweat rivers down Hana's forehead, and the tightness in her face looks more like concentration than rage.

I sit on a sloped stool in the corner of the room. She snorts. I ignore her.

Xandra's eyes dance behind her closed lids, her veins way too purple against her still-ashen skin. She's been in and out–a good sign, according to Hana. If she passed out and stayed unconscious, there might be no saving her.

I have no idea what happened. All I can think about is the rumor I heard back in Tansy Beach, that Prince Xander fainted when he saw a portrait of his mother. Once I discovered the portrait wasn't seen so much as burned, I figured the faint was an exaggeration, too. After all, she would've told me about that.

Or so I thought.

Looking at her now… I have no idea. Queen Maris hovered for the first few minutes until one of the other lords pulled her away to finish their meeting. Maybe she looked reluctant. I don't know her well enough to say. All I know is that she offered a couple of sentences and disappeared. There's no one to ask but Xandra, who hasn't yet stayed awake longer than to swallow a few sips of water.

"Something's wrong, isn't it?" I ask.

"I'm not talking to you without her." Hana spares me a glance. "Sorry."

She may as well have said yes. Something is wrong with our baby, and Xandra didn't tell me.

Xandra lurches up off the table with a weak cough then drops back down. Before she can hit the hard surface, Hana manages to slide what passes for a pillow around here under her skull. Her eyes flutter wildly.

The healer holds a waterskin to her lips. I creep closer. It has to be this time. Every time she passes back out, Hana looks more worried. Any more, and she'll twist her face all the way off.

Xandra drinks greedily, water pouring down her chin. When the skin is empty, Hana pulls it away. Xandra gestures, hums softly, and it fills once more.

Hana offers me a smile pounded thin from stress.

I race to Xandra's other side, cramming myself between the wall and the jut of the bed. A shelf pokes into my shoulder. "How are you? What happened?"

"Fainted." She coughs again, her gaze still muzzy with something worse than sleep. "All better now." She starts to push up.

"I wouldn't." Hana lowers her back down.

"Why?" I demand.

Xandra shoots me a look. She was about to ask that.

"I said I wouldn't talk to you until she was awake." Hana runs a hand over Xandra's bare stomach. "I've got news."

My blood freezes. "Bad news."

She shrugs. "Depends on how you look at it."

"Tell us." Xandra clings to the waterskin, empty once again.

"I feel a heartbeat." Hana drags her hand over and down. "And another one."

The pieces float together slowly. "Twins?"

"Twins," she confirms.

"Twins," Xandra says wonderingly, staring down at her stomach.

Two babies. A boy and a girl? Two girls or two boys? No matter what, two little voices screaming for me in the night. Two pairs of feet finding fumbling first steps.

Two members of our family in one fell swoop.

"Good news, then." Hana smiles, then starts mixing something else in her heavy mortar.

"I think so." Xandra looks up at me, tears shining in her eyes.

Words snarl in my throat. I can only take her hand and nod. There's no way to say I'd take triplets, quadruplets, as many as she has in a heartbeat without losing my grip on something I can't quite name but I know threatens to unmake me entirely.

"How are we going to handle twins?" Xandra laughs, half-nerves and half-excitement.

"Carefully," I reply, my voice rough. "And without a lot of sleep."

"Speaking of that." Hana turns back, daubing a green mixture onto a cloth. "I'm a little surprised your healer at home didn't talk to you about rest already."

"Rest?" Xandra's hazel eyes dart to me, too fast to read the expression within.

Still, tension prickles up my spine. In the rush, I almost forgot we were here because she fainted. Because something is wrong.

"You ought to have been on bed rest a couple of weeks ago." Hana lays the cloth over Xandra's forehead. "I don't know if it's your scribing work or what, but your body has not developed to support a single baby well, much less two. This is going to be a very fraught pregnancy."

The linen bandages she bound her chest with. The magic, which no one really understands. Years of training and acting like a man.

"That is strange," she murmurs.

And I know. Miralyn, the palace healer, absolutely told her to stay in bed. Right on the timeline Hana suggested, I'd bet. And not only did Xandra ignore that, she didn't even bother to tell me she was ignoring it.

"Take one of these every day." Hana shakes a small pile of pills onto a clean fabric, then winces when the bottle stops spitting them. "Every other day. And come to me when you run out. There are… simpler, slightly less effective versions I might be able to scrounge together."

I open my mouth to object—she needs them!—but the look on Hana's face silences me. This is a war zone. Any medicine spent on others can't be used for soldiers.

"Can I lie down a moment longer?" Xandra asks.

Hana glances around and then looks out the window. "Of course. Just—"

"Don't touch anything," I finish for her.

She nods, scoops up the pieces of armor she shed to work on Xandra more easily, and leaves.

"What the fuck were you thinking?" I hiss.

"That my meetings with the healer were private for a reason?" Holding the cloth to her forehead, Xandra sits up, clearly struggling less than she was a moment ago.

"You're at risk." I wriggle out from behind the table. "Our baby— babies–are at risk."

"A calculated risk." She narrows her eyes at me. "Or did you think being prince of a country at war was a safe position to occupy? I assure you, that's less true when you're not fifth in line."

I grit my teeth. "Oh, wonderful. You're throwing jabs at my ability to inherit. If being first in line means all of this, I don't want it."

"Don't lie to me. You want it more than anything. Every prince does."

"You did." I step between her and the door. She's not leaving until she agrees to follow Hana's orders. "Not everyone."

"My apologies, I didn't mean to imply you wanted something."

I spit a bitter, burning laugh. She has seen more clearly through me than even I thought. "And I didn't mean to imply you might ever need to trust someone else. Deeply sorry."

"I trust." She dodges left, then right, but between all the furniture and shelves, she can't get around me. "By the Goddess, Finn, what do you think you're going to do? Trap me in here?"

"If that is what it takes to make you rest, I will." I cross my arms. "I won't allow you to destroy yourself. Not when I know better."

"You won't allow me." She repeats the words softly, almost to herself, disbelief dripping from every letter. "Who are you to *allow* me anything?"

"Your mate." I tug her collar aside to reveal the sun-shaped mark she's ceased covering. "The father of your twins. You're risking their lives as well as your own."

"Don't you dare accuse me of that." She curls her arm protectively around her stomach. "I know what my limits are. I'll stop when I need to."

"Will you?" I take a step closer. "Or will you faint in a cellar, surrounded by the leaders of a foreign kingdom, when you said you were going to fucking lunch?"

"Plans changed! And they are not foreign to me." She juts her chin out at me, eyes blazing. I've never seen her this angry. She could burn the entire world away.

And I don't move. Let her burn. This is where I belong. If she won't listen to reason, she has to listen to muscle.

She looks me up and down and then scoffs. "A jailer. That's what you'll be, then. Another jailer to add to my list."

"That's not—"

"Isn't it?" She throws her scowl like a knife. "All my life, there has been someone—some *man*—between me and the rest of the world. Protecting me, or so he claimed."

"I am nothing like your father." My voice rumbles out of me like a peal of thunder.

"No?" She steps closer, presses her chest against mine. "Then step aside."

I don't. I can't. She will run right back to her mother, to her work, and I will have lost my only chance. Adrenaline and instinct braid in my veins, keeping me put.

"Exactly." She turns away from me and walks toward the shuttered window. "You want to talk about trust, Finn? Then trust me. Let me make my own choices. Be my mate. My partner."

I clench my fists until my nails chew into my palms. I know there's another option, and I need to hear it.

She sits on the edge of the bed. "Or be my jailer. You won't be able to keep me here. And as soon as you slip up, I will run. Farther and faster than you can believe. Imagine how much danger that will put us all in."

She sounds tired now. Furious, but tired of being furious. Like a fight she's been engaged in for too long won't end.

"Or, hell, just crawl back home. Let me have these babies by myself." She looks at the shuttered window. "I will do that before I spend the rest of my life fighting you. The choice is yours."

I open my mouth to answer.

38

IMPOSSIBLE COMPROMISE

Xandra

THE ONLY STILL POINTS IN THE ROOM ARE FINN'S ICE-BLUE EYES, wavering with an indecision that threatens to gut me.

Twins. The only explanation for why this pregnancy has already been so hard on me, an explanation so obvious I should have seen it coming. Corwyn's mother was Father's twin. They run in his family.

But even twins, I can—will–raise alone if he forces me. I have my mother beside me again. Even with all the questions still unanswered between us, I know she will do anything for her grandchildren. I will be able to run, if he makes me, because she will throw every available resource at me to do so.

Perhaps I have no training in parenthood. Perhaps I assumed for my whole life that I would adopt some orphan, or make one of Vedran's children my heir, when the time came. But anything is better than trading one prison for another. I won't do it.

These thoughts are much easier to hold on to when I don't look at Finn. I can do this without him—but there is a part of me, one that seems to have taken up residence in my gut, that screams to say whatever I must to make him stay.

I can, but it's simply a prison of my own design rather than his.

"You know there's only one of those options I can choose," he whispers.

I've hurt him by doing this. A tired ember of anger flames back to life, too weak to power me to do anything but face his gaze once more.

"And which is that?"

"Staying." He shakes his head, somewhere between disbelief that I have to ask and that he has to say it. "Backing off. Letting you make your own choices."

I clutch the thin blanket on the bed in one hand and try to keep the rush attached to his words from overwhelming me. Tears prick, and my mark sings to kiss him.

With all the willpower I have left, I stay seated. This is the barest minimum. I won't reward him for it.

"But—"

"But?" I repeat.

"But." He crosses his arms, muscles tensing beneath the skin, and I am reminded again just how little I could force the issue if I wanted to. The spike of want in my gut goes equally ignored. "I'm not going to stand here and let you compare me to your father."

"You're doing what he did, and I am getting tired of repeating myself." More accurately, I'm just getting tired, but I will not tell him that. Not now.

"No, I'm not, and if you'd let me finish a Goddess-damned thought, I could tell you why."

I gesture flippantly at him. I already know there's nothing he can say.

"King Alden wanted you to stay where he could control you, right?" Finn says. "Where he could get what he wanted out of you—a viable heir."

Older memories fight to my lips. He was protecting me, or at least it seemed that way when I was younger. If I had been raised as a girl, I would've been subject to the marriage market from my name day on. A token, traded between the other great houses as they saw fit to show who was leading the race to the throne. Doing this may have been painful in its own way, but in others, it was safer.

And then my cheek stings with the ghost of his palm.

"Right." Finn takes my silence as all the answer he needs. "That's not—I'm—fuck." He sits on the floor, his back against the door.

My immediate thought is that he's playing for pity, but I've never seen Finn do anything like that before. He wouldn't bother.

"Anwen could explain this right." He smiles tiredly. "Or Candace. Hell, I bet she already knows whatever I'm trying to say."

His siblings. "What do they have to do with this?"

"Nothing." He sighs. "Everything. I'm not sure."

"If you don't know what you're saying, I'd rather just leave." I either need to lie down or walk to clear the remains of the fuzz from my head. The thick smell of herbs in here is pleasanter than the cellar, but fresh air is what I need.

"Fine, then you get the shitty version." He sits up, resting his arms on his bent knees. "I grew up as the last resort. In theory, Ingrid could inherit, but nobody wanted her to. I was the last real line of defense. But with you, with them,"—he nods to my stomach—"I'm it. And that means I need to take care of the three of you like I'm everyone. Enough. I don't know."

There's no hint of irony in his voice, no feigned sarcastic distance. He means this completely. He wants to be my—our–world. No secondary motive.

And that doesn't change anything.

"You're not it." I stand slowly.

He raises his eyebrows.

I put my hand on my stomach. "They have both of us. I have myself. This fantasy you have—it's impossible."

"So I can't want it?" He climbs to his feet as well.

"Not with me." I shrug. "I lived my life behind walls. Now I'm out, and there is a whole, real world to explore. You could never be my everything because I won't shrink my life like that again."

He swallows. Something in his posture shifts, tightens. "I understand."

We hold that position, out of arms' reach, just looking at each other, for a long, hard moment.

"I've already given you my answer." He steps away from the door. "Just… will you try to rest as much as you can? When they don't need you anywhere else?"

His words sound like they're being dragged from the depths of the ocean. The Finn of a few months ago would've already snapped something cutting and sauntered out. He's trying.

That thing in my gut, the one that wants to throw myself at him and weep, begs me to try as well.

"When I can," I say.

"Thank you." Relief hangs so thick on his words I can taste it. "Now, let's give Lieutenant Hana her house back before she guts us for it."

* * *

I DO GO BACK TO THE ROOM, AND I DO MEAN TO LIE DOWN. I EVEN manage it, for a few minutes. But my mind won't stop racing, and the air in the converted playhouse reeks of ill-washed bodies and old linens. So I crawl out of bed, struggle into a cleanish dress—thank the Goddess common women don't often bother with anything stiffer than wooden stays—and walk out into Tarrin.

This far from the seashore, salt barely tinges the air. Instead, all the smells are green—trees I've read about rather than seen, grass trampled under the feet of the army suddenly squatting in this tiny border town. I take deep breaths, savoring its newness. The familiar, ambient heat doesn't rock me like that of the kitchen, and stretching my legs abates the lingering dregs of nausea in the back of my throat.

"Anica!" Sanja calls.

I find her crouched before a tub of water, surrounded by a small army of children. Most are toddlers, far too many to be hers. One girl of about twelve clutches a bar of soap clearly responsible for the few suds in the tub.

"Do you think we'll have time to finish that letter later?" Communication through the mind-link within Moonlight Hollow is hard enough; across pack lines is so unreliable that these ancient forms are more useful.

"If you ever escape bath duty," I say with a smile.

She laughs. "When I offered to help one neighbor, I didn't expect half the village to take me up on it."

I take a step forward but hesitate. Water bubbles on my fingertips. Powers are a rare blessing in Tansy Beach, a sign from the Goddess that you have been chosen. Lord Denidor has spent a lifetime crowing about his powers, despite his usually unblessed line. As a prince, mine ended more than a few arguments. As a farmer's daughter, they'll only cause questions.

One of the toddlers shrieks at the top of their lungs, and the girl drops the soap in the dirt.

I'm not worrying about questions like that anymore.

I curl water out of the air and around the soap, washing it clean before the girl can even scoop it off the ground. She and Sanja both stare at me, open-mouthed.

"Rare knack in my family." I smile self-consciously. "Mostly, I helped with the watering. And it makes all my ink last longer."

Ela nods numbly. "I've never truly seen anyone with the magic."

"Well, would you like to see what the magic can do for bath time?" I roll up my sleeves and kneel beside the tub.

As with all things, the novelty wears off quickly. Sanja and the girl —Petra, I learn—can't stare at me while there's a job to do. We settle into an easy rhythm. Petra holds the children. Sanja washes. And I control the water, rinsing them clean. Once Sanja realizes I've never done anything like this—or even really interacted with children this young before—she explains what she's doing as she does it. How to handle different children, when to inspect their cries and when to ignore them, which of the sweet, hidden folds and rolls of cloaking fat need to be scrubbed to keep them well.

It is a little like fighting. There's nothing but sensory input and the task at hand. I cannot relax, cannot let my guard down. At any moment, one of the children might squirm out of Petra's grasp or start throwing a tantrum or simply need something. Sounds, smells, and textures surround me.

Visceral.

By the time we are done, I wish the other half of the village had taken Sanja up on her offer as well. I stand slowly, dusting off my hands. "I am more than happy to help, next time this comes up."

Ela smiles gratefully. "I will be sure to find you when it does."

My chest warms. I smile back at her.

Petra struggles to lift the massive basin, and dirt-stained water sloshes over the edge.

"Oh, let me." I grab the two handles—barely, it's massive—and hum a soft tune to make the water float slightly above the bottom, lightening the load.

"Thank you, miss." Petra curtsies.

I wink at her. "If I get wet, I can dry off much easier."

"You are too kind." Sanja dries her hands. "Just dump it at the edge of the woods, if you can."

"I'll bring the tub right back here." I march toward the forest, humming under my breath to keep the water aloft. Magic exhaustion is a distant memory, but despite what I told Finn, I really don't want to overtax myself physically. The basin alone is enough weight.

At the tree line, I set it down and coax the water out of the metal. If I spread it out, I can grow these trees here a little more and add a shred of protection to this tiny capital. I smooth it slowly into a line while studying the trees for signs of dehydration.

"This is not what we agreed to," someone says, low and urgent.

All council meetings happen in that cellar, and that's not a soldier's diction. I inch forward, trying to see what's going on.

The edge of a tunic pokes into view around a trunk, hemmed in scarlet like all three rebel lords. My heart charges into my throat.

"You said Astralis would—"

In my distraction, my control slips, and all the water crashes to the ground. I wince and duck behind a tree, but it's already too late.

"Another time," the first voice says. Two sets of footsteps depart.

Who the hell is Astralis?

3 9

HARD REALITIES

Finn

I grunt as I lift one of the last crates of supplies off the back of the cart at the edge of Tarrin. Something inside shifts heavily against my chest.

"I would offer to help," the driver says, "but there's a reason I only do the smuggling." She raises her arms, displaying how thin they are.

I shake my head as I struggle a few steps forward. "You have a princess's arms, if nothing else."

Princess Joli Som, last in line for the throne of Lightning Cape, laughs and throws a few locks of her pinned, dark brown hair over her shoulder. "Most people don't risk talking to me that way."

I heft the box higher in lieu of a response. Obviously, an actual tanner wouldn't tease a princess, even if she was perched on the back of a dirty hay cart, wearing leather pants and a stained tunic. A princess who introduced herself as "Joli, the one keeping you all fed." Who I only recognized from being forced to learn royals' faces. At least her status is apparently well enough known that I didn't give myself away just from mentioning it.

Damn this box. I can barely think straight under its weight.

"Most people aren't carrying half an army in a single crate. What the hell is in here?"

She laughs again. "Weapons. I stumbled across a cache, and I know they won't fight with their hands now, but a war has a way of complicating people's principles."

"Goddess above." I drop the crate just over the pile of logs that will one day be Tarrin's wall. It's about three feet high now and sprouts more every single day. "Couldn't have warned me?"

"I wanted to see if people from Dun's Crossing turn as red as they say." She grins at me. "They do, by the way."

She's either extremely smart or she recognizes me.

Or she knows how rare blonde hair is on this side of the border.

Better safe than sorry, either way. When Lieutenant Sime gave me this job this morning, he warned me that the smuggler was troublesome. She has a way of distracting people, making every job take twice as long. In some ways, she reminds me of Ingrid, but she's at the end of an even longer line—eight Soms children, I believe. On the upside, that means I have some idea of how to deal with her.

"Glad I could amuse you." That should give her nothing to bounce off.

She shakes her head at me, almost knowingly. I toss her a tired smile and think about how often Lightning Cape came up during the council meetings back in Tansy Beach. Corwyn swore up, down, and sideways that Alpha Iraj would send men any day now, that he'd promised them to Tansy's cause. But here is his daughter, smuggling for the other side. Does her father know? Is Alpha Iraj just waiting for a winner to become apparent and playing his chances until then?

There's no way of knowing. Asking Joli will only get me more trouble—and a higher chance of being caught.

"Well, thanks," I tell her.

With a sigh, she says, "Tell them the next shipment won't be for two weeks. Supply chain issues."

"Will—"

She hops onto the cart, spurs the horse attached to the front—all sleek lines and dappled hair, just as fast-looking as Lightning Cape horses are rumored to be—and trundles away as fast as a hay cart can.

"—do," I finish. She's even more like Ingrid than I thought. I dust off my hands and head back into Tarrin.

Only to see Xandra bent over her makeshift desk in the center of town, scribbling out another missive. It's been almost a week since our talk, and she's resting *more*, I guess. But she was resting almost less than I am, so it's hard to see the difference. Something hot and tight bubbles in my throat—more arguments, more attempts to make my point. But she's clearly not going to listen.

"Where are you?" I ask Elian through the mind-link. The troubles everyone has been having with them don't seem to affect us, probably because Dun's Crossing isn't at war with itself.

"The ring," he replies.

I arrive at what passes as a training ground here—a flat ring of dirt, outside the main town, where General Zdenko drills soldiers day in and day out—shortly. Milo, as Elian is now known around camp, quickly turned from a leatherworker and underground brawler, landing him right back amidst the soldiers. His white fur flashes amidst all the reds and muddy browns. Despite Joli's prediction, those in Moonlight Hollow haven't abandoned their convictions about fighting as wolves just yet.

"Can you step out?" I ask him.

Elian moves like a flash, abandoning the careful circle he was weaving around his opponent in favor of a brutal leg-sweep, followed by his teeth around the other wolf's neck.

"Good," General Zdenko barks from his position in the rare shade on the opposite side of the circle. "But that wolf could stand back up. In an actual fight, break his legs."

I grimace as Elian shifts, pulls on a loose robe from a pile, and jogs over to me. That sounds like the sort of order that would leave the mess we had after the battle at Tansy Tower.

"What can I do for you?" Elian asks.

My tongue threatens to jump down my throat, the very idea of asking Elian anything abruptly ridiculous, but I force it to obey. "What's something Howell does that you hate?"

He leads me a little farther from the ring. "Chews with his mouth open when he's distracted."

"Bigger than that. Something that really pisses you off." Scares him, I should say, but then my tongue really will mutiny.

Elian thinks for a moment. "He used to not come home for a day or two at a time. No warning, would just say he was busy. Drove me up the Goddess-damned wall."

"I didn't know that." I glance at him. Why didn't he tell me?

He shrugs. "I asked you for advice about the chewing thing once, and you asked me if I'd ever met you before. Didn't seem like the sort of thing you'd want to talk about."

That same hot feeling sears my throat. I was busy; I didn't know Howell—but all my excuses feel like bullshit. "Apologies."

Elian raises his eyebrows. "Accepted. But why do you ask?"

I force the words out through my teeth before I can back down. "How did you make him stop?"

"Make him?" Elian scoffs. "I can't make him do anything."

"You just talked to him?" Sour resignation fills my gut.

"Tried that." He shakes his head. "He didn't even listen. No, I started locking the door after he'd been out for twenty-four hours. If he wanted to come back, he'd have to go through me."

"And that worked? He didn't just get pissed?"

"Oh, he was furious. So was I. But that opened both of us up like nothing else had, and we were finally able to talk." Elian laughs. "You think Xandra's stubborn? You should have seen Howell when I started with him."

"I don't think getting her angry will help." There's no point in denying what I'm actually asking him about anymore. "I have very much already tried that."

"Maybe she's got a different thing that will uncork her." Elian leans against a pole set deep in the ground to support the growing wall. "You just asked about Howell."

"Thank you so much," I snap. "I'm aware they are different people.

I just made the mistake of thinking you might have something useful to add."

Elian punches me in the shoulder—not hard enough to knock me off my feet, but more than hard enough to bruise.

"What the hell?" I growl.

"Ready to get out of your own way?" he asks. "I'm more than happy to hit you again, if not."

Xandra's words echo through my mind. I want this—I want her. And that, apparently, means enduring Elian's jibes.

"What, then?" I spit. "What pearl of insight do you have for me?"

"That the Goddess doesn't care what genders our mates are, but the world does. We're raised one way—man and woman, passels of babies, the whole nine yards. And I had to lock Howell out of our room because neither of us was ever taught to talk to men we loved. I needed to bash him over the head with it until that conditioning cracked."

"Xandra isn't—"

"But she was," he interrupts. "Twenty-three years, she lived as a man. Was treated like a man by everyone she met. That's bound to leave a mark."

"But—"

"But nothing." He crosses his arms. "I'm telling you that you don't have the mate bond we were raised to believe we should have. It's going to take more work, more time, for you two to figure out how to talk to each other. You can take that and run with it, or you can stand here and argue with me."

"Milo. Silas." General Zdenko dips half a bow as he steps up to us —enough not to insult me, if I cared about that sort of thing, but not enough to indicate to anyone else what he was doing. No one has told the other lords who I am yet, but they've puzzled out that I'm the father, so they've started treating me with this grudging respect. "Is all well?"

"Of course. I just needed to discuss a few personal matters with an old friend." Elian claps me on the shoulder. He's always been a better liar than I am.

"Yes." He looks back and forth between us, his eyes sharp. "Well, Silas, have you seen our fighters? Do you think you might someday find yourself amongst them?"

"Someday." His sharp command to break legs churns through me. "If I am more needed there than I am here."

"With your… wife. Of course." He scans me again, like he's trying to recognize me. "You've certainly got the build of a fighter."

"Have you ever skinned a cow?" Elian asks. "Try doing it without muscles."

Zdenko grimaces. "I was simply curious if Silas here had any thoughts about our fighting."

The way he says *our* makes it very clear that neither Elian nor I are included within that. I should refuse completely. It's better for my cover, and I don't like the way Zdenko looks at either of us.

"I know you prefer to fight in wolf form, but it seems like you're ignoring the potential advantage of magic," I say. After all I've seen, I'm not going to deny the obvious. Powers make any fight easier, and taking your own away just seems like self-sabotage.

Zdenko snorts then goes vague with a mind-link. One of the other fighters shifts and joins us.

"Dmitry, show them what you can do with water."

The man, Dmitry, puts out his hand and closes his eyes. After several seconds of silence, he conjures a few beads of water and then makes them swirl in a circle. When he releases them, they disappear back into the air, and he pants like he's just run several miles.

"Dmitry is one of our strongest." Zdenko gestures him back to the fighting, and the warrior leaves. "Wolves even the playing field. But thank you for your words of… wisdom, Silas."

He strides away, leaving me thinking about everything I've seen Xandra do with half the effort.

40

DISCOVERED

Xandra

"Oh," Finn half-gasps.

Things have been tense between us since he learned just how much time I'm supposed to be spending in bed, nearly two weeks ago now, but I still take his hand. "You will get used to the feeling, I promise."

He screws up his face as Vedran dances fingers through the air. I can barely feel the distant prickle of magic. Ever since he and Elian arrived, we've resumed our normal morning routine of glamors, just a different set than before. Finn, though, has never been included in the process.

Not until he mentioned the lingering gazes of Princess Joli and General Zdenko a few days ago. She was likely just trying to get under his skin, as she does with all the new laborers we send her way, but I have never fully trusted Lord Zdenko.

"Won't everyone notice I look different?" He squirms slightly as the illusion starts to take shape.

Vedran makes a small, displeased noise in the back of his throat. "I am no street conjurer."

I shoot a smile at my friend. "He means to say that he knows how to disguise you in a way that cloaks your identity from any who might recognize you without drawing attention to the change. That is why it takes so long—Vedran is an artist."

He offers me a slim smile in return. Finn, by comparison, peeks one eye open and looks at me.

"That makes sense," he says after a few long heartbeats. There's something soft, almost thoughtful, in his eyes that I don't understand.

As I open my mouth to ask what it is, a mind-link crackles through my thoughts.

"Wolf approaching... fast... from Tansy Beach."

I shoot to my feet. Finn tries to follow, but Vedran holds him down in a way Finn's face makes clear is far more a product of surprise than Vedran's strength.

"Can you stop him?" Mother asks. Of everyone here, she is always the clearest.

"Alone, Your Majesty. Should we?"

"Catch him at the border. Bring me what message he carries."

"We have to go to the palace," I say.

"Agreed," Finn mumbles.

Vedran huffs, and his hands turn faster. After a few agonizing moments, he steps back, and I look into a near-stranger's face instead of Finn's. Chin rounded, eyebrows darkened but softer, eyes a shade less pure. Years of seeing a stranger's face in the mirror still haven't prepared me. My world tips sideways.

"Go," Vedran says.

The wolf. The message. I pull Finn from his seat and run before the sideways feeling can catch me totally. I can even ignore the flicker of his frown when I start rushing.

He doesn't argue, though. That's all I ask.

What seems like all of Tarrin crowds the central square by the time we reach it. After nearly two weeks here, though, we are known quantities. People part for the daughter of Luna Maris's nursemaid and her foreign mate.

Finn starts pulling in another direction. I resist until I realize he's caught sight of Lieutenant Sime, moving urgently, and is following in his wake.

The message. Lieutenant Sime must be the messenger. My heart races unevenly.

He reaches the single step up to the palace just as the door opens. Mother stands there, dressed as she always is in a simple gown and leather armor, flanked by Lord Denidor, with undersecretary, and Lord Andrija.

Lieutenant Sime kneels. A beat of silence passes as he clearly attempts to relay the message through the mind-link. Mother frowns, those new lines carving deeper into her cheeks.

"I have nothing to hide from these people who have taken such good care of me," she says finally. "Speak the message aloud."

Whispers ripple through the crowd. Everyone knew about the trouble with mind-links, but no one knew it was affecting her. Not even me. My few failed mind-links take on a different tenor in my memory.

"Remand Prince Xander to my care," Lieutenant Sime says slowly, "or pay the consequences for holding him."

Whispers turn to murmurs then shouts. *"Prince Xander? What happened to Prince Xander? Why do they think we have him?"*

My face burns—no, my skin, as if I've spent too long in the sun. My heart flies, barely beating. The shouts build to a wall of noise I could not puncture if I wanted to, and I am certain I don't. It is as if I'm watching Mother's portrait burn again. Unconsciousness grabs for me with proprietary fingers, and I bat them away only with the strength of my desire not to give Finn another reason to keep me in bed. And, perhaps, my desperate need not to give a soul in this crowd a reason to look at me. Vedran's charms have protected me for my whole life, but they now feel like gauze. Flimsy, fragile, liable to be ripped away at any second.

Father knows where I am.

He's going to kill these people to get to me.

"Peace, please," Mother calls.

Quiet stumbles over the crowd rather than falling like a sheet of metal. Murmured conversations remain in small pockets.

"I apologize for the upset this has caused." She folds her hands in front of her, scanning her people. Her gaze lands on me. I cannot meet it. "Rest assured that I will get to the bottom of King Alden's implications and keep this violence from reaching you to the best of my ability."

More murmurs. Some of gratitude. Heads nod, and the peace she called for does seem to creep amongst these people on quiet feet.

I've never seen loyalty like this before. I wonder how long it will last when they realize she's lying to protect me.

"Council meeting," she flutes. "Now."

I do not need to look at her to know I am expected there. Finn starts to release me—he has never yet been invited into one—but without his hand in mine, I will collapse. I cling tighter, and a smile flickers across his mouth.

Together, we walk into the palace. Since the meeting in the basement where I fainted, council meetings have begun taking place in a central room here, one that looks like it was once a pantry, which Vedran managed to ward against prying ears. It's still small, especially with the round table crammed into the center, but it has a pair of windows that let in a blessed breeze. Mother, the three rebel lords, Denidor's undersecretary, Finn, and I all squeeze inside. Lord Denidor casts a searching glance at Finn, but when Mother does not object, neither does he.

"I thought we would have more time," she mutters as she takes her seat.

"We were seen crossing the Grayhead," I somehow say with a tongue made of stone.

"Wonderful." Lord Andrija shakes his head. "He likely searched farther east, did not find anything, and just assumed you were here."

"I'm surprised he did not also ask for—Silas," Mother says.

"He's scared of losing Dun's Crossing's support," Finn replies.

A beat of silence. Lord Denidor narrows his eyes at Finn, clearly trying to make the connection. I thank the Goddess for Vedran's work and whatever time it has bought us.

"Does he know about Tarrin?" Lord Andrija asks.

"He didn't when we left." Finn shrugs.

I could kiss him, if my body weren't made of heavier stone than my tongue. Orchestrating responses seems impossible.

"That's why we've been keeping him on his side of the Grayhead," General Zdenko hisses. "Once he crosses, there will be no hiding the truth."

Mother drops her head into her hands. Ice steals through my veins, the first sensation I've truly felt since Lieutenant Sime spoke my doom. Our doom.

"The truth?" Finn asks.

Another kiss. I'll tally them, pay when this is over and I can think straight again.

"This is all we have," Mother says grimly.

He frowns. "According to rumor—"

"Alpha Octavio of Oakspring Dunes is so caught up in his wife's illness he barely knows there's a civil war on his doorstep," Lord Andrija spits.

"And Birchmint Valley holds themselves so strictly isolated that they wouldn't know to contradict us," General Zdenko adds sourly.

And they were rumored to be allied with no others. Not by name, that is. They have all the fighting forces of one third of Tansy Beach, no more.

We sought the aid of Dun's Crossing. We must have looked like an unstoppable war machine.

My stomach curdles. Sick bites at the back of my tongue, but I swallow it. I'm growing more accustomed to its waves, more able to resist them for a few minutes at least.

"If King Alden makes good on his threat, we will fall," Mother says.

"So we shall keep him from doing that." Lord Denidor eyes me for a long moment.

"No," Finn and Mother say in unison.

In my spinning thoughts, I have missed something.

"It is the simplest way to solve our problem," Lord Denidor says. "Give him what he wants, and he will drop the threat."

Lord Denidor wants to turn me over.

The moment the thought occurs to me, it seems so blindingly obvious. I am very nearly far enough along that Father can't destroy the pregnancy without killing me along with my babies. He'll be furious, and I cannot expect kind treatment, but it will save Mother, save all these people. It is the simplest, cleanest, clearest solution.

I will lose all chance at happiness, but having had that for even the short time I did is a blessing I never expected. If this is all I can get, I'll warm myself with the memories on my cold throne.

"I will not abandon my daughter to him a second time. Not when I have just gotten her back." Mother throws her words at Lord Denidor like knives. "I did not even believe violence was the way to proceed. This is your war, yours and Zdenko's. You will find another way around."

The burning in Mother's eyes will comfort me when I meet the ice of Father's, but my decision is made.

41

SACRIFICE

Finn

WE LEAVE THE COUNCIL MEETING WITH NO ANSWERS. ANDRIJA, WHO I'M starting to believe might just be an idiot, seems convinced we can send Alden a fake prince. Denidor didn't suggest a plan other than sending Xandra away. Zdenko kept offering more and more brutal military methodologies to keep Alden on the other side of the river—which Luna Maris mostly refused, even though she looked more tired and resigned every time she did. It was a slice of what every council meeting here has been like, I could tell.

Except for Xandra, sitting beside me and clinging to my arm, getting paler and paler. I couldn't believe she didn't collapse when Sime reported the message, much less that she didn't leave to get sick. The meeting stretched so long that people had to bring us lunch, and exhaustion drags her steps.

I start to lead her back to our room without saying anything. She has to lie down, and she has to know that.

She shakes her head. "We need… to talk. Go somewhere private."

One glance at her face tells me there's no point in arguing. She looks like she's going to be sick any second, but her jaw is set, and so are her brows. Elian's advice echoes through my mind. Fucking useless.

I lead her toward the southeast edge of the wall. It's being built facing the Grayhead, so from southeast to northeast. A few spans here, at the farthest edge, are complete, towering ten feet in the air, but work is happening to the north, and the span directly to the south is still only about a foot tall. I help her cross it, then lean her against the finished wall so she can catch her breath.

My chest aches, maybe the mark, as I look at her. She's passed pale and gone straight to gray, the red in her auburn hair making her look like a day-old corpse. Every movement trembles. She doesn't even fight me when I lower her to sit on an abandoned, rotted log. Long moments of ragged breathing pass, and the slice of her visible collarbone only makes me sick. She hasn't been eating enough for three, and it is starting to show.

Finally, she lifts her head off the wall and looks at me. "We have to leave. Elian and Vedran should stay, assist however they can, but —"

"No."

Her exhausted eyes spark. "You're not even willing to listen to me?"

"Look at you!" I gesture vaguely at her. "One meeting and a walk across town. That's more than you can handle."

"That meeting was monstrously long and directly followed one of the worst pieces of news I've ever received." Weakly, she crosses her arms. "I think I am doing miraculously well, and you should take this as a positive sign."

"Conjure enough water to see yourself in, then tell me that." Those hot words burn in my throat again. "And no matter what, he'll kill our babies."

She shakes her head. "I talked to Miralyn about how pregnancies end. If we evade his men for a little while, he will not be able to focus on Moonlight Hollow, and by the time we reach him, ending the pregnancy will sincerely risk killing me with it."

I stare at her. The light in her eyes looks manic, almost inhuman, like an escaped prickle of Vedran's magic. She can't actually be serious.

"We barely escaped them for a day and a half of straight fucking running."

"They knew where we started from," she replies.

The sun beats down on my shoulders, inflaming the heat inside me. "So you want to die."

"What?"

"If he cannot kill our babies, he will kill you."

"Father would never—"

"I've watched enough beatings to know!" I roar.

Xandra doesn't flinch. She blazes up in response. I cut her off before she can argue.

"Sometimes, Mother hit Raven like she wanted to pass the time, or like she wanted to teach a lesson, or like she was irritated. And sometimes, she hit her like she knew she was going to kill her someday, and she didn't particularly care if that day was today." I meet Xandra's gaze and hold it. "When he hit you, his shoulders were loose, his swing easy, his face liquid with rage. He wasn't holding back. The only thing that saved you was ending the pregnancy."

"I don't believe you." She spits the words like she can't get them out fast enough. "I think you'd say anything to keep me in bed."

"Have I been acting like that? Have I said shit about how much time you spend running around?" I pace the ground in front of her, trying to work off some of the burning. It doesn't abate. "I would keep you in bed if I could—for your safety, and theirs. Does that make me such a monster?"

"Ignoring me does." Xandra struggles to her feet. I lurch forward, grab her arm for support as she sways, and she glares at me. "Treating me like I'm going to break does. Would you have treated Xander like this?"

I don't let go. Better she be furious with me than collapse out here. "Maybe I fucking should've."

She laughs acidly. "You would have looked like a fool. I did not need you then, and I don't now."

"I would expect you to be a better liar after all this time." Despite her glare, she leans heavily on my hold, clearly needing it.

"And I would expect you to be a better listener." She looks out at the trees in the distance, not tired out but still alive with anger. "If you won't come with me, I will go alone. I would rather have these babies, raise them, and live a life with them. When Father dies, you could even return to court. But I won't let these people die on my behalf just because you say so."

Then go. The words boil behind my lips. I want them, need to taste their bloody barbs scraping over my tongue. It's what she deserves. She doesn't listen to me—to anyone–and obviously, she needs to make her own mistakes to figure out she should. Let her discover just how much of a mess she's going to find herself in without me watching her back.

Ready to get out of your own way now? Elian asks in my memory.

That might be what I want to say to her. Hell, it might be what she deserves. I don't know. But that's what she's expecting—that, or me rolling over to do whatever she wants. Because she wasn't just raised male, she was raised as a prince. Crown prince. I remember just how fucking spoiled Kieran used to be; it was like everything in the castle existed only to please him, and if it didn't, it better get out of his way.

"I don't want you to do that," I say simply.

She huffs a breath. "When you are ready to tell me something I don't already know, you can find me packing up my things."

"No, I—" Words. Fucking words. Of course, that would be what I needed in the end.

I love you.

Those are too big. Too much. I don't even really know if they're true or if they're just the biggest thing I can say right now.

"It's not that I don't trust you," I say instead.

"Oh, we're having this conversation again." She rolls her eyes.

"Can you please listen?" I snap.

She looks at me, surprise plain on her face. "I don't think I've ever heard you say please before."

"Don't get used to it," I grumble. "I trust you. Completely. I know you'll make the best choice according to your priorities and carry it through to the best of your ability."

"But I have silly priorities that don't include your rules." She shakes her head. "Finn—"

"They include me," I blurt. "They just don't include you."

She blinks. Clearly, she wasn't expecting me to say that.

"I don't want to control you." The words come easier now, not pretty but true. "I think that's bullshit, and neither of us would enjoy it. But your whole life, you've come last. After your people, after your parents, after your legacy. I don't want to control you; I just want you to have someone telling you that you belong higher on that list."

"I'm the crown prince," she says, almost like a shield.

"You're Xandra. My mate. And you're at the top of my priority list." I stroke my thumb along the soft skin of her arm. "All I ever want is to put you at the top of yours. Honestly, forget about having me on there, if that's what it takes. Just include you. Sometimes."

She looks at me, and I watch something break in her eyes, but softly, like an egg cracking as a chick tries to escape. Fuck, I feel naked. More naked than I do without my clothes. All the soft parts are laid out, waiting for her to smash them.

She sways and then sits without my having to suggest it. "If I were higher on my list—"

"I wouldn't have shit to say about what you do." I crouch in front of her.

She takes a long, slow breath. Then another. "That… makes sense."

"Thank the Goddess," I say.

Xandra offers me a tired smile. "You really trust me?"

"With my life." Now, that's easy to say. "Just not with yours."

She leans forward and kisses me, just as soft as the break in her eyes or the heart I dropped on the ground in front of her.

4 2

———

TOGETHER

Xandra

I don't intend anything when I kiss Finn, other than to steal his words away. They taste like my first sip of sourplum brandy, warm as the covers on a cool night but burning all the way down. Safe and terrifying in a single breath.

So I try to swallow them with the ginger-and-moss taste of his mouth, but that's the very same. Warm, soft and sharp. My impossible mate.

He is right. In my life, I have always come last. Perhaps someone telling me I should feels an awful lot like control. The line between that and freedom is far thinner than I thought.

I kiss him again, drinking down the pain-pleasure of his mouth alone. He grabs my hips, hard fingers softening at the last moment as he realizes I am something he wants to be careful with.

"No." The word garbles against his lips, and painfully, I pull back. "No. Do not treat me like that."

"Like I,"—he swallows—"care about you?"

His unfinished sentence bursts in my chest. "Like I'm not your equal."

"Are you saying you'll never be gentle with me?" He smirks.

"Not if you talk to me like that." I kiss the smirk away. "And I'm telling you that you already know how to make me scream. Isn't that letting you take care of me?"

His pale eyes darken with the implication, and his hands tighten on my hips. "Oh, I'll take care of you."

In one smooth motion, he drags me off the log and lays back in the emerald grass. I sit straddling his hips with a soft jolt that, yes, does make my head spin. He eyes me for a moment, then rolls us over.

A heartbeat passes. He waits for me to object. Goddess, I want to, but he's right. Again. So, instead, I answer by dragging my blouse up over my head and starting on the tie to my skirt.

He needs no further invitation. Heat prickles down my spine as his mouth crashes back down onto mine. His whole body melts into mine—warm, heavy, and familiar. Mine.

I tear through the tie on my skirt and begin on his pants as we kiss like this is our last chance. Like he holds my last breath of air between his teeth, like I am the last meal he will ever eat. Heat turns to an incandescent burn, and I remember why I still drink sourplum brandy.

Sometimes, the best thing one can do in this life is burn. Hot, bright, and fast. Defiant of what the world decrees for you. Finn sinks teeth into my lower lip and pulls back sharply with a lance of pain. I take the split second he's away from me to meet his gaze.

No, the best thing in life is not to burn. It's to burn together with someone one… cares about.

I wrap my arms around Finn's neck and bite him back until I draw blood hotter than his words, colder than the fire building between my legs. My tongue slides along his lower lip before darting into his mouth, rich with ginger and moss.

"Xandra," he rasps, clutching at the layers of open fabric barely separating us.

His cock juts against my hip, and I grind against it. He blows out a sharp breath through gritted teeth.

I want to have time. To go slowly, to enjoy every second. But we weren't given the luxury of mating during peacetime. Our story is one of war, one of stolen seconds between battles. Of protecting each other when we cannot protect ourselves.

Moments together can feel like lifetimes when it's the right person on top of me, panting his breath into my mouth, dripping his sweat onto my forehead. I grab at every inch of Finn I can reach just to be closer, and he hisses when I scratch.

"Everyone is going to know," he murmurs against my lips.

"Good." I spread my legs, welcoming him between them.

He slots into place. I reach into his pants, free his cock, and stroke it to the rhythm of our mouths. The rhythm of our heartbeats. The judder in his kiss sends fire curling through my veins.

I need him. In all the physical ways my body screams at me and so much more. Words can't contain the gulf of need I didn't even realize hid behind my ribcage until he looked at me and told me I always came last.

Not anymore.

Finn thrusts his cock inside me in one smooth motion. A moan tears from my throat, barely smothered by his mouth, and my muscles squeeze around him in something terrifyingly like relief. His hands roam over my body as I wrap my legs around him, and he sets a punishing pace. Grass around me turns into nothing but green smears as he fucks me into the dirt, ruthless and hungry and like this is everything he, too, has been waiting for.

Every thrust pushes me closer to the apex. My breath comes in shallow rasps. He groans, mumbling wordless nothings against me. Our kiss devolves into an excuse to keep ourselves as close as possible, both of us too far gone to remember anything but the fire building between us.

"Finn!" I shout, my back arching off the grass. Pleasure rips my body to shreds and laces it back together again slightly new in a spasm of tingling skin and clenching muscles. He digs his nails into my sides as he slams home one last time and follows me over the edge.

I open my eyes and find him looking down at me with delicate, dazed love.

Soon, he rolls off me, and I lie in the grass on my side, just watching him. Vedran's magic is fading, as it usually does. We ought to go to him to refresh it, but I can't imagine getting up yet. Not when Finn is here, when we're together, and when no one can reach us for a brief moment.

Finn's hair is growing out, corn silk strands clouding his icy eyes. He is so pale, as if he were born to fade into the background as he so likes to. I trail a finger over the curve of his bicep, up the breadth of his shoulder. Anyone who overlooks him is a fool.

"I noticed you before you noticed me," I say.

He raises a spent eyebrow. I smile.

"From across that very first ball. You noticed me after I began making a ruckus, right?"

He nods.

"I saw you when I walked in."

The memory spreads out before my eyes. One of the first formal balls Father let me attend after Kieran took the throne, and our world started knitting itself back together. In a sweltering room full of royals in glittering gowns and perfectly tailored jackets, the night breeze whispering in through the windows was not nearly enough to offset the body heat of the crowd. I thought my heart might crawl out of my mouth. I'd never seen so many people who didn't owe Father their loyalty—I was going to be caught.

Some squire bugled our arrival. Every face in the room turned toward us. King Alden's mysterious son, finally out in the world? They had to see him—me.

Every face, that is, except one.

"You didn't turn when they announced us," I say.

"Apologies?"

I shake my head, savoring that first sight of his broad shoulders in a dark jacket, the pale fuzz of his hair barely contrasting his skin. I knew, right then, that I needed to make him talk to me that night.

"It made me want to know you." I trace the angle of his jaw. "To find out how you didn't care."

He snorts. "Stubbornness, mostly."

"I know that now." I shove him gently. Exhaustion still slows me down. Perhaps I will rest after this. "Then, it was mysterious."

"How mysterious is it that I was avoiding your father?"

"Why?" Curiosity sparkles through me.

"I bet you a kiss you can guess." He twirls a lock of my hair around one of his fingers.

"He raked you over the coals for impropriety last you saw him?"

"Kieran did the raking after we left, but basically." He laughs. "I wasn't in the mood to get into trouble."

"Well, I was." I steal the kiss I've earned from his lips, but now that he's been mentioned, Father hangs in the air between us. Silence falls, drags. It's hard to think of anything but the message he sent.

"How did he know we were here?" Finn asks eventually.

I tug my blouse back into place. "As Lord Andrija said—"

"Andrija's an idiot," he says dismissively. "And Alden is a perfectionist. This is the last place he wants you to be—he would've gone through every kingdom to the east and northeast before turning here."

He's not exactly wrong. As much as my being here poses a risk to Mother, it is perhaps more dangerous to Father. If he knew anything about what Mother was actually doing, he would know how it would appeal to me. I frown. "Are you suggesting someone informed him we were here?"

Finn shrugs. "I don't exactly have any proof."

A conversation floats back to me, one I haven't made any sense of yet. "I overheard one of the lords talking to someone I couldn't see. He said it was not what they agreed to, and that the stranger had promised some strange word would… do something."

"Strange word?"

That was the day we last fought, when I was running away from everything Finn had said. Combined with my earlier faint, I don't remember much of it. "Astra-something?"

His eyebrows jump like tiny frogs. "Astralis?"

"Yes!" I grin for a heartbeat. "How did you know that?"

"I found a note in the Old South Tower—"

My heart skips a beat. "You entered it?"

"Is now really the time for superstition?" He shoots me a dry look.

Every time is the time for ill-luck superstitions, but I would rather hear what he found than be teased. I'll fix the issue of our luck tonight. With a shrug, I gesture for him to go on.

"I assumed it was ancient, but it said something about reaching M, doing something soon, and then Astralis."

"M for Maris?" I roll onto my back to give my aching arms a break.

"Potentially," he says. "Only one way to find out."

"Ask Mother?"

"I meant look into this in general. Clearly, whatever Astralis is has followed us here." Finn shifts up onto his side, as if he cannot endure being unable to see my face for longer than a moment. Lit by the sun like this, he doesn't look like the ice everyone accuses Dun's Crossing of. He looks like gold.

"I bet we can do it," I say with a smile. "Together."

Even though he didn't win, Finn brushes a kiss over my lips. "Together."

43

SEEING AND SEEN

Finn

A FEW DAYS AFTER XANDRA AND I TALKED OUTSIDE THE WALL, I DIVE AT Lieutenant Sime with my jaws open wide. He rolls out of the way with a soft grunt, reddish fur just whistling through my teeth.

"Good," General Zdenko says. "Now, push that advantage."

An advantage isn't one until you push it, Father says in my memory. *I thought you wanted to fight, Finn.*

Like I did back then, I shove both voices out of my mind and dart in the opposite direction of Sime's roll before he finishes. But he's too Goddess-damned fast; I'm not able to get behind him before he finds his feet again. His tail lashes, and he bares his teeth. I swipe out with a claw, hoping to steal a little distance from his gleaming canines.

Buy some time if you need to think, Anwen says, voice cracking with puberty.

Sime spots the heartbeat of hesitation and lunges. Fuck, he's fast. I don't have time to get out of the way.

I charge toward him, leading with my shoulder. Something crunches. Maybe his teeth.

"There it is!" Zdenko shouts. "This is a fucking brawl; stop fighting pretty."

Sime snarls with bloodstained, broken teeth. I scythe up with a claw instead of posturing. At the last second, though, I retract my claws. The blow still knocks him back with a hacking cough, but no matter what Zdenko says, we're sparring. Sime's on my side.

As much as I can believe anyone is before we know more about Astralis.

"All right," Zdenko calls.

I pad over to Lieutenant Sime and help him to his feet as much as I can without hands. By the look he shoots me, he can tell I'm thinking we're both on the same side, and he appreciates it.

Zdenko marches up to us, wearing a scarlet-hemmed tunic and leather armor so engraved in elaborate scrolling patterns reminiscent of their embroidery that it's difficult to believe he will never fight in it. Almost a shame.

Xandra thinks Zdenko is our best target because, of the lords here, he's the only one of an age to take the throne himself and enjoy a good, long reign. Andrija is pushing forty, and Denidor is older than that. She also can't stop holding his tactics against him. He is vicious—he only sounded pleased when I broke Sime's teeth—but I'm less sold. Zdenko strikes me as nothing more than a general. Smart, big-picture thinker, determined to do whatever it takes to get the job done, but not the kind of man who shapes dynasties.

Truth be told, if he wanted the throne this badly, I think he would have slit Xandra and King Alden's throats years ago.

"Lieutenant, admirable work, as always," Zdenko says. "Watch your back left—Silas may not have known enough to go for it, but others might." He nods sharply to Sime, who nods in return before trotting off to join the small crowd of wolves watching the example bouts Zdenko arranged for training today. "Silas."

His gaze is sharp on my fur. There are a lot of reasons I'm here. The wall doesn't need me today. Lying in bed with Xandra mostly leads to having sex, which certainly doesn't constitute the sort of rest Hana meant. I need to make sure nobody has a chance to ask me to tan anything, and with all the leaders marching around in leather, that gets harder and harder.

But most of all, Xandra is sure the person she heard mention Astralis was one of the lords, and her choice is Zdenko. I'm here to check him out. I stand patiently in front of him, waiting for him to wave me away because it's not like I'm going to listen to him.

"How has it taken this long for you to join our ranks?" He asks with a scraped sliver of a smile.

Flattery. I half-smother a yawn.

"Understood." He crosses his arms and looks me over. "Allow me to guess—you cut your teeth in bar fights?"

I nod. Easier than explaining how many of the world's finest tutors tried and failed to teach me anything.

"It shows. You're strong, and you know when to play dirty, but you fight like you're not quite sure where your hands went." He gestures at the other wolves. "There are many reasons we do not fight in human form, but that is an important one of them. We have nothing to miss. The sooner you get that straight, the sooner you become the fighter I can see." He turns on his heel to face the others. "Ante! Marko! Two minutes, then you fight."

I know a dismissal when I see one. But I am halfway back toward the waiting wolves before I realize why Zdenko bothered to give me advice—he doesn't know who I am. He doesn't look at me and see, as I once heard myself called, the Prince of Eye Rolls. He doesn't assume I've already stopped listening. That was why I was hearing Father and Anwen—they tried, for a little while, to convince me to listen. They gave up, of course, but they tried.

Strange. Just as strange as the faint glow of warmth the attention left behind.

I join Elian in the crowd. *"That's my bout done."*

"He said I fight enough," Elian huffs. *"None for me today."*

"Then should we get going?"

"No time like the present."

We peel off from the group, headed for the spot in the woods that has become the unofficial bathroom of those at the ring. I almost don't want to go, but I promised Xandra. Once we're out of sight, we loop back toward town. Fighting under Zdenko is one thing; I might be able to get a sense of his character, but nothing more. No, Xandra asked us to search Zdenko's room, once we had an alibi.

The lords each occupy a house adjacent to Luna Maris's "palace." Denidor to the west, Zdenko to the north, and Andrija to the east. Xandra pointed them out to me on our evening walk yesterday. She has been trying to rest more, but she says if she doesn't get out at least once a day, she's going to lose what little sanity she has left.

Maybe I've started looking forward to them.

"There." I nudge Elian toward Zdenko's house. Usually, a pair of soldiers would stand at the front and back gates, but ever since Alden's threat, there just aren't enough bodies to guard the perimeter and hold training simultaneously. His house is completely open.

We shift, and I grab the bag of clothes I stashed nearby. Once we're decent enough that any staff won't assume the worst upon finding us, I point at an open window on the second floor.

"Apparently, he's superstitious," I say, *"and that's the luckiest room in the house."*

Elian eyes the ten feet of stone wall below it, covered only by a vined trellis. *"Of course it is."*

We dart in through the gate and over to our makeshift ladder. Elian goes first—the wood creaks under his hands, which isn't promising for when I entrust my weight to it. But I stabilize the sides as he climbs, ducking low so no one walking by will see me until I realize the full-grown adult shimmying up the wall will probably catch any nearby eye.

With a final shudder, the trellis goes still. Elian shoots me a thumbs-up then grabs it from the top.

I promised Xandra.

Slowly, I scale the grid of aging wood. Splinters jut into my palms. It grumbles like it's waiting for a chance to dump me on my ass. Once, it actually starts to tip out from the wall, and Elian has to drag it back before I end up in Hana's house with a broken bone or three.

But somehow I make it to the top and scramble in through the open window—another superstition.

Inside looks more like a barracks than a noble's bedroom, except for the number of beds. A carpet that clearly used to cover the floor has been rolled up and leans against the wall. The fireplace lays dark —perfectly reasonable, in this heat—and a corner of a colorful, mosaic mantel peeks out from under the drab cloth thrown over it. A battered chest holds his clothes because the wardrobe is full of weapons he is forbidden to use. Maps plaster the walls over murals.

Elian whistles lowly. "Do you think he shits the war, too?"

I nudge him. *"Quiet. He might have staff."*

Looking at this, though, that's hard to believe. A few half-empty mugs sit here and there. Dirty clothes mound in a corner. No one is cleaning up after him.

With any luck, that means he hasn't bothered to get rid of anything incriminating.

"You start on that side." I gesture toward the fireplace. *"I'll take this one."*

"I'm keeping anything funny I find," he warns.

I don't bother telling him not to. Zdenko doesn't seem like a man with a sense of humor.

A bell rings in the distance. Vedran convinced everyone in Tarrin that it was a sacred tradition amongst his people to ring bells every fifteen minutes today. It was Xandra's idea. I watch Elian's eyes narrow and his focus sharpen. We get three of those, no more, and we have to be gone.

One down.

Sifting through layers of military errata, I can't believe they've only been in Tarrin for a few months. That, or I'll die before accepting an invitation to visit his manor. He must build up a mess around him like it's his job.

But I promised Xandra. And I promised her that I would do this so she didn't have to. So we could scratch Zdenko off our list and figure out who we're really dealing with—or, I suppose, confirm that she's right.

At the second bell, I ask Elian through the mind-link, *"Have you found anything?"*

"I'm not sure," he replies. *"What the hell is this?"*

I turn to see him holding what looks like a strip of bark off what Xandra called a laughing cedar. Scratched—or maybe burnt—onto it are….

"Letters. And, let me guess, they don't make any sense?"

He nods. "Like someone threw a dictionary at a tree."

I smirk. "I know where we need to go."

* * *

"In the Old South Tower, I read a pamphlet on how to pass messages more securely than letters when mind-links couldn't be trusted." I lead Elian to a laughing cedar with thick, blue-green moss on only one half of its trunk. "Do you have a knife?"

He hands it over. I didn't exactly leave with one, and Silas has little more than what he showed up with. Carefully, I cut away the bark just below the moss.

"This moss is a natural adhesive. They pull the bark off, write on it, and then paste it back in place." After a few slices, a long strip falls away—marked all over with more dark letters. "And for a little extra security, they encode it."

Elian stares at me as I replace the letters with their opposite from the other end of the alphabet, and a message starts to take shape.

"Lightning," it reads. *"Much has changed. Meet me when the demon's roadweed kisses the Gray."*

I have to ask Xandra, but I think that's tonight.

4 4

VOICES IN THE DARK

Xandra

"The symbol of Lord Denidor's house is lightning," I grumble as I wedge myself into the Y-shaped branch Finn has picked out for us to watch this meeting from.

"All the more reason to be here." Finn scans the horizon intently. "Since we found the first bark in Zdenko's room."

The branch squishes my hips in a way I know means I will have to relieve myself before long. "And what reason would Lord Denidor and General Zdenko have for using this method of communication?"

"Mind-links within Moonlight Hollow have been spotty, too," Finn replies.

I bite down on my sigh and settle in. Below us, as it always does before the full moon, the Grayhead starts flooding its banks just enough to reach the itching roadweed leaves curled around the base of the reedy graylaurels. Parsing the message was so easy, I have to wonder why they bothered to encode it at all. And this secret trunk method Finn dredged up, I don't believe it has been used since the Old South Tower was sealed. There is no reason for General Zdenko, a modern man for all his flaws, to use any of this. And yet, the first strip of bark was in his room. None of this makes any sense.

But Finn brought the information to me as soon as he had it. When I told him I would also be watching the meeting, he only asked for time to make sure we could hide safely. And, for all I am beginning to develop a very personal hatred of this branch, it is safe. It barely rustled when I lowered my growing weight onto it.

In the same way Finn agreed to search General Zdenko's room, though, I know he believes other suspects are more likely, I'll watch this meeting and see what comes of it. Because he came to me. Because he asked.

"How long do we have left?" Finn pushes pale hair out of his face.

I close my eyes. I've only read about this happening, but I can feel the water as if it's humming under my skin. "Half an hour, perhaps."

He hums. "How should we pass the time?"

"I could explain to you all the political reasons why it makes no sense for Lord Denidor to be at the heart of this." I open my eyes and smirk at him. "His son, Petar, isn't quite able to take the throne legally, did you know? And yet, he's close enough that no one would accept Denidor on the throne."

"But—" Finn shakes his head with a smile. "Nope. I am not having this conversation again."

"Damn." I laugh. "I almost had you."

"Almost." He looks at me, eyes soft in the moonlight. "Are you sure this is comfortable for half an hour?"

"Comfortable?" I rub my rumbling stomach. "Certainly not. But survivable."

His gaze drops to my hand. After a long moment of quiet, he says, "Have you started thinking about names?"

No. The answer leaps to my lips, but even as I think it, I know it's a lie. I thought about names when I was a child, skimming ancient family trees. When we fled Tansy Tower. The moment Hana said the word *twins*.

"Here and there," I reply.

His answering smile is soft and grateful. "So have I."

"Tobias?" I guess.

"I'd have to call him Toby." The branch underneath us quivers softly as we both laugh. "What are you thinking?"

Which to tell him? "I've always liked Maja. Perhaps Maja and Mislav, if they are a boy and a girl?"

Finn screws up his face. "Mislav? Do you want him to be teased mercilessly?"

I swat him. "Mislav was my great-grandfather's name, and he wore it proudly."

"I bet it was easier to be proud of a hundred years ago." He shakes his head. "I am not calling my son Mislav. What about Caleb?"

This time, I grimace. "That sounds like an herb no one wants in their poultice."

Rustling leaves don't cover his laughter. "I was almost named Caleb."

"And it's rank egotism." I grin at him. "No Caleb. But you don't mind Maja?"

"Well, that depends." He runs his hand softly over my stomach. "Would she be called Maja Mlakar…or Maja Solberg?"

I whip my gaze up to him. That is two steps to the left of a proposal. In the forest dark, Finn's expression is unreadable, like water shadowed by overhanging branches. But he said it quietly, with that jagged edge of being wrenched from his throat. As if, until the moment the words left his lips, he wasn't quite certain he was going to say them.

"What if—"

We hear another rustle, louder than anything we've made in this tree. I freeze. Finn whirls toward the meeting place he had put his back to.

Stepping out of a bush and batting its grabbing branches away is Lord Denidor, for once without his undersecretary. He is unmistakable in the moonlight—graying hair, aristocratic posture rather than military, crisply clean clothes smudged here and there with the dirt of travel.

"He's early," Finn hisses under the roar of the river.

I nod. It is strange. Lord Denidor has always been punctual, but rarely early. That is an honor he reserved exclusively for meetings with Father alone. The meetings he deemed important enough to his advancement. As we watch, Lord Denidor fixes his hair in the tumultuous reflection of the Grayhead, then paces in tight lines.

"He's nervous," I murmur. Or at least, I believe he is. This is not a posture I have seen on Lord Denidor before.

Finn tenses. He starts to shift in front of me, then shifts back. My mark hums. He's listening. So will I.

Where he cannot see me, I shift ever so slightly behind him. Wedged as I am, I cannot escape quickly. Perhaps a little added protection isn't the worst idea.

Something splashes, and my heart leaps. The person Lord Denidor is meeting with is crossing the Grayhead? He is a traitor twice over? And as soon as the treasonous wolf speaking with him shifts, we will know who to blame.

But the second figure that steps out wears a cloak and walks on two human legs. I grit my teeth.

"Denidor," they say.

Lord Denidor bows slightly. "I would have expected a warning about Alden's threat."

"Why?" The other person laughs, though I can only tell by their shaking shoulders. The roar of the river strips out most of the sound of their voice. "You told me she was here. You had to know something would come of that."

"The queen is up in arms. She won't turn over the prince— princess." Lord Denidor begins pacing again as my blood boils. "I would like a kingdom for Petar to rule."

"Then we have to empty the thrones." The cloaked person shakes their head, and their hood shifts back. The profile of a face edges into view. A face I know far too well.

Caramel-colored hair. Pale brown eyes. Mother's chin.

The man Lord Denidor is planning the destruction of the whole kingdom with, the murder of myself and my parents with, is my own Beta.

My vision goes red. I lunge forward, hair prickling out of my skin in thick gouts as the shift starts to take me before I can even consciously think of it. I know how to defeat Corwyn better than any other wolf on this planet. He is a pile of smirking meat to me.

Strong hands catch my shoulders as the branch bounces. Finn's. I snarl at him. *"Release me!"*

It doesn't matter that we don't have a mind-link. He tightens his grip like he can read my mind. I reach up, claws shining sharp in the night air, and claw at the backs of his hands.

"What was that?" Denidor hisses.

Good. Let them come here.

Finn shoots me a look so sharp it even punctures the animal rage clouding my senses. I grab hold of my shift, arresting it midway. From his bag, he grabs a fistful of something and scatters it at the base of the tree just before Corwyn parts the bushes to search. A pair of small mammals dart out of the trunk to gather or inspect whatever it was.

"Chipmunks," Corwyn says dismissively. "Seems one of them dropped some nuts."

A low growl rumbles deep in my throat. How did Corwyn sneak by me for so long if he is this foolish? Finn remains taut next to me, one hand still on my shoulder. Corwyn releases the bushes and steps away.

"That seems quite a coincidence." Denidor doesn't look away from our tree. "I have never before seen chipmunks here."

"You're right." Corwyn rolls his eyes. "It is far likelier that Astralis's enemies trained a pair of animals to cover their tracks."

"I thought you said no one knew what Astralis was." Denidor's voice takes on an unfamiliar edge of panic. "This only works if no one knows."

"And it is a good thing your iron nerves are helping us keep that secret." Corwyn glances over his shoulder at the river. "Look, I have a long run back. You said you have news?"

"I am not sure we should—"

"I am not coming back," he replies with sharp finality.

Denidor looks at us—near us—again.

Quickly, Denidor lays out a sketch of the plans we have been making in the council meetings. He skips details, but not nearly enough that Corwyn does not have every shred of information he needs.

He always seemed to be two steps ahead of what Moonlight Hollow would do next.

"Drive them toward the southern end of the river," he says. "And quickly. Alden is ravenous. Keeping him on our side of the river has been harder and harder."

I blink. What—

"And the Alpha and Luna still live." Denidor nods, and revulsion crashes through me.

Corwyn is extending the war. Dragging out the blood until he has what he wants. My teeth grow until they bite into my lip, and copper blood stains my chin. Finn rubs soothing circles into my shoulder, as if that could even touch what I have learned about a man I once counted as nearly my brother.

"Astralis is nothing without our members in position." Corwyn claps Denidor on the shoulder. "Stay the course, and we will all get what we want in the end."

"Stay the course." Denidor repeats the words like a mantra.

Corwyn steps into the brush, and a few moments later, I hear that splashing again. He's gone. Denidor mumbles to himself, too soft for us to hear, before fleeing the clearing as well.

Finn releases my shoulder. The soft ache of a bruise hums into my knowledge. He looks at me, silently asking how furious I am with him.

My mind whirls. We know more than we would have, had he not stopped me.

But I am going to kill those two if it is the very last thing I do.

4 5

THICKER THAN WATER

Finn

"WHAT?" LUNA MARIS STRUGGLES UP ONTO HER ELBOW, SLEEP clouding her eyes and strands of her hair stuck to her cheek.

"Denidor, Mother," Xandra says urgently. "And Corwyn. They are working against the entire kingdom to not only create this war but drag it out as long as possible."

I stand by the window we climbed through, half-wishing this was happening in Dun's Crossing. Kieran would already be up, on his feet. He would have men charging for Denidor already, scouts headed into Tansy Beach to alert King Alden, on the off chance that might make a difference. I would know what to say to convince him.

She blinks once, twice. Xandra seizes an empty cup on the barrel serving as a bedside table, fills it with water, and holds it to her mother's lips. Luna Maris takes the cup and drinks slowly.

When she is done, she looks at each of us. "How sure are you?"

"Sure enough to wake you in the dead of night." Xandra straightens. "We saw them. We heard them say that they had to empty the thrones."

Luna Maris pales slightly. She doesn't look anything like a warrior queen now, just like every royal does when they remember this job comes with a reasonable expectation of premature death. Scared.

"And you have proof?" she asks.

"We have a message they sent to arrange the meeting," Xandra says.

"We can get it," I say. Elian and I returned the bark to the tree, so no one knew we'd seen it and the meeting would still happen.

Luna Maris purses her lips. "Anything else?"

"The word of two royals," Xandra says. "Notes in the Old South Tower—you know Corwyn always laughed at those superstitions."

"He did, but—" She sits up. "That is not enough to accuse these two in public. Corwyn is not even a member of my court."

Xandra raises her chin, looking surprisingly like Xander for the first time in a while. "Lord Denidor is, and a dangerous one. I know we can prove it, if an accusation is made and a search can be undertaken."

Moonlight hits both of their faces. Xandra has so many of her mother's features, but on her, they all look sharper. Like someone filed down the excess, leaving only the finest point behind. Xandra is an arrow, whistling toward her target. Luna Maris….

"Lord Denidor holds the allegiance of the majority of our men," she says.

Luna Maris just whistles. I've seen her type a hundred times. She was raised to mate up and reap the rewards, not to do anything after that. Mother tried to raise Candace to be one of those women. Luna Maris seems to have enough of a heart in her chest that the conditioning didn't quite work on her. But she's pretended it did for too long. She can rebel against King Alden, but not against the men supporting her rebellion.

"Traitorous men," Xandra hisses. "If they are his, we don't need them."

"And he has General Zdenko's ear," Luna Maris continues like she can't even hear her daughter. "So any we didn't lose in accusing Denidor would go when Zdenko sided with him."

"And if Father knew what he had in his own court—"

"He would pull your cousin in closer," she snaps. "Do not kid yourself. If he will lay hands on you, there is little else he won't do."

"I do not believe that." Xandra takes a step closer to her mother, her chin still high. "Is Moonlight Hollow not about finding a better way? We cannot just allow this to happen, allow Denidor to snap up the pieces when he empties the thrones."

Luna Maris takes her daughter's hand tiredly. "If I move against him now, I give him an excuse to take me out even sooner. Paranoid queen turns on her own, loses her mind in her fervor for so-called freedom. They will look like heroes for cutting me down. I believe you, my darling, but that means nothing."

There it is. I'm sure Xandra is right—a full search would turn up enough to prove what Denidor is doing. The bark is an old method, but it wasn't that difficult to figure out. And Luna Maris doesn't have the guts to take that risk.

"But—"

I step forward and put a hand on Xandra's shoulder. "We all need rest."

She wheels on me, eyes blazing, for the second time tonight. I don't have the words to convince her. I just know that look in Luna Maris's eyes. I've practiced it enough. Resignation. The boredom of a creature that's found itself caught in the same old trap. For all Xandra's fire, there's no use in fighting.

"All right." Xandra's free hand clenches and unclenches. "Be on your guard, at least, Mother."

"I always am," the Luna replies.

We leave the way we came in—out the first-floor window, dodging patrols until we reach the garden gate, and jumping that into Tarrin proper. As soon as our boots touch dirt, Xandra explodes.

"We cannot just allow them to get away with this!"

"And I don't intend to." I start leading her toward our quarters. We really do need rest. "But you weren't going to make her understand."

Xandra shakes her head. "You don't know her like I do."

"I know royals. I know what my mother would've done." I shrug.

"Even rebel kingdoms are stagnant. It takes something—or someone —exceptional to change that."

"I don't believe that." She sets her jaw, fury still burning. The backs of my hands ache from where she clawed them.

She is that someone exceptional. That truth pounds through me, steady as a heartbeat. If somebody had woken her up with the same news, she would be on her feet. King Alden is a moron for many reasons, and one of them is wasting her like he did.

"Your mother is not our only option," I say.

She raises an eyebrow. "This, from the man who wouldn't let me murder them both when we had a chance?"

"She said we didn't have enough proof." I shrug as we step up to the door. "We can find that proof."

"You saw how alert Denidor was. His manor will be guarded endlessly, perhaps even warded."

"Can we convince him we're on his side?" I lower my voice as we step into the converted hall. The heavy hush of a few dozen sleeping people hangs in the air, punctured only by arrhythmic snores.

"I doubt I could," she murmurs. "And I doubt you're enough of a liar."

I want to object, but just picturing the man makes my teeth itch to tear his throat out. In the tree, I was holding myself back as much as I was holding her.

"We could win over one of his secretaries?"

Xandra and I toss plans back and forth all the way to our tiny room in whispers. We undress while discussing if it's worth attempting to fake evidence. She argues that planted proof is likely to fall apart as we slide into bed together. I suggest Kieran might loosen his moratorium on getting involved if he knew what was really going on while her eyes start to flicker shut.

Midway through a sentence, no closer to an answer than when we were in Queen Maris's room, Xandra's words stumble into nothing-ness, and her mouth goes slack. She's started passing out nearly the moment her head hits the pillow. That's just proof that she should be resting more.

But my mind won't shut up. It races like a pup chasing its tail, spinning through options. Anwen would know what to do—if I could reach him. He was always the best schemer. Candace would know just how real Denidor's nerves are and how to use them against him. Kieran would bring the whole weight of Dun's Crossing down on traitors like Corwyn and Denidor. Even Ingrid would have some insane, explosive idea that would at least move us forward.

Once I'm sure Xandra is fully asleep, I slip out of bed. The cot creaks softly. She stirs, grabs my pillow, but doesn't wake. A little fresh air and movement will help.

I creep out into the night and just start walking. Distantly, in the back of my mind, a piece of me wonders if the others reach for the rest of our talents when in trouble. If Candace wishes for Kieran's diplomatic skill or Ingrid's bombast. Am I the only one who thinks about them when I get stuck?

Maybe that's why I end up being compared to them all the time. They all have specific, distinctive strengths. I have a lungful of night air and a restless mind.

Supplies of everything are low in Tarrin, but I'd give almost anything for a tavern. A drink, a laugh, and some music. Maybe Elian has something. He'll just about kill me for waking him up like this, but that might be worth it to get out of my own head for a minute.

My feet carry me toward the northern side of camp before I realize it's the murmur of voices drawing me there. They're upbeat rather than bleary with sleep. Maybe my wish has been granted, and someone has set something up.

I turn the last corner and remember a conversation I had with Lieutenant Hana earlier today. Another shipment of supplies, coming in late to ease the crossing. I traded shifts with Ilja, one of the other general laborers, when I found the message in Zdenko's room.

High, clear laughter slices through the night. Princess Joli again. Has it really been that long?

A few men laugh with her, and that sounds a hell of a lot better than anything else I have going on. I roll up my sleeves and saunter up.

"Need some extra hands?"

Joli lights up when she sees me, like I'm who she's been waiting for. "And here I heard you were too busy to bother with a lowly smuggler like me."

I frown. We've barely spoken. "Apologies?"

"Accepted." She flounces down off the edge of the cart—covered, this time—and toward me. "We always need more hands. You take the position inside and hand the supplies down to these other lugs."

That is the best way to do it, when we have the manpower. There's nothing exactly wrong with what she's saying, just a troublesome glint to her smile that, after the fucking night I've had, looks more like the shine off a knife than off a gemstone.

"Am I missing something?" I ask.

She laughs. "Oh, I knew I liked you. Go."

That is most certainly not an answer, but Ilja is looking at me like I have two heads, so I duck the one I have and climb into the cart. Like she said last time, no one else dares talk to a princess like I do, even if she doesn't much act like one.

Outside, the laughter spins up again—apparently, Ilja is such a comically poor card player that people are beating him between trips —and I roll out my shoulders. Joli is strange, but I sincerely doubt she's dangerous. She has none of Corwyn's or Denidor's political poise. Astralis, whoever else they may be, seems to prefer that in its operatives.

One box. Two. I beat Ilya at a hand of cards, then return to the cart.

"Don't hit me," someone says through the mind-link.

Not someone—Ingrid, crawling out from between two barrels with an impish smile on her face.

"Joli really is a great smuggler."

46

MEETING THE FAMILY

Xandra

Morning arrives far too quickly for how late I tumbled into bed. Sunlight pries at my eyelids, and the waking-up noises of the people around our small room hammer on my eardrums. Slowly, I sit up.

My first thought is, *I have to relieve myself.*

My second is, *Where is Finn?*

The covers next to me are undisturbed, the pillow undented. He came to bed with me last night. I may be tired, but I'm sure of that. My heart skips a few beats. He wouldn't have gone to face Denidor alone, would he?

The twins in my stomach make it very clear that relieving myself is a necessity, not something I can pause to consider like the whereabouts of my missing mate. I hurry to the small bathroom I now share with everyone else sleeping here; luckily, the swell of my belly lets me cut the line of morning shufflers.

I return to the room and find no new signs of Finn. Bruises stand out, round and purple, where he grabbed my shoulder. Last night, I

289

could only think of how he was restraining me—how angry was he? I throw on a blouse and skirt and warn Vedran we will likely be late for our usual enchantments this morning through the stuttering mind-link.

A pair of voices puncture the quiet morning clamor. They're not any louder than the others, really, just sharper. Tinged with the hard edge of argument—and too far away for me to hear any details yet. I pad to the door and press my ear against it.

Smells fill my nose. Some, bathroom-ward, I push aside. Through the fog of other bodies, I smell what I'm hoping for—ginger and moss.

Finn. Alive. And angry.

The voices draw closer. The other is higher, lighter. Finn sounds more animated than he is with anyone but me and Elian. I frown.

"You heard Joli," the higher voice says. "Taking me back is going to be much harder."

Princess Joli? The smuggler?

Finn groans. "Harder doesn't mean impossible."

The board right outside our door creaks, and I shoot back before one of them can open the door directly into my face. Finn steps in first, a sleepless night hanging in heavy bags under his eyes. Behind him—

"Princess Ingrid?" I say disbelievingly.

She bounces in. "Apparently, I'm not supposed to be called that here."

Finn rubs his face and sits on the bed. Instantly, I understand a few important details. However, and why ever, Princess Ingrid has arrived here, Finn has spent the whole night trying to convince her to go back and failed.

"Should I take that to mean you're staying?" I bow—out of habit.

She fakes a curtsy, though she wears a pair of grubby, masculine trousers. "I seem to be bringing my dear brother around to that point."

"Tell her," Finn says. "You wanted to meet her so badly; tell her why you're here."

"I did want to meet you." Ingrid looks me up and down slowly, appraisingly. "Properly, I mean."

I straighten, despite my mussed hair and half-tied clothes. "You have met me. Properly, I mean."

"I met you as Xander." She drifts slightly to the left, then to the right. A barely subtler version of circling me. "Not Anica."

"Xandra," I correct. "And if you think I am not who I was then, you're going to find yourself badly mistaken."

She meets my gaze. Her eyes are the same blue as all the true Solbergs, but on her, they make me think more of cloudless skies than frozen lakes. No less exacting, no less sharp. Just deceptively safe—at first glance. Princess Ingrid has a reputation as the least welcoming Solberg for a reason. I've even heard some call her the missing princess because of how little she is sometimes seen.

"What is Finn's worst trait?" she asks.

A test. A challenge. Certainly not what I need this morning, but Ingrid gives the strong sense of someone who would not let Finn or anyone else dictate the timing of this.

"His defensiveness," I reply. "And his best is his thoughtfulness."

"Thoughtful?" She snorts. "Have you met Finn before?"

"And how was Kieran before Raven?" I step closer to her. "Anwen before Estrella?"

She eyes me for a long moment.

Then, she throws her arms around me. "I knew I was going to like you."

"Next time you suspect you like a pregnant woman, I would advise against an early morning quiz." Still, I hug her back. Accepting affection like this still feels strange, but there's something about Ingrid that makes her undeniable. A bit like a cat who has decided they like you; earning that is enough of a chore that refusing them any attention they deserve seems cruel.

"Is he really thoughtful now?" she murmurs in my ear.

"The most thoughtful," I reply, looking over her shoulder at him. He has his head in his hands, but he is peeking out through his fingers, and I can see the sliver of his smile. For all his dramatics, he's pleased. He wanted her to like me–and for me to like her.

No matter what I told her, this is the first member of his family I've truly met. Something zings inside me. Ingrid may, someday, be my sister-in-law.

How strange.

She releases me. "I am here to help with the war effort. Once I heard Finn was here—"

"You heard that?" My eyebrows shoot up.

"King Alden sent a letter." She waves her hand dismissively, like this is not world-shaping news. "Anyway, once I heard that, I figured there was more to this civil war than a land dispute, and I was bored."

"You were bored." I look at Finn again. He shrugs helplessly. This is how the missing princess acts around those she has chosen, it seems. More like a kitten than a cat.

She nods. "Joli made a joke, last I saw her, so I reached out to see if it was true, and it was, and now I'm here!"

"She is not here to help with the war effort," Finn says tiredly. "She can't even fight."

"I've been working on it." She crosses her remarkably thin arms. "But, fine, he said I'd be more useful with some kind of scheme the two of you are cooking up?"

"She will be." This, Finn says with a heavy note of certainty. Whatever impression he fears Ingrid is making, he is telling me, she is clever and competent. And I believe it. Only rarely have I met royals who seem this flighty without hiding something underneath.

"All right." I look out our narrow window, bisected by one of the makeshift walls, at the rising sun. "But first, I am due to see Lieutenant Hana."

"The healer," Finn tells Ingrid. To me, he says, "I'll take her to Zlata for a job."

Zlata, our quartermaster, won't know what to do with Ingrid. "Can I say she is your sister?"

"Ma'am, yes, ma'am." Ingrid salutes me teasingly.

I leave for Lieutenant Hana's with a soft smile on my face. Ingrid is going to complicate our already precarious situation. There are only so many royals we can pack into one war camp before someone starts wondering if Tarrin isn't hiding Prince Xander after all. But the ease with which she accepts that I am the man she met and the woman she is meeting now goes a long way to make up for any trouble.

* * *

Lieutenant Hana opens her door, her dark red hair pulled loosely away from her face.

"Good morning." I slip inside.

"I would be better if I hadn't sat up all night with the Balogs' squalling infant."

I hop up onto the table, as she has always asked me to do so far. "I don't believe I've met them."

"You would not have. They live in Alnwick, up the river." She pulls down her usual array of metal and stone implements.

"So you traveled?" Since I won't rest, she—and Finn—have insisted on weekly appointments. This is my third, since fainting, and I am beginning to adjust to her. Small talk seemed far from the realm of possibility, at first. She is even busier and more businesslike than Miralyn. But every question I have asked is met with a frank, sometimes even voluble, response. I've learned she grew up in an apothecary, that she has a mate trapped in Tansy Beach, and that she was a laundress in the palace. "How? The Grayhead is treacherous this time of year."

"Not for me." She grins proudly as she gestures for me to lift my shirt. "And certainly not for *Laurel*."

I obey her instruction, and she smooths something cold over my exposed stomach. "I thought your mate's name was Julija."

"It is." She smiles. "*Laurel* is my ship. You remember how I said I grew up in an apothecary?"

I nod and lean back.

"Floating apothecary. We sailed up and down the Grayhead, stopping for a few days in every town, administering to whoever needed us." She gestures to the walls of bottles. "These all come from her. My brother kept her in dock, never took to the trade. The first thing I did when I got here was hunt him down, and he told me to take the whole damn ship."

"Is there anything you cannot do?" I wince slightly as she presses down on my stomach. Perhaps another trip to the bathroom is in order shortly.

"More than I can count." She smiles wryly. "But I suppose a healing, fighting ship captain is a bit impressive."

"A bit." I laugh. "I read books and write letters, nothing more. For half your skills, I'd sell anything I own."

She shakes her head. "The twins feel strong. One of them has opinions about all the pushing. I wouldn't guess that you could feel it yet, but he's kicking me."

"He?" My breath catches. I have a son.

"I would guess." She shrugs. "All old wives' superstitions, though. His size, his activity, how low you're carrying."

A son. He springs fully formed into my mind's eye—Finn's hair, his sharp cheekbones. My eyes, the Mlakar nose. Our son.

Tears prick at my eyes. With a smile, Hana offers me a handkerchief and continues her examination. Not a mocking smile, either, like I might've expected from someone like her. Someone accomplished and worldly. She smiles at me like she's watching a dear friend receive good news.

Perhaps I have managed to make a friend.

47

TRADING BLOWS

Finn

"Duck!" I snarl at Ingrid through the mind-link as my blunted practice sword, courtesy of Lightning Cape, slams into her shoulder again.

"That's a little high for ducking." She flips a thick braid over her shoulder and huffs out a breath. "Shouldn't I parry?"

"Someone as strong as me would smash through any defense you managed to pull up, and then it would just be your own sword in your neck." I shove sweat-soaked hair out of my face. "I thought you said you'd been training."

"I've been training for one year." She lowers the tip of her sword to the grass. "That does not exactly replace a lifetime."

Irritation surges through me once again that Candace and Ingrid were only given the bare essentials. She knows where to put a dagger to disable someone in close quarters, knows how to run and howl for help… the rest, she's scraped out for herself over the past year.

"And I'm not much of a trainer." But I'm not exactly going to turn her over to Zdenko, and though Elian offered, I know they would end up talking about jousting instead of anything else. "All right. When you are facing a stronger opponent—"

"Who says you're stronger than me?" She smirks and curls her arm to show off a more impressive swell of muscle than I anticipated.

I roll up the sleeve of my loose tunic and show her mine. Nearly twice the size.

"See?" she says, like she was right.

I shake my head. "When you are facing a stronger opponent, don't waste your energy parrying. They're always going to break through it. You want to dodge and get inside their guard."

"People keep saying that but never tell me how." An edge of real frustration creeps into her voice.

"How?" my childish words echo in my mind. *"I know what, Father, but how?"*

"Figure it out, Finn. Kieran needs prep before we meet with the envoy."

I take a deep breath. "You need a hole in their guard, which is hard, but not impossible to get without parrying. Put your sword up. I'm going to be you. You be the stronger opponent."

That makes her smile. She settles into a workable defensive stance and beckons me forward.

I fake left and then lunge right. Her sword cleaves down where I would've been. With the momentum of my movement, the momentum of her swing, I hit the side of her knee, bare-knuckled. She yelps as her leg crumples for a heartbeat. With an armored shoulder, I knock her sword away just enough to get in close and pull a dagger from my belt. Almost before she has her feet back underneath her, I press the equally blunted blade to her throat.

"Damn," she mumbles.

"That was a combo I came up with when I was younger." I pull the dagger away and step back. "When everyone else was still stronger than me."

"You came up with it?" She rubs her throat. "I would've expected a move like that from Anwen."

"He always went for the tutor's bad knee. But sometimes, you don't get to do the careful lead-up and watch your enemy until you find their weakness. Everyone's knee is bad if you hit it right."

She nods and pulls her waterskin off her belt. After a few sips, she pours more on her face. "So, you watched him while you were training?"

I look away. It's easier than saying that I watched him from a high tower because the tutor had strict priorities, handed down by Father: Kieran got the most time, then Anwen, then me.

"Ah." But I don't need to say it. She grew up there, too. "Well, then I'm surprised we didn't run into each other."

"You watched him, too?" I raise an eyebrow at her.

"All three of you." She shrugs. "Whenever I could. Mother kept me busy."

Ingrid and I have never been close. She had Candace, her hobbies, and Mother's attention most of the time. I had myself. Until this moment, I've never considered that to be something of a blessing.

"Did you ever ask to join?"

She throws back her head and laughs. "Can you imagine? I think Mother might've dragged me out with Raven. Better off stealing glimpses—but you know that."

I look at my sister with new eyes. How many times were we watching the same things from different windows? How many of her activities, her endless hobbies, were to fill the time until our family needed her again?

"That's why I'm here," I say slowly.

"To get better at fighting?" She caps her waterskin and grabs her sword again.

To stop watching from windows. Because Xandra and the twins mean there will always be a place for me.

"Certainly not if I'm sparring with you." I lift my sword. "Again. This time, try to get inside my guard."

She shakes her head. "All right, but—"

I hold up my hand. Footsteps rustle through the grass. When I turn, Lord Denidor and his constant undersecretary stand a few feet away from the ring we laid out roughly in sticks.

"Silas," he says. "And, what was it, Vivian? Please, do not let me interrupt. I was merely curious."

"That's him," I tell Ingrid through the mind-link.

She tenses, her knuckles going white around her sword. *"Then we'd better give him a show."*

"Damn right."

"Of course," I call.

Ingrid comes at me before I'm ready, brow furrowed in concentration. Too direct. Her feint looks like a misstep, not an actual change of direction. I bring my arm up to block her blow, and she spins away.

Denidor's gaze burns into my back. Anwen would want him to underestimate us. I want him scared.

I throw myself at Ingrid, chopping through the air in heavy swings. She weaves between them. I recognize her jousting footwork —steady, but complex and almost quicker than the eye can follow. Still, I manage to drive her so close to the edge of the circle that a twig snaps under her heel.

She grimaces. Then, she does something I'm actually not expecting: she throws her sword like a spear. I dodge it almost effortlessly, but by the time I've looked back at her, she is tumbling away in a forward roll.

"Dammit." I spin

Ingrid rolls to her feet, unarmed. But I'm off balance now. She goes left. I swing left.

And it was a fucking feint. She's already at my right, fist whistling into the tendons of my knee. Pain ribbons up my leg, braided tightly with tingling numbness. I falter.

Cold metal presses against my throat. Ingrid grins at me, chest heaving.

"Bad form to disarm yourself." I smirk at her. "But otherwise—"

"Otherwise, I fucking beat you!" Her grin is incandescent.

Denidor clears his throat behind us. Ingrid's smile dies. We both turn.

"I have never seen a fight quite like that." He takes a step forward, his hands folded behind his back. "Silas, I know you are a tanner, so handling a blade falls near your area of expertise, but Vivian, how did you develop such skills?"

"I'm a dancer," she says through gritted teeth. "I use ribbons in my routines. It's really not so different."

"Hmm." Denidor offers us a sharp sickle of a smile. "Two such talents in one family really is a blessing. Are your parents proud?"

"We lost them both," I reply. "There was a storm."

"How awful." I want to knock the look of mock pity off his face. "I suppose that is why Vivian moved here with you."

"It is." She slings an arm around my shoulder. "We're all each other has in this world."

"Such a fragile family line." He tuts. "But I am sure they watch over you from above."

Ingrid swallows a snort. Whatever our real parents are doing in the sky, there is very little kindly watching-over. More spitting and sneering, if I had to bet.

"As you've said, my sister and I are hardy enough." I lift the sword slightly, just enough to make Denidor retreat a step. As expected. In this place, he wouldn't know the difference between a blunted blade and a real one. "And my Anica is proof the family line is in no danger."

"That she is." He raises his hands, and a faint spray of water spatters across his face a heartbeat later, conjured from nothing. "Apologies. The heat."

It is sweltering out here, but Xandra mentioned him taking any excuse to show off his magic. I nod like I understand.

"You must miss home," he says.

"Our house was—"

"Dun's Crossing, I mean," he interrupts with a sly smile. "You are from there, are you not? I know I could never survive away from even my manor as long as you have. How many years was it again?"

"Three," I reply tightly. "You are right, Lord Denidor, about the heat. We really ought to stop for today."

Ingrid nods, barely not glaring at Denidor. I can't blame her. The more I look at him, the more I wish I'd let Xandra loose two nights ago. Let his blood water this dirt. Let his family line turn "fragile."

We turn away from him, and the hairs on the back of my neck prickle, but I don't look.

What was that he said about being unable to live without his manor?

OUTSIDE THE LINES

Xandra

"He said he couldn't live without it, Mother." I lean forward over the breakfast I've been picking at. One of the twins—our son, perhaps—apparently hates the smell of the tiny fish I used to love. "Why did you select Tarrin as your base camp, anyway?"

"Proximity to the border." She sips her tea primly, and I know she's lying.

"And proximity to Lord Denidor's manor?"

"He may have suggested this location because he was familiar with the townspeople." She sets her cup down. "But that's far from evidence, and if this costume has made you forget, you are the heir to now both kingdoms, in some ways. Entering the grounds of his manor could be seen as an act of war."

"If we are caught."

She scoffs. "I have perhaps never met a man more paranoid than Lord Denidor."

"So there is no point in trying?" I stare her down, trying to decipher her hesitation. Finn says there is no point in arguing with her, that she's resigned, but if that were true, she wouldn't have rebelled against Father in the first place. Right? "I thought this project meant everything to you. Defending it against an attack I swear to you is happening should be your first priority."

"He needs Moonlight Hollow to exist to be able to rule it, and I am not so foolish as to miss an assassination attempt," she says quietly. "Today, right now, my priority is to have a pleasant breakfast with my daughter."

It's slippery, but she's saying no. If I bring it up again, I run the risk of ending our twice-weekly breakfasts entirely. And when I haven't been pushing her to pursue Denidor, they've been…well, they've been a reprieve from the general tension that pervades the air here. Every day, reports come in that Father's scouts are getting bolder, trying harder to cross the river. No rumbles of troop movements follow behind; Mother sent an official denial of my presence in camp, but obviously, that won't hold against fucking Corwyn's word for long. She called me heir to both kingdoms, but I think there is no point in pretending any longer that Corwyn has not usurped my position in Tansy Tower.

"Now, how are my grandchildren?" Mother asks.

* * *

I brace my heels on the corners of Lieutenant Hana's table a week later. A week of nothing but stalling and denial.

"You're tense," she notes as she prepares her usual brew in a mortar.

"Everyone in Tarrin is tense," I reply through gritted teeth. "King Alden may attempt to 'liberate' Prince Xander at any moment."

Time hasn't decreased the frequency of scouts, either. One made it halfway across the Grayhead before being stopped yesterday.

"You have the queen's ear, do you not?" She exposes my stomach.

"I thought I did." No matter how I approach Mother, I always get the same answer—Denidor will not bring down Moonlight Hollow. Or so Mother says.

Cold rivers across my stomach as always. "And what would you try, if she would listen to you?"

I glance at her. I've never seen her closer than a stone's throw away from Denidor, but she takes her orders from Zdenko, as all the soldiers in town do. Could she be here to win my confidence, like we wanted to win Denidor's?

Her soft smile when she told me about my son hums through my memory. No, she couldn't. I know the smiles of those who dream of your death, and that was not it.

"I want to search Lord Denidor's manor," I say.

Hana just hums, massaging the goo into my skin. No judgment. Barely even a reaction.

"I caught him at a meeting discussing treason. The murder of Luna Maris." There is no point in holding back now. "And my mate heard him allude to the importance of his manor. He visits twice a week. Did you know that? Luna Maris herself admitted Tarrin was a suggestion by Lord Denidor."

"What would you need to do this?" A new note of tension creeps into her voice. Have I misjudged her?

"A way out of camp. A distraction for Lord Denidor, most likely." I swallow. "And an escort. You have heard the rumors of rogues."

She inclines her head, but she doesn't need to. A kingdom in turmoil like this always attracts them. "You have the services of a lieutenant in the Luna Queen's army at your beck and call."

I blink. "I—you? You would escort us?"

"Can you get the rest of these pieces yourself?" she asks.

Between Finn, Elian, Vedran, and, hell, Ingrid, I'm sure we can. I nod.

"You and your babies both seem well." Lieutenant Hana's face hardens. "And I would rather disobey my queen than watch her fall to an enemy she is too stubborn to see."

* * *

THE SPIRES OF LORD DENIDOR'S MANOR, SEAT OF HOUSE BREKALO, split the sky as we climb the last hilly rise. My stomach roils with the swaying of the horse underneath me. Running is so often easier than riding that I am unused to its rolling gait. Only two hours' ride, and I have had to stop to be sick quietly three times. At least now, I am too empty to be forced to stop again.

"Looks familiar," Elian mutters.

As he says it, I realize what he means—the manor is a mirror image of Tansy Tower itself. Not perfectly, but a near enough copy that an outsider can spot it at a glance.

"I bet it's decorated the same, too," Finn replies.

Lieutenant Hana, at our head, remains quiet as she has through most of the trip. Vedran and Ingrid stayed behind; with so many rogues on the loose, it made sense to only bring those with the ability to protect themselves, and Finn insisted that leaving Ingrid alone at Tarrin would be a mistake that we would regret within an hour of our departure. The three of them ride in a loose circle around me, as they have since we left. So far, we've heard a few howls and found footprints, but we haven't been attacked.

The ride home at sunset will be far more dangerous.

"I will take that bet," I say with as much gusto as I can muster. "Someone would have commented on it by now if so."

He puts out his hand, and I shake my head. When we stop, I'll seal the deal. For now, these reins are my only lifeline.

Luckily, we arrive before even my empty stomach riots beyond my control. Lieutenant Hana leads us around the back and lets us in through a small entrance in the high wall.

"I escorted him here once. His chief guard gave me a short briefing on their security measures. They mostly manage people getting in. Once we're inside, we should be set. He refuses to pay a staff to tend the place when he's not here."

"He is a tight fist." I look up at the spires. They're far too familiar when I cannot see the differences. Perhaps I'll be sick for another reason entirely.

Lieutenant Hana dismounts and ties her horse to a post.

Finn leaps down beside her and then reaches up to wrap his hands around my waist. I traded the skirts I've been wearing for trousers, so I mounted this beast myself, but I barely want to fight the offer of help. The ground seems much farther away than it was when I first climbed up.

He pulls me down, and I collide softly with his chest. The faux Tansy Tower behind him sends my mind spinning, imagining a different life. One where I was always Princess Xandra and our mating was cause for celebration. One where he carries me over the threshold of the tower, as old customs dictate, to welcome in a long life of prosperity.

"Step where I step," Lieutenant Hana says when Elian lands beside us.

He throws her a salute, which she accepts like it's genuine. I'd rather not shatter the illusion that Elian means anything without a wink, for now.

She begins a complex dance across the courtyard. At first, I think she's stepping on particular stones to avoid some nasty trap Denidor set. Perhaps she is, for some of them. But she flattens herself against the wall in places, and I look to the skies, trying to find what she's hiding from.

Soldiers—marching along the top of the high wall. Soldiers Tarrin needs. He is too greedy to pay to have his manor cleaned more than a few hours before he arrives, but arms, he will keep for himself without so much as flinching.

The babies in my stomach leap at the idea of ending his worthless reign. I lurch forward—they moved! I have never felt that before!

Elian catches me by the arm, keeping me from tumbling out of the shadows the lieutenant tucked us into. "Come on, I can't ride back already."

"We'd be beheaded for treason if caught."

He laughs disbelievingly, more air than sound. "Right. Of course, we would. And nobody thought to tell me that?"

"You would've complained the whole way," Finn hisses. "Or wear something foolish around your neck."

Elian rubs his throat. "A gorget doesn't sound like such a bad idea."

"Keep moving," Hana spits, already on the next stone.

In silence, we follow her the rest of the way to a simple, wooden door which would lead to a staircase in Tansy Tower. Here, it opens into some kind of minor pantry. Jars of preserved fruit gather dust on shelves.

Lieutenant Hana bends over, catching her breath. I snatch Finn's hand and pull him back a pace.

"I felt the babies," I whisper. "They moved."

The slow smile spreading over his face is more beautiful than any sunrise I've ever seen. He places a gentle hand on my stomach, but they are still now.

"Next time," I promise him.

"I'll hold you to that."

"We should split up," Elian declares. "This place is huge, and we should try to get out before dark."

After dark, the rogues will be far braver.

Elian nods at Finn and me. "Xan—uh, Anica, you take Silas."

Lieutenant Hana glances at us, eyes dancing with calculation. Elian winces. Finn loops his arm through mine. My stomach sinks. It was only a matter of time, but alone behind enemy lines is no safe place for her to learn the truth.

After a long moment, Lieutenant Hana bows. "Your Highness."

Relief disappears under a new cloud of concern. I lurch forward and pull her out of the gesture. "That is not—I would not like to be treated any differently than I have been, titles included."

A muscle in her jaw flickers. "Then I should call you Anica?"

That smile. "Xandra. In private. If you would like to."

Finn's hold on me tightens, but Lieutenant Hana nods.

"Thank you for trusting me." She looks at Finn and Elian. "And you?"

"Prince Finn," he murmurs. "My Beta, Elian."

Elian offers his own sweeping bow. "Finn won't want a title, but you can call me whatever you like."

Lieutenant Hana nods slowly, clearly piecing together the sequence of events. Vedran, likely. Perhaps even Ingrid.

"I will go with Elian," she says finally.

Tension whooshes out of the room like a released breath, even as Elian fakes offense at not being given a title. His dramatized complaints echo through the halls as we step out into House Brekalo.

4 9

HOUSE BREKALO

Finn

Xandra and I creep through the musty halls of Lord Denidor's manor. Thick curtains hang shut over every window, making the place feel like a tomb, even though I can see lines of bright summer sunlight around them. Her hand trembles slightly on my arm.

"Are you all right with Hana knowing the truth?" I ask.

She laughs self-consciously. "That is not precisely how I would have handled the conversation, given the choice, but it certainly could have gone worse."

"She seems to be on our side." I open a door and glance inside. Another sitting room. Smart money would bet secrets will be in offices, maybe libraries, so I shut it again. "For now."

"I trust her." For all her shaking, those words sound rock-solid.

"Why?"

Xandra brushes her free hand over her stomach as I peek in on what turns out to be a closet. "She's my friend."

"I remember being your friend," I say with a smile. "It included a lot more drinking games and a lot less unqualified trust."

She nudges me. "Lieutenant Hana is *my* friend. You were Xander's."

Somehow, that makes sense.

Goddess above, if my siblings thought their mates were complicated.

We check a few more rooms. I can't even hear Elian and Hana anymore, just our muted footsteps. I hope Hana is right that there's no one in here. The dust means we are leaving a trail a mile wide to follow.

Eventually, we reach a three-way intersection of halls.

"If he was trying to avoid accusations of copying Tansy Tower, his office might be in the opposite location of Father's," Xandra says. "Which I would guess means the northwestern most tower, at the bottom. Or in the middle, if he wanted to avoid the bad luck of the bottom."

"Then we should start there and work our way up." I turn toward what I hope is the northwest.

Xandra stumbles slightly to keep up and clutches her stomach. "Oh, now!"

"Now?"

"Kicking!"

I forget about the tower, the funerary feeling in the air, the war waiting for us outside, and put my hand on her stomach as fast and gently as I can.

Our fingers overlap. She slides hers out of the way, and soft pressure bumps into my palm. Once. Twice. Then, it stills.

Our babies.

I meet Xandra's gaze. In the dim, her hazel eyes look like night, shining with stars—or tears. My throat closes around a soft, choked noise. The little lives inside her aren't just an idea anymore. They are real enough to react, to touch me even through her.

"I will always take care of you," I murmur, not sure whether I'm talking to Xandra or our children.

She nods, and I realize it doesn't matter. We are a family. She will take care of me, I'll take care of her, and both of us will burn the world down for our twins. I kiss her softly.

Something clanks further off in the manor, and we jump apart.

"Apologies," Elian says through the mind-link. *"That was me."*

"Elian," I explain.

She exhales. "Tell him to watch his step. I thought—"

"Soldiers." I nod and start to warn him.

She shakes her head. "Denidor was obviously trying not to copy Tansy Tower entirely, but it's still similar enough. I thought it was Father."

That feeling, I know all too well. My chest aches, and I take her hand to continue down the hall I chose, but she leads me down a different path. I still expect Father to swing around corners with murder on his face at home, even though he's dead.

"If he is here, I'll knock him out," I say.

"Don't you dare." She squeezes my hand. "I deserve the chance far more than you."

I laugh. "All yours. I'll clean up whatever's left."

"If there is any." She smirks and then looks around the dour hall. "You know, I've never been here because heirs don't visit the manors of other houses. I should not be here until I take the throne."

"I could call you Your Majesty, if you like." I rub a small circle on the back of her hand.

She giggles. "And make me a cape from one of these curtains?"

"Taking them down would be enough of a blessing that I am happy to."

"It is still different," she says. "I should have my Beta by my side. And…."

She doesn't need to finish the sentence. She was never supposed to have a mate. My mark throbs, but I hold on to her hand.

"Do you wish that was how everything had turned out?" I ask.

"I wish the lives lost in this war could be spared," she says. "But I wouldn't wish away you or the twins."

Relief surprises me, and I shove it away. I should know better by now. "What if you could have both?"

She hums thoughtfully. "I'm not sure I could accept being under Father's rule. He was better before Mother left. Simply protective. But it's hard to imagine going back now." She touches her cheek.

It takes all my willpower not to crush her fingers. Corwyn, Denidor—they're traitors, betraying their people to grasp at power. Ending their pathetic lives will be a pleasure. But Alden is the bastard I've been dreaming about. He betrayed his family for his Goddess-damned reputation. If the war ends with him still on the throne, I'll be hard pressed not to plan his assassination.

"What about you?" Xandra asks. "Did you ever imagine taking the throne?"

"Twice, maybe." I shake my head. "If someone managed to take out Father, Kieran, and Anwen, it was made very clear that I wouldn't stand a chance. No, the only way I took the throne was if I killed them myself."

She laughs. "Alpha Finn, the Killer King."

"Atop a throne I'd dye red with my enemies' blood." I smile, but that's something I considered once. Not seriously, but I knew I would never be able to get rid of the three of them clever enough to seem innocent. If I became Alpha, I would have to embrace my murderous path there. Become a greater villain than Father ever was.

"Noble Tansy Beach would be compelled to fight you," she says, mock-seriously.

"I would expect nothing less." I laugh. "No, I figured the likeliest path for me was castle layabout. I considered becoming a drunk for a while, just to really meet expectations."

"Oh, I can see that." Her giggle echoes dully off the walls. "Did you have a drunken mate in these fantasies?"

"Not frequently. Lying about is easier alone." After Elian met Howell, though, I sometimes imagined myself with a companion.

"That sounds lonely," she says. "It was what you wanted?"

"What I expected."

She slows and then nods at a staircase. "That is the northwestern most tower. Real work awaits. So I am only going to ask once, and you can tell me you won't answer." Xandra takes a deep breath. "What did you want, Finn?"

Naïve visions of myself as someone important dance through my head. The position always changed—Beta, spymaster, general, whatever I thought I might be good at that day. All that mattered was that I'd been picked for it. Just me, on purpose. And that it meant I was always needed at the heart of things.

Xandra looks at me through the darkness. She's my mate, the mother of my children. If there's one person in this world I should be able to tell anything to, it's her.

"I won't—can't answer," I say.

"I understand." She turns and starts marching up the staircase.

Regret scorches through me, but the words won't come any easier just because I'd like to say them. If I tell her, she'll just offer me some pity position in a court that may never exist, and I'll never know if she wanted to give it to me or just wanted me to get what I wanted. There is no unbiased decision-making; that's why I stopped dreaming about any of that shit. Kieran would've given me damn near whatever title I wanted, and it wouldn't have meant a thing. I'll either get there someday or I won't. Simple.

The door on the first floor yields a room shockingly like Alden's *kafi* chamber. Xandra rushes to the second floor, even though I can see all the stairs are exhausting her, and throws open that door.

"His office," she declares.

It's richly decorated, covered in lightning symbols, and crowded. It's full of bookshelves, a pair of desks, a quilt of rugs, with a crowded mantel over the fireplace.

"I hope the sun sets slowly," I say as I release her hand.

The bookshelves hold nothing but history books, mostly of his family. None of the knickknacks seem magical. Comparing the handwriting on the papers in the two desks reveals that Denidor himself only uses one of them, but neither contains detailed sketches of assassination plans.

"Undersecretary Matej," I read from the signature on a letter.

Xandra frowns at me. "*Undersecretary?*"

"That, or he writes the letter 'S' like the word 'under.'" I show her the paper.

"Matej…he is the one Denidor always has by his side. But it's strange to have an undersecretary so close." She stares around the room. "Keep looking."

None of the many spindly tables or painted chests holds anything useful. The tapestries only have walls behind them. Finally, in frustration, I start rolling up the rugs.

"Xandra." A tiny trapdoor, maybe two feet by two feet, comes into view at the center of the room. I yank it open to find—

A book.

I pull it out and recognize the title. "This one is already on the shelf."

She grabs the other copy and joins me on the floor. "Are they different?"

We flip through slowly, page by page. Same, same, same.

Xandra gasps. I stare at the pair of identical House Brekalo family trees, trying to see what she sees.

"There." She points to her copy, a tiny blue star next to Denidor's name. "That marks that he was born with powers."

I look at mine.

No star in sight.

50

SETTING THE TRAP

Xandra

Hana looks at me in blank disbelief. "He has been lying for all these years?"

"Undersecretary Matej is responsible for every drop of water Lord Denidor has ever controlled." The more I say it, the truer it sounds. Even with a horse rocking unpleasantly underneath me, my voice doesn't shake. It makes sense. If he was as strong as he claimed, it would be virtually impossible for Petar to have such weak powers.

She blows out a long, slow breath. I watch Finn and Elian exchange a look. He'll explain to his Beta what this means, how much it will destroy Denidor in the eyes of Moonlight Hollow. We do not even need to prove his involvement with Astralis any longer.

A howl splits the night. I sniff—wild fur, matted with dust. Rogues.

Hana urges her horse into a trot, then a canter. As promised, mine immediately follows her lead. The wilderness whips past me at a dizzying rate.

A shape lunges from the trees, and a horse screams. It's a far higher-pitched, more human sound than I ever would have antici-pated. It shivers up my spine so sharply that I don't even notice the world turning on its side, the leather slipping from between my legs, until I hit the ground hard enough to jar my skull and knock the breath from my lungs.

I look up into a pair of yellow eyes, a dull brown muzzle slicked with blood. My stomach aches.

Instinct roars into place where my thoughts should be, and I explode into a shift without a second thought.

More horses scream, but I don't know whether they're hurt or just scared. Adrenaline pulses through me. Everything else falls away. I swipe out with a paw and knock the rogue back from my horse. It snarls at me.

Moss and ginger fill my nose. Finn looms large between the rogue and me, his saliva dripping red with blood.

I step up beside him and bare my teeth at the rogue. I don't need protection now. I need to feel the rush of being alive.

"Run, your—Xandra," Hana snaps.

"We can handle three rogues," I reply.

"And the eight more that are closing in?"

I lunge at the rogue in front of me, going for his throat, but scent the air as I go. Hana has a stronger nose than I, but there is an awful lot of rogue stink in the air. Certainly more than three.

Instead of clamping down, I shove the rogue back with my open jaw, then take off running. Finn growls one last time before bolting after me, Elian hot on his heels. Hana covers us from behind, but before I can tell her we need her just as much as we need the rest of us, my vision goes gray at the edges.

I blink, and it clears, but the attendant vertigo does not. I trip over my own paws, nearly landing face-first in the dirt. Too much exer-tion. More than I've tried since Finn discovered the healer's orders.

He takes the scruff of my neck gently between his teeth and hauls me back onto my feet. Worry clouds his still so blue eyes. I shake my head. There is no stopping, not with howls still issuing up from every angle. Not with the vicious, wet sounds of a feast behind us.

He growls a gentle warning at me, and I wish we could speak like this.

Someday, perhaps.

For now, it does not matter that I should rest. He said it himself. He cannot carry me over longer distances, and regardless, I don't especially believe that riding nude into Tarrin on the back of a wolf would convince anyone that we left for perfectly average reasons. The last thing we need is for Denidor to suspect what we've discovered tonight.

I brace myself against Finn's shoulder, using the rhythmic movement of his muscles as the only steady point in my universe, and run. Hana will tell me how worried I should be about the pinching in my stomach when we reach Tarrin.

* * *

"How did it feel?" Hana runs cold hands over my bare stomach while I stare out the window over her shoulder the next day. I am due in a council meeting… now, but she insisted on an appointment once Finn told her about the pain I mentioned.

"Like a pinch, deep in my gut." If I am not there, Finn will have to present the plan we spent half the night coming up with himself, and he is far less likely to succeed alone.

Hana's brow furrows, deeper than I've seen before, and I forget about the council meeting for a heartbeat. She's truly worried.

"What?"

She shakes her head. "You need to rest, Xandra. It is no longer a recommendation. It is an order."

"Or what?" My gut sinks as I ask the question. I think I can already read the answer in her furrowed brow.

"Or you are going to lose these babies," she says seriously. "If you do not also lose yourself."

I have to tell Finn.

I can't. Our whole plan hinges on me, there, in the battle.

"Thank you," I say. "I will… do what I can."

Hana's concerned frown follows me out of her house and into the tight, warded pantry. Everyone else is already there. Mother sits in her usual seat, but the worry of the past few weeks leaves deeper and deeper marks on her every day. I think there might be more gray in her hair than when I saw her yesterday, and the bags beneath her eyes are certainly deeper.

Andrija sits at the opposite end, already looking sullen, likely because it wasn't his idea to call the meeting in the first place. Finn stands against the wall, and his eyes light up when he sees me. The two seats before him are clearly set aside for us, but he is learning; if he sat, Denidor would have legal precedent to call the meeting to order despite my absence.

Denidor, of course, perches at the heart of a tight trio. He, Zdenko, and Matej seem to be nearly sharing the same seat, they sit so close together. Finn was right—Zdenko is not the ringleader here, and perhaps I should've seen that in the way he looks to Denidor before speaking on anything but military matters.

I lock eyes with the older councilor as I enter. He scans me up and down. I stand proudly. It does not matter what news I've just received; I know the secret he has spent his whole life hiding, and I am going to destroy him with it before he has the chance to touch my family.

"Thank you for waiting," I say as I march to my seat at Mother's right hand and take it. "Silas and I have a plan for how to face King Alden's army—and win."

Finn sits beside me and begins marshaling the little markers Ingrid started whittling for us the moment we returned within mind-link range and could tell her what we were thinking. The only markers not already on the board are small, splintery boats.

"We have not been making full use of the resources at our disposal."

As I explain, Mother's eyebrows creep slowly up her forehead. Not with disdain or displeasure, but simply in surprise. I am suggesting a strategy which comes from none of our illustrious forefathers, which was written in no book in our library.

At one point, Andrija thumps his hand against the table, sending a few markers flying, and declares that he's been *saying* this—despite the fact I have heard him mention the many boats available to the people of Tarrin exactly never.

Still, I incline my head and give him the credit he craves. If he thinks it was his idea, we can count on his support. And with every word I speak, Finn nods or sets another marker on the map, underscoring my points with simple, quiet support. I glance at him a few times—so much of this plan was his idea. Does he not want credit? But he simply smiles up at me and waits for me to continue.

I believed him, that day just outside the wall of Tarrin. But now, watching him cede the floor to me so completely, I know there is nothing underhanded or controlling in his desire to protect me. He just…

He just loves me.

The realization rocks me enough that I have to grab the table to keep my feet, but I keep talking. I've maintained a perfect face for too long to stumble here.

"And that's where you come in, Lord Denidor." I tap the blue ribbon of the Grayhead on the map. "The final advantage we need to turn the tide against their superior numbers."

Mother claps her hands together once. "I knew you were brilliant, but you may have just saved all our lives."

"It must be put to a vote," Zdenko declares. "I see many holes in the defenses you present."

"Where?" Finn gestures to the map.

Zdenko purses his lips and then points to a few ships. "There are gaps through which they might slip past us."

I adjust the ones he indicates. His plan leaves an opening to the north, but Father tends to forget the north, especially when the south is made to look more appealing. "Is that better?"

Zdenko grunts softly. He didn't expect me to have an answer so quickly.

"And what if King Alden is able to muster his own response?" Denidor blusters.

"You are so strong, Lord Denidor. How could he possibly muster an impressive enough response to counter you?" I bat my eyes, a trick I've seen a million women use on me and never had the chance to try myself.

Denidor narrows his gaze at me. Perhaps I should've asked Finn what my attempt looked like before unveiling it.

"A vote," Mother says. "We shall do this properly, as the hopefully final birthing pain of our new kingdom. All in favor of this plan?"

She raises her own hand immediately. I raise mine, unsure if I am truly allowed a vote in this new arrangement.

"I suggested the same months ago." Andrija raises his hand grumpily.

"The people here are not combatants," Zdenko says. "They will not be able to handle their ships in battle conditions."

"I've seen farmers and blacksmiths at your training session," Finn replies. "Can you not train a fisherman?"

Zdenko clenches his jaw, but Finn has him. Either he admits weakness or comes to our side. Slowly, Zdenko raises his hand.

All eyes turn to Denidor. He stares at the map, eyes darting this way and that, clearly searching for a reason to object. We have offered him a place at center stage, and he cannot take it—but to refuse it will draw as many eyes as acceptance, if not more.

He raises his hand. "I will lend my magic to the cause, as you wish, Luna Maris."

"The motion passes." Mother stands. "In two weeks, we land a blow against my former husband the likes of which he cannot imagine."

"For Moonlight Hollow." I stand as well.

"For Moonlight Hollow," the rebel councilors and Finn echo.

51

LOVE

Finn

Xandra leans on my arm as we duck out of the "palace" and into the blistering sun. As soon as the door shuts behind us, I can't hold it in anymore. I grin. Xandra laughs when she sees it, leaning on me even more heavily.

He took the bait. Denidor is ours—in two weeks, which is what we need to train the various captains and convince Alden to make the first move.

"Did you see his face?" she asks.

I twist mine into a mockery of it—barely restrained anger behind a mask of politeness. "Matej looked like he was going to shit himself."

Her giggles make her miss a step, and I catch her. Just like I did last night, when the run clearly almost wiped her out. Two weeks seems much longer now—Xandra needs her rest, and she needs it soon. But if we said any quicker, Denidor would've torn us to shreds.

"He didn't even mention my powers," she says breathlessly.

"He's not bright enough." I roll my eyes, glad we didn't have to pull out the fawning flattery we'd planned for that. Just watching her bat her eyelashes at him once was enough for me. "We had him where we wanted him the second we pulled out the little ships."

"We have to tell everyone." Her gaze goes hazy with a mind-link as she relays the news to Vedran and Hana.

"Denidor bit," I tell Ingrid and Elian. *"Two weeks."*

After I receive their affirmatives, I reach out to Ingrid alone. *"If you're in our room right now, get gone."*

"Ew," she replies.

I chuckle and look at my mate. She's still struggling through the mind-link confusion, which means I can study the brownish-red curls of hair framing her cheeks and the thousand different colors in her hazel eyes uninterrupted. She kept looking at me in the meeting, like she was waiting for me to chime in, but I just wanted to listen to her talk. It was like the fire I saw in her, standing up to Alden, but a little more restrained. Like a controlled burn to save a forest rather than a wildfire. The sort of thing a person could sustain over a lifetime—that inspires a kingdom to follow them to the ends of the earth.

"What are you staring at?" Her eyes clear, and she smirks.

"The reason I just kicked Ingrid out of our room." I smirk back at her.

Her eyes darken with want, and that's all the invitation I need. Let the whole town know I'm fucking my mate—if Denidor thinks we're celebrating, maybe he'll finally be as scared as he should've been when he first took aim at her.

I wind an arm around her shoulders, slip the other under her legs, and pick her up.

"F—Silas!" she squeals.

I jog toward our room, trying to jounce her as little as possible. "This isn't protective—I'm tired of waiting."

She swallows audibly and knots her fingers in my hair. The tiny sparks of pain only spur me faster. She is brilliant, gorgeous, and we are so close to having everything we want. Waiting is a waste of everyone's time.

I shoulder open the door and dart through the labyrinthine halls.

Our door barely closes at the best of times, so opening it with her in my arms barely requires a pause. Once inside, I bend to kiss her.

She holds up her hand to stop me. Worry clouds her face. "Hana is worried. She says, if I don't rest… the babies and I are in danger."

My stomach swoops. I knew it was worse, but I didn't expect it to be that bad.

She studies my face, her frown deepening as she does. "I am going to try."

And she told me. As soon as she could, without telling our enemies. No hiding, no lying. Her eyes beg me to trust that she will do her best.

I take a deep breath. "And I will help you, however I can."

A smile lights up her face in a way that makes everything else worth it. I lower her onto the bed and claim her mouth.

Xandra arches up into me, the growing swell of her stomach pressing between us. I groan. She needs to be carefu—

Her words from the last time we did this echo in my mind. I'm not supposed to treat her like she's breakable.

Maybe this is what all my strength is good for.

I spin her around on the bed so her back is facing me, controlling every second of the spin and her landing. She grunts softly then giggles and twists her face in the pillow to peer at me.

"What are you doing?"

"Celebrating." I kiss the back of her neck, drinking in her taste, feeling her movement underneath me. This way, all she can do is lie still and accept the attention I give her. I hold my body just slightly up, brushing against hers without crushing it into the bed. A perfect balance.

She hums into the thin pillow, and her eyes flutter shut. I unlace her blouse from behind, baring the curve of her spine. She is already softer than she was the first time I tasted her, and I take my time with it. I lick, suck, and nibble along her spine, mapping the new softness. Xandra writhes slowly beneath me, moving to a song neither of us can hear, sinuous as a snake. Her answering moans are soft, growing slowly louder. We can take our time. No one will need us for a long time yet.

I lick a stripe up her back, then lean in to whisper in her ear, "Have you considered that this is a benefit of staying in bed all the time?"

Her answering chuckle is low and throaty, all hunger. It shoots straight to my cock. "I might, if you give a convincing enough argument."

The challenge makes my mouth water. Thank the Goddess we've got time. Xandra doesn't know what she's just unleashed.

I unfasten her skirt slowly, then slide it down off her hips while still laving her back with attention. Then, when she is boneless underneath me, I grab both of her lower thighs and push her up into a half-kneeling position, her face smashed into the pillow.

This time, there's no yelp, no question, just a wanton groan. Her wetness glistens in the low light of our room. I lick my lips and bury my face between her thighs.

She rocks back into me, chasing the pressure. I tease her, dragging her higher. At this angle, I can reach beneath her, play with her taut nipples, and I happily take advantage. She keens like she did that first night, a sound I've realized means she's approaching overwhelm.

Good. If she's going to be overwhelmed with anything, it should be pleasure. It's sweat torture, my tongue between her legs and my hands on her breasts. I wind my other arm under her shoulders, taking a little more of her weight, so I can fuck her as hard as she deserves without any danger. She nuzzles toward it, then bites down. A throbbing ache I hope turns into a teeth-shaped bruise takes up residence in the muscle.

My cock screams for release. I don't have a hand to tend to it. Every inch of my body is hers, devoted to pushing her closer toward the edge or keeping her from getting hurt when she falls off.

We have time.

I pull my face reluctantly from between her legs. She echoes my disappointment with a high whine that dies when I line up my cock and sink quickly up to the hilt. She swallows me down, her core as hungry as her eyes. So hot, so wet. So much like coming home.

She rolls her hips against me, and I start moving. Her heartbeat, fast but not frenetic, under my palm sets our pace. She groans, begging for more, faster, but she won't release her grip on my arm long enough to use her words.

Of course, she doesn't have to. I want to see her explode, fall apart. My hips speed, chasing the rhythm that makes her face go slack—like that. I release her breast and thread my hand between her legs, then bend over her to shower her neck in kisses again. I nibble on her earlobe, brush my lips across her cheek, wish I could taste the moans pouring from her lips at this angle.

At least watching is damn near as good.

A few heartbeats after I find her speed, my fingers dancing over where she needs them most, the slack expression on her face twists into one of pure euphoria. A laughing smile, bright tears at the corners of her eyes, her mouth open around my name.

I slam into her one last time and follow her over the edge. That smile burns through my veins like a shot as I shake apart inside her.

It takes all the strength I have left to roll to the side rather than collapsing on top of her.

She rolls to face me, eyes soft and sleepy, and drags her fingers along my jaw. "I love you, Finn Solberg."

Warmth ribbons through my chest, and I kiss her. She loves me. I knew it, deep in that instinctual place that the Haze calls out, but to hear her say the words, watch her lips curl into a smile around them…it's more of a miracle than anything else I've seen so far, like she keeps saving up a little more magic to impress me again.

Then, I release her, and a beat of silence passes. Xandra looks at me intently.

I'm supposed to say it back to her.

Ice wraps a cold hand around the base of my spine. She is so beautiful like this, so soft and open. Just waiting for me to meet her where she is. To admit the thing I've suspected ever since we started pretending to be Silas and Anica.

I love her. Goddess above, it's impossible not to.

And when I open my mouth to say the words, nothing but air comes out.

She keeps staring at me, a furrow growing between her eyebrows.

"You know," I mumble.

"I'm not sure I do." She sits up, holding the sheet to her chest.

I've said things around this half a dozen times now. Implied I'd like to spend the rest of my life with her. But coming at it head on, telling her that I'm far past anything the mark or paternal responsibility would do to me, that she could take my heart in her hand and crush it to dust if she wanted to, feels like the last line I haven't crossed. Until I say those words, I might be able to escape without getting hurt.

Even though she said them first. Even though I know the truth.

Stupid.

"I—" My mouth tastes like acid. Her confusion turns to frustration.

"Understood." She stands, her hands shaking as she gets dressed. "I am going to go sleep in someone else's room tonight. You take your time and think about what I might or might not know without you ever getting up the courage to tell me."

Holding the tie of her skirt in her hands, she slams out of our room.

I drop back onto the bed with a groan.

5 2

———

LEADING THE CHARGE

Xandra

I ROLL OVER IN A SOFTER BED THAN I'VE SLEPT ON IN WEEKS AND FACE the first rays of morning sun. Straw still crunches under my cheek. This bed is thicker, but it is made of all the same materials as the thin one Finn and I—

My bite sears, and I close my eyes again. Yesterday, I thought something had changed. That he was done running away. Perhaps I should stop hoping he will ever be exactly what I want.

"I know you're awake, darling," Mother says.

I grumble softly in response. She is already out of bed, sitting at a combined vanity-desk and readying herself for the day, checking her face in a bowl of water someone else summoned while writing some letter blindly.

"Can I ask why I had the pleasure of a day with you yesterday?" Her voice is soft, nonjudgmental. There's a reason I went to her rather than Hana or Vedran. I didn't want to hear about how I should be more careful, how half-measures would hurt us both. I simply....

I wanted my mother.

With my eyes still closed, I say, "Finn."

She hums understandingly. "Your father and I fought all the time in the early days."

"About what?" Neither of them have ever talked about that period in their lives much.

"Oh, everything." She chuckles. "I had already spent half my life arguing against his and his father's policies. He just didn't know it because I wasn't allowed into the council chamber with my father."

When Father first took the throne, he was a recently injured war hero, young and impetuous. Mother was a court lady, a perfect match for him. All my early memories show them in perfect harmony; I just assumed they had always been that way.

But I can picture this woman, the one pulling leather armor on over her head even though she will likely never see battle, standing outside the council chamber, getting angrier and angrier. Rehearsing arguments in her head until Father returned. Honing her words to a dagger's point.

"I wish I'd known you then," I say softly.

"We would've been wonderful friends," she says.

That strikes an off chord in my chest somehow, like it wasn't the right answer. I push the feeling aside and roll over to watch her, just the way I did when I was small.

"Did he accept you right away?"

Mother scoots back on her chair and pats the front of it between her knees, also like she did when I was little. On tired feet, I wobble across the room and sit before her. She threads fingers into my hair and starts braiding. "We started planning a wedding the very next day. But if Finn is too much of a fool—"

I remember my certainty in the meeting, warm and solid. Finn loves me. I don't doubt that. He simply won't say it. "He's not a fool. He's just scared. Or stubborn. Or both."

"That, I can help you with." Her chuckle turns wry. "Allow me to guess—you are right about something, and he refuses to admit it?"

"Yes!" I lurch forward, and she tugs on my hair to pull me back into place.

My chest aches again, sweeter this time. I've seen the other court ladies do this with their own daughters a thousand times, wondered what it felt like. It is the gentlest correction. An invitation into a club that I thought was barred.

"You could keep telling him how right you are." I can hear her smile. "Or you can give him space. He will miss you–and soon." Something in her voice breaks, and I wonder just how painful the months of her absence from me were for her. "And missing you will give him time to think. To wonder if this is really what he would like to plant his flag on."

Someone raps on the door. Mother hands me the strands of my braid, which I hold delicately, not sure what move will cause it all to unravel. She opens the door but positions it and herself such that I am invisible to whoever waits outside.

"Luna Maris," says a crisp voice, military, but not one I recognize. I can't see them either. "There is news from Tansy Beach."

"Tell me."

"King Alden is ill. He coughs into a handkerchief that he hides quickly and remains often in bed. Rumor says that he has been complaining of headaches."

My stomach falls as Mother exchanges a few final words with the messenger. Hiding the handkerchief can only mean one thing. Blood. Combined with the headaches, the symptoms are all too familiar Lord Juraj complained of the exact same troubles just before he—

The door shuts, and Mother sits behind me once more, but she doesn't pick up the braid I'm holding. She simply sits.

"Did you hear about Lord Juraj?" I ask quietly.

"We did."

Her simple words muffle any others, thick and dampening as the blanket of white I saw on my one trip to Snowcrest Canyon. She is thinking the same thing I am. Perhaps Lord Juraj was poisoned. If he was, Father has been, too. Or perhaps Father spent too much time around a sick man.

Regardless, a man we have both loved—may both love—is dying.

My cheek burns in the shape of his hand. I have so many good memories of him. Will that be my last?

"Will you—do you miss him?" I ask finally.

She offers a long, slow sigh in return and then remains quiet for so long that I start to wonder if she is going to answer at all. "He is a difficult man to miss," she says.

"I don't know if I agree."

Slowly, with a slight tremble in her hands, she retakes my braid. "How so?"

"I keep expecting him to appear." My face quirks up into half a smile. I don't know whether I'm afraid of it or hoping for it.

"He is quite a presence. I've never seen him enter a room without gathering up all the attention for himself."

I shake my head, and she pulls me softly back into position again. "I don't think I mean like that."

"I have grown used to being unfair to him," she admits to the back of my head. "It is certainly the more popular opinion here."

"I'm sure you can't get through a conversation with Lord Andrija otherwise."

She laughs soundlessly. "Very true. But your father took the attention for a reason and not simply because it was what his father trained him to do. It was a shield. Every eye on him stayed away from you or me."

"Exactly." I barely resist the urge to nod. "And he had the best eye for presents."

"Goddess above, did he." In the reflection of the water, I watch her reach for her collarbone, where the jeweled necklace he gave her for their tenth anniversary always used to hang. I didn't even realize until this moment that she hasn't been wearing it. Part of me wonders if that, too, wasn't Denidor's idea. Some twisted approximation of loyalty. "Yet somehow, he never had the foggiest idea of what he might want."

"Though he was lovely about whatever I decided to get him." A parade of ill-formed attempts lined his nightstand every time I saw it. Awkward chunks of whittled wood, misspelled cards, a blade like Corwyn's which I've never seen him wear. He displayed them like trophies anyway.

Mother ties off the thick tail of my braid and rests her hands on my shoulders. "Your father was a complicated man."

And there it is. He *was* complicated. We haven't talked of him in anything but past tense since the messenger interrupted. As if he is already gone.

Perhaps he is. I haven't seen the man we're talking about since the morning Tansy Tower woke up to Mother's letter.

"Did you know?" I find myself asking.

"Know what?" She smooths my rumpled shirt.

"What leaving would do to him."

Her hands still. In the bowl of water, I watch her gaze grow distant, as if she's mind-linking someone. I know she is just lost in the past. Not for the first time, I hunt for myself in her face. I have Father's eyes, Father's hair, Father's nose. Some have said I have Father's mouth, but I think that was more about how I spoke. Finn says he sees her in me, though, so I look again at this face I've always found so foreign and so familiar.

For the first time, with my hair pulled back like hers usually is, I can see pieces of what he means. I have her cheekbones, though the skin has been fletched away from mine by stress and weeks of nausea. The fine point of my chin, which I've always resented, is aristocratic on her face. And my eyes are all Father in color, but their soft, almond shape belongs to her.

Side-by-side, for the very first time, we look like mother and daughter.

And so I know, in the timber of her sigh, what she is going to say to my question.

"Yes and no."

A political answer. Even though we are alone, with no one watching, she has to hedge her bets. Just a little bit.

"I suspected he would be angry," she continues. "Furious. That there would be retaliation. But I thought, after a few months, once I could lure him to the negotiating table, he would listen. That we could split peaceably, perhaps even simply become sovereign pieces of one kingdom."

As she talks, the similarities I noticed seem to drift away. I can't imagine how she thought that. Perhaps I wouldn't have guessed just how awful things have become. Certainly, until the moment I saw him raise his hand, I would never have expected him to hit me. But with all his pride, all his anxiety about the Mlakar line, I could have told her that there would be no peace without blood unless she came home.

And just like that, I know that I will not avoid Finn until he is able to admit what we both already know. I am still angry with him, but there is one thing he and I have that Mother and Father never did— understanding. It was hard won, and I am sure it's not perfect yet, but I know exactly what he would do if I left him.

He would fight me every step of the way out the door, and if I insisted it was what I wanted, he would let me go. He loves me too much to force my hand.

I deserve better than relying on my own knowledge for the rest of my days, but on the back of that knowledge, I will wait until he realizes the truth. On the back of that knowledge, I suspect it won't be long.

"I think I will miss him," Mother says, and it takes me a moment to realize she is still talking about Father.

"It might not be over yet," I say. "Lord Juraj took a long time to die. This may all end in two weeks, and there may be an antidote."

She slides my braid over my shoulder and tucks a flower into it. "Perhaps."

I don't say what I'd like to say—that we could intervene sooner, try to save him. I might try on my own, if I think he'll believe me. But there's nothing I can say to convince Mother to do anything but wait two weeks and hope for the best.

Instead, I simply say, "We should adjust the plan. Corwyn will lead the troops instead."

"That's very clever, darling." She kisses me on the side of the head, and I know we made the right choice, not telling her the true intent of our plan.

5 3

WITHOUT HER

Finn

AFTER A DAY OF MY BITE ACHING, XANDRA RETURNS TO OUR ROOM. SHE doesn't mention what happened. Since not mentioning things is my specialty, I decide to follow her lead.

And for one night, that feels almost normal.

But a second day passes. A third. I train with Elian and Ingrid in out-of-the-way corners of the camp that Denidor somehow always seems to find anyway. I get used to the tingling of Vedran's magic on my skin, disguising my face just enough that we can scrape another few days closer to this whole plan coming together.

Xandra still doesn't say anything. She just eats meals with me, laughs at my jokes, puts my hand on her stomach so I can feel the twins kick. A couple of times, when she does that, I open my mouth in the hope and with a prayer that the words can sneak out before my brain notices. Every time, she looks up at me like she's waiting, and they die on my tongue.

The faint flicker of disappointment in her gaze becomes familiar, and that makes me as sick as she is.

Or, I should say, *was*. A week after we set our plan in place, her morning sickness disappears like someone shut a curtain on it. Her dizziness worsens, and she starts getting intense cravings for hyper-specific foods, often ones that take Hana, Luna Maris, and Vedran together to produce. But she no longer turns green every time we pass the main communal kitchen, and Hana says we should take that as a good sign.

In private, I ask Hana whether it's a good enough sign that I shouldn't be worried about bed rest anymore. Her expression tells me all I need to know.

Once, Xandra says she loves me again. I challenge her to an arm-wrestling competition, for old times' sake, and after winning a few in a row, I let her win and blame her success on our son. Or maybe both of the twins working in tandem against me. She laughs so hard that she has to wipe tears from her eyes, and that's when it slips out of her mouth again.

I wait for her to look surprised or embarrassed. I wait for the answer to come automatically to my lips. Neither happens. She just looks at me, sighs softly, and challenges me to another round.

On the morning of the battle we planned together, we wake up together. She brushes a kiss across my cheek and rolls out of bed.

Outside, I can hear the rest of Tarrin in a furor. This is the most fragile part. On the opposite side of the Grayhead, Tansy Beach's armies stand ready. They've planned their attack for tomorrow, and they think they're perfectly hidden in the trees as they prepare. The element of surprise is one of our only allies.

Which is, of course, why we told Denidor we'd be attacking in the afternoon instead of the morning. Xandra thought he wouldn't risk being so obvious in his double-cross and that we should've just told him the wrong day, but I wouldn't be surprised if he and Corwyn and whatever the fuck Astralis is are planning to end the Mlakar line in this fight. This way, the shift seems normal, and he doesn't have the time to alert the other side.

"Hana offered to help me get ready," Xandra says.

My bite throbs. Our whole plan falls apart if she's not in this fight, and it kills me to have her there. "How are you feeling?"

She offers me a thin smile. "Like winning my kingdom back."

That is not enough of an answer for her to disappear on, but she turns to walk out the door, and I can't say the only three words that will stop her.

Instead, I drag myself to the only two people in this camp I know will tell me the whole truth, without trying to be careful about my feelings.

* * *

"Oh." Ingrid studies me for a moment. "You're an idiot."

"Concurred." Elian nods.

"Bastards."

She shrugs. "You asked us. What else did you expect?"

"A little compassion?" I grumble. "Maybe understanding?"

"Oh, I understand," Elian says. "You're scared shitless of her. Still."

"Not *of* her." I chuck a straw-stuffed pillow at him. "For her, maybe?"

"Or of admitting you care about someone," Ingrid adds. "Which makes sense, given that you're too scared to look awake in most meetings."

"I've changed my mind." I stand up. "I do not want to talk about this. I will solve the problem myself."

Elian grabs my wrist and looks at me seriously. All the turmoil of the last few months makes that expression suit his face in a way it didn't use to. He's grown up.

"Listen to me," he says. "You love her, right?"

It's easier to nod than open my mouth.

"We are all marching to our potential deaths today. It is a good plan, but we are massively outnumbered, and there will be Dun's Crossing soldiers on that field." He meets my gaze. "Do you really want to die without ever telling her that?"

* * *

Laurel's deck rocks softly under my feet, buoyed by the rapids of the Grayhead. Hana stands a few feet away, proud at the helm of her ship. She's one of several dozen folks from Tarrin who nearly tripped over themselves to loan their boats to the cause when we asked. Every scrap of leather armor, mostly from the closets of Queen Maris and the rebel lords, has gone to them; they will be the only ones in human form in the battle.

At the front edge, Vedran's brow knits in concentration. He is weaving a massive spell with the help of one woman in the village who knows a few charms. It doesn't have to hold for long—just long enough for us to launch all our ships before anyone on the far side notices we're moving—but clearly, even that is a struggle.

"We're in position," Xandra says beside me. Sunlight, wavy like we're underwater through Vedran's magic, catches on the angles of her face. Her stomach is undeniable now, painfully visible under the thin blouse I know will shred the moment she shifts.

My heart crawls into my throat. A shift won't be enough to protect her. Nothing will. We are marching toward our deaths. Every instinct in my body screams to grab her and run.

But she wants to be here. She belongs here, among her people, winning them a better life. I have to trust her.

Vedran exhales slowly and lowers his arms, releasing the spell.

I have to tell her I love her before I run out of time.

"Wait!" I shout.

"For what?" Vedran hisses.

I ignore him and turn to Xandra. She looks at me with wide, worried eyes.

"I love you," I say like it's the easiest thing in the world.

Maybe it has been all along. I just needed to get out of my own way.

Her worry melts into a soft smile as she cups my cheek. "I know."

I can't do anything but laugh at that. "Does that mean I can skip the rest of the speech?"

"Oh, no, if there is a speech, I intend to hear it." She crosses her arms.

Vedran grunts with effort, but the corners of his grimace are turning up into a smile. He is happy for Xandra—just not my timing.

"I'll keep it short," I say to both of them. "Hana!"

"Yes?"

"Is it true that ship's captains can perform marriages?"

Hana gives me a hard, sharp, soldier's smile. A last drink before the suicide mission smile—with a softness around the edges that doesn't quite click to me but makes Xandra's eyes suddenly watery. "Yes, it is. Sanja, take the helm."

I turn back to my mate. "There's no excuse for how long this has taken me."

"No, there is not," she replies with a smirk, her hand on her stomach.

I put my hand on top of hers. "I knew ages ago. When we got here —before that, if I'm being honest. I love you. I want to spend my life with you, however short that's going to be. And I don't intend to die without ever knowing how your thoughts feel inside my head."

Her answering smile is indulgent, overwhelmed, thrilled. "Mother told me to stay away from you. I couldn't because I couldn't risk losing how well you understand me. So I doubt I have to tell you what I think."

"That I am an idiot who should've listened to you?"

She kisses me soundly. "That you are an idiot who should've known there was nothing to be afraid of."

Hana steps up in front of us, a length of thick rope for docking a ship in her hands. "We are going to have to do this a little nontraditionally."

"For us?" Xandra asks wryly. "What a surprise."

Hana shakes her head. "Hold hands. I have to remember the words." She ties us together quickly, almost roughly, with the rope. It scrapes at my skin, leaving marks I hope linger long after this.

"Since we do not have the luxury of time," she glances at Vedran, "can you both repeat after me and insert the appropriate names?"

We nod.

"I pledge my love and life to you."

Our voices ring out in discordant harmony, coming together on all the most important words. I hold her hazel gaze as I swear to love her again, like I should have before.

"I promise to be ever at your side," Hana says, "no matter the storm."

I squeeze Xandra's hands as I repeat the words.

"I bet this puts most of the other storms to shame," she whispers to me when she's done.

"I won't take that," I reply. "I don't want to win if the whole world lights on fire."

She laughs, and Hana waits with surprising patience for us to finish.

"I thank the Moon Goddess for joining our two hearts," Hana ends.

I spent so long cursing her. Wishing not only that I didn't have Xandra, but that I didn't have anyone. Elian and Ingrid are right; I am an idiot.

"I bind my heart to yours for all time."

Xandra barely finishes the words before she throws herself at me to seal the vows with a kiss. Aniseed and clover burst on my tongue as I reach out tentatively for our very first mind-link.

"Xandra?"

"I'm here," she replies.

"The spell is coming down," Vedran grunts.

5 4

FALSE FACE

Xandra

LIEUTENANT HANA GRABS ONE END OF THE ROPE BINDING FINN AND I together, yanks, and the whole tie comes undone in a heartbeat. But even as Vedran's glamor shimmers into nothingness, as the other boats appear on either side of us, I can still feel the scrape of that sailing rope on my skin. Under it. In my very mind.

I glance at Finn. He glances back at me, apology and love in one gaze. He knows he'll be apologizing for how long this took for a very long time.

I can't wait.

A howl goes up on the far side of the Grayhead. It's Corwyn's scouts spotting us.

The water churns under our feet. Denidor's—Matej's power—pushing the massive line of ships forward, spanning more of the border than I dreamed when we came up with this idea.

I throw myself into a shift, Finn next to me. The river hums in my blood, and so does he. My mate. My husband. The father of our children.

One last fight. If this doesn't work, all is lost. If it does, we may finally get to relax.

With my head back, I scream a howl at the sky.

The wolves of Tansy Beach hit the frothing waters of the Grayhead. As anticipated, the current shoves them back, us forward. Matej really is impressive; I'm not surprised Denidor took advantage of him as he did when he found the young man in his ranks. It's not that dissimilar from what my parents did to Vedran as a child.

And it will destroy the people's faith in him. A wolfish smile spreads over my lips.

A few enemy wolves slip through Matej's control and scramble up the sides of our ships. Built low, both to navigate the dangerous river and for passing wolves to be able to board, they make quick work of the sides. We always knew they would, even with Lieutenant Hana yanking the tiller back and forth to try to shake them off. I skitter across the deck and find myself face-to-face with the snarling maw of a dripping Tansy Beach wolf.

"This war is being fought falsely," I try to tell him. *"The king has been poisoned; he's being lied to."*

There is no response but a dive for my throat, which I am forced to roll backward to protect. My stomach lurches. Though I couldn't train properly, I spoke to Hana often over the past two weeks—she told me how to fight while keeping that which is most important, my babies, safe. I curl around them now, taking a glancing scrape across my spine instead.

Adrenaline thrums. I roll back onto my feet and dart at the enemy, using all the tricks of movement my feet always craved but I couldn't use against Vedran. The Grayhead's waters move like my very own blood—hard, fast, and unyielding. I slash across the other wolf's chest, drawing ruby on my claws.

"Behind you!" Finn shouts through the mind-link.

I whirl to the side, trying to see both enemies at once. A wolf in Dun's Crossing gray drips river water and blood as he charges me. The other takes advantage of my distraction and leaps for my hindquarters.

Finn hits him midair, smashing him to the deck and leaving me to deal with his pack mate. I tuck and roll, remembering a maneuver Ingrid talked about for days after she mastered it. The Dun's Crossing wolf sails over my head, and I flick my nose to the side.

Water rises off the surface of the river and snatches him from the deck. He won't drown—I carve a space for his bloodstained snout below the waves—but he will remain there until the fight ends.

Kieran's men aren't evil. None of these wolves is, with the exception of the few who led us all here.

"We are wasting time," I tell Finn as he snarls over the wolf he tackled. *"Denidor awaits."*

"I'll protect your back."

My paws slide on the slick wood as I take off running along the line of ships. It is so much easier to trust him now that he's in my head, now that I can hear the ring of truth in his very thoughts. But in this, I would've trusted him months ago. Perhaps when he beat me at that very first party.

The first gap looms. I need all my strength for what comes after we reveal Denidor; the water can't catch me. And the more I run, the more my vision tilts, no longer quite matching up with the sway of the ship.

I should be in bed.

My people need me.

I jump.

My knees ache, and my stomach lurches as I land hard on the next deck. Finn lands harder, water sloshing up over the low sides. A wolf so red with blood I don't even know whose side he's on lunges at me, and Finn knocks the blow away before it reaches me.

"I could have taken that," I snap at him.

"I know," he replies while wrestling the wolf to the ground.

No explanation. No apology. I already know everything he is going to say—that he loves me, and that I am needed for bigger things than this.

Even better, I finally know that he's right.

I keep running, trusting him to follow behind. Two more ships separate us from Lord Denidor. He sensed something was wrong when the plan relied so heavily on him and insisted on helming his own vessel. General Zdenko expanded the distance between the ships, stretching it to the absolute maximum of what a reasonable person would agree to. They tried to keep us away.

They should have tried harder.

I hurtle over the next jump. The edge of my vision tinges gray for the heartbeat of empty air before I land. When I do, I see a broad Tansy Beach wolf towering over the slim figure at the helm.

Petra. Sanja's daughter. She was supposed to be on our ship!

My vision goes red as I charge the other wolf. All peace leaves my mind. He might be my man, but that makes him my problem to put down. The stink of copper only makes me hungry as I sink teeth into his shoulder, and dodging the wide swing of his claws is like second nature. As Elian once suggested, I jump and slam my back legs directly into the other wolf's chest when he tries to back up to reposition.

His paws skid. I call more water under his feet, and a tiny shape charges past me.

Petra shoves the enemy wolf back, sending him sliding into the water with a barely audible *splash*. She turns back to me, tears in her eyes, and mouths a thank you that disappears under the noise of battle.

My stomach clenches. She is too young for this.

"Ingrid!" I shriek through our new mind-link.

"Congratulations on the wedding," she replies, like we are not in the middle of a war.

"Two ships north of Hana's," I reply. *"The girl at the helm needs protection."*

Ingrid doesn't reply, and that's how I know she understands. Finn lands on the stern behind me, and we take off running, side by side. The final jump comes easier and harder. The darkness at the edges of my vision doesn't fade quite as quickly as it did before. I am on a time limit.

On a high platform, towering over the battle like a king, Denidor stands in human form. He swishes his hands back and forth like he is conducting a symphony, and he looks like a fool.

Our powers are a gift. A true blessing from the Goddess, handed out carefully to those who are dear to Her. She knows we understand their value, unlike those in other kingdoms who have bred them into half the population.

Denidor spat in the face of that. He's lucky we have other enemies to face today.

"I'll find Matej." Finn leaps through an open trapdoor to the lower portion of Denidor's boat to find the undersecretary.

I scale the high platform Denidor stands atop. He's no fool—he built it so a wolf could get up and down. Otherwise, everyone would know he intended to stay clean and above the fray, pretending to be our savior.

He turns as I reach the top, and surprise flashes across his face. "I told Luna Maris I had no need of a bodyguard."

"I am not here to protect you," I snarl, waiting for Finn's signal.

His eyebrows raise. "Xander."

"Xandra."

He waves a hand flippantly—far outside his rhythm, nothing the water would reply to. I lunge forward before I can stop myself, hungry to snap it right off.

The water shifts underfoot.

"I found him," Finn says.

Soon. Finn needs control of Matej. Then, no one will look twice at me for feeding the Grayhead the blood of this liar.

"I know." I circle Denidor slowly. *"I know everything."*

Something like fear replaces the surprise on his face, and I drink it down hungrily. "Secrets are a politician's bread and butter—not that you would be old enough to understand that."

I spit a rasping, lupine laugh at him. *"I have been a secret since I was born. I've just never been a traitor or a blasphemer.:*

He pales.

"Almost," Finn grunts over mind-link. *"He's a fighter."*

"Potent words from a disinherited former prince." Denidor fights to hang onto his composure, to pretend like he's still stirring the waves driving the endless supply of enemy wolves back. "If you had any proof, they just might be intimidating."

"Proof like Undersecretary Matej?"

Denidor's laughter strikes something cold into my heart. It's not terrified–not defensive. He should be shaken. Are we wrong?

"He will never turn on me," Denidor declares. "I own him."

"Got him," Finn declares.

"He doesn't need to," I tell Denidor with a vicious smile as the river starts to calm, and wolves pour into the water from the far side.

"Lord Denidor?" someone asks. "Why have you stopped?"

He freezes, his hands still aloft mid-gesture. "Ah, I am beginning to weaken—"

"Liar!" I shout through every mind-link I can reach. *"Lord Denidor has no more magic than this ship."*

Finn bursts out of the trapdoor, wearing a robe with Matej scruffed in one hand. "This is the man who's been working all of Lord Denidor's magic."

Perhaps this is too much hope, but I think I see relief in Matej's bruised eyes as he flicks his hand and the water around him leaps to attention.

"Now you," I tell the so-called lord in front of me.

Denidor moves his hands. It's pitiful, a desperate imitation by a man already ruined. Nothing so much as twitches.

Gasps pock the decks. Even the wolves in the now-forgiving Grayhead seem to slow.

I lift my chin and stare out over the carnage. *"I am your heir. The man you've known as Xander, the woman you've known as Anica. And I will lead you to safety.'*

Until this moment, I intended to seize the Grayhead. Wrest control of it, force it to obey. But with the scent of blood so thick in the air, with victory on my tongue, I don't want to make any more enemies.

I extend myself to the water like I am asking it to dance, and the water reaches back.

The current is mine.

And then I smell it on the wind—balsam and salt.

5 5

TRUST ME

Finn

Xandra turns abruptly north, her nose pointed at the sky. *Corwyn.*

The skin on the back of my neck prickles as I drop back into a shift. Matej isn't going to cause any more trouble. He fought like hell until I wrestled him down, and then I didn't even have to convince him to prove to everyone what Denidor had made him do.

But Corwyn is trouble. He deserves to die here, in the cinders of the fake war he created for power. One of us should kill him. Xandra, for how long he lied. Me, for how hard he made reaching my mate. Or for that damn look in his eye that made me want to kill him every time he saw it.

And he's north. Where the only hole in our defenses is.

"This is a trap," I tell her.

She's not listening. She's too busy scrambling down off Denidor's platform, not even bothering to kill him. Judging by the furious eyes turning his way, the wolves on both sides circling the base like sharks, I don't think we need to.

349

Last time we were here, Corwyn and Denidor in our grasp, I held her back. We would've lost. We didn't have the plan, the time, or the numbers. Now, we do.

So when she looks at me, not even bothering with a mind-link, I know what she's asking. She wants me to let her go. Even though I watched her struggle landing the last jump and can see the tiredness bowing her shoulders from holding the whole current under her sway. It's impressive, incredible—and her stomach swings, painfully vulnerable, with our children inside.

I can say no here. Just like she could've refused to marry me.

But neither of us really can.

I dart forward to meet her, press my shoulder into hers, and we run. Our feet land in steady rhythm. Before I even ask her to, she jumps for the shore—two leaps, instead of the dozen or so it would take across ship-back. She's promising I can trust her.

All I can do is follow and hunt the trees for an ambush. Corwyn isn't a good enough fighter to risk taking us alone. I knocked him on his ass by myself.

At the end of our line, one ship drifts too far from the others. My instincts scream. The human at the helm is well and cleanly dressed, like I haven't seen anyone in Tarrin other than Luna Maris and the lords. This is his ship.

"I know him too well," Xandra says. *"He cannot surprise me."*

And she leaps headlong into the water. I grit my teeth and follow. This time, instead of trying to drown me, the current offers me a helping hand. I barely have to paddle to the floating snare.

We scramble onto the deck, and a familiar, coppery-tan wolf steps out with a smile.

"I was wondering if you would—"

The time for talking is over. Xandra launches herself at him, teeth bared. I dart to the other side, Corwyn's exit.

And he moves like fucking lightning. Like he most certainly did not, that night on the beach. Xandra clamps her teeth around empty air, and I stare into Corwyn's burning eyes, barely a maw's length away.

"Only a fool shows the enemy everything," he says.

I choke down a retort about only fools monologuing during battle in favor of a clouting paw across his snout. He whips his head out of the way, turning something that should've knocked him down into a glancing blow. Xandra lines up behind him, so I keep his attention on me by ramming my shoulder into his chest.

That lands. It's too human of a move for him to predict. As he coughs, Xandra bites into his haunch, and the reek of copper fills the air.

He doesn't howl in pain. He just swings back at her, freeing his leg when she dodges.

"Did you think you were the only one with a mage?" He barely bleeds as he dances back a few steps, sizing us up. *"Astralis's resources are vast."*

"Vast enough to betray your people?" Xandra seems to relax—until Corwyn's gaze darts to me, and she leaps.

Like he was waiting for it, he rolls out of the way. I snarl at him and scrape claws across his passing ribs, but it barely seems to make a dent. Fucking mage. He must have something strengthening his hide.

She doesn't give up her attack. Instead, she lands neatly enough to spring into another dive in a whirlwind of claws. I read her movements in her muscles, in the whispers of thought I can half-hear through the mind-link. Staying behind Corwyn, picking up the pieces when he dodges, is all I can do.

And he fucking laughs in both our minds. *"Is it really betrayal to free someone from a leader like Uncle Alden?"*

She howls. *"He trusted you!"*

I don't wait for her next attack. He is too focused on her to see my bite coming. I sink my fangs deep into his neck—or as deep as I can before the vibration, a sickening version of Vedran's glamor, becomes too intense to bear. Blood sheets over my tongue.

He rips free, and I watch the wound start to knit, but far more slowly than the others. I shoot her a grim smile.

"If he knew enough not to, he'd have been chosen by Astralis, not me," Corwyn replies, voice slightly ragged.

"If you were chosen," she snarls, *"you should've said no."*

Corwyn tries to dart back, but I move behind him. He slams into the wall of my body, and even magic isn't enough to move me. Xandra hits him next, claws seeking the rend I've left in his neck. More blood spatters the deck.

"And that is why you need to die, cousin," he replies. *"You have no vision."*

He explodes out of the pin in a flurry of copper-colored fur. Xandra skids across the wood, flat on her stomach. He darts left, a third point to our triangle.

I should go after him. He's cocky—already gloating like he's won.

"Are you all right?" I ask.

She struggles to her paws. I can see the uneven rise and fall of her chest from here, read the extra sway in her legs. *"Ask me when he's dead."*

"I suppose I should thank you, Finn," Corwyn says before I can tell her he's not worth it.

"For the scar I gave you last time, or the one I just gave you on your neck," I spit as I lunge at him again.

If she won't leave, I'll end this.

"For showing me 'Prince Xander's' truth. It made this all much easier."

He darts to the side, slashing out at me as he goes, and I barely catch the railing. The raging Grayhead spits at me—without Xandra by my side, I'll die in seconds.

"Perhaps you should be wondering why I never trusted you enough," Xandra says.

"Oh, that's simple." Corwyn feints at her, circling around. *"You've always been too terrified to do what needs to be done."*

I scrape my feet back underneath me, my side screaming from his claws. Hits that should be dropping him only slow him—but I've fought bastards so drunk they can't feel pain before. I just need him a little slower.

"Put more water on the deck," I tell Xandra. *"Anything to trip him up."*

Water starts creeping over the sides of the ship. Wood creaks as she carves gaps between boards. Corwyn starts to look toward the sound, but she interrupts him.

"What am I too scared to do? What did Astralis promise you to make you sell everyone out?"

He laughs again, grating, and I realize what that look in his eyes I hate so damn much is. He is always about to start laughing.

"They want everything, dear cousin." He darts forward, then back again. He's testing her defenses. His claws catch on a split board, and he stumbles for a heartbeat. *"King Gavin was a fool—he tried to steal the world in broad daylight. All the cleverest people know you do that from the shadows."*

Goddess above, how did nobody hit him before now?

"I'll push him back," Xandra tells me.

She doesn't need to finish the thought. I can see the rivulets of water running toward the river, the gap in the railing from where I clawed at it. I just step aside as she lunges at him, and he dances back.

"They realized I was being wasted under your father," he says. *"They chose me."*

Fuck.

I understand what he's saying.

If some group had come to me months ago, said I was the one they'd been looking for, the only one, wasted where I was....

"You are not him," Xandra says.

I look at her. Recognition glows in her eyes as she slashes at her cousin, forcing him back another inch. She doesn't need the mind-link to read my every thought.

Maybe I don't need it either. And maybe I would've stopped before civil war. But I know why he said yes, at least at first.

Which is why I know, a heartbeat before it happens, that we've made a mistake.

Corwyn follows Xandra's gaze, waiting as always for the moment where everyone forgets about him. He sees me just as his claw catches in a split board, and I watch him trace the crack with his foot, feeling how new it is. His gaze narrows, fury swallowing all hints of smugness.

I wanted the look gone.

He roars as he charges Xandra. She starts to roll to protect herself, but he's too fast.

His claws flash silver. Droplets of red chase the movement.

Xandra falls, curled around her stomach.

"Stand and fight me!" Corwyn bellows.

I race to her side, even though I know it's only going to make him angrier. My blood is all ice. My mate. Our babies.

"Help me up," she murmurs when I reach her.

Every instinct in my body screams no, but I trust the sharpness in her eyes. She knows—

She shudders, whines. Some new pain wracks her.

"What's happening?"

"I...I don't know. It almost feels like...." She shakes again.

Labor. She's barely four months pregnant, and it feels like labor.

"Stand!" Corwyn yells.

"Denidor is lost," I shout back. *"Everyone knows he lied. He's probably dead already. You should be running, not screaming at us."*

Some of the fight leaks out of Corwyn's stance, and I turn to my mate.

"You need to go."

She looks up at me, rage and confusion in her gaze. *"We can end this!"*

"You are putting yourself last." Something taut builds up in my throat, like tears a wolf cannot cry. *"If you stay, you will die. All three of you. Please, trust me this time."*

Her stare doesn't soften. It simply drifts over my shoulder, where I know Corwyn stands. My heartbeat runs ragged, matching the uneven rhythm of her breath. I have no doubt she could kill him. We could kill him. But she is not a price I'm willing to pay, not even for the sake of two kingdoms.

Xandra looks back at me, and I know her decision is made.

5 6

WEAKNESS

Xandra

FINN'S EYES BURN INTO MINE, THAT IMPOSSIBLE BLUE, COLD AS ICE AND hot as the center of a flame. My heart aches. Another spasm wracks me.

They are just like Hana described. A wave of agony, rippling through my abdomen, so potent I can barely think. The pain of the scratches Corwyn left behind disappears under each.

It feels like labor. So early our babies will certainly die.

Finn is right.

And I cannot reach Hana on my own.

"*All right,*" I tell him. "*I will go—but only if you come with me.*"

Corwyn lunges at us, snarling. "*I am no mere ornament you can ignore. I will slaughter you both and bless the new world with your blood.*"

Finn whips around, shoulders him back. The blood Corwyn promised drips down Finn's silver fur, but he doesn't even grimace as he turns back to me. "*I can end this.*"

"*You are one of my priorities,*" I reply. "*And I need you to watch my back.*"

Finn wedges his nose underneath me, helping me up. It's a silent agreement. Over his back, I meet Corwyn's gaze.

"I am sad for you, cousin."

He sneers. *"Sad for me? Uncle Alden never saw how fucking weak you are. This will be all the proof I need—if I even march home in time."*

My legs shake underneath me as I stand. Another spasm—another contraction. Trembling whines slip from my lips.

Perhaps Corwyn is right.

"No." Finn holds me up, unshaken. *"You, all alone? You're the weak one. Good luck."*

The threat in his final sentence catches Corwyn—and me—off guard. Corwyn's defenses slacken, and Finn's shoulder, pressed against mine, shifts.

I stumble forward a step. He looks back at me. I know what he is going to say before he says it.

In the heat and danger of battle, blood in the air and wolves howling in pain in every direction, I shift into a fragile, vulnerable human and climb onto Finn's back. He sprints off the boat almost before I tighten my fingers in his fur.

Almost.

He yells through the mind-link for Hana to be ready for us. For Elian and Vedran to close in on Corwyn's position and finish what we couldn't. After a heartbeat of hesitation, he shouts the same to whatever Dun's Crossing soldiers can hear him. In breathless gasps, he recounts what he knows, what Corwyn did.

Affirmatives trickle in from all sides as we pass Denidor's ship, his platform now occupied by Matej.

I can barely hear them. Every bounce of Finn's back sends lightning bolts of pain up my spine. I chew on my lip to deafen my screams and plead with the little lives inside me.

"My son. My daughter." I've been imagining one of each, though Hana isn't sure yet. *"Not now. I love you too much to lose you to this. I know it hurts, just endure a little longer."*

I know the answering shrieks I hear are my own mind, but they sound like the souls I've been entrusted with suffering. My gut twists.

I hunch and get sick just off Finn's side. Blood ribbons his fur, hot and wet, and I wish I had a hand to press to my stomach. They need my comfort.

Between spasms, shrieks, and waves of sickness, I sing a little lullaby I half-remember Mother crooning over me when I was small. "Sleep, sweet pup. Dream, sweet pup. Mother will watch the moon until morning brings her sun."

Tears streak down my face. I was so selfish, so foolish not to listen to Finn sooner. Never again. They are my priorities–now and forever.

Hana's boat comes into view, and I choke on a sob of relief.

"Brace," Finn says.

I tighten my grasp on him for the final leap. His muscles bunch, lengthen, and we soar.

When we land, I scream.

Hana is already there, her hands like ice as she lifts me off Finn's back. Is she truly that cold, or am I on fire? For some strange, cruel reason, she sets me on my feet.

"You need to walk." Her voice is low, urgent. "It will help." She wraps a sheet around me.

I stumble forward. My legs feel like tree trunks, heavy and wooden. She leads me to the cabin near the back which Finn and other men spent days loading with all the supplies from her house. She's our traveling apothecary. The wounded sprawl on bolted beds and cots around it already, tended by other hands. I catch myself on one, and something sticky coats my fingers.

Hana just keeps pushing me forward. The cabin is even warmer, with shelves lined with iron-barred bottles to keep them from sliding on the waves. She says something to Finn, and he lifts me onto an empty cot.

I scream as another contraction pounds through me.

"How far apart?" Hana asks.

I shake my head. Time is a concept lost in the sea of pain. I can tell her about the current of the Grayhead outside, how it slips toward me and away with each wave of pain, as if it can't quite decide whether to help or take its opportunity to run. It is a familiar friend, a dog nudging my leg at the dinner table. I stroke it absently, my thoughts drifting.

"She was conscious when I warned you," Finn replies instead.

Light spears through me—Hana lifting my eyelids. When did I close them? I squint at her.

"She's conscious now. I'm just not sure how long that will last." Hana fastens leather cuffs around my ankles, a band around my head. "Just to keep you from rolling away."

I try to nod, but the leather holds me back. "Sleep, sweet pup."

"Rest, sweet pup," Hana replies gravely.

I can almost feel Finn's confusion, but I am not quite certain how I found my lips anymore, so I cannot explain.

"Cold water," Hana barks. "Hot wine."

Finn, barely a blur in my vision, spins to obey.

Hana leans closer. Her features smear, and for a moment, I think she is Mother. But no. Mother is elsewhere in the battle, above and away, watching but not with blood on her paws. She considered it. I warned her. Denidor…Denidor intends to empty her throne.

"Denidor is gone," Finn says, answering a question I didn't know I spoke aloud.

"Dead?" Hana swipes something freezing softly over my stomach. I keen—it feels like knives.

"Not sure. Most likely." Finn thumps something down. "What next?"

"Put korallion in some of the wine. A cup."

I spasm, and the knives light with unholy fire. Someone shrieks. Perhaps it's me.

"Drink."

Someone plugs my nose and tips a cup to my lips. Hot liquid pours down my throat. I struggle to swallow instead of drowning. My insides burn, and I do not know what to blame anymore.

Sleep, sweet pup. Dream, sweet pup.

Words volley back and forth over my head, increasingly unfamiliar. Willow bark, cave cotton, aga spider. Finn's steady, quick steps pause only for the creak of old metal and scrape of glass. Hana's touch is everywhere, a freezing counterpoint to the burning. Water drips into my eyes, or from it, as if the Grayhead has reached up into me and taken control instead. It can bear the pain I can't.

Mother will watch the moon until morning brings her sun.

I am weak. Too weak for this. I choke on another drink, spit half of it up, and am forced to take it again. My children, my babies, are going to tear through me for the reward of a single, pained breath. I will lose everything in a single blow.

Corwyn deserves to die. I whisper a prayer to the Goddess that someone will end him—someone other than Finn. He shouldn't muffle the taste of grief with revenge when I am gone.

"I need you to breathe." Hana grabs my chin, yanking my attention back to the agony of the present.

I gasp in a breath. My lungs sear. Had I forgotten?

"Fuck," Finn mutters.

"Don't worry so much," Hana replies as she releases me. "Our prince was a bookworm, but our princess is a fucking fighter."

I smile. Perhaps. I want to smile, and that is all I can really muster right now. The spasms seem to draw closer together. Handfuls of heartbeats separate them now. Shouldn't they be farther apart? Why won't anyone do anything about the half-dozen knives in my gut?

Hana's voice grows sharper, Finn's footsteps faster. Distantly, I think something has changed. I gulp down another mouthful of air, in case that's the problem.

They don't slow, and another spasm sends me twisting into myself. My mind launches itself away from the pain.

Once, I asked Mother why she never had another child. Before she told me what the healers said to her, her face twisted up in a grimace I had never seen on her before. I didn't understand it then. Now, I know it was a memory much like this. Pain without end or beginning. A price no person should have to pay.

For my children, I would pay it a hundred times.

I never thought I would get the chance. Father told me I would have to adopt someday. An orphan, he said. Some lost child no one would miss, with as much of my coloring as I could find. I was to give the child our name and let his past die.

Sometimes, I allowed myself to think about that child. Who he might be before I laid hands on him. Whether that life might have, in the end, been a better one than what I could provide in a palace.

And at other times, I simply wondered who he would be. If he would, by some act of the Goddess, end up with my curls or my smile. I wondered what would make him smile in the first place.

Now, there is a little boy—perhaps two, perhaps beside his sister—fighting for life alongside me. We have an equal chance of ever learning what makes the other smile.

You, I tell my twins. *You and your father made me smile.*

Someone takes my hand. I cling to the pressure. Another spasm will come soon. Counting is beyond me, but I can feel the rhythm of the waves, and they come in time. I brace for the pain.

And it doesn't come.

My breath catches. I start to relax, and the torment slams through me. I shriek, but that heartbeat of delay seems to have sapped some of its power.

The next spasm comes another heartbeat late. I can still feel the knives in my stomach, but it's like someone is trickling ice water down their blades, numbing the incisions. A sigh of relief gusts into my hair. Someone drags a kiss across my forehead.

Slowly, painfully, the contractions slow. I can shape thoughts in the moments between them. I can hear something other than my blood and my screams. I can open my eyes.

Hana pushes drenched hair back from her brow and drops into a chair. Finn lingers by my bedside, his hand in mine, close enough to be the lips I felt on my skin. He's gotten a robe at some point, and it clings to him in splatters of blood and sweat.

"I love you," I say.

His answering smile is exhausted. "I love you too."

5 7

EYE OF THE STORM

Finn

XANDRA LOOKS LIKE SHE'S BEEN MAULED, BUT THEN, THAT MIGHT BE because she has been. I'm glad when her eyes flutter shut again because it means she can't see the gory wreck of her abdomen and thighs. Blood coats the table, the floor, so much of it I can't believe she's still with us. But her face isn't bunched in pain anymore, and though Hana hasn't said anything yet, I recognize it when she staggers back from Xandra.

It's a soldier's stumble away from battle. Blank disbelief that you get to live another day. Celebration comes later.

I push streaky, auburn hair off Xandra's forehead and kiss her again, thanking the Goddess and every single star that she listened to me. That she trusted me. Hana wouldn't look like that if all three of them weren't going to make it through this.

A high howl pierces the abrupt quiet of the healer's cabin and the quiet of the world outside the cabin. I pry open the door and peek outside without releasing Xandra's hand.

Wolves of every color line the deck. Some lay fallen. Others stand.

Still others throw themselves over the side and begin paddling back across the Grayhead. But no one is fighting.

"It's over," someone says breathlessly. *"Tansy Beach raised the white flag."*

"Send a messenger," Luna Maris decrees. *"Peace talks start at sunrise."*

I glance back at Xandra and Hana. A tiny smile creases Xandra's lips. Hana seems to have slumped even more. They heard.

"Corwyn?" I ask Elian privately.

"The bastard escaped," he spits. *"Or somebody got to him before I did, but he wasn't where you said he would be."*

Escaped sounds about right. I crack my knuckles and stare at the wolves paddling away across the Grayhead. If he's as smart as he seems to think he is, he won't show his face here again.

"Apprehend General Zdenko," Xandra says tiredly, with an echo I know means she's talking to her mother and me. *"I am in the apothecary, but I will come to you."*

"Come to you?" I demand so Hana is aware.

She cracks an eye open, still sharp enough to fight.

"We need to… to root out the conspirators." Xandra starts to sit up, then falls back with a small yelp. I'd blame the leather restraints, if not for her grimace.

Hana jumps deftly to her feet and back to work. "I slowed the damage, but you are not well. The twins will likely still come early."

"Mother needs me."

"Does she?" I close the door and return to Xandra's side. Fuck, we were so close to losing her. She's still gray, and she holds my hand with all the strength of a kitten.

"Yes." All the strength missing from her hand is in her voice. In her eyes.

Goddess above, she's right.

We've been living in Luna Maris's shadow for months now. We've seen the way she works. And, over and over, we've been disappointed by it.

I look at Hana. "Can we get her up?"

Hana scowls. "I might have a chair. But she needs time to recover."

After sponging as much blood as we can off her and applying a few bandages—not tight, the pressure could work against all Hana's medicines—we help Xandra into a soft robe and a chair with two wheels where its back legs should be. I tell Luna Maris in no uncertain terms that she can bring Zdenko to Hana's ship if she wants to see Xandra.

By the time we wheel Xandra out, shock is turning into excitement. Drinking songs rumble from a few nearby boats. I watch men and women clap each other on the shoulders in celebration and laugh.

Xandra grins at them, her arms folded tightly around her stomach. She glances out over the water, and it finally settles back into its normal rhythm, like she just remembered she was controlling it.

It's a fucking miracle.

But that miracle has to wait because Luna Maris vaults onto the deck with a small squadron of guards, led by Lieutenant Sime, which parts to reveal Zdenko in manacles.

"What happened?" Luna Maris demands, scanning Xandra desperately.

"Your nephew," I reply sharply before cutting the connection and leaving Xandra to answer the rest, if she wants. Luna Maris's decision to stay safely away from the fighting seemed smart before—she could see the whole field and make tactical decisions. Now, I just keep comparing her unscratched leather armor to Xandra's stained robe.

Bigger fish to fry. I step forward while the two of them talk and eye Zdenko. Even from the deck, I watched the life go out of Denidor when we revealed him. Zdenko is a fighter—still proud, even in chains.

"Astralis," I say.

His perfect posture flickers. Shit, is that shock or confusion?

"Confusion," Xandra whispers in the back of my mind.

I let my real smile turn sharp as I face the former general. "You really expect me to believe you know nothing?"

He lifts his chin. "I do not even know what language you spoke."

It looks true. That flicker is gone; he's happy to meet my gaze, and he's not flinching.

"What was your relationship with Lord Denidor?"

Zdenko spits on the ground. "I wish I'd never heard the blasphemer's name."

That has to be about Denidor's false powers. "Then you'll have no problem telling us everything you know about him."

"Or else what?"

I take a step closer to the man. My shoulder aches, and so do my ribs, but I still have an inch over him, and I make sure to use it. "Would you like to find out?"

The question is all Anwen, bordering on Father, but that doesn't feel as unpleasant as it used to. They are the people I had to learn from. Of course, I resemble them in some ways.

Zdenko gulps audibly. "I took his advice. Often. More often than I took the advice of the queen."

Luna Maris whirls, but I hold up a hand behind my back, asking for one more minute with Zdenko. She stops.

Thank the Goddess. I didn't think that would work.

"Anything else?" I ask.

He glances over my shoulder at her, then down at Xandra. I let him. He may not know who else I am, but he knows she is my mate. He should know just how little I'm willing to be fucked with right now.

"I gave him reports on troop movements before anyone else," Zdenko says. "Provided personal guard for his manor and exchanged messages with him through the bark of a tree."

I take a step back. He had no idea we knew about the tree. We left the original sliver of bark behind. And Goddess only knows what it says now, so if he is telling us that, I believe him.

"He was a patsy," I tell everyone—Xandra, Luna Maris, the fighters slowly gathering around our little display. "For Lord Denidor, Lord Corwyn, and a group named Astralis that wanted to destroy both kingdoms."

Surprise whispers through the crowd. There's no point in hiding what we know now—and certainly no point in letting Corwyn weasel his way back in somewhere.

"He'll be put under formal investigation," Xandra says. "But not to death."

I smile back at her. She holds her mother's hand now, and Luna Maris's face is tight with worry, but Xandra only looks confident.

"Luna?" someone asks. Someone who clearly didn't hear everything that happened on Denidor's ship.

"It shall be as my daughter, Princess Xandra, and her mate, Prince Finn, say." Luna Maris smiles out at her people. "Tomorrow, we discuss peace. The day after, we face the future—hopefully as a kingdom united once more!"

Cheers go up from this ship, from other ships as the news spreads. Ingrid slips out of the crowd and waves at me, Elian by her side. Vedran nods once, sharply, like everything has been set to rights.

A chant of "Luna Maris" echoes, and I realize that's not quite the case. I turn away from the celebrations, toward Xandra and her mother, and usher them back toward the cabin. At least there's privacy there.

"What's going on?" Xandra asks, the wheels of her chair squeaking along.

"We need to discuss the peace talks, don't we?" I say while we're still within earshot of everyone. "I don't really think waiting for Andrija will help anyone."

She huffs a tired laugh and allows me to keep rolling her. I wonder how she'll feel when she knows the whole truth.

It doesn't matter. I know I'm right.

Inside the cabin, the cheers are muted but not silenced. The boat rocks as Hana—or, hopefully, someone else while Hana naps—starts steering it to shore.

"I have not heard whether your father would be well enough for a parley," Luna Maris says.

Xandra swallows. "If he isn't, and Corwyn is gone, they'll send one of the other councilors, but there is no way of knowing who."

"Isn't there?" I look at her.

She frowns at me. She knows I'm up to something, just not what. "House Dolenec will barely have finished swearing in their new councilor since Lord Juraj's death. Lord Kresimir would normally be my choice, but the war against Moonlight Hollow particularly damaged his lands; he'll be unfair in negotiations."

I nod. "So they'll send Edvard."

"He's the only choice." Xandra shakes her head. "What difference does it make?"

"Luna Maris, did you know that?"

She raises her eyebrows. "If I had taken some time, I could have puzzled it out."

"Maybe." I look between the two of them, so similar and so different. "Let me ask you a new question: why did you leave without Xandra?"

"Lord Denidor said—" She pauses, goes slightly pale. "I am sorry."

"I'm not angry anymore." Xandra looks at me, confused. "And I don't know what Finn is getting at."

I kneel in front of her chair. "If anyone asked you to leave the twins behind in the same situation, what would you say?"

"No," she says slowly, "and that anyone who wanted me to do that didn't understand the project I was building. The purpose of something like Moonlight Hollow is to be better than the old ways, and starting it with old cruelties will make it the same before long."

"I think both of you should go to the peace talks tomorrow." I stare up at Xandra. "And once the two kingdoms are reunited, you should think about who is really the best leader for what this place could be."

Luna Maris makes a sound behind me. Surprise, disgust—I don't really care. I've seen kingdoms under all kinds of leadership, traveling with Kieran to try to right Father's wrongs. I know a dream like Moonlight Hollow dies under Luna Maris and thrives under Xandra.

I look up at my wife to try to read her thoughts on her face and find her ashen.

"What is it?"

She shakes her head, tears filling her eyes. "Didn't you hear him?"

"Him?"

"Alden," Luna Maris says numbly.

"He's dying." Xandra looks at me with wild eyes. "Now."

I shift before she does. We can't run the distance to Tansy Tower in time any other way, and I'm not letting her go alone.

5 8

RACE AGAINST TIME

Xandra

"*ALEXANDER*," FATHER SAID ACROSS MILES OF MIND-LINK, HIS VOICE THIN with exhaustion or the unstable magic connecting us. *"Alexander, Maris, my time has come."*

I'm sure he knew that those words would send me running. They have. My whole body burns as I run, not as bad as it burned just riding on Finn's back on the way to Hana's side, but bad enough. Her warnings carve lines of fire into my skin. I should be resting.

But he is my father. He is dying.

"Hold on another few minutes," I call back through whatever mind-link still connects us. *"Just another few minutes."*

The run from the Grayhead to Tansy Tower will take hours. We could've run it in one night if I hadn't needed to rest last time. But if I keep begging him for another few minutes, and another, he'll be there when we arrive.

My eyes burn as badly as my limbs, as the screaming muscles of my stomach. I start to slow.

Finn slows beside me, a ghost in the darkness.

Why am I running? Why am I risking the lives we just barely managed to snatch from the brink for him? He hasn't earned it.

When I learned he was sick, I asked Mother if she missed him. I wanted to know if I did. If I could. I am still nowhere near sure.

When he hit me, I hated him. There's no point in lying about that now. Perhaps I've always hated him a little.

"Are we stopping?" Finn asks.

"I don't know."

The moon shines down on me with the Goddess's cold light. I want a hand to hold, a warmth to guide my path. But the Goddess is distant, watching and intervening only rarely. She has no answers for me.

"What changed?" he asks.

"He did." I can only see his eyes, furious as he crossed the room. His hand drawing back. I wish I could stop running toward him.

I want to be at the side of the man who raised me when he dies, but I don't know if I already was there when *that* man died.

Finn trots up alongside me. The Goddess's light turns his coat to glistening metal, an impossibility I want to stare at for the rest of my days. Something twinges in my gut—a lingering spark of the pain that almost destroyed everything. A reminder that I can't just run and pray.

"Did he?" Finn asks.

My tongue curls around the words *of course* and releases them. I don't feel like I recognize the man Father turned into, but Mother was only gone for three short months before he hit me. Three dances of the Goddess overhead. He couldn't have changed so much, so fast.

He never would have hit me before, but he did yell. He did forbid me things I wanted so desperately I begged him for them. He did talk over me, seal me away, place Corwyn ahead of me like he would've preferred his nephew as his son.

And I loved him through all of it.

"My father was a monster," Finn says. *"And the whole world knew it. He and I never had the best relationship. Him dying...it made my life a better in a lot of ways. But I still cried after I heard the news."*

His eyes shine, and I know he's never said that to anyone else before. I picture him, three years younger, the Goddess's light on his blond hair as he sobs in private, grieving a man the world celebrates the death of. My heart aches.

"*It is different,*" I say. "*My father wasn't—isn't all bad.*" I take a few steps forward.

"*Just answer one question.*" Finn circles slightly in front of me, cutting off my path. I have to stop or run into him. "*What are you hoping for?*"

The question takes my breath away. If he didn't force me to stop, I still would have. The thousand answers bursting through my brain are too much to bear while running.

I want him to be the man he was before, to be stripped bare by his pain.

I want to hit him like he hit me.

I want to laugh in his face as he dies.

I want to see his face one more time while it's still moving.

"*I don't know,*" I repeat.

One of the twins kicks, which is a painful highlight to how little I'm sure of tonight. Everything was planned. How can it have worked out and still feel like it is crashing down around my shoulders? I am winning and losing at the same time on a bet I don't remember making.

"*I couldn't hate my father when he died,*" Finn says quietly. "*After? Now? Sure. I know that he ruined half the world because he wanted to. That he tortured some of my siblings and countless other people who didn't deserve it. But that first night, I couldn't.*"

The stars twinkle softly down at us, the souls of all we've lost. So many they blanket this night in their glow. Somewhere up there is King Gavin, monster and man. A father, grieved by his son.

I take a deep breath and meet Finn's gaze. "*I don't know what I want from him, but I have to see him to find out.*"

Finn steps out of my path. "*Lead the way.*"

* * *

THE RHYTHMIC EBB AND FLOW OF MY PAIN BECOME ALMOST SOOTHING after hours of running. I know which parts of my stride stretch Hana's careful stitches, which ones let them relax. The twins kick whenever we pause—often, because I want to be there, but I will not risk everything to do so—as if they are asking whether we are there yet. Finally, though, Tansy Tower rises over the horizon.

"Father?" I ask.

"Alexander." Warmth and weakness braid together in his voice. *"They will open the gates for you."*

We sprint through halls I still know like the back of my hand despite the months away. Staff skitters out of our lupine way, and no one stops us.

"Where is the prince?" someone mutters as we pass.

I wonder why they don't recognize me then remember the swell of my stomach. He didn't tell anyone why I left.

My heart burns with something other than exertion as I round the final corner to his room, Finn hurries behind me.

A steward stands in the hall with a robe over his arm. When he sees both of us, his gaze goes distant with a mind-link, and another steward hurries out with a second robe a moment later. Finn and I shift and slide the offerings on. They are Tansy Beach indigo, like Father is staking his claim.

I push open the door to his bedroom, and the reek of sickness hits me before anything else. A fire roars in the grate, making the room far too warm for the season. Miralyn looks up when we enter, dark bags under her eyes and a wet cloth in one hand. I can read on her face that she's tried everything to save him.

"Alexander," Father rasps.

I take a step forward, and he comes into view past his hangings.

It's like looking at a ghost already. He is wasted, his cheeks sunken into his skull, the broad shoulders I always envied narrowed and slumped. A small army of pillows holds him nearly sitting, but he's slipped down them. His nightshirt is stained with some medicine and speckles of ruby blood that match the pile of crumpled handkerchiefs at his feet. There's no point in taking them away now. He stands at the doorway between life and death.

My gut screams to rush to him. I take Finn's hand and stand my ground.

"Alexandra," I say.

"Alexandra." He extends a weak hand clutching another spattered handkerchief. "I am sorry."

I will not lose him while I hate him.

My feet fly across the carpet. Miralyn clears a path and then drags a chair into position at his side when she sees how unsteady I am. I take Father's hand, the very same one he cracked across my cheek, and rub the freezing twigs of his fingers.

"I chased you away," he mumbles. "Maris will never come back."

Mother didn't even start to move, despite her stricken look, when we both received Father's message.

"You were scared," I reply. "Too scared."

"Too scared for you and your mother both." A tear drips down his cheek, the first I've ever seen him shed. "I made so many mistakes. You were right to go."

I put my other hand on my stomach. I will not hate him now, but I won't disagree with that either. Away from him was the only place I could've found all the happiness I did.

"Is your Finn here?" Father's eyes search the room.

I swallow. He should be able to see Finn, mere feet from the end of his bed. "Yes."

"You will treat her well. Better than any other woman has been treated," he says to the air, something of the old iron in his voice. "Or I will escape the sky to remind you of this moment."

"I will." Finn looks at me as he speaks.

"And you will lead our people well," Father says to me. "Carry on the Mlakar line."

My chest squeezes. All my life, I have been nothing but a continuation of the Mlakar line, the next step in a dynasty. Even on his deathbed, as he whispers apologies for his mistakes, he can't let go of that.

"I will lead," I say, my voice shaking. "But there are more important things than our line."

He looks up at the ceiling for a long moment. "Your baby. Have you named it?"

"Babies," I reply carefully. "I am having twins."

He takes a deep breath and then hacks blood into a handkerchief. Miralyn starts to stand to tend to him, but I grab a clean cloth, conjure water, and dampen his forehead before she can. I will not hate him before I lose him, and that means seeing all the pieces of the whole. He is the man who raised me and the one who hit me.

"Tell them I loved them," he says. "Despite everything, I do. Just as I love you. My Alexandra."

"I love you, too."

He squeezes my hand, fingers as weak as a fresh shoot, and then releases it.

The firelight dancing over his face makes it impossible to tell when the life leaves his eyes. He doesn't speak again, doesn't even move. I don't know how long I sit beside him, holding his hand, occasionally swiping water off his brow. All I know is that one of our sons has a name.

5 9

A NEW DAWN

Finn

MIRALYN MOVES FIRST. SHE CROSSES THE ROOM SLOWLY AND SHUTS Alden's eyes. That's the first time I realize how sore and shaking my knees are from a long night ended by standing at the foot of his bed, clutching one of the posts for support and watching Xandra's stony face.

Her lips part around a soft sob now, caught in the first glow of morning light.

Like Miralyn broke some kind of spell, Xandra throws herself out of her chair and at me. I barely manage to unfreeze my arms in time to catch her. She impacts hard, both of us stumbling. Her chest heaves with tears.

"I'm so sorry," I murmur into her hair.

She just holds me tighter. My chest aches. I look over her shoulder at Miralyn.

"Is her room...?"

Miralyn nods. Xandra's room is still hers. I lift her gently. She still clings to my neck, and I begin the long walk there. The soldiers outside react dramatically when we step out. They're waiting for news.

I think I recognize one of them from my night in a cell. They can wait until the Goddess Herself tells them, for all I care.

The winding halls of Tansy Tower are familiar enough to me that I reach Xandra's door before she stops crying. The door swings open on silent hinges—someone has been taking care of them, or they would've stuck. It didn't seem like Alden was lying, but between that and the flurry of clothes still scattered across the front room, clearly untouched since the night Xandra left, the last of my doubts die.

Mother turned Raven's room into a private study the day she left. Before Father left to confront Kieran, I heard him talking about taking over Kieran's.

I put Xandra on the bed, my stomach churning. Acid burns through me. She just lost her father. I can't be jealous now that hers was more than mine ever could've been.

"Sit with me," she says. It's not a question.

I do. She grabs me again, dragging me closer, and I stroke her back. Slowly, softly, in time with my own breath instead of her frantic ones. She shudders in my arms. We need to get back to Hana soon. I don't know how long she slowed the birth for, and I don't trust Miralyn like I do—

"Thank you," Xandra says.

I blink. "For what?"

"For telling me I didn't have to hate him," she mumbles. "Or stop hating him after."

I kiss the top of her head. I don't know if I've ever done anything worse. It was what Xandra needed to hear, so I told her, but thinking about it makes me sick. No one should've mourned Father.

She pulls back and looks at me. "You're upset."

"I just watched a man die." I shrug. "You're upset."

As soon as I say it, I know I've made a mistake. Her eyes narrow as she sees right through me.

"Tell me."

"I'm glad he apologized." That's true. I want her to have everything.

"But?"

"But you are too smart for your own good." I shake my head. "We can talk later."

"We will." She holds my gaze, her hazel eyes still full of tears. "And now."

She needs to rest, not worry about me. There's only one way to stop her now. "I'll tell you if you agree to become Luna."

Her mouth opens. Her tears shine in the morning light flooding in through parted curtains. I saw her face when I suggested it the first time; she doesn't think she's ready, and she won't do it to her mother.

"Only if you become my Alpha."

My stomach drops. That was the one detail I wasn't thinking about. A life at the center of everything, by her side. No more disappearing into the background.

But her eyes burn like they did when she asked me to leave Corwyn behind. My mark screams. This is my mate, my wife. There's no life she leads that I don't lead with her.

"I wish I'd hated my father the whole time," I whisper. "I wish he would've apologized."

Her lips turn up into a smile. "He should have."

And she kisses me as tears burn in my eyes. I drop onto the bed, fold myself around her. Falling asleep is a threat the second I hit the mattress. Twenty-four hours of running, fighting, bleeding, worrying. I got married today. I gained a kingdom, lost a fight, nearly watched my wife and children die.

I told a secret I thought I'd take to the grave.

And she loves me anyway. She loves me just as much as she did before I asked her to leave the fight, as much as she did when I told her the truth as advice she needed to hear. I thread gentle fingers into the mats of blood and dirt in her hair and kiss her. After a day like today, I need her more than I need sleep.

She seems to feel the same.

We touch each other slowly, soft as the morning sunlight. She traces the line of my jaw with a broken nail, and I barely wince when she scrapes over a cut I don't remember receiving. I kiss every inch of her face, covering her in me so she remembers that she will never be alone.

I drag my teeth over the mark I left on her so long ago, the ridges of the sun emblazoned on her skin. When she first showed it to me, my world turned upside down. I never want it put back the way it was.

Our robes melt away at some point. The day's hurts ravage our skin. I lave attention around Hana's neat stitch work, careful not to disturb a thread.

Xandra puts a hand on my head. I pause.

"I want to call our son Alden," she says.

I brush a kiss along a stretch of unbroken skin. "I like that name."

Her choked laugh paints a picture of her smile in my mind so vivid that I don't even need to look. Silently, with my head against the swell of her stomach, I make promises to the twins.

Alden will be twice the man his grandfather was or more—either grandfather. And we'll tell him about them both. Xandra's right. Putting the truth off doesn't make it any easier to say. And the other one, whether a boy or a girl, will grow up Alden's equal. Tansy Beach's inheritance rules are already strange enough. Twins Alphas don't seem that crazy.

And I will love you so much, I tell them both. *I already do.*

One of them—Alden, maybe—kicks me in the cheek, and I smile.

Xandra just cards her fingers through my hair, patient for once in her life, like she knows what's going on. Maybe she talks to them all the time. Maybe she can't stop thinking about how close we came to losing them either.

The early morning paints her skin gold. We have to be back in time for the peace talks. Tomorrow, we'll have all the time in the world. Today, we've got a world to build.

I kiss down the slope of her stomach and between her legs. She gasps and grabs my shoulders, scraping the slash Corwyn left behind. My hiss of pain only makes her rock against me.

My tongue dances against her, lapping up her flavor. Aniseed and clove, the perfect combination. Warm and cold, sweet and sharp. Her voice wings between those high, fragile noises I know mean I'm on the right track and notes lower than the deepest valley when I find where she needs me most. A blend of contradictions, just like she is. Want builds in my gut as I move faster, chasing more and more sounds from her lips.

She trembles, on the edge of an explosion. Faster, faster.

And then she stops. Gently, she pulls me out from between her legs. Tear tracks streak her cheeks, but her pupils are blown wide and dark with hunger.

"I need to hear you say it."

"I love you," I say instantly.

She shakes her head with a laugh. "Not that, though I certainly don't mind."

Half my brain is in my cock. I shake my head. I can't keep up with her.

"Say you'll do this with me." She bites her swollen lower lip like she's not sure what my answer is going to be. "Lead with me."

Five months ago, I was a leftover prince with no prospects, hiding from the Haze. Now, somehow, I'm smiling as I say, "Of course."

Her smile explodes across her face. Even the tear tracks, shining with new wetness, glow. I surge up her body to kiss her.

"I love you," she says to me.

"I certainly don't mind," I reply.

She bites my lip, hard, but barcly hard enough to notice through all the other aches and pains. If I feel like this, she must be miserable. But she still winds her arms around my neck and pulls me closer.

I shift her a few inches up the bed, laying her head on the pile of pillows, and cradle her hips as I line myself up. A horn blows outside, a low, mournful note. The king is dead.

But Tansy Beach, Moonlight Hollow, the future is very much alive. In the gasps between our mouths, in the lives cradled between our bodies as I slide home.

Home. This kingdom, whatever it ends up being, is now my home. Maybe more than Dun's Crossing ever was.

Xandra and I rock together. Gentle, for once in our relationship. There will be time for everything she wants—everything we both want—but right now, we just need to feel each other. To careen over the edge together, not like a fiery explosion, but like the softly dawning sun.

I hold her as we shake apart together.

60

THE LAST HAZE

Ingrid

Seven months later...

"Come dance." Candace grins at me and holds out her hands.

"Do I have to?" I run my fingers up and down the stem of my goblet, wishing it was the neck of my lute, and look around at the glittering array of nobles packed into the half-constructed ballroom of the new Moonlight Tower, heart of the united Moonlight Beach.

The twins, Alden and Lucian, squirm in their parents' arms, clearly no happier with their name-blessing party than I am. They're only a few months old, and they look like mismatched cherubs in their long, ceremonial dresses. Alden inherited Finn's hair and Xandra's eyes, and Lucian the opposite. They might be the center of attention, but at least they don't have to make small talk.

Candace smiles "There are people to meet."

And a Haze coming in, which she doesn't need to say. I can feel it prickling over my skin, even if I couldn't see it through the open windows. Yet another reason not to be in this ballroom. Finding my mate doesn't sound like the worst thing in the world, but the few

Hazes I've been through so far have mostly been a great excuse for a run.

"You aren't going to let this go, are you?" I ask her.

She shakes her head with a playful smile.

"Fine." I take her hand. "But I hope you know finding Hollis has turned you into a terrible matchmaker."

"Did I tell you I think I found someone for Eva?" she asks, her eyes glowing.

"Did I tell you I think you should just set her up with one of your birds and call it a day?"

She swats my arm. "I want her to be happy."

I glance across the ballroom at where Candace's new best friend entertains a small crowd with Hollis. "She is."

Her answering huff tells me there's no getting through to her. She won't listen when I tell her I'm happy either. A mate might be nice—not that the early experiences of any of my siblings make the process seem all that pleasant—but I have enough in my life.

Or I would, if every single member of my family didn't insist on dragging me to these parties.

Candace tugs me across the ballroom to a group in orange and white. I search my memory for who those belong to. They're familiar, I just—

"Ingrid!" Joli jumps out of the group as we approach, grinning.

"I should've known you'd be here." That makes this the group from Lightning Cape, the neighboring kingdom that mostly stayed out of the civil war rocking Moonlight Beach. "It's not like they could keep you out."

She laughs, but the quick glance over her shoulder might as well be a glowing sign—her family doesn't know about her smuggling. I nod. They won't find out from me. Joli is a couple of years younger than me, and I can't imagine what would've happened if Mother found out about half my hobbies when I was her age.

Candace tugs me gently away from my friend, and I shoot her a look.

"Joli is lovely," she says through the mind-link, *"but she's not who I want you to dance with."*

"I thought I was supposed to dance with you."

Candace doesn't bother responding. My surprise and her pretense are all just a game at this point. Goddess, she really is a matchmaker.

"Prince Amval Som." She dips into a low curtsy. "I would like for you to meet my sister, Princess Ingrid Solberg."

At least she calls me her sister without flinching again. Someday, she will take Hollis's name. For now, she simply introduces herself as Candace and lets everyone else make of that what they will.

I wish she were still home. I wish I saw her outside of these parties, where all she can think of is making me happy in the exact same way she is.

Prince Amval bows, deep and formal. "It is my honor."

He's got a nice voice, low and smooth. It matches his eyes, that strange, amber-caramel color I've only ever seen in Lightning Cape and rare even there. I offer him a perfunctory curtsy. "Nice to meet you, too."

Other than his eyes and his voice, every inch of him is stiff. Starched doublet, unmoving coif of dark brown hair, posture so upright it gives the walls of this tower a run for their money. He looks like someone unwrapped him for the first time tonight.

"What brings you to Moonlight Beach?" he asks.

Candace tightens her grip on my arm just slightly. She knows me too well to give me a chance to run. "I wanted to see a half-built palace."

The serenity in Amval's eyes flickers with confusion. "I would have thought it was your brother."

Fuck, he doesn't even have a sense of humor. "I've actually been avoiding him all night."

"Oh." Amval almost frowns, but his mouth doesn't quite seem to know the shape. He's too polite for it.

If Mother were standing at my elbow instead of Candace, the grip on my arm would've started cutting off blood flow to my hand. Candace just shakes her head, but I can see the smile pulling at her mouth. She thinks I'm funny, even if this prince as dull as sand doesn't.

"If I spent time with him, I'd lose time with the building," I continue, my smile growing. "We can talk when he visits me."

"What have you learned?" Amval asks.

If it weren't for the looking-for-a-lifeboat desperation in his voice, I would almost admire the attempt. Most people have politely found an excuse to walk away by now.

"Well, I think they ought to put a fourth wall on before it rains."

Candace breaks with a snort that would've made Mother turn purple. Normally, I don't think about Mother this much, but I can see some of her face in these people. She was a mid-rank noble on the border of Lightning Cape and Dun's Crossing, no real relation, but there's still something familiar.

I crush the thought. It might be the only thing that could make this party worse.

Amval clears his throat. "I see. This was all a convoluted lie."

"Joke," I say with a smile. "They're called jokes."

"Only if they're funny," he replies.

* * *

OCEAN-COOLED AIR WHIPS MY SKIN AS I SHIMMY OUT OF MY DRESS, JUST past where I think the people still at the party can see. Instinct sings in my blood. The night beckons. I probably could've resisted longer, but I'll see my nephews tomorrow, and I was running out of *convoluted lies* to keep anyone from asking me to dance.

Only if they're funny, he said. Like he actually has a personality under all that starch.

I shake off one of a thousand boring conversations at a party where no one is allowed to say anything interesting and fold my dress. The moon hangs high overhead. Tonight, there is no small talk. No mannerly princes trying to polite me into being the mannerly princess they expect.

There is only the Goddess and me.

I shift. My world expands. There are dozens, maybe hundreds, of other wolves here in the night with me. Foreign trees and grasses are barely strange to my paws. Speed courses through me, and I take off.

Running is always a blessing. During the Haze, it feels a little like magic. I am nothing more than another puff of white fog, drifting in off the sea. A piece of this place. I don't have to think about where to set my feet, when to breathe, who might be looking. I just am.

The wind shifts, and I freeze.

Basil and something acrid, almost burnt, like the remains of a fire.

My heart skips a beat.

My mate is here.

I whip around and run. The scent is powerful, unavoidable, all-consuming. How didn't I smell it before now? How have I walked anywhere on this planet without smelling it? I crash through high grass, unseeing, relying totally on my nose. Fronds whip at me, scratching my skin. I could not care less.

He's here.

I nearly crash into him. There is no visibility in the grass, just the faint hissing of other wolves somewhere nearby. I take a step, alone, and then there he is.

Tall. Proud. Fur so dark I have no idea if it's brown or black.

Mine.

I throw myself at him, shifting midair. He follows a half second behind, and my mouth crashes into his

On my tongue, his smell transforms. The basil is herbal and wild. The char isn't the death of something but the potential for it again, fire starters and embers kept banked. I devour it as he shoves his hands into my hair and rolls on top of me. Strong, long-fingered hands. Claiming hands that hold me down in the whispering grass, hidden from the world by his body.

I grab at him blindly. If I've learned one thing tonight, it's that eyes are useless. My fingertips map the contours of his muscles, weaving down his back and along his stomach. The steep V leading me between his legs and the coarse curls I find there. He moans as I brush them, and the sound is better than anything I've ever played.

To hear it again, I brush lower and lower. He is already hard under my touch. Something inside me clenches. I've been too busy to bother learning this like I've learned everything else I came across. It's too dangerous with someone you don't want to marry, too time-consuming to just dabble at.

But I take every new project headfirst.

I wrap my hand around his cock and stroke. He jerks into the motion. A new sound bubbles up in my throat. It's a moan, hungry and wanting. It disappears into his mouth, and he kisses me even harder.

He palms one of my breasts, rolls a thumb over my nipple like he's plucking a string. I bow for him as new sensations rocket through me. I've never felt alive like this before, every inch of my body alight.

I think he grins. I smile back at him. *More.*

But he can't hear my silent plea, and I won't give up his mouth long enough to speak it. His fingers dance over my breasts like he's making his own map, playing me like I intended to play him. That electric, alive feeling builds and builds. I roll my hips up into him, keep a steady rhythm on his cock, beg with my body.

He won't listen—or he wants to make me wait.

But he is my mate as much as I am his, so he is going to learn.

I shift my legs, rub his tip through the wetness gathering there. A growl rips from his mouth—wanting, not warning. Without another heartbeat of hesitation, I line him up and fit him inside.

My voice breaks on a cry as he fucks me. Pressure burns into plea-sure, too much becoming just enough in a span of heartbeats. We were made to fit each other, and Goddess above, we do. Our harsh breath blends with the rustling grass, the wind blowing it overhead to create a dome of perfect privacy. I cling to him, meet every thrust with force. My hips sting from the impact of his.

Instinct storms my thoughts. I release his mouth, searching for any inch of skin I can reach. Some impossible climax is coming; I need to find somewhere to bite.

The same urge seems to have captured him. He buries his face in my chest hungrily, leaving the expanse of his neck exposed. I curl around him to reach it.

His cock drives deeper, hitting something new inside me.

Only his throat in my mouth muffles my scream. Teeth pierce flesh as I shake, ecstatic, electric, more than I've ever been before.

ALSO BY BELLA MOONDRAGON

The Alpha King's Breeder series:

Bought by the Alpha: The Alpha King's Breeder Book 1

Loved by the Alpha: The Alpha King's Breeder Book 2

Lost by the Alpha: The Alpha King's Breeder Book 3

Luna of the Alpha: The Alpha King's Breeder Book 4

Legacy of the Alpha: The Alpha Kings's Breeder Book 5

Daughter of the Alpha: The Alpha King's Breeder Book 6

Descendants of the Alpha: The Alpha King's Breeder Book 7

Shadow of the Alpha: The Alpha King's Breeder Book 8

Son of the Alpha: The Alpha King's Breeder Book 9

Spare of the Alpha: The Alpha King's Breeder Book 10

Claimed by the Alpha: The Alpha King's Breeder Book 11

Atonement for the Alpha King: The Alpha King's Breeder Book 12

Rejected by the Alpha: The Alpha King's Breeder Book 13

Abducted by the Alpha: The Alpha King's Breeder Book 14

Abandoned by the Alpha: The Alpha King's Breeder Book 15

Wolf Shifter Fairy Tale Retellings series

Beauty and the Alpha Beast

Sleeping Beasty

Tangling With the Alpha

The Luna's Vampire Prince series:

The Culling

The Kingdom

The Conquered

Pregnant With Four Alphas' Babies

Chosen As the Breeder

Mated to Four Alphas

Threats Against the Breeder

At War for the Breeder

The Stolen Breeder

Four Alphas, Four Babies

Becoming the Luna Queen

Descendants of the Breeder

Desired by the Devil series

Whispers of the Devil

Banter of the Devil

Murmurs of the Devil

The Mafia Kings series

Indebted to the Mafia King

Loved by the Mafia King

Claimed by the Mafia King

Secrets of the Mafia King

Burned by the Mafia King

Kidnapped by the Mafia King

Dark Stalker Romance series

Tempted by Sin

Fated to Sin

Secret Billionaires series

Finding the Secret Billionaire by Olivia Bhelle Kildare

Falling for My Secret Billionaire by Bella Moondragon

Driven by the Secret Billionaire by ID Johnson

Wolf Shifter Alpha Kings series

Ravens and Ruins

Sundrops and Shadows

Snowflakes and Sabotage

The Vampire King's Feeder series

Claiming the Alpha's Daughter

Loving the Alpha's Daughter

Finding the Alpha's Daughter

Bewitching the Alpha's Son

Writing as B. Moon

The Boy Who Died

Sign up for Bella's newsletter here.

Or get a free novella from The Alpha King's Breeder series when you sign up here:
The Beta and the Maid

Follow Bella on Facebook here.

Follow Bella on Bookbub here.

9 798889 871065 1